Praise for *Delirium*

'Lauren Oliver is the rising star of young adult fiction . . .
[*Delirium*] deftly conjures up a recognisably dystopian
parallel to our own world, as convincingly terrifying as the
North America of Margaret Atwood's *The Handmaid's Tale*.'
Sunday Times

'Prepare to pull a sickie and be rooted to your chair with one
of the most addictive books we've come across in ages . . . A
recklessly romantic, smart, poignant and tense read from one
of the most exciting writers around . . . Clever, moving and
incredibly addictive.'
Heat

'A dystopian Romeo and Juliet story that deserves
to be as massive as *Twilight*.'
Stylist

'This novel had me glued to my bed from start to finish;
I whirred through 450 pages in less than 24 hours.'
Easy Living

'Hugely compelling and addictive.'
Bookseller's Choice, *The Bookseller*

'Lauren Oliver truly is a phenomenal writer.'
thecrookedshelf.blogspot.com

'This has to be one of the most original fiction concepts
for a long time . . . It will sti— the emotions and remind
you why you —
New—

'A beautifully written a—
that fans of Marga— —ood will devour.'
Best

'An original and fast-moving read from a very talented writer.'
Sun

'I didn't leave my bedroom all weekend after I picked up this Margaret Atwood meets *Twilight* novel. Ah-ma-zing.'
Grazia

'Lauren Oliver's futuristic vision, set in an alternate but recognisable America, is chillingly realised.'
Marie Claire

'Lauren Oliver's *Before I Fall* was one of *Bella*'s favourite books of last year and this follow-up doesn't disappoint.'
Bella

'Lauren Oliver can do no wrong. As long as she keeps writing with the same haunting, poetic prose, I will keep reading.'
wondrousreads.com

'If you fall in love with one book this year, let it be this one.'
narrativelyspeaking.blogspot.com

'Clever, imaginative novel . . . the movie must surely be just around the corner.'
Daily Mail

'This thought-provoking read will change the way you feel about Valentine's Day.'
Bliss

Visit
www.laurenoliverbooks.com
www.Facebook.com/LoveDelirium
for the latest news, competitions and exclusive material
from Lauren Oliver

Delirium

LAUREN OLIVER

HODDER

First published in America in 2011 by HarperCollins Children's Books
A division of HarperCollins Publishers.
First published in Great Britain in 2011 by Hodder & Stoughton
An Hachette UK company

First published in paperback in 2011

8

A geographical note about the description of Portland, Maine:
Although many of the larger geographical areas indicated in this book do, in fact,
exist (such as Tukey's Bridge, the Cove, Munjoy Hill, and the neighborhood of
Deering Highlands), as I had the pleasure to discover while staying there to research
this book, most (if not all) of the streets, landmarks, beaches, and universities are
of my own invention. To the residents of Portland: Please excuse the fictional
liberties I have taken with your wonderful city, and I'll see you soon.

The lines from 'i carry your heart with me (i carry it in)'
Copyright 1952, © 1980, 1991 by the Trustees for the E.E. Cummings Trust,
from *Complete Poems: 1904–1962* by E.E. Cummings, edited by George J. Firmage.
Used by permission of Liveright Publishing Corporation.

A CIP catalogue record for this title is available from the British Library.

B format 978 0 340 98093 4
A format 978 1 444 73605 2
Ebook 978 1 444 72065 5

Printed and bound in the UK by Clays Ltd, St Ives plc

Hodder & Stoughton policy is to use papers that are natural, renewable
and recyclable products and made from wood grown in sustainable
forests. The logging and manufacturing processes are expected to conform
to the environmental regulations of the country of origin.

Hodder & Stoughton Ltd
338 Euston Road
London NW1 3BH

www.hodder.co.uk

For all the people who have infected me with
amor deliria nervosa in the past
—you know who you are.
For the people who will infect me in the future
—I can't wait to see who you'll be.
And in both cases:
Thank you.

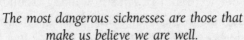

*The most dangerous sicknesses are those that
make us believe we are well.*

– Proverb 42, *The Book of Shhh*

It has been sixty-four years since the president and the Consortium identified love as a disease, and forty-three since the scientists perfected a cure. Everyone else in my family has had the procedure already. My older sister, Rachel, has been disease free for nine years now. She's been safe from love for so long, she says she can't even remember its symptoms. I'm scheduled to have my procedure in exactly ninety-five days, on September 3. My birthday.

Many people are afraid of the procedure. Some people even resist. But I'm not afraid. I can't wait. I would have it done tomorrow, if I could, but you have to be at least eighteen, sometimes a little older, before the scientists will cure you. Otherwise the procedure won't work correctly: people end up with brain damage, partial paralysis, blindness, or worse.

I don't like to think that I'm still walking around with the disease running through my blood. Sometimes I swear I can feel it writhing in my veins like something spoiled, like sour milk. It makes me feel dirty. It reminds me of children throwing tantrums. It reminds me of resistance, of diseased girls dragging their nails on the pavement, tearing out their hair, their mouths dripping spit.

And of course it reminds me of my mother.

After the procedure I will be happy and safe forever. That's what everybody says, the scientists and my sister and Aunt Carol. I will have the procedure and then I'll be paired with a boy the evaluators choose for me. In a few years, we'll get married. Recently I've started having dreams about my wedding. In them I'm standing under a white canopy with flowers in my hair. I'm holding hands with someone, but whenever I turn to look at him his face blurs, like a camera losing focus, and I can't make out any features. But his hands are cool and dry, and my heart is beating steadily in my chest – and in my dream I know it will always beat out that same rhythm, not skip or jump or swirl or go faster, just *womp, womp, womp*, until I'm dead.

Safe, and free from pain.

Things weren't always as good as they are now. In school we learned that in the old days, the dark days, people didn't realize how deadly a disease love was. For a long time they even viewed it as a *good* thing, something to be celebrated and pursued. Of course that's one of the reasons it's so dangerous: *It affects your mind so that you cannot think clearly, or make rational decisions about your own well-being.* (That's symptom number twelve, listed in the *amor deliria nervosa* section of the twelfth edition of *The Safety, Health, and Happiness Handbook,* or *The Book of Shhh,* as we call it.) Instead people back then named other diseases – stress, heart disease, anxiety, depression, hypertension, insomnia, bipolar disorder – never realizing that these were, in fact, only symptoms that in the majority of cases could be traced back to the effects of *amor deliria nervosa.*

Of course we aren't yet totally free from the *deliria* in the United States. Until the procedure has been perfected, until it has been made safe for the under-eighteens, we will never be totally protected. It still moves around us with invisible, sweeping tentacles, choking us. I've seen countless uncureds dragged to their procedures, so racked and ravaged by love that they would rather tear their eyes out, or try to impale themselves on the barbed-wire fences outside of the laboratories, than be without it.

Several years ago on the day of her procedure, one girl managed to slip from her restraints and find her way to the laboratory roof. She dropped quickly, without screaming. For days afterward, they broadcast the image of the dead girl's face on television to remind us of the dangers of the *deliria.* Her eyes were open and her neck was twisted at an unnatural angle, but from the way her cheek was resting against the pavement you might otherwise think she had lain down to take a nap. Surprisingly, there was very little blood – just a small dark trickle at the corners of her mouth.

Ninety-five days, and then I'll be safe. I'm nervous, of course. I wonder whether the procedure will hurt. I want to get it over with. It's hard to be patient. It's hard not to be afraid while I'm still uncured, though so far the *deliria* hasn't touched me yet.

Still, I worry. They say that in the old days, love drove people to madness. That's bad enough. *The Book of Shhh* also tells stories of those who died because of love lost or never found, which is what terrifies me the most.

The deadliest of all deadly things: It kills you both when you have it and when you don't.

two

*We must be constantly on guard against the Disease;
the health of our nation, our people, our families,
and our minds depends on constant vigilance.*

– 'Basic Health Measures,' *The Safety, Health,
and Happiness Handbook, 12th edition*

The smell of oranges has always reminded me of funerals. On the morning of my evaluation it is the smell that wakes me up. I look at the clock on the bedside table. It's six o'clock.

The light is grey, the sunlight just strengthening along the walls of the bedroom I share with both of my cousin Marcia's children. Grace, the younger one, is crouched on her twin bed, already dressed, watching me. She has a whole orange in one hand. She is trying to gnaw on it, like an apple, with her little-kid teeth. My stomach twists, and I have to close my eyes again to keep from remembering the hot, scratchy dress I was forced to wear when my mother died; to keep from remembering the murmur of voices, a large, rough hand passing me orange after orange to suck on, so I would stay quiet. At the funeral I ate four oranges, section by section, and when I was left with only a pile of peelings heaped on my lap I began to suck on those, the bitter taste of the pith helping to keep the tears away.

I open my eyes and Grace leans forward, the orange cupped in her outstretched palm.

'No, Gracie.' I push off my covers and stand up. My stomach is clenching and unclenching like a fist. 'And you're not supposed to eat the peel, you know.'

She continues blinking up at me with her big grey eyes, not saying anything. I sigh and sit down next to her. 'Here,' I say, and show her how to peel the orange using her nail, unwinding bright orange curls and dropping them in her lap, the whole time trying to hold my breath against the smell. She watches me in silence. When I'm finished she holds the orange, now unpeeled, in both hands, as though it's a glass ball and she's worried about breaking it.

I nudge her. 'Go ahead. Eat now.' She just stares at it and I sigh and begin separating the sections for her, one by one. As I do I whisper, as gently as possible, 'You know, the others would be nicer to you if you would speak once in a while.'

She doesn't respond. Not that I really expect her to. My aunt Carol hasn't heard her say a word in the whole six years and three months of Grace's life – not a single syllable. Carol thinks there's something wrong with her brain, but so far the doctors haven't found it. 'She's as dumb as a rock,' Carol said matter-of-factly just the other day, watching Grace turn a bright-coloured block over and over in her hands, as though it was beautiful and miraculous, as though she expected it to turn suddenly into something else.

I stand up and go toward the window, moving away from Grace and her big, staring eyes and thin, quick fingers. I feel sorry for her.

Marcia, Grace's mother, is dead now. She always said she never wanted children in the first place. That's one of the downsides of the procedure; in the absence of *deliria nervosa*, some people find parenting distasteful. Thankfully, cases of full-blown detachment – where a mother or father is unable to bond *normally*, *dutifully*, and *responsibly* with his or her children, and winds up drowning them or sitting on their windpipes or beating them to death when they cry – are few.

But two was the number of children the evaluators decided on for Marcia. At the time it seemed like a good choice. Her family had earned high stabilization marks in the annual review. Her husband, a scientist, was well respected. They lived in an enormous house on Winter Street. Marcia cooked every meal from scratch, and taught piano lessons in her spare time, to keep busy.

But, of course, when Marcia's husband was suspected of being a sympathizer, everything changed. Marcia and her children, Jenny and Grace, had to move back with Marcia's mother, my aunt Carol, and people whispered and pointed at them everywhere they went. Grace wouldn't remember that, of course; I'd be surprised if she has any memories of her parents at all.

Marcia's husband disappeared before his trial could begin.

It's probably a good thing he did. The trials are mostly for show. Sympathizers are almost always executed. If not, they're locked away in the Crypts to serve three life sentences, back-to-back. Marcia knew that, of course. Aunt Carol thinks that's the reason her heart gave out only a few months after her husband's disappearance, when she was indicted in his place. A day after she got served the papers she was walking down the street and – *bam!* Heart attack.

Hearts are fragile things. That's why you have to be so careful.

It will be hot today, I can tell. It's already hot in the bedroom, and when I crack the window to sweep out the smell of orange, the air outside feels as thick and heavy as a tongue. I suck in deeply, inhaling the clean smell of seaweed and damp wood, listening to the distant cries of the seagulls as they circle endlessly, somewhere beyond the low, grey, sloping buildings, over the bay. Outside, a car engine guns to life. The sound startles me, and I jump.

'Nervous about your evaluation?'

I turn around. My aunt Carol is standing in the doorway, her hands folded.

'No,' I say, though this is a lie.

She smiles, just barely, a brief, flitting thing. 'Don't worry. You'll be fine. Take your shower and then I'll help you with your hair. We can review your answers on the way.'

'Okay.' My aunt continues to stare at me. I squirm, digging my nails into the windowsill behind me. I've always hated being looked at. Of course, I'll have to get used to it. During the exam there will be four evaluators staring at me for close to two hours. I'll be wearing a flimsy plastic gown, semi-translucent, like the kind you get in hospitals, so that they can see my body.

'A seven or an eight, I would say,' my aunt says, puckering her lips. It's a decent score and I'd be happy with it. 'Though you won't get more than a six if you don't get cleaned up.'

Senior year is almost over, and the evaluation is the final test I will take. For the past four months I've had all my various board exams – math, science, oral and written proficiency, sociology and psychology and photography (a specialty elective) – and I should be getting my scores sometime in the next few weeks. I'm pretty sure I did well enough to get assigned to a college. I've always been a decent student. The academic assessors will analyse my strengths and weaknesses, and then assign me to a school and a major.

The evaluation is the last step, so I can get paired. In the coming months the evaluators will send me a list of four or five approved matches. One of them will become my husband after I graduate college (assuming I pass all my boards. Girls who don't pass get paired and married right out of high school). The evaluators will do their best to match me with people who received a similar score in the evaluations. As much as possible they try to avoid any huge disparities in intelligence, temperament, social background, and age. Of course you do hear occasional horror stories: cases where a poor eighteen-year-old girl is given to a wealthy eighty-year-old man.

The stairs let out their awful moaning, and Grace's sister, Jenny, appears. She is nine and tall for her age, but very thin: all angles and elbows, her chest caving in like a warped sheet pan. It's terrible to say, but I don't like her very much. She has the same pinched look as her mother did.

She joins my aunt in the doorway and stares at me. I am only five-two and Jenny is, amazingly, just a few inches shorter than I am now. It's silly to feel self-conscious in front of my aunt and cousins, but a hot, crawling itch begins to work its way up my arms. I know they're all worried about my performance at the evaluation. It's critical that I get paired with someone good. Jenny and Grace are years away from their procedures. If I marry well, in a few years it will mean extra money for the family. It might also make the whispers go away, singsong snatches that four years after the scandal still seem to follow us wherever we go, like the sound of rustling leaves carried on the wind: *Sympathizer. Sympathizer. Sympathizer.*

It's only slightly better than the other word that followed me for years after my mom's death, a snakelike hiss, undulating, leaving its trail of poison: *Suicide.* A sideways word, a word that people whisper and mutter and cough: a word that must be squeezed out behind cupped palms or murmured behind closed doors. It was only in my dreams that I heard the word shouted, screamed.

I take a deep breath, then duck down to pull the plastic bin from under my bed so that my aunt won't see I'm shaking.

'Is Lena getting married today?' Jenny asks my aunt. Her voice has always reminded me of bees droning flatly in the heat.

'Don't be stupid,' my aunt says, but without irritation. 'You know she can't marry until she's cured.'

I take my towel from the bin and straighten up. That word – *marry* – makes my mouth go dry. Everyone marries as soon as they are done with their education. It's the way things are. 'Marriage is Order and Stability, the mark of a Healthy society.' (See *The Book of Shhh*, 'Fundamentals of Society,' p. 114). But the thought of it still makes my heart flutter frantically, like an insect behind glass. I've never touched a boy, of course – physical contact between uncureds of opposite sex is forbidden. Honestly, I've never even talked to a boy for longer than five minutes, unless you count my cousins and uncle and Andrew Marcus, who helps my uncle at the Stop-N-Save and is always picking his nose and wiping his snot on the underside of the canned vegetables.

And if I don't pass my boards – *please God, please God, let me pass them* – I'll have my wedding as soon as I'm cured, in less than three months. Which means I'll have my wedding *night*.

The smell of oranges is still strong, and my stomach does another swoop. I bury my face in my towel and inhale, willing myself not to be sick.

From downstairs there is the clatter of dishes. My aunt sighs and checks her watch.

'We have to leave in less than an hour,' she says. 'You'd better get moving.'

three

Lord, help us root our feet to the earth
And our eyes to the road
And always remember the fallen angels
Who, attempting to soar,
Were seared instead by the sun and, wings melting,
Came crashing back to the sea.
Lord, help root my eyes to the earth
And stay my eyes to the road
So I may never stumble.

– Psalm 24
(From 'Prayer and Study,' *The Book of Shhh*)

My aunt insists on walking me down to the laboratories, which, like all the government offices, are lumped together along the wharves: a string of bright white buildings, glistening like teeth over the slurping mouth of the ocean. When I was little and had just moved in with her, she used to walk me to school every day. My mother, sister, and I had lived closer to the border, and I was amazed and terrified by all the winding, darkened streets, which smelled like garbage and old fish. I always wished for my aunt to hold my hand, but she never did, and I had balled my hands into fists and followed the hypnotic swish of her corduroy pants, dreading the moment that St. Anne's Academy for Girls would rise up over the crest of the final hill, the dark stone building lined with fissures and cracks like the weather-beaten face of one of the industrial fishermen who work along the docks.

It's amazing how things change. I'd been terrified of the streets of Portland then, and reluctant to leave my aunt's side. Now I know them so well I could follow their dips and curves with my eyes closed, and today I want nothing more than to be alone. I can smell the ocean, though it's concealed from view by the twisting undulations of the streets, and it relaxes me. The salt blowing off the sea makes the air feel textured and heavy.

'Remember,' she is saying for the thousandth time, 'they want to know about your personality, yes, but the more generalized your answers the better chance you have of being considered for a variety of positions.' My aunt has always talked about marriage with words straight out of *The Book of Shhh*, words like *duty*, *responsibility*, and *perseverance*.

'Got it,' I say. A bus barrels past us. The crest for St. Anne's Academy is stenciled along its side and I duck my head quickly, imagining Cara McNamara or Hillary Packer staring out the dirt-encrusted windows, giggling and pointing at me. Everyone knows I am having my evaluation today. Only four are offered throughout the year, and slots are determined well in advance.

The makeup Aunt Carol insisted I wear makes my skin feel coated and slick. In the bathroom mirror at home, I thought I looked like a fish, especially with my hair all pinned with metal bobby pins and clips: a fish with a bunch of metal hooks sticking in my head.

I don't like makeup, have never been interested in clothes or lip gloss. My best friend, Hana, thinks I'm crazy, but of course she *would*. She's absolutely gorgeous – even when she just twists her blond hair into a messy knot on the top of her head, she looks as though she's just had it styled. I'm not ugly, but I'm not pretty, either. Everything is in-between. I have eyes that aren't green or brown, but a muddle. I'm not thin, but I'm not fat, either. The only thing you could definitely say about me is this: I'm short.

'If they ask you, God forbid, about your cousins, remember to say that you didn't know them well . . .'

'Uh-huh.' I'm only half listening. It's hot, too hot for June, and sweat is pricking up already on my lower back and in my armpits, even though I slathered on deodorant this morning. To our right is Casco Bay, which is hemmed in by Peaks Island and Great Diamond Island, where the lookout towers are. Beyond that is open ocean – and beyond *that*, all the crumbling countries and cities ruined by the disease.

'Lena? Are you even listening to me?' Carol puts a hand on my arm and spins me in her direction.

'Blue,' I parrot back at her. 'Blue is my favourite colour. Or green.' Black is too morbid; red will set them on edge; pink is too juvenile; orange is freakish.

'And the things you like to do in your free time?'

I gently slip away from her grasp. 'We've gone over this already.'

'This is important, Lena. Possibly the most important day of your whole life.'

I sigh. Ahead of me the gates that bar the government labs swing open slowly with a mechanized whine. There is already a double line forming: on one side, the girls, and fifty feet away, at a second entrance, the boys. I squint against the sun, trying to locate people I know, but the ocean has dazzled me and my vision is clouded by floating black spots.

'Lena?' my aunt prompts me.

I take a deep breath and launch into the spiel we've rehearsed a billion times. 'I like to work on the school paper. I'm interested in photography because I like the way it captures and preserves a single moment of time. I enjoy hanging out with my friends and attending concerts at Deering Oaks Park. I like to run and was a co-captain of the cross-country team for two years. I hold the school record in the 5K event. I often babysit the younger members of my family, and I really like children.'

'You're making a face,' my aunt says.

'I love children,' I repeat, plastering a smile on my face. The truth is, I don't like very many children except for Gracie. They're so bumpy and *loud* all the time, and they're always grabbing things and dribbling and wetting themselves. But I know I'll have to have children of my own someday.

'Better,' Carol says. 'Go on.'

I finish, 'My favourite subjects are math and history,' and she nods, satisfied.

'Lena!'

I turn around. Hana is just climbing out of her parents' car, her blonde hair flying in wisps and waves around her face, her semi-sheer tunic slipping off one tan shoulder. All the girls and boys lining up to enter the labs have turned to watch her. Hana has that kind of power over people.

'Lena! Wait!' Hana continues barreling down the street, waving at me frantically. Behind her, the car begins a slow revolution: back and forth, back and forth, in the narrow drive until it is facing the opposite direction. Hana's parents' car is as sleek and dark as a panther. The few times we've driven around in it together I've felt like a princess. Hardly anyone has cars anymore, and even fewer have cars that actually *drive*. Oil is strictly rationed and extremely expensive. Some middle-class people keep cars mounted in front of their houses like statues, frigid and unused, the tires spotless and unworn.

'Hi, Carol,' Hana says breathlessly, catching up to us. A magazine pops out of her half-open bag, and she stoops to retrieve it. It's one of the government publications, *Home and Family*, and in response to my raised eyebrows she makes a face. 'Mom made me bring it. She said I should read it while I'm waiting for my evaluation. She said it will give the right impression.' Hana sticks her finger down her throat and mimes gagging.

'Hana!' my aunt whispers fiercely. The anxiety in her voice makes my heart skip. Carol hardly ever loses her temper, even for a minute. She whips her head in both directions, as though expecting to find regulators or evaluators lurking in the bright morning street.

'Don't worry. They're not spying on us.' Hana turns her back to my aunt and mouths to me, *Yet*. Then she grins.

In front of us, the double line of girls and boys is growing longer, extending into the street, even as the glass-fronted doors of the labs swoosh open and several nurses appear, carrying clipboards, and begin to usher people into the waiting rooms. My aunt rests one hand on my elbow lightly, quick as a bird.

'You'd better get in line,' she says. Her voice is back to normal. I wish some of her calmness would rub off on me. 'And Lena?'

'Yeah?' I don't feel very well. The labs look far away, so white I can hardly stand to look at them, the pavement shimmering hot in front of us. The words *most important day of your life* keep repeating in my head. The sun feels like a giant spotlight.

'Good luck.' My aunt does her one-millisecond smile.

'Thanks.' I kind of wish Carol would say something else – something like, *I'm sure you'll do great*, or *Try not to worry* – but she just stands there, blinking, her face composed and unreadable as always.

'Don't worry, Mrs. Tiddle.' Hana winks at me. 'I'll make sure she doesn't screw up too badly. Promise.'

All my nervousness dissipates. Hana is so relaxed about the whole thing, so nonchalant and normal.

Hana and I go down toward the labs together. Hana is almost five-nine. When I walk next to her I have to do a half skip every other step to keep up with her, and I wind up feeling like a duck bobbing up and down in the water. Today I don't mind, though. I'm glad she's with me. I'd be a complete wreck otherwise.

'God,' she says, as we get close to the lines. 'Your aunt takes this whole thing pretty seriously, huh?'

'Well, it is serious.' We join the back of the line. I see a few people I recognize: some girls I know vaguely from school; some guys I've seen playing soccer behind Spencer Prep, one of the boys' schools. A boy looks my way and sees me staring. He raises his eyebrows and I drop my eyes quickly, my face going hot all at once and a nervous itch working in my stomach. *You'll be paired in less than three months*, I tell myself, but the words don't mean anything and seem ridiculous, like one of the Mad Libs games we played as children that always resulted in nonsensical statements: *I want banana for speedboat. Give my wet shoe to your blistering cupcake.*

'Yeah, I know. Trust me, I've read *The Book of Shhh* as much as anyone.' Hana pushes her sunglasses up onto her forehead and bats her eyelashes at me, making her voice supersweet: '"Evaluation Day is the exciting rite of passage that prepares you for a future of happiness, stability, and partnership."' She drops her sunglasses back down on her nose and makes a face.

'You don't believe it?' I lower my voice to a whisper.

Hana has been strange recently. She was always different from other people – more outspoken, more independent, more fearless. It's one of the reasons I first wanted to be her friend. I've always been shy, and afraid that I'll say or do the wrong thing. Hana is the opposite.

But lately it's been more than that. She's stopped caring about school, for one thing, and has been called to the principal's office several times for talking back to the teachers. And sometimes in the middle of talking she'll stop, just shut her mouth as though she's run up against a barrier. Other times I'll catch her staring out at the ocean as though she's thinking of swimming away.

Looking at her now, at her clear grey eyes and her mouth as thin and taut as a bowstring, I feel a tug of fear. I think of my mother floundering for a second in the air before dropping like a stone into the ocean; I think about the face of the girl who dropped from the laboratory roof all those years ago, her cheek turned against the pavement. I will away thoughts of the illness. Hana isn't sick. She can't be. I would know.

'If they really want us to be happy, they'd let us pick ourselves,' Hana grumbles.

'Hana,' I say sharply. Criticizing the system is the worst offense there is. 'Take it back.'

She holds up her hands. 'All right, all right. I take it back.'

'You *know* it doesn't work. Look how it was in the old days. Chaos all the time, fighting, and war. People were miserable.'

'I said, I take it back.' She smiles at me, but I'm still mad and I look away.

'Besides,' I go on, 'they do give us a choice.'

Usually the evaluators generate a list of four or five approved matches, and you are allowed to pick among them. This way, everyone is happy. In all the years that the procedure has been administered and the marriages arranged, there have been fewer than a dozen divorces in Maine, less than a thousand in the entire United States – and in almost all those cases, either the husband or wife was suspected of being a sympathizer and divorce was necessary and approved by the state.

'A *limited* choice,' she corrects me. 'We get to choose from the people who have been chosen for us.'

'Every choice is limited,' I snap. 'That's life.'

She opens her mouth as though she's going to respond, but instead she just starts to laugh. Then she reaches down and squeezes my hand, two quick pumps and then two long ones. It's our old sign, a habit we developed in the second grade when one of us was scared or upset, a way of saying, *I'm here, don't worry.*

'Okay, okay. Don't get defensive. I love the evaluations, okay? Long live Evaluation Day.'

'That's better,' I say, but I'm still feeling anxious and annoyed. The line shuffles slowly forward. We pass the iron gates, with their complicated crown of barbed wire, and enter the long driveway that leads to the various lab complexes. We are headed for Building 6-C. The boys go to 6-B, and the lines begin to curve away from each other.

As we move closer to the front of the line, we get a blast of air-conditioning every time the glass doors slide open and then hum shut. It feels amazing, like being momentarily dipped head to toe in a thin sheet of ice, popsicle-style, and I turn around and lift my ponytail away from my neck, wishing it weren't so damn hot. We don't have air-conditioning at home, just tall, gawky fans that are always sputtering out in the middle of the night. And most of the time Carol won't even let us use those; they suck up too much electricity, she says, and we don't have any to spare.

At last there are only a few people in front of us. A nurse comes out of the building, carrying a stack of clipboards and a handful of pens, and begins distributing them along the line.

'Please make sure to fill out all required information,' she says, 'including your medical and family history.'

My heart begins to work its way up into my throat. The neatly numbered boxes on the page – Last Name, First Name, Middle Initial, Current Address, Age – collapse together. I'm glad Hana is in front of me. She begins filling out the forms quickly, resting the clipboard on her forearm, her pen skating over the paper.

'Next.'

The doors whoosh open again, and a second nurse appears and gestures for Hana to come inside. In the dark coolness beyond her, I can see a bright white waiting room with a green carpet.

'Good luck,' I say to Hana.

She turns and gives me a quick smile. But I can tell she is nervous, finally. There is a fine crease between her eyebrows, and she is chewing on the corner of her lip.

She starts to enter the lab and then turns abruptly and walks back to me, her face wild and unfamiliar-looking, grabbing me by both shoulders, putting her mouth directly to my ear. I'm so startled I drop my clipboard.

'You know you can't be happy unless you're unhappy sometimes, right?' she whispers, and her voice is hoarse, as though she's just been crying.

'What?' Her nails are digging into my shoulders, and at that moment I'm terrified of her.

'You can't be really happy unless you're unhappy sometimes. You know that, right?'

Before I can respond she releases me, and as she pulls away, her face is as serene and beautiful and composed as ever. She bends down to scoop up my clipboard, which she passes to me, smiling. Then she turns around and is gone behind the glass doors, which open and close behind her as smoothly as the surface of water, sucking closed over something that is sinking.

four

The devil stole into the Garden of Eden.
He carried with him the disease – amor deliria nervosa –
in the form of a seed. It grew and flowered into a
magnificent apple tree, which bore apples as bright as blood.

– From *Genesis: A Complete History of the World*
and the Known Universe, by Steven Horace, PhD,
Harvard University

B y the time the nurse admits me into the waiting room, Hana is gone – vanished down one of the antiseptic white hallways and whisked behind one of the dozens of identical white doors – although there are about a half-dozen other girls milling around, waiting. One girl is sitting in a chair, hunched over her clipboard, scribbling and crossing out her answers, and then rescribbling. Another girl is frantically asking a nurse about the difference between "chronic medical conditions" and "pre-existing medical conditions." She looks like she's on the verge of having some kind of fit – a vein is standing out on her forehead and her voice is rising hysterically – and I wonder whether she's going to list *a tendency toward excessive anxiety* on her sheet.

It's not funny, but I feel like laughing. I bring my hand to my face, snorting into my palm. I tend to get giggly when I'm extremely nervous. During tests at school I'm always getting in trouble for laughing. I wonder if I should have marked that down.

A nurse takes my clipboard from me and flips through the pages, checking to see that I haven't left any answers blank.

'Lena Haloway?' she says in the bright, clipped voice that all nurses seem to share, like it's part of their medical training.

'Uh-huh,' I say, and then quickly correct myself. My aunt has told me that the evaluators will expect a certain degree of formality. 'Yes. That's me.' It's still strange to hear my real name, *Haloway*, and a dull feeling settles at the bottom of my stomach. For the past decade I've gone by my aunt's name, Tiddle. Even though it's a pretty stupid last name – Hana once said it reminded her of a little-kid word for peeing – at least it isn't associated with my mother and father. At least the Tiddles are a real family. The Haloways are nothing but a memory. But for official purposes I have to use my birth name.

'Follow me.' The nurse gestures down one of the hallways, and I follow the neat *tick-tock* of her heels down the linoleum. The halls are blindingly bright. The butterflies are working their way up from my stomach into my head, making me feel dizzy, and I try to calm myself by imagining the ocean outside, its ragged breathing, the seagulls turning pinwheels in the sky.

It will be over soon, I tell myself. *It will be over soon and then you'll go home, and you'll never have to think about the evaluation again.*

The hallway seems to go on forever. Up ahead a door opens and shuts, and a moment later, as we turn a corner, a girl brushes past us. Her face is red and she's obviously been crying. She must be done with her evaluation already. I recognize her, vaguely, as one of the first girls admitted.

I can't help but feel sorry for her. Evaluations typically last anywhere from half an hour to two hours, but it's common wisdom that the longer the evaluators keep you, the better you're doing. Of course, that isn't always true. Two years ago Marcy Davies was famously in and out of the lab in forty-five minutes, and she scored a perfect ten. And last year Corey Winde scored an all-time record for longest evaluation – three and a half hours – and still received only a three. There's a system behind the evaluations, obviously, but there's always a degree of randomness to them too. Sometimes it seems the whole process is designed to be as intimidating and confusing as possible.

I have a sudden fantasy of running through these clean, sterile hallways, kicking in all the doors. Then, immediately, I feel guilty. This is the worst of all possible times to be having doubts about the evaluations, and I mentally curse Hana. This is her fault, for saying those things to me outside. *You can't be happy unless you're unhappy sometimes. A limited choice. We get to choose from the people who have been chosen for us.*

I'm *glad* the choice is made for us. I'm glad I don't have to choose – but more than that, I'm glad I don't have to make someone else choose *me*. It would be okay for Hana, of course, if things were still the way they were in the old days. Hana, with her golden, halo hair, and bright grey eyes, and perfect straight teeth, and her laugh that makes everyone in a two-mile radius whip around and look at her and laugh too. Even clumsiness looks good on Hana; it makes you want to reach out a hand to help her or scoop up her books. When I trip on my own feet or spill coffee down the front of my shirt, people look away. You can almost see them thinking, *What a mess.* And whenever I'm around strangers my mind goes fuzzy and damp and grey, like streets starting to thaw after a hard snow – unlike Hana, who always knows just what to say.

No guy in his right mind would ever choose me when there are people like Hana in the world: it would be like settling for a stale cookie when what you really want is a big bowl of ice cream, whipped cream and cherries and chocolate sprinkles included. So I'll be happy to receive my neat, printed sheet of 'Approved Matches.' At least it means I'll end up with *somebody.* It won't matter if nobody ever thinks I'm pretty (although sometimes I wish, just for a second, that somebody would). It wouldn't matter if I had one eye.

'In here.' The nurse stops, finally, outside a door that looks identical to all the others. 'You can leave your clothing and things in the antechamber. Please put on the gown that is provided for you, with the opening to the back. Feel free to take a moment, have some water, do some meditation.'

I imagine hundreds and hundreds of girls sitting cross-legged on the floor, hands cupped on their knees, chanting *om,* and have to stifle another wild urge to laugh.

'Please be aware, however, that the longer you take to prepare, the less time your evaluators will have to get to know you.'

She smiles tightly. Everything about her is tight: her skin, her eyes, her lab coat. She is looking straight at me, but I have the impression that she isn't really focusing, that in her mind she's already tick-tocking her way back to the waiting room, ready to bring yet another girl down yet another hallway, and give her this same spiel. I feel very lonely, surrounded by these thick walls that muffle all sounds, insulated from the sun and the wind and the heat, all of it perfect and unnatural.

'When you're ready, go on through the blue door. The evaluators will be waiting for you in the lab.'

After the nurse clicks away I go into the antechamber, which is small and just as bright as the hallway. It looks like a regular doctor's examination room. There's an enormous piece of medical equipment squatting in the corner, emitting a series of periodic beeps, a tissue-paper-covered examination table, a stinging, antiseptic smell. I take off my clothes, shivering as the air-conditioning makes goose bumps pop up all over my skin, the fuzz on my arms standing up a little straighter. Great. Now the evaluators will think I'm a hairy beast.

I fold my clothes, including my bra, in a neat pile and slip on the gown. It's made of super-sheer plastic, and as I wrap it around my body, securing it at the waist with a knot, I'm fully aware that you can still see pretty much everything – including the outline of my underwear – through its fabric.

Over. Soon it will be over.

I take a deep breath and step through the blue door.

It's even brighter in the lab – dazzlingly bright, so the evaluators' first impression of me must be of someone squinting, stepping backward, bringing her hand to her face. Four shadows float in a canoe in front of me. Then my eyes adjust and the vision resolves into the four evaluators, all sitting behind a long, low table. This room is very large, and totally empty except for the evaluators and, in the corner, a steel surgical table that's been shoved up against one wall. Dual rows of overhead lights beat down on me, and I notice how high the ceiling is: at least thirty feet. I have a desperate urge to cross my arms over my chest, to cover myself up somehow. My mouth goes dry and my mind goes as hot and blank and white as the lights. I can't remember what I'm supposed to do, what I'm supposed to say.

Fortunately, one of the evaluators, a woman, speaks first. 'Do you have your forms?' Her voice sounds friendly, but it doesn't help the fist that has closed deep in my stomach, squeezing my intestines.

Oh, God, I think. *I'm going to pee. I'm going to pee right here.* I try to imagine what Hana will say after this is over, when we're walking through the afternoon sunshine, with the smell of salt and sun-warmed pavement heavy on the air around us. 'God,' she'll say. 'That was a waste of time. All of them just sitting there staring like four frogs on a log.'

'Um – yes.' I step closer, feeling like the air has turned solid, resisting me. When I'm a few feet away from the table, I reach out and pass the evaluators my clipboard. There are three men and one woman, but I find I can't focus on their features for too long. I scan them quickly and then shuffle backward again, getting only an impression of some noses, a few dark eyes, the winking of a pair of glasses.

My clipboard bobs its way down the line of evaluators. I squeeze my arms to my sides and try to appear relaxed.

Behind me, an observation deck runs along the back wall, elevated about twenty feet off the ground. It is accessed through a small red door high up beyond the tiered rows of white seats that are obviously meant to hold students, doctors, interns, and junior scientists. Not only do the lab scientists perform the procedure, they do checkups afterward and often treat difficult cases of other diseases.

It occurs to me that the scientists must perform the cure here, in this very room. That must be what the surgical table is for. The fist of anxiety starts closing in my stomach again. For some reason, though I've often thought about what it would be like to be cured, I've never really thought about the procedure itself: the hard metal table, the lights winking above me, the tubes and the wires and the pain.

'Lena Haloway?'

'Yes. That's me.'

'Okay. Why don't you start by telling us a little about yourself?' The evaluator with the glasses leans forward, spreading his hands, and smiles. He has big, square white teeth that remind me of bathroom tiles. The reflection in his glasses makes it impossible to see his eyes, and I wish he would take them off. 'Talk to us about the things you like to do. Your interests, hobbies, favourite subjects.'

I launch into the speech I've prepared, about photography and running and spending time with my friends, but I'm not focusing. I see the evaluators nodding in front of me, and smiles beginning to loosen their faces as they take notes, so I know I'm doing fine, but I can't even hear the words that are coming out of my mouth. I'm fixated on the metal surgical table and keep sneaking looks at it from the corner of my eye, watching it blink and shimmer in the light like the edge of a blade.

And suddenly I'm thinking of my mother. My mother had remained uncured despite three separate procedures, and the disease had claimed her, nipped at her insides and turned her eyes hollow and her cheeks pale, had taken control of her feet and led her, inch by inch, to the edge of a sandy cliff and into the bright, thin air of the plunge beyond.

Or so they tell me. I was six at the time. I remember only the hot pressure of her fingers on my face in the nighttime and her last whispered words to me. *I love you. Remember. They cannot take it.*

I close my eyes quickly, overwhelmed by the thought of my mother, writhing, and a dozen scientists in lab coats watching, scribbling impassively on notepads. Three separate times she was strapped to a metal table; three separate times a crowd of observers watched her from the deck, took note of her responses as the needles, and then the lasers, pierced her skin. Normally patients are anesthetized during the procedure and don't feel a thing, but my aunt had once let slip that during my mother's third procedure they had refused to sedate her, thinking that the anesthesia might be interfering with her brain's response to the cure.

'Would you like some water?' Evaluator One, the woman, gestures to a bottle of water and a glass set up on the table. She has noticed my momentary flinch, but it's okay. My personal statement is done, and I can tell by the way the evaluators are looking at me – pleased, proud, like I'm a little kid who has managed to fit all the right pegs in all the right holes – that I've done a good job.

I pour myself a glass of water and take a few sips, grateful for the pause. I can feel sweat pricking up under my arms, on my scalp, and at the base of my neck, and I pray to God they can't see it. I try to keep my eyes locked on the evaluators, but there it is in my peripheral vision, grinning at me: that damn table.

'Okay now, Lena. We're going to ask you some questions. We want you to answer honestly. Remember, we're trying to get to know you as a *person*.'

As opposed to what? The question pops into my mind before I can stop it. *As an animal?*

I take a deep breath, force myself to nod and smile. 'Great.'

'What are some of your favourite books?'

'*Love, War, and Interference*, by Christopher Malley,' I answer automatically. '*Border*, by Philippa Harolde.' It's no use trying to keep the images away: they are rising now, a flood. That one word keeps scripting itself on my brain, as though it is being seared there. *Pain*. They wanted to make my mother submit to a fourth procedure. They were coming for her on the night she died, coming to bring her to the labs. But instead she had fled into the dark, winged her way into the air. Instead she had woken me with those words – *I love you. Remember. They cannot take it.* – which the wind seemed to carry back to me long after she had vanished, repeated on the dry trees, on the leaves coughing and whispering in the cold grey dawn. 'And *Romeo and Juliet*, by William Shakespeare.'

The evaluators nod, make notes. *Romeo and Juliet* is required reading in every freshman-year health class.

'And why is that?' Evaluator Three asks.

It's frightening: that's what I'm supposed to say. It's a cautionary tale, a warning about the dangers of the old world, before the cure. But my throat seems to have grown swollen and tender. There is no room to squeeze the words out; they are stuck there like the burrs that cling to our clothing when we jog through the farms. And in that moment it's like I can hear the low growl of the ocean, can hear its distant, insistent murmur, can imagine its weight closing around my mother, water as heavy as stone. And what comes out is: 'It's beautiful.'

Instantly all four faces jerk up to look at me, like puppets connected to the same string.

'Beautiful?' Evaluator One wrinkles her nose. There's a zinging, frigid tension in the air, and I realize I've made a big, big mistake.

The evaluator with the glasses leans forward. 'That's an interesting word to use. Very interesting.' This time when he shows his teeth they remind me of the curved white canines of a dog. 'Perhaps you find suffering beautiful? Perhaps you *enjoy* violence?'

'No. No, that's not it.' I'm trying to think straight, but my head is full of the ocean's wordless roaring. It is growing louder and louder by the second. And now, faintly, it's as though I can hear screaming as well – like my mother's scream is reaching me from across the span of a decade. 'I just mean . . . there's something so sad about it . . .' I'm struggling, floundering, feeling like I'm drowning now, in the white light and the roaring. Sacrifice. I want to say something about sacrifice, but the word doesn't come.

'Let's move on.' Evaluator One, who sounded so sweet when she offered me the water, has lost all pretense of friendliness. She is all business now. 'Tell us something simple. Like your favourite colour, for example.'

Part of my brain – the rational, educated part, the logical *me* part – screams, *Blue! Say blue!* But this other, older thing inside of me is riding across the waves of sound, surging up with the rising noise. 'Grey,' I blurt out.

'Grey?' Evaluator Four splutters back.

My heart is spiraling down to my stomach. I know I've done it, I'm tanking, can practically see my numbers flipping backward. But it's too late. I'm finished – it's the roaring in my ears, growing louder and louder, a stampede that makes thinking impossible. I quickly stammer out an explanation. 'Not grey, exactly. Right before the sun rises there's a moment when the whole sky goes this pale nothing colour – not really grey but sort of, or sort of white, and I've always really liked it because it reminds me of waiting for something good to happen.'

But they've stopped listening. All of them are staring beyond me, heads cocked, expressions confused, as though trying to make out familiar words in a foreign language. And then suddenly the roaring and the screaming surge and I realize I haven't been imagining them all this time. People really are screaming, and there's a tumbling, rolling, drumming sound, like a thousand feet moving together. There's a third sound too, running under both of those: a wordless bellowing that doesn't sound human.

In my confusion everything seems disconnected, the way it does in dreams. Evaluator One half rises from her chair, saying, 'What the hell . . . ?'

At the same time, Glasses says, 'Sit down, Helen. I'll go see what's wrong.'

But at that second the blue door bursts open and a streaming blur of cows – actual, real, live, sweating, mooing cows – come thundering into the lab.

Definitely a stampede, I think, and for one weird, detached second feel proud of myself for correctly identifying the noise.

Then I realize I'm being charged by a bunch of very heavy,

very frightened herd animals, and am about two seconds from getting stomped into the ground.

Instantly I launch myself into the corner and wedge myself behind the surgical table, where I'm completely protected from the panicked mass of animals. I poke my head out just a little so I can still see what's going on. The evaluators are hopping up onto the table now, as walls of brown and speckled cow flanks fold around them. Evaluator One is screaming at the top of her lungs, and Glasses is yelling, 'Calm down, calm down!' even though he's grabbing onto her like she's a life raft and he's in danger of sinking.

Some of the cows have wigs hanging crazily from their heads, and others are half-swaddled in gowns identical to the one I'm wearing. For a second I'm sure I'm dreaming. Maybe this whole day has been a dream, and I'll wake up to discover that I'm still at home, in bed, on the morning of my evaluation. But then I notice the writing on the cows' flanks: NOT CURE. DEATH. The words are written in sloppy ink, just above the neatly branded numbers that identify these cows as destined for the slaughterhouse.

A little chill dances up my spine, and everything starts clicking into place. Every couple of years the Invalids – the people who live in the Wilds, the unregulated land that exists between recognized cities and towns – sneak into Portland and stage some kind of protest. One year they came in at night and painted red death skulls on every single one of the known scientists' houses. Another year they managed to break into the central police station, which coordinates all the patrols and guard shifts for Portland, and move all the furniture onto the roof, even the coffee machines. That was pretty funny, actually – and pretty amazing, since you'd think

Central would be the most secure building in Portland. People in the Wilds don't see love as a disease, and they don't believe in the cure. They think it's a kind of cruelty. Thus the slogan.

Now I get it: the cows are dressed up as us, the people being evaluated. Like we're all a bunch of herd animals.

The cows are calming down somewhat. They're not charging anymore, and have begun to shuffle back and forth in the lab. Evaluator One has a clipboard in her hand, and she's swooping and swatting as the cows butt up against the table, mooing and nipping at the papers scattered across its surface – the evaluators' notes, I realize, as a cow snaps up a sheet of paper and begins to rip at it with its teeth. Thank God. Maybe the cows will eat up *all* the notes, and the evaluators will lose track of the fact that I was completely tanking. Half-concealed behind the table – and safe, now, from those sharp, stamping hooves – I have to admit the whole thing is kind of hilarious.

That's when I hear it. Somehow, above the snorting and stomping and yelling, I hear the laugh above me – low and short and musical, like someone sounding out a few notes on a piano.

The observation deck. A boy is standing on the observation deck, watching the chaos below. And he's *laughing*.

As soon as I look up, his eyes click onto my face. The breath whooshes out of my body and everything freezes for a second, as though I'm looking at him through my camera lens, zoomed in all the way, the world pausing for that tiny span of time between the opening and closing of the shutter.

His hair is golden brown, like leaves in autumn just as they're turning, and he has bright amber eyes. The moment I see him I know that he's one of the people responsible for this. I know that he must live in the Wilds; I know he's an Invalid. Fear clamps down on my stomach, and I open my mouth to shout something – I'm not sure what, exactly – but at precisely that second he gives a minute shake of his head, and suddenly I can't make a sound. Then he does the absolutely, positively unthinkable.

He *winks* at me.

At last the alarm goes off. It's so loud I have to cover my ears with my hands. I look down to see whether the evaluators have seen him, but they're still doing their little tabletop dance, and when I look up again, he's gone.

five

Step on a crack, you'll break your mama's back.
Step on a stone, you'll end up all alone.
Step on a stick, you're bound to get the Sick.
Watch where you tread, you'll bring out all the dead.

– A common children's playground chant,
usually accompanied by jumping rope or clapping

That night, I have the dream again.

I'm at the edge of a big white cliff made out of sand. The ground is unsteady. The ledge I'm standing on is starting to crumble, to flake away and tumble down, down, down – thousands of feet below me, into the ocean, which is whipping and snapping so hard it looks like one gigantic, frothing stew, all whitecaps and surging water. I'm terrified I'm going to fall, but for some reason I can't move or back away from the edge of the cliff, even as I feel the ground sifting away from underneath me, millions of molecules rearranging themselves into space, into wind: any second I'm going to fall.

And just before I know that there's nothing underneath me but air – that at any split second I'm going to feel the wind shrieking around me as I drop down into the water – the waves lashing underneath me open up for a moment and I see my mother's face, pale and bloated and splotched with blue, floating just below the surface. Her eyes are open, her mouth is split apart as though she is screaming, her arms are extended on either side of her, bobbing in the current, as though she is waiting to embrace me.

That's when I wake up. That's when I always wake up.

My pillow is damp, and I've got a scratchy feeling in my throat. I've been crying in my sleep. Gracie is folded next to me, one cheek squashed flat against the sheets, her mouth making endless, noiseless repetitions. She always gets into bed with me when I'm having the dream. She can sense it, somehow.

I brush her hair away from her face and pull the sweat-soaked sheets away from her shoulders. I'll be sorry to leave Grace when I move out. Our secrets have made us close, bonded us together. She is the only one who knows of the Coldness: a feeling that comes sometimes when I'm lying in bed, a black, empty feeling that knocks my breath away and leaves me gasping as though I've just been thrown in icy water. On nights like that – although it is wrong and illegal – I think of those strange and terrible words, *I love you*, and wonder what they would taste like in my mouth, try to recall their lilting rhythm on my mother's tongue.

And of course I keep her secret safe. I'm the only one who knows that Grace isn't stupid, or slow: there's nothing wrong with her at all. I'm the only one who has ever heard her speak. One night after she'd come to sleep in my bed I woke up in the very early morning, the nighttime shadows ebbing off our walls. She was sobbing quietly into the pillow next to me, pronouncing the same word over and over, stuffing her mouth with blankets so I could barely hear her: 'Mommy, Mommy, Mommy.' As though she was trying to chew her way around it; as though it was choking her in her sleep. I'd put my arms around her and squeezed, and after what felt like hours she exhausted herself on the word and fell back to sleep, the tension in her body slowly relaxing, her face hot and bloated from the tears.

That's the real reason she doesn't speak. All the rest of her words are crowded out by that single, looming one, a word still echoing in the dark corners of her memory. *Mommy.*

I know. I remember.

I sit up and watch the light strengthen on the walls, listen for the sounds of the seagulls outside, take a drink from the glass of water next to my bed. Today is June 2. Ninety-four days.

I wish, for Grace, the cure could come sooner. I comfort myself by thinking that someday she will have the procedure too. Someday she will be saved, and the past and all its pain will be rendered as smoothly palatable as the food we spoon to our babies.

Someday we will all be saved.

By the time I drag myself down to breakfast – feeling as though someone is grinding sand into both of my eyes – the official story about the incident at the labs has been released. Carol keeps our small TV on low while she makes breakfast, and the murmur of the newscasters' voices almost puts me back to sleep. *"Yesterday a truck full of cattle intended for the slaughterhouse was mixed up with a shipment of pharmaceuticals, resulting in the hilarious and unprecedented chaos you see on your screen."* Cue: nurses squealing, swatting at lowing cows with clipboards.

This doesn't make any sense, but as long as no one mentions the Invalids, everyone's happy. We're not supposed to know about them. They're not even supposed to *exist*; supposedly, all the people who live in the Wilds were destroyed over fifty years ago, during the blitz.

Fifty years ago the government closed the borders of the United States. The border is guarded constantly by military personnel. No one can get in. No one goes out. Every sanctioned and approved community must also be contained within a border – that's the law – and all travel between communities requires official written consent of the municipal government, to be obtained six months in advance. This is for our own protection. Safety, Sanctity, Community: that is our country's motto.

For the most part, the government has been successful. We haven't seen a war since the border was closed, and there is hardly any crime, except for the occasional incident of vandalism or petty theft. There is no more hatred in the United States, at least among the cured. Only sporadic cases of detachment – but every medical procedure carries a certain risk.

But so far, the government has failed to rid the country of the Invalids, and it is the single blemish on the administration, and the system in general. So we don't talk about them. We pretend that the Wilds – and the people who live there – don't even exist. It's rare to hear the word even spoken, except when a suspected sympathizer disappears, or when a young diseased couple is found to have vanished together before a cure can be administered.

One piece of really good news is this: all of yesterday's evaluations have been invalidated. All of us will receive a new evaluation date, which means I get a second chance. This time I swear I'm not going to screw it up. I feel completely idiotic about my meltdown at the labs. Sitting at the breakfast table, with everything looking so clean and bright and normal – the chipped blue mugs full of coffee, the erratic beeping of the microwave (one of the few electronic devices, besides the lights, Carol actually allows us to *use*) – makes yesterday seem like a long, strange dream. It's a miracle, actually, that a bunch of fanatical Invalids decided to let loose a stampede at the exact moment I was failing the most important test of my life. I don't know what came over me. I think about Glasses showing his teeth, and the moment I heard my mouth say, 'Grey,' and I wince. *Stupid, stupid.*

Suddenly I'm aware that Jenny has been talking to me.

'What?' I blink at Jenny as she swims into focus. I watch her hands as she cuts her toast precisely into quarters.

'I said, what's wrong with you?' Back and forth, back and forth. The knife dings against the edge of the plate. 'You look like you're about to puke or something.'

'Jenny,' Carol scolds. She is at the sink, washing dishes. 'Not while your uncle is eating breakfast.'

'I'm fine.' I rip off a piece of toast, slide it across the stick of butter that's getting melty in the middle of the table, and force myself to eat. The last thing I need is a good old family-style interrogation. 'Just tired.'

Carol turns to look at me. Her face has always reminded me of a doll's. Even when she's talking, even when she's irritated or happy or confused, her expression stays weirdly immobile. 'Couldn't sleep?'

'I slept,' I say. 'I just had a bad dream, that's all.'

At the end of the table, my uncle William starts up from his newspaper. 'Oh, God. You know what? You just reminded me. I had a dream last night too.'

Carol raises her eyebrows, and even Jenny looks interested. It's extremely unusual for people to dream once they've been cured. Carol once told me that on the rare occasions she still dreams, her dreams are full of dishes, stacks and stacks of them climbing toward the sky, and sometimes she climbs them, lip to lip, hauling herself up into the clouds, trying to reach the top of the stack. But it never ends; it stretches on into infinity. As far as I know, my sister Rachel never dreams anymore.

William smiles. 'I was caulking the window in the bathroom. Carol, you remember I said there was a draft the other day? Anyway, I was piping in the caulk, but every time I finished, it would just flake away – almost like it was snow – and the wind would come in and I'd have to start all over. On and on and on – for hours, it felt like.'

'How strange,' my aunt says, smiling, coming to the table with a plate of fried eggs. My uncle likes them super runny, and they sit on the plate, their yolks jiggling and quivering like hula-hoop dancers, spotted with oil. My stomach twists.

William says, 'No wonder I'm so tired this morning. I was doing housework all night.'

Everyone laughs but me. I choke down another bit of toast, wondering whether I'll dream once I've been cured.

I hope not.

This year is the first year since sixth grade that I don't have a single class with Hana, so I don't see her until after school, when we meet up in the locker room to go running, even though cross-country season ended a couple of weeks ago. (When the team went to Regionals it was only the third time I'd ever been out of Portland, and even though we went just forty miles along the grey, bleak municipal highway, I could still hardly swallow, the butterflies in my throat were so frantic.) Still, Hana and I try to run together as much as we can, even during school vacations.

I started running when I was six years old, after my mom committed suicide. The first day I ever ran a whole mile was the day of her funeral. I'd been told to stay upstairs with my cousins while my aunt prepared the house for the memorial service and laid out all the food. Marcia and Rachel were supposed to get me ready, but in the middle of helping me dress they'd started arguing about something and had stopped paying me any attention at all. So I had wandered downstairs, my dress zipped halfway up my back, to ask my aunt for help. Mrs. Eisner, my aunt's neighbor at the time, was there. As I came into the kitchen she was saying, 'It's horrible, of course. But there was no hope for her anyway. It's much better this way. It's better for Lena, too. Who wants a mother like that?'

I wasn't supposed to have heard. Mrs. Eisner gave a startled little gasp when she saw me, and her mouth shut quickly, like a cork popping back into a bottle. My aunt just stood there, and in that second it was as though the world and the future collapsed down into a single point, and I understood that this – the kitchen, the spotless cream linoleum floors, the glaring lights, and the vivid green mass of Jell-O on the counter – was all that was left now that my mother was gone.

Suddenly I couldn't stay there. I couldn't stand the sight of my aunt's kitchen, which I now understood would be *my* kitchen. I couldn't stand the Jell-O. My mother *hated* Jell-O. An itchy feeling began to work its way through my body, as though a thousand mosquitoes were circulating through my blood, biting me from the inside, making me want to scream, jump, squirm.

I ran.

Hana, one foot on a bench, is lacing up her shoes when I come in. My awful secret is that I like to run with Hana partly because it's the single, sole, solitary shred of a thing that I can do better than she can, but I would never admit that out loud in a million years.

I haven't even had a chance to put my bag down before she's leaning forward and grabbing my arm.

'Can you believe it?' She's fighting a smile, and her eyes are a pinwheel of colour – blue, green, gold – flashing like they always do when she's excited about something. 'It was definitely the Invalids. That's what everybody's saying, anyway.'

We're the only people in the locker room – all the sports teams have finished their seasons – but I instinctively whip my head around when she says the word. 'Keep your voice down.'

She pulls back a little, tossing her hair over one shoulder. 'Relax. I did recon. Even checked the toilet stalls. We're in the clear.'

I open up the gym locker I've had for all my ten years at St. Anne's. At its bottom is a film of gum wrappers and shredded notes and lost paper clips, and on top of that, my small limp pile of running clothes, two pairs of shoes, my cross-country team jersey, a dozen half-used bottles of deodorant, conditioner, and perfume. In less than two weeks I'll graduate and never see the inside of this locker again, and for a second I get sad. It's gross, but I've actually always loved the smell of gyms: the industrial cleaning fluid and the deodorant and soccer balls and even the lingering smell of sweat. It's comforting to me. It's so strange how life works: you want something and you wait and wait and feel like it's taking forever to come. Then it happens and it's over and all you want to do is curl back up in that moment before things changed.

'Who's everybody, anyway? The news is saying it was just a mistake, a shipping error or something.' I feel the need to repeat the official story, even though I know just as well as Hana that it's BS.

She straddles the bench, watching me. As usual, she's oblivious to the fact that I hate it when other people see me change. 'Don't be an idiot. If it was on the news, it definitely isn't true. Besides, who mixes up a cow and a box of prescription meds? It's not like it's hard to tell the difference.'

I shrug. She's right, obviously. She's still looking at me, so I angle slightly away. I've never been comfortable with my body like Hana and some of the other girls at St. Anne's, never gotten over the awkward feeling that I've been fitted together just a little wrong in some very key places. Like I've been sketched by an amateur artist: if you don't look too closely, it's all right, but start focusing and all the smudges and mistakes become really obvious.

Hana kicks one leg out and begins stretching, refusing to let the issue drop. Hana's more fascinated with the Wilds than anyone I've ever met. 'If you think about it, it's pretty amazing. The planning and all that. It would have taken at least four or five people – maybe more – to coordinate everything.'

I think briefly of the boy I saw on the observation deck, of his flashing, autumn-leaf-coloured hair, and the way he tipped his head back when he laughed so I could see the vaulted black arch of his mouth. I told no one about him, not even Hana, and now I feel I should have.

Hana goes on, 'Someone must have had security codes. Maybe a sympathizer—'

A door bangs loudly at the front of the locker room, and Hana and I both jump, staring at each other with wide eyes. Footsteps click quickly across the linoleum. After a few seconds of hesitation, Hana launches smoothly into a safe topic: the colour of the graduation gowns, which are orange this year. Just then Mrs. Johanson, the athletic director, comes around the bank of lockers, swinging her whistle around one finger.

'At least they're not brown, like at Fielston Prep,' I say, though I'm barely listening to Hana. My heart is pounding and I'm still thinking about the boy, and wondering whether Johanson heard us say the word *sympathizer*. She doesn't do anything but nod as she passes us, so it seems unlikely.

I've learned to get really good at this – say one thing when I'm thinking about something else, act like I'm listening when I'm not, pretend to be calm and happy when really I'm freaking out. It's one of the skills you perfect as you get older. You have to learn that people are *always* listening. The first time I ever used the cell phone that my aunt and uncle share, I was surprised by the patchy interference that kept breaking up my conversation with Hana at random intervals, until my aunt explained that it was just the government's listening devices, which arbitrarily cut into cell phone calls, recording them, monitoring conversations for target words like *love*, or

Invalids, or *sympathizer*. No one in particular is targeted; it's all done randomly, to be fair. But it's almost worse that way. I pretty much always feel as though a giant, revolving gaze is bound to sweep over me at any second, lighting up my bad thoughts like an animal lit still and white in the ever-turning beam of a lighthouse.

Sometimes I feel as though there are two me's, one coasting directly on top of the other: the superficial me, who nods when she's supposed to nod and says what she's supposed to say, and some other, deeper part, the part that worries and dreams and says 'Grey.' Most of the time they move along in sync and I hardly notice the split, but sometimes it feels as though I'm two whole different people and I could rip apart at any second. Once I confessed this to Rachel. She just smiled and told me it would all be better after the procedure. After the procedure, she said, it would be all coasting, all glide, every day as easy as one, two, three.

'Ready,' I say, spinning my locker closed. We can still hear Mrs. Johanson shuffling around in the bathroom, whistling. A toilet flushes. A faucet goes on.

'My turn to pick the route,' Hana says, eyes sparkling, and before I can open my mouth to protest, she lunges forward and smacks me on the shoulder. 'Tag. You're it,' she says, and just as easily spins off the bench and sprints for the door, laughing, so I have to run to catch up.

Earlier in the day it rained, and the storm cooled everything off. Water evaporates from puddles in the streets, leaving a shimmering layer of mist over Portland. Above us the sky is now a vivid blue. The bay is flat and silver, the coast like a giant belt cinched around it, keeping it in place.

I don't ask Hana where she's going, but it doesn't surprise me when she starts winding us toward Old Port, toward the old footpath that runs along Commercial Street and up to the labs. We try to keep on the smaller, less trafficked streets, but it's pretty much a losing game. It's three thirty. All the schools have been released, and the streets surge with students walking home. A few buses rumble past, and one or two cars squeeze by. Cars are considered good luck. As they pass, people reach out their hands and brush along the shiny hoods, the clean, bright windows, which will soon be smudged with fingerprints.

Hana and I run next to each other, reviewing all the day's gossip. We don't talk about the botched evaluations yesterday, or the rumours of the Invalids. There are too many people around. Instead she tells me about her ethics exam, and I tell her about Cora Dervish's fight with Minna Wilkinson. We talk about Willow Marks, too, who has been absent from school since the previous Wednesday. Rumor is that Willow was found by regulators last week in Deering Oaks Park after curfew — with a boy.

We've been hearing rumours like that about Willow for years. She's just the kind of person people talk about. She has blonde hair, but she's always colouring different streaks into it with markers, and I remember once on a freshman class trip to a museum, we passed a group of Spencer Prep boys and she said, so loud one of our chaperones could have easily heard, 'I'd like to kiss one of them straight on the lips.' Supposedly she was caught hanging out with a boy in tenth grade and got off with a warning because she showed no signs of the *deliria*. Every so often people make mistakes; it's biological, a result of the same kind of chemical and hormonal imbalances that occasionally lead to Unnaturalism, to boys being attracted to boys and girls to girls. These impulses, too, will be resolved by the cure.

But this time it is serious, apparently, and Hana drops the bomb just as we turn onto Center: Mr. and Mrs. Marks have agreed to move the date of Willow's procedure up by a full six months. She'll be missing graduation day to get cured.

'Six months?' I repeat. We've been running hard for twenty minutes, so I'm not sure if the heavy thumping in my chest is a result of the exercise or the news. I'm feeling more out of breath than I should be, like someone's sitting on my chest. 'Isn't that dangerous?'

Hana tips her head to the right, gesturing the way to a shortcut through an alley. 'It's been done before.'

'Yeah, but not *successfully*. What about all the side effects? Mental problems? Blindness?' There are a few reasons why the scientists won't let anyone under the age of eighteen have the procedure, but the biggest one is that it just doesn't seem to work as well for people younger than that, and in the worst cases it's been known to cause all kind of crazy problems. Scientists speculate that the brain and its neuro-pathways are still too plastic before then, still in the middle of forming themselves. Actually, the older you are when you have the procedure, the better, but most people are scheduled for the procedure as close as possible to their eighteenth birthday.

'I guess they think it's worth the risk,' Hana says. 'Better than the alternative, you know? *Amor deliria nervosa*. The deadliest of all deadly things.' This is the catchphrase that's written on every mental health pamphlet ever written about the *deliria*; Hana's voice is flat as she repeats it, and it makes my stomach dip. All of yesterday's craziness has made me forget Hana's comment to me before the evaluations. But now I remember, and remember how strange she looked too, eyes cloudy and unreadable.

'Come on.' I feel a straining in my lungs and my left thigh is starting to cramp. The only way to push through it is to run harder and faster. 'Let's pick it up, Slug.'

'Bring it.' Hana's face splits into a grin, and both of us start pumping faster. The pain in my lungs swells up and blossoms until it feels like it's everywhere, tearing through all my cells and muscles at once. The cramp in my leg makes me wince every time my heel hits the pavement. It's always like this on miles two and three, like all the stress and anxiety and irritation and fear get transformed into little needling points of physical pain, and you can't breathe or imagine going farther or think anything but: *I can't. I can't. I can't.*

And then, just as suddenly, it's gone. All the pain lifts away, the cramp vanishes, the fist eases off my chest, and I can breathe easily. Instantly a feeling of total happiness bubbles up inside of me: the solid feeling of the ground underneath me, the simplicity of the movement, rocketing off my heels, pushing forward in time and space, total freedom and release. I glance over at Hana. I can tell from her expression that she's feeling it too. She has made it through the wall. She senses me looking and whips around, her blonde ponytail a bright arc, to give me the thumbs-up.

It's strange. When we run I feel closer to Hana than at any other time. Even when we're not talking, it's like there's an invisible cord tethering us together, matching our rhythms, our arms and our legs, as though we're both responding to the same drumbeat. More and more it has been occurring to me that this, too, will change after our procedures. She'll retreat to the West End and make friends with her neighbors, with people richer and more sophisticated than I am. I'll stay in some crappy apartment on Cumberland, and I won't miss her, or remember what it felt like to run side by side. They've warned me that after my procedure I may not even like running anymore, period. Another side effect of the cure: people often change their habits afterward, lose interest in their former hobbies and things that had given them pleasure.

'The cured, incapable of strong desire, are thus rid of both remembered and future pain' ('After the Procedure,' *The Safety, Health, and Happiness Handbook*, p.132).

The world is spinning by, people and streets, a long, unfurling ribbon of colour and sound. We run past St. Vincent's, the biggest all-boys school in Portland. A half-dozen boys are outside playing basketball, lazily dribbling the ball around, calling to one another. Their words are a blur, an indistinct series of shouts and barks and short bursts of laughter, the way that boys always sound whenever they're together in groups, whenever you only hear them from around corners or across streets or down the beach. It's like they have a language all their own, and for about the thousandth time I think how glad I am that segregation policies keep us separate most of the time.

As we run by I think I sense a momentary pause, a fraction of a second when all their eyes lift and turn in our direction. I'm too embarrassed to look. My whole body goes white-hot, like someone's just stuck me headfirst into an oven. But a second later I feel their eyes sweeping past me, a wind, latching on to Hana. Her blonde hair flashes next to me, a coin in the sun.

The pain is creeping back into my legs, a leaden feeling, but I force myself to keep going as we round the corner of Commercial Street and leave St. Vincent's behind. I feel Hana straining to keep up next to me. I turn my head, barely managing to gasp out, 'Race you.' But as Hana pulls up, arms pumping, and nearly passes me, I put my head down and lunge forward, cycling my legs as fast as I can, trying to suck air into my lungs, which feel like they've shrunk to the size of a pea, fighting the screaming in my muscles. Blackness eats the edges of my vision, and all I can see is the chain-link fence that rises up in front of us suddenly, blocking our path, and then I'm reaching out and thwacking it so hard it begins to shake, turning around to yell, 'I won!' as Hana pulls up a second behind me, gasping for breath. Both of us are laughing now, hiccuping and taking huge gulping breaths of air as we pace around in circles, trying to walk it off.

When she can finally breathe again, Hana straightens up, laughing. 'I let you win,' she says, an old joke of ours.

I toe some gravel in her direction. She ducks away, shrieking. 'Keep telling yourself that.'

My hair has come out of its ponytail and I wrestle it out of its elastic, flipping my head down so I get the wind on my neck. Sweat drips down into my eyes, stinging.

'Nice look.' Hana pushes me lightly and I stumble sideways, whipping my head up to swipe back at her.

She sidesteps me. There's a gap in the chain-link fence that marks the beginning of a narrow service road. This is blocked with a low metal gate. Hana hops it and gestures for me to follow. I haven't really been paying attention to where we are: the service drive threads down through a parking lot, a forest of industrial Dumpsters and cargo storage sheds. Beyond those is the familiar string of white square buildings, like giant teeth. This must be one of the side entrances of the lab complex. I see now that the chain-link fence is looped on top with barbed wire and marked at twenty-foot intervals with signs that all read: PRIVATE PROPERTY. NO TRESPASSING. AUTHORIZED PERSONNEL ONLY.

'I don't think we're supposed to—' I start to say, but Hana cuts me off.

'Come on,' she calls out. 'Live a little.'

I do a quick scan of the parking lot beyond the gate and the road behind us: no one. The small guard hut just past the gate is also empty. I lean over and peek inside. There's a half-eaten sandwich sitting on wax paper, and a stack of books piled messily on a small desk next to an old-fashioned radio, which is spitting static and patchy bits of music into the silence. I don't see any surveillance cameras, either, though there must be some. All the government buildings are wired. I hesitate for a second longer, then swing myself over the gate and catch up to Hana. Her eyes are lit up with excitement, and I can tell that this was her plan, and her destination, all along.

'This must be how the Invalids got in,' she says in a breathless rush, as though we've been talking about yesterday's drama at the labs all this time. 'Don't you think?'

'Doesn't seem like it would have been hard.' I'm trying to sound casual but the whole thing – the empty service road and the enormous parking lot, shimmering in the sun, the blue Dumpsters and the electrical wires zigzagging across the sky, the sparkling white slope of the lab roofs – makes me uneasy. Everything is silent and very still – frozen, almost, the way things are in a dream, or just before a major thunderstorm. I don't want to say it to Hana, but I'd give pretty much anything to head back to Old Port, to the complex nest of familiar streets and stores.

Even though there's no one around, I have the impression of being watched. It's worse than the normal feeling of being observed in school and on the street and even at home, having to be cautious about what you do and say, the close, blocked-in feeling that everyone gets used to eventually.

'Yeah.' Hana kicks at the packed dirt road. A plume of dust puffs up, resettles slowly. 'Pretty crappy security for a major medical facility.'

'Pretty crappy security for a petting zoo,' I say.

'I resent that.' The voice comes from behind us, and both Hana and I jump.

I spin around. The world seems to freeze for an instant.

A boy is standing behind us, arms crossed, head cocked to the side. A boy with caramel-coloured skin and hair that's a golden-brown colour, like autumn leaves getting ready to fall.

It's him. The boy from yesterday, from the observation deck. The Invalid.

Except he isn't an Invalid, obviously. He's wearing a short-sleeved blue guard's uniform over jeans, and he's got a laminated government ID clipped to his collar.

'I leave for two seconds to get a refill' – he gestures to the bottle of water he's holding – 'and I come back to find a full-fledged break-in.'

I'm so confused I can't move or speak or do anything. Hana must think I'm scared, because she jumps in quickly, 'We weren't breaking in. We weren't doing anything. We were just running and we . . . um, we got lost.'

The boy crosses his arms in front of his chest, rocking back on his heels. 'Didn't see any of the signs outside, huh? "No Trespassing"? "Authorized Personnel Only"?'

Hana looks away. She's nervous too. I can feel it. Hana's a thousand times more confident than I am, but neither of us is used to standing in the open and talking to a boy, *especially* not a boy-guard, and it must have occurred to Hana that he already has plenty of grounds to arrest us.

'Must have missed them,' she mumbles.

'Uh-huh.' He raises his eyebrows. It's obvious he doesn't believe us, but at least he doesn't look angry. 'They're pretty subtle. Only a few dozen of them. I can see how you might not have noticed.'

He looks away for a second, squinting, and I get the feeling he's trying to stop himself from laughing. He's not like any guard I've ever seen – at least, not the typical guards you see at the border and all around Portland, fat and scowly and old. I think about how sure I was yesterday that he came from the Wilds, the solid certainty deep inside of me.

I was wrong, obviously. As he turns his head I see the unmistakable sign of someone who is cured: the mark of the procedure, a three-pointed scar just behind the left ear, where the scientists insert a special three-pronged needle used exclusively for immobilizing the patient so that the cure can be administered. People show off their scars like badges of honor; you hardly see any cureds with long hair, and the women who haven't lopped off their hair entirely are careful to wear it pulled back.

My fear recedes. Talking to a cured isn't illegal. The rules of segregation don't apply.

I'm not sure if he has recognized me or not. If so, he hasn't given any sign of it. Finally I can't take it anymore and I burst out, 'You. I saw you—' At the last second I can't finish the sentence. *I saw you yesterday.*

You winked *at me.*

Hana looks startled. 'You two know each other?' She shoots a look at me. Hana knows I've hardly ever exchanged two words with a boy before, unless it's 'Excuse me' in the street or 'Sorry for stepping on your toes' when I trip on somebody. We're not supposed to have more than minimal contact with uncured boys outside of our own families. Even after they've been cured, there's hardly a need or excuse for it, unless we're dealing with a doctor or teacher or someone like that.

He turns to look at me. His face is completely professional and composed, but I swear I see something flickering in his eyes, a look of amusement or pleasure. 'No,' he says smoothly. 'We've never met. I'm sure I would remember.' The flash in his eyes is back – is he laughing at me?

'I'm Hana,' Hana says. 'And this is Lena.' She jabs me with an elbow. I know I must look like a fish, standing there with my mouth gaping open, but I'm too outraged to speak. He's lying. I *know* he's the one I saw yesterday, would bet my life on it.

'Alex. Nice to meet you.' Alex keeps his eyes on me as he and Hana shake hands. Then he extends a hand to me. 'Lena,' he says thoughtfully. 'I've never heard that name before.'

I hesitate. Shaking hands makes me feel awkward, like I'm playing dress-up in an adult's too-big clothing. Besides, I've never actually touched skin-to-skin with a stranger. But he's just standing there with his hand out, so after a second I reach out and shake. The moment we touch, a tiny electrical shock buzzes through me, and I pull away quickly.

'It's short for Magdalena,' I say.

'Magdalena.' Alex tips his head back, watching me from narrowed eyes. 'Pretty.'

I'm momentarily distracted by the way he says my name.

In his mouth it sounds musical, not clunky and angular, the way my teachers have always made it sound. His eyes are a warm amber colour, and as I look at him I have a sudden, flashing memory of my mother pouring syrup over a stack of pancakes. I look away, feeling ashamed, as though he has somehow been responsible for dredging the memory up, has reached in with his hand and wrenched it from me. Embarrassment makes me feel angry, and I press on, 'I *do* know you. I saw you yesterday in the labs. You were on the observation deck, watching – watching everything.' Again, my courage fails me at the last second and I don't say, *Watching me.*

I can feel Hana glaring at me, but I ignore her. She must be furious I haven't told her any of this.

Alex's face doesn't change. He doesn't blink or drop his smile for even a fraction of a second. 'Case of mistaken identity, I guess. Guards aren't allowed in the labs during evaluations. Especially not part-time guards.'

For a second longer we stand there, staring at each other. Now I know he's lying, and the easy, lazy grin on his face makes me want to reach out and slap him. I ball my fists and suck in a deep breath, willing myself to stay calm. I'm not the violent type. I don't know why I'm feeling so aggravated.

Hana jumps in, breaking the tension. 'So this is it? A part-time security guard and some "Keep Out" signs?'

Alex keeps his eyes on me a half second longer. Then he turns to look at Hana as though noticing her for the first time. 'What do you mean?'

'I would have thought the labs would be better protected, that's all. It doesn't seem like it would be too hard to break into this place.'

Alex raises his eyebrows. 'Thinking about making the attempt?'

Hana freezes, and my blood goes to ice. She has gone too far. If Alex reports us as potential sympathizers, or trouble-makers, or anything, we're in for months and months of surveillance and investigation – and we can kiss our chances of passing the evaluations with decent scores good-bye. I picture a lifetime of watching Andrew Marcus fish snot out of his nose with a thumbnail and feel queasy.

Alex must sense our fear, because he raises both hands. 'Relax. I was kidding. You don't exactly seem like terrorists.' It occurs to me how ridiculous we must look in our running shorts and sweaty tank tops and neon sneakers. Or at least, I must look ridiculous. Hana looks like a model for athletic wear. Again, I feel a fit of blushing coming on, followed by a surge of irritation. No wonder the regulators decided on the segregation of boys and girls: otherwise, it would have been a nightmare, this feeling angry and self-conscious and confused and annoyed all the time.

'This is just the loading area, anyway, for freight and stuff.' Alex gestures beyond the line of cargo sheds. 'Real security starts closer to the facilities. Full-time guards, cameras, elec-trified fence, the whole shebang.'

Hana doesn't look at me, but when she speaks I can hear the excitement creeping into her voice. 'The loading area? Like, where the deliveries come?'

In my head I start praying, *Don't say anything dumb. Don't say anything dumb. Do not mention the Invalids.*

'You got it.'

Hana dances on her feet, shifting her weight back and forth. I try to shoot her a warning look, but she avoids my eyes.

'So this is where the trucks come? With medical equipment and . . . and other stuff?'

'Exactly.' Again I have the impression of something flickering behind Alex's eyes, even as the rest of his face stays totally neutral. I don't trust him, I realize, and again wonder why he is lying about being in the labs yesterday. Maybe only because it's forbidden, like he said. Maybe because he was laughing instead of trying to help out.

And maybe, after all, he really doesn't recognize me. We made eye contact for only a few seconds, and I'm sure to him I was only a blurry, in-between face, easy to forget. Not pretty. Not ugly, either. Just plain, like a thousand other faces you would see on the street.

He, on the other hand, is most definitely not in-between. There's something insane to me about standing in the open talking to a strange boy, even if he *is* cured, and though my head is whirling, it's like my vision gets razor sharp, making everything look ultra-detailed. I notice the way a piece of his hair curls around his scar, like a frame; I notice his large brown hands and the whiteness of his teeth and the perfect symmetry of his face. His jeans are faded and belted low on his hips, and the laces in his sneakers are the weirdest ink-colour blue, like he has coloured them in with a pen.

I wonder how old he is. He looks my age, but he must be slightly older, maybe nineteen. I wonder, too – a brief, flitting thought – whether he's already been paired. But of course he has; he must have been.

I've been staring at him accidentally and he turns suddenly to look at me. I drop my eyes, feeling a quick and irrational terror that he has managed to read my thoughts.

'I'd love to look around,' Hana hints not-so-subtly. I reach out and pinch her when Alex isn't looking and she shrinks away, giving me a guilty look. At least she doesn't start grilling him about what happened yesterday, and get us thrown in jail or dragged through an interrogation.

Alex tosses his water bottle in the air, catches it in one hand. 'Trust me, there's nothing to see. Unless you're a fan of industrial waste. There's plenty of that around here.' He tips his head toward the Dumpsters. 'Oh – and the best view of the bay in Portland. We've got that going for us too.'

'Really?' Hana wrinkles her nose, momentarily distracted from her detective mission.

Alex nods, tosses the bottle again, catches it. As it arcs through the air the sun winks through the water like light from a jewel. '*That* I can show you,' he says. 'Come on.'

All I want is to get out of here, but Hana says, 'Sure,' so I trudge along after her, silently cursing her curiosity and fixation with all things Invalid-related and vowing never to let her pick our running route again. She and Alex walk in front, and I pick up scattered bits of their conversation: I hear him say he takes classes at one of the colleges but miss what he says he studies; Hana tells him we're about to graduate. He tells her he's nineteen; she says that we're both turning eighteen in several months. Thankfully, they avoid talking about the botched evaluations yesterday.

The service road connects with another, smaller drive, which runs parallel to Fore Street, slanting steeply uphill toward the Eastern Promenade. Here there are rows of long, metal storage sheds. The sun is flat and high and unrelenting. I'm incredibly thirsty, but when Alex turns around and offers me a sip from his water bottle, I say, 'No,' quickly and too loud. The thought of putting my mouth where his mouth has been makes me feel anxious all over again.

As we come up to the top of the hill – all three of us panting a little from the climb – the bay unfolds to our right like a gigantic map, a sparkling, shimmering world of blues and greens. Hana gasps a little. It really is a beautiful view: unobstructed and perfect. The sky is full of poufy white clouds that make me think of feather pillows, and seagulls turn lazy arcs over the water, patterns of birds forming and dissolving in the sky.

Hana walks forward a few feet. 'It's amazing. Gorgeous, isn't it? No matter how long I live here I never get used to it.' She turns and looks at me. 'I think this is my favourite way to see the ocean. Middle of the afternoon, sunny and bright. It's just like a photograph. Don't you think, Lena?'

I'm feeling so relaxed – enjoying the wind at the top of the hill, which sweeps over my arms and legs and makes me feel cool and delicious, enjoying the view of the bay and the high, blinking eye of the sun – I've almost forgotten that Alex is with us. He's been hanging back, standing a few feet behind us, and ever since we came up the hill he hasn't said a word.

Which is why I nearly jump out of my skin when he leans forward and directs a single word into my ear: 'Grey.'

'What?' I whirl around, my heart pounding. Hana has turned back to the water and is going on about wishing she had her camera and how you never seem to have anything you really need. Alex is bent close to me – so close I can see his individual eyelashes, like perfect brushstrokes on a canvas portrait – and now his eyes are literally dancing with light, burning as though on fire.

'What did you say?' I repeat. My voice comes out a croaky whisper.

He leans another inch closer, and it's like the flames seep out of his eyes and light my whole body on fire. I've never been this close to a boy before. I feel like fainting and running all at the same time. But I can't move.

'I said, I prefer the ocean when it's grey. Or not really grey. A pale, in-between colour. It reminds me of waiting for something good to happen.'

He does remember. He *was* there. The ground seems to be dissolving under my feet the way it does in the dream about my mother. All I can see are his eyes, the shifting pattern of shadow and light turning there.

'You lied,' I manage to croak out. 'Why did you lie?'

He doesn't answer me. He pulls away a few inches and says, 'Of course it's even prettier at sunset. Around eight thirty the sky looks like it's on fire, especially at Back Cove. You should really see it.' He pauses, and though his voice is low and casual I get the feeling he's trying to tell me something important. 'Tonight it will probably be amazing.'

My brain grinds into action, slowly processing his words, the way he's emphasizing certain details. Then it clicks: he has given me a time and a place. He's telling me to meet him. 'Are you asking me to—?' I start to say, but just then Hana runs back up to me, grabbing my arm.

'God,' she says, laughing. 'Can you believe it's after five already? We've got to *go*.' She's dragging me backward before I can respond or protest, and by the time I think to look over my shoulder to see if Alex is watching or giving me any kind of sign, he has disappeared from view.

six

Mama, Mama, help me get home
I'm out in the woods, I am out on my own.
I found me a werewolf, a nasty old mutt
It showed me its teeth and went straight for my gut.

Mama, Mama, help me get home
I'm out in the woods, I am out on my own.
I was stopped by a vampire, a rotting old wreck
It showed me its teeth, and went straight for my neck.

Mama, Mama, put me to bed
I won't make it home, I'm already half-dead.
I met an Invalid, and fell for his art
He showed me his smile, and went straight for my heart.

– From 'A Child's Walk Home,' *Nursery Rhymes*
and Folk Tales, edited by Cory Levinson

That evening I can't concentrate. When I'm setting the table for dinner, I accidentally pour wine in Gracie's juice cup and orange juice in my uncle's wineglass, and while I'm grating cheese I catch my knuckles so many times in the teeth of the grater my aunt finally sends me out of the kitchen, saying she'd prefer not to have a topping of skin for her ravioli. I can't stop thinking about the last thing

Alex said to me, the endlessly shifting pattern of his eyes, the strange expression on his face—like he was inviting me. *Around eight thirty the sky looks like it's on fire, especially at Back Cove. You should really see it . . .*

Is it even remotely, conceivably possible he was sending me a message? Is it possible he was asking me to meet him?

The idea makes me dizzy.

I keep thinking, too, about the single word, directed low and quietly straight into my ear: *Grey*. He was there; he saw me; he *remembered* me. So many questions crowd my brain at once, it's like one of the famous Portland fogs has swept up from the ocean and settled there, making it impossible to think normal, functional thoughts.

My aunt finally notices something's wrong. Just before dinner I'm helping Jenny with her homework, as always, testing her on her multiplication tables. We're sitting on the floor of the living room, which is squashed up right next to the 'dining room' (an alcove that barely holds a table and six chairs), and I'm holding her workbook on my knees, reciting the problems to her, but my mind is on autopilot and my thoughts are a million miles away. Or rather, they're exactly 3.4 miles away, down at the marshy edge of Back Cove. I know the distance exactly because it's a nice run from my house. Now I'm calculating how quickly I could get down there on my bike, and then beating myself up for even considering the idea.

'Seven times eight?'

Jenny pinches her lips together. 'Fifty-six.'

'Nine times six?'

'Fifty-two.'

On the other hand, there's no *law* that says you can't speak to a cured. Cureds are safe. They can be mentors or guides to the uncureds. Even though Alex is only a year older than I am, we're separated, irreparably and totally, by the procedure. He might as well be my grandfather.

'Seven times eleven?'

'Seventy-seven.'

'Lena.' My aunt has squeezed out of the kitchen, past the dining room table, and is standing behind Jenny. I blink twice, trying to focus. Carol's face is tight with concern. 'Is something the matter?'

'No.' I drop my eyes quickly. I hate it when my aunt looks at me like that, like she's reading all the bad parts from my soul. I feel guilty just for thinking about a boy, even a cured one. If she knew, she would say, *Oh, Lena. Careful. Remember what happened to your mother.* She would say, *These diseases tend to run in the blood.* 'Why?'

I keep my eyes trained on the worn carpet underneath me. Carol bends forward, swoops up Jenny's workbook from my knees, and says loudly in her clear, high voice, 'Nine times six is fifty-four.' She snaps the workbook closed. 'Not fifty-two, Lena. I assume you know your multiplication tables?'

Jenny sticks her tongue out at me.

My cheeks start heating up as I realize my mistake. 'Sorry. I guess I'm just kind of . . . distracted.'

There's a momentary pause. Carol's eyes never leave the back of my neck. I can sense them burning there. I feel like I'll scream, or cry, or confess, if she keeps staring at me.

Finally she sighs. 'You're still thinking about the evaluations, aren't you?'

I blow the air out of my cheeks, feel a weight of anxiety

ease off my chest. 'Yeah. I guess so.' I venture a glance up at her, and she smiles her little skittering smile.

'I know you're disappointed you have to go through the process again. But think about it this way – this time you'll be even more prepared.'

I bob my head and try to look enthusiastic, even though a little, pinching feeling of guilt starts nipping at me. I haven't even thought about the evaluations since this morning, not since I found out the results would be discounted. 'Yeah, you're right.'

'Come on, now. Dinnertime.' My aunt reaches out and passes a finger over my forehead. Her finger is cool and reassuring, and gone as quickly as the lightest stirring of wind. It makes the guilt flare up full force, and in that moment I can't believe I was even *considering* going to Back Cove. It's the absolute, 100 percent wrong thing to do, and I stand up for dinner feeling clean and weightless and happy, like the first time you feel healthy after a long fever.

But at dinner my curiosity – and with it, my doubts – return. I can barely follow the conversation. All I can think is: *Go? Don't go? Go? Don't go?* At one point my uncle is telling a story about one of his customers, and I notice everyone is laughing so I laugh too, but a little too loud and long. Everyone turns to look at me, even Gracie, who puckers her nose and tilts her head like a dog sniffing at something new.

'Are you okay, Lena?' my uncle asks, adjusting his glasses as though hoping to bring me into clearer focus. 'You seem a little strange.'

'I'm fine.' I push around some ravioli on my plate. Normally I can put away half a box myself, especially after a long run (and still have room for dessert), but I've barely managed to choke down a few bites. 'Just stressed.'

'Leave her alone,' my aunt says. 'She's upset about the evaluations. They didn't exactly turn out as planned.'

She lifts her eyes to my uncle, and they exchange a quick glance. I feel a rush of excitement. It's rare for my aunt and uncle to look at each other like that, a wordless glance, full of meaning. Most of the time their interactions are limited to the usual thing – my uncle tells stories about work, my aunt tells stories about the neighbours. *What's for dinner? There's a leak in the roof. Blah blah blah.* I think that for once they're going to mention the Wilds, and the Invalids. But then my uncle gives a minute shake of his head.

'These kinds of mix-ups happen all the time,' he says, staking a ravioli with his fork. 'Just the other day, I asked Andrew to reorder three cases of Vik's orange juice. But he goes and gets the codes wrong and guess what shows up? Three cases of baby formula. I said to him, I said, "Andrew . . ."'

I tune the conversation out again, grateful that my uncle is a talker, and happy that my aunt has taken my side. The one good thing about being kind of shy is that nobody bugs you when you want to be left alone. I lean forward and sneak a glance at the clock in the kitchen. Seven thirty, and we haven't even finished eating. And afterward I'll have to help clear and wash the dishes, which always takes forever; the dishwasher uses up too much electricity, so we have to do them by hand.

Outside, the sun is streaked with filaments of gold and pink. It looks like the candy that gets spun at the Sugar Shack downtown, all gloss and stretch and colour. It *will* be a beautiful sunset tonight. In that moment the urge to go is so strong, I have to squeeze the sides of my chair to keep from suddenly springing up and running out the door.

Finally I decide to stop stressing and leave it to luck, or fate, or whatever you want to call it. If we finish eating and I'm done cleaning up the dishes in time to make it to Back Cove, I'll go. If not, I'll stay. I feel a million times better once I've made the decision, and even manage to shovel down a few more bites of ravioli before Jenny (miracle of miracles) has a sudden late burst of speed and cleans her plate, and my aunt announces I can clear the dishes whenever I'm ready.

I stand up and start stacking everyone's plates. It's almost eight o'clock. Even if I can wash all the dishes in fifteen minutes – and that's a stretch – it will still be difficult to get to the beach by eight thirty. And forget about making it back by nine o'clock, when the city has a mandated curfew for uncureds.

And if I got caught on the streets after curfew . . .

The truth is, I don't know *what* would happen. I've never broken curfew.

Just as I've finally accepted that there's no way to get to Back Cove and back in time, my aunt does the unthinkable. As I'm reaching forward to take her plate, she stops me. 'You don't have to clean the dishes tonight, Lena. I'll do them.'

As she's speaking, she reaches out and puts a hand on my arm. Just like earlier, the touch is as fleeting and cool as wind.

And before I can think about what this means, I'm blurting out, 'Actually, I have to run to Hana's house really quick.'

'Now?' A look of alarm – or suspicion? – flickers across my aunt's face. 'It's nearly eight o'clock.'

'I know. We – she – she has a study guide she was supposed to give me. I just remembered.'

Now the look of suspicion – it *is* suspicion, definitely – makes itself comfortable, drawing Carol's eyebrows together, cinching her lips. 'You don't have any of the same classes. And your boards are over. How important can it be?'

'It's not for class.' I roll my eyes, trying to conjure up Hana's nonchalance, even though my palms are sweating and my heart is jerking around in my chest. 'It's like a guide full of pointers. For the evaluations. She knows I need to prep more, since I almost choked yesterday.'

Again, my aunt directs a small glance at my uncle. 'Curfew's in an hour,' she says to me. 'If you get caught out after curfew . . .'

Nervousness makes my temper flare. 'I *know* about curfew,' I snap. 'I've only been hearing about it for my whole life.'

I feel guilty the second that the words are out of my mouth, and I drop my eyes to avoid looking at Carol. I've never spoken back to her, have always tried to be as patient and obedient and good as possible – have always tried to be as *invisible* as possible, a nice girl who helps with the dishes and the little kids and does her homework and listens and keeps her head down. I know that I owe Carol for taking Rachel and me in after my mother died. If it wasn't for her, I'd probably be wasting away in one of the orphanages, uneducated, unnoticed, destined for a job at a slaughterhouse, probably, cleaning up sheep guts or cow crap or something like that. Maybe – maybe! – if I was lucky, I'd get to work for a cleaning service.

No foster parent will adopt a child whose past has been tainted by the disease.

I wish I could read her mind. I have no idea what she's thinking, but she seems to be analysing me, attempting to read my face. I think, *I'm not doing anything wrong, it's harmless, I'm fine,* over and over, and wipe my palms on the back of my jeans, positive I'm leaving a sweat mark.

'Be quick,' she says finally, and as soon as the words are out of her mouth I'm off, jetting upstairs and switching my sandals for sneakers. Then I bang back down the stairs and fly out the door. My aunt has barely had time to take the dishes into the kitchen. She calls something to me as I blur past her, but I'm already pushing out the front door and don't catch what she says. The ancient grandfather clock in the living room starts booming out just as the screen door swings shut behind me. Eight o'clock.

I unlock my bike and pedal it down the front path and out into the street. The pedals creak and moan and shudder. This bike was owned by my cousin Marcia before me and must be at least fifteen years old, and leaving it outside all year isn't doing anything to preserve it.

I start cruising in the direction of Back Cove, which is downhill, fortunately. The streets are always pretty empty at this time of night. For the most part, the cureds are inside, sitting at dinner, or cleaning up, or preparing for bed and another night of dreamless sleep, and all the uncureds are home or on their way there, nervously watching the minutes swirl away toward nine o'clock curfew.

My legs are still aching from my run earlier today. If I make it to Back Cove on time and Alex is there, I'm going to be a complete mess, sweaty and disgusting. But I keep going anyway. Now that I'm out of the house I push all my doubts and questions out of my mind and focus on hauling ass as fast as my cramping legs will allow me, spinning down through the vacant streets toward the cove, taking every shortcut I can think of, watching the sun descend steadily toward the blazing gold line of the horizon, as though the sky – a brilliant, electric blue at this point – is water, and the light is just sinking through it.

I've only been out at this hour a few times on my own, and the feeling is strange – frightening and exhilarating at the same time, like talking to Alex out in the open earlier this afternoon: as though the revolving eye that I know is always watching has been blinded just for a fraction of a second, as though the hand you've been holding your whole life suddenly disappears and leaves you free to move in any direction you want.

Lights sputter in windows around me, candles and lanterns, mostly; this is a poor area, and everything is rationed, especially gas and electricity. At a certain point I lose sight of the sun's position beyond the four- and five-storey buildings, which grow more densely packed after I turn onto Preble: tall, skinny, dark buildings, pressed up against one another as though already preparing for winter and huddling for warmth. I haven't really thought about what I'll say to Alex, and the idea of standing alone with him suddenly makes my stomach bottom out. I have to pull my bike up abruptly, stop and catch my breath. My heart is pounding frantically. After a minute's rest I keep pedaling, slower now. I'm still about a mile away but the cove is visible, flashing off to my right. The sun is just teetering over the dark mass of trees on the horizon. I have ten, fifteen minutes tops until total darkness.

Then another thought nearly stops me, hitting me straight like a fist: he won't be there. I'll be too late and he'll leave. Or this will turn out to be a big joke, or a trick.

I wrap one arm around my stomach, willing the ravioli to stay put, and pick up speed again.

I'm so busy circling one foot after the other – left, right, left, right – and doing a mental tug-of-war with my digestive tract, that I don't hear the regulators coming.

I'm about to speed through the long-defunct traffic light at Baxter when I am suddenly dazzled by a wall of zipping, bouncing light: the beams of a dozen flashlights directed into my eyes, so I have to skid abruptly to a halt, lifting a hand to my face and nearly flipping over the handlebars – which would be a real disaster, since in my rush to get out of the house I forgot to bring my helmet.

'Stop,' the voice of one of the regulators barks out – the leader in charge of the patrol, I guess. 'Identity check.'

Groups of regulators – both volunteer citizens and the actual regulators employed by the government – patrol the streets every night, looking for uncureds breaking curfew, checking the streets and (if the curtains are open) houses for unapproved activity, like two uncureds touching each other, or walking together after dark – or even two cureds engaging in 'activity that might signal the re-emergence of the *deliria* after the procedure,' like too much hugging and kissing. This rarely happens, but it *does* happen.

Regulators report directly to the government and work closely with the scientists at the labs. Regulators were responsible for sending my mother off for her third procedure; a passing patrol saw her crying over a photograph one night right after her second failed treatment. She was looking at a picture of my father, and she'd forgotten to close the curtains all the way. Within days, she was back at the labs.

Normally it's easy to avoid the regulators. You can practically hear them from a mile away. They carry walkie-talkies to coordinate with other patrolling groups, and the static interference of the radios going on and off makes it sound like a giant buzzing den of hornets is heading your way. I just wasn't paying attention. Mentally cursing myself for being so stupid, I fish my wallet out of my back pocket. At least I remembered to grab *that*. It's illegal to go without ID in Portland. The last thing anybody wants is to spend the night in jail while the powers that be try to verify your validity.

'Magdalena Ella Haloway,' I say, trying to keep my voice steady, as I pass my ID to the regulator in charge. I can hardly make him out behind his flashlight, which he keeps trained on my face, forcing me to squint. He's big; that's all I know. Tall, thin, angular.

'Magdalena Ella Haloway,' he repeats. He flips my ID over between his long fingers and looks at my identity code, a number assigned to every citizen of the USA. The first three digits identify your state, the next three your city, the next three your family group, the next four your identity. 'And what are you doing, Magdalena? Curfew's in less than forty minutes.'

Less than forty minutes. That must mean it's almost eight thirty. I shift on my feet, trying hard not to betray impatience. A lot of the regulators – especially the volunteer ones – are poorly paid city techs: window washers or gas-meter readers or security guards.

I take a deep breath and say as innocently as possible, 'I wanted to take a quick ride down to Back Cove.' I do my best to smile and look kind of stupid. 'I was feeling bloaty after dinner.' No point in lying any more than that. I'll just get myself in trouble.

The lead regulator continues to examine me, the flashlight directed glaringly at my face, my ID card in his hand. For a second he seems to waver, and I'm sure he's going to let me go, but then he passes my ID to another regulator. 'Run it through with SVS, will you? Make sure it's valid.'

My heart plummets. SVS is the Secure Validation System, a computer network where all the valid citizenships, for every single person in the entire country, are stored. It can take twenty to thirty minutes for the computer system to match codes, depending on how many other people are calling into the system. He can't really think I've forged an identity card, but he's going to waste my time while someone checks.

And then, miraculously, a voice pipes up from the back of the group. 'She's valid, Gerry. I recognize her. She comes into the store. Lives at 172 Cumberland.'

Gerry swings around, lowering his flashlight in the process. I blink away the floating dots in my vision. I recognize a few faces vaguely – a woman who works in the local dry cleaners and spends her afternoons leaning in the doorway, chewing gum and occasionally spitting out into the street; the traffic officer who works downtown near Franklin Arterial, one of the few areas of Portland that has enough car traffic to justify one; one of the guys who collects our garbage – and there, in the back, Dev Howard, who owns the Quikmart down the street from my house.

Normally my uncle brings home most of our groceries – canned goods and pasta and sliced meats, for the most part – from his combo deli and convenience store, Stop-N-Save, all the way over on Munjoy Hill, but occasionally, if we're desperate for toilet paper or milk, I'll run out to the Quikmart. Mr. Howard has always creeped me out. He's super-skinny and has hooded black eyes that remind me of a rat's. But tonight I feel like I could hug him. I didn't even think he knew my name. He's never said a word to me except, 'Will that be all today?' after he has rung up my purchases, glowering at me from underneath the heavy shade of his eyelids. I make a mental note to thank him the next time I see him.

Gerry hesitates for a fraction of a second longer, but I can see that the other regulators are starting to get restless, shifting from foot to foot, eager to continue the patrol and find someone to bust.

Gerry must sense it too, because he jerks his head abruptly in my direction. 'Let her have the ID.'

Relief makes me feel like laughing, and I have to struggle to look serious as I take my ID and tuck it into place. My hands are shaking ever so slightly. It's strange how being around the regulators will do that to you. Even when they're being relatively nice, you can't help but think of all the bad stories you've heard – the raids and the beatings and the ambushes.

'Just be careful, Magdalena,' Gerry says, as I straighten up. 'Make sure you're home before curfew.' He tilts his flashlight into my eyes again. I lift my arm to my eyes, squinting against the dazzle. 'You wouldn't want to get into any trouble.'

He says it lightly, but for a moment I think I hear something hard running under his words, a current of anger or aggression. But then I tell myself I'm just being paranoid. No matter what the regulators do, they exist for our protection, for our own good.

The regulators sweep away in a group around me, so for a few seconds I'm caught up in a tide of rough shoulders and cotton jackets, unfamiliar cologne and sweat-smells.

Walkie-talkies sputter to life and fade away again around me. I catch snippets of words and broadcasts: *Market Street, a girl and a boy, possibly infected, unapproved music on St. Lawrence, someone appears to be dancing . . .* I get bumped side to side against arms and chests and elbows, until finally the group passes and I'm spit out again, left alone on the street as the regulators' footsteps grow more distant behind me. I wait until I can no longer hear the fuzz of their radio chatter or their boots hitting the pavement.

Then I take off, feeling again a lifting sensation in my chest, that same sense of happiness and freedom. I can't believe how easy it was to get out of the house. I never knew I could lie to my aunt – I never knew I could lie, period – and when I think about how narrowly I escaped getting grilled by the regulators for hours, it makes me want to jump up and down and pump my fist in the air. Tonight the whole world is on my side. And I'm only a few minutes from Back Cove. My heart picks up its rhythm as I think about skidding down the sloping hill of grass, seeing Alex framed against the last, dazzling rays of sun – as I think about that single word breathed into my ear. *Grey.*

I tear down Baxter, which loops around the last mile down to Back Cove. And then I stop short. The buildings have fallen away behind me, giving way to ramshackle sheds, sparsely situated on either side of the cracked and run-down road. Beyond that, a short strip of tall, weedy grass slants down toward the cove. The water is an enormous mirror, tipped with pink and gold from the sky. In that single, blazing moment as I come around the bend, the sun – curved over the dip of the horizon like a solid gold archway – lets out its final winking rays of light, shattering the darkness of the water, turning everything white for a fraction of a second, and then falls away, sinking, dragging the pink and the red and the purple out of the sky with it, all the colour bleeding away instantly and leaving only dark.

Alex was right. It was gorgeous – one of the best I've ever seen.

For a moment I can't move or do anything but stand there, breathing hard, staring. Then a numbness creeps over me. I'm too late. The regulators must have been wrong about the time. It must be after eight thirty now. Even if Alex decides to wait for me somewhere along the long loop of the cove, I don't have a prayer of finding him and making it home before curfew.

My eyes sting and the world in front of me goes watery, colours and shapes sloshing together. For a second I think I must be crying, and I'm so startled I forget everything – forget about my disappointment and frustration, forget about Alex standing on the beach, the thought of his hair catching the dying rays of sun, flashing copper. I can't remember the last time I cried. It's been years. I wipe my eyes with the back of my hand, and my vision sharpens again. It's just sweat, I realize, relieved; I'm sweating, it's getting in my eyes. Still, the sick, leaden feeling won't work its way out of my stomach.

I stay there for a few minutes, straddling my bike, squeezing the handlebars hard until I'm a little bit calmer. Part of me wants to say, screw it, to shove off, both legs extended, and go flying down the hill toward the water with the wind whipping up my hair – screw curfew, screw the regulators, screw everyone. But I can't; I couldn't; I could never. I have no choice. I have to get home.

I maneuver my bike around in a clumsy circle and start

back up the street. Now that the adrenaline and excitement have faded, my legs feel like they're made out of iron, and I'm panting before I've gone a quarter of a mile. This time I'm careful to stay alert for regulators and police and patrols.

On the way home I tell myself that it's probably for the best. I must be crazy, zooming around in the half dark just to meet up with some guy on the beach. Besides, everything has been explained: he works at the labs, probably just snuck in on evaluation day for some completely innocent reason – to use the bathroom, or refill his water bottle.

And I remind myself that I probably imagined the whole thing – the message, the meeting up. He's probably sitting in his apartment somewhere, doing course work for his classes. He's probably already forgotten about the two girls he met at the lab complex today. He was probably just being nice earlier, making casual conversation.

It's for the best. But no matter how many times I repeat it, the strange, hollow feeling in my stomach doesn't go away. And ridiculous as it is, I can't shake the persistent, needling feeling that I've forgotten something, or missed something, or lost something forever.

seven

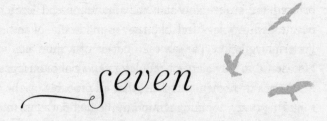

Of all the systems of the body – neurological, cognitive, special, sensory – the cardiological system is the most sensitive and easily disturbed. The role of society must be to shelter these systems from infection and decay, or else the future of the human race is at stake. Like a summer fruit that is protected from insect invasion, bruising, and rot by the whole mechanism of modern farming; so must we protect the heart.

– 'The Role and Purpose of Society,' *The Book of Shhh*, p.353

I was named after Mary Magdalene, who was nearly killed from love: 'So infected with *deliria* and in violation of the pacts of society, she fell in love with men who would not have her or could not keep her.' (*Book of Lamentations*, Mary 13:1).

We learned all about it in Biblical Science. First there was John, then Matthew, then Jeremiah and Peter and Judas, and many other nameless men in-between.

Her last love, they say, was the greatest: a man named Joseph, a bachelor all his life, who found her on the street, bruised and broken and half crazy from *deliria*. There's some debate about what kind of man Joseph was – whether he was righteous or not, whether he ever succumbed to the disease – but in any case, he took good care of her. He nursed her to health and tried to bring her peace.

By this time, however, it was too late. She was tormented by her past, haunted by the loves lost and damaged and ruined, by the evils she had inflicted on others and that others had inflicted on her. She could hardly eat; she wept all day; she clung to Joseph and begged him never to leave her, but couldn't find comfort in his goodness.

And then one morning, she woke and Joseph was gone – without a word or an explanation. This final abandonment broke her at last and she fell to the ground, begging God to put her out of her misery.

He heard her prayers, and in his infinite compassion he instead removed from her the curse of *deliria*, with which all humans had been burdened as punishment for the original sin of Eve and Adam. In a sense, Mary Magdalene was the very first cured.

'And so after years of tribulation and pain, she walked in righteousness and peace until the end of her days.' (*Book of Lamentations*, Mary 13:1).

I always thought it was strange that my mother named me Magdalena. She didn't even believe in the cure. That was her whole problem. And the Book of Lamentations is all about the dangers of *deliria*. I've done a lot of thinking about it, and in the end I guess I've figured out that despite everything, my mother knew that she was wrong: that the cure, and the procedure, were for the best. I think even then she knew what she was going to do – she knew what would happen.

I guess my name was her final gift to me, in a way. It was a message.

I think she was trying to say, *Forgive me*. I think she was trying to say, *Someday, even this pain will be taken away*.

You see? No matter what everyone says, and despite everything, I know she wasn't all bad.

The next two weeks are the busiest of my life. Summer explodes into Portland. In early June the heat was there but not the colour—the greens were still pale and tentative, the mornings had a biting coolness—but by the last week of school everything is technicolour and splash, outrageous blue skies and purple thunderstorms and ink-black night skies and red flowers as bright as spots of blood. Every day after school there's an assembly, or ceremony, or graduation party to go to. Hana gets invited to all of them; I get invited to most, which surprises me.

Harlowe Davis – who lives with Hana in the West End, and whose father does something for the government – invites me to come over for a 'casual good-bye thing.' I didn't even think she knew my name – whenever she's talking to Hana her eyes have always skated past me, like I'm not worth focusing on. I go anyway. I've always been curious about her house, and it turns out to be as spectacular as I imagined. Her family has a car, too, and electric appliances everywhere that obviously get used every day: washers and dryers and huge chandeliers filled with dozens and dozens of lightbulbs. Harlowe has invited most of the graduating class – there are sixty-seven of us in total and probably fifty at the party – which makes me feel less special, but it's still fun. We sit in the backyard while the housekeeper runs in and out of the house with plates and plates of food – coleslaw and potato salad and other barbecue stuff – and her father turns out spare ribs and hamburgers on the enormous smoking grill. I eat until I feel like I'm about to burst and have to roll backward onto the blanket I'm sharing with Hana. We stay there until almost curfew, when the stars are peeking through a curtain of dark blue and the mosquitoes rise up all at once and we all go shrieking and laughing back into the house, slapping them away. Afterward I think it's one of the nicest days I've had in a long time.

Even girls I don't really like – like Shelly Pierson, who has hated me since sixth grade, when I won the science fair and she took second place – start being nice. I guess it's because we all know the end is close. Most of us won't see one another after graduation, and even if we do it will be different. *We'll* be different. We'll be adults – cured, tagged and labeled and paired and identified and placed neatly on our life path, perfectly round marbles set to roll down even, well-defined slopes.

Theresa Grass turns eighteen before school ends and gets cured; so does Morgan Dell. They're absent for a few days and come back to school just before graduation. The change is amazing. They seem peaceful now, mature and somehow remote, like they're encased in a thin layer of ice. Only two weeks ago Theresa's nickname was Theresa Gross, and everyone made fun of her for slouching and chewing on the ends of her hair and generally being a mess, but now she walks straight and tall with her eyes fixed straight in front of her, her lips barely curled in a smile, and everyone shifts a little in the halls so she can pass easily. Same thing goes for Morgan. It's like all their anxiety and self-consciousness has been removed along with the disease. Even Morgan's legs have stopped trembling. Whenever she used to have to speak in class, the trembling would get so bad it would rock the desk. But after the procedure, just like that – *whoosh!* The shaking stops. Of course they're not the first girls in our class to get cured – Eleanor Rana and Annie Hahn were both cured way back in the fall, and half a dozen other girls have had the procedure this past semester – but in them the difference is somehow more pronounced.

I keep going with my countdown. Eighty-one days, then eighty, then seventy-nine.

Willow Marks never comes back to school. Rumours filter back to us – that she had her procedure and it turned out fine; that she had her procedure and now her brain is going haywire, and they're talking about committing her to the Crypts, Portland's combo prison-and-mental-ward; that she ran away to the Wilds. Only one thing is for sure: the whole Marks family is under constant surveillance now. The regulators are blaming Mr. and Mrs. Marks – and the whole extended family – for not instilling in her a proper education, and only a few days after she was supposedly found in Deering Oaks Park, I overhear my aunt and uncle whispering that both of Willow's parents have been fired from their jobs. A week later we hear that they've had to move in with a distant relative. Apparently people kept throwing rocks at their windows, and a whole side of their house was written over with a single word: SYMPATHIZERS. It makes no sense, because Mr. and Mrs. Marks were on record insisting that their daughter have the procedure early, despite the risks, but as my aunt says, people get like that when they're scared. Everyone is terrified that the *deliria* will somehow find its way into Portland on a large scale. Everyone wants to prevent an epidemic.

I feel bad for the Marks family, of course, but that's the way things are. It's like the regulators: you may not like the patrols and the identity checks, but since you know it's all done for your protection, it's impossible *not* to cooperate. And it may sound awful, but I don't think about Willow's family for long. There's just too much end-of-high-school paperwork to file, and nervous energy, and lockers to clean out and final exams to take and people to say good-bye to.

Hana and I can barely find time to run together. When we do, we stick to our old routes by silent agreement. She never mentions the afternoon at the labs again, to my surprise. But Hana's mind has a tendency to skip around, and her new obsession is a collapse at the northern end of the border that people are saying might have been caused by Invalids. I don't even consider going down to the labs again, not for one single solitary second. I focus on everything and anything besides my lingering questions about Alex – which isn't too hard, considering that I now can't believe I spent an evening biking up and down the streets of Portland, lying to Carol and the regulators, just to meet up with him. The very next day it felt like a dream, or a delusion. I tell myself I must have gone temporarily insane: brain scramble, from running in the heat.

On graduation day Hana sits three rows ahead of me at the commencement ceremony. As she files past me to take her seat she reaches out for my hand – two long pumps, two short ones – and when she sits down she tilts her head back so I can see that she has taken a marker and scrawled on the top of her graduation cap: THANK GOD! I stifle a laugh, and she turns around and makes a pretend-stern face at me. All of us are giddy, and I've never felt closer to the St. Anne's girls than that day – all of us sweating under the sun, which beams down on us like an exaggerated smile, fanning ourselves with the commencement brochures, trying not to yawn or roll our eyes while Principal McIntosh drones on about 'adulthood' and 'our entrance into the community order,' nudging one another and tugging on the collars of our scratchy graduation gowns to try to let some air down our necks.

Family members sit in white plastic folding chairs, under a cream-white tarp fluttering with flags: the school flag, the city flag, the state flag, the American flag. They applaud politely as each graduate goes up to receive her diploma. When it's my turn I scan the audience, looking for my aunt and my sister, but I'm so nervous about tripping and falling as I take my place on the stage and reach for the diploma in Principal McIntosh's hand, I can't see anything but colour – green, blue, white, a mess of pink and brown faces – or make out any individual sounds beyond the *shush* of clapping hands. Only Hana's voice, loud and clear as a bell: 'Hallelujah, Halena!' That's our special pump-you-up chant that we used to do before track meets and tests, a combination of both of our names.

Afterward we line up to take individual portraits with our diplomas. An official photographer has been hired, and a royal blue backdrop set up in the middle of the soccer field, where we all stand and pose. We're too excited to take the pictures seriously, though. People keep doubling over laughing in their pictures, so all you can see is the crown of their heads.

When it's my turn for a picture, at the very last second Hana jumps in and throws one arm around my shoulders, and the photographer is so startled he presses down on the shutter anyway. *Click!* There we are: I'm turning to Hana, mouth open, surprised, about to laugh. She's a full head taller than me, has her eyes shut and her mouth open. I really do think there was something special about that day, something golden and maybe even magic, because even though my face was all red and my hair looked sticky on my forehead, it's like Hana rubbed off on me a little bit – because despite everything, and just in that one picture, I look pretty. More than pretty. Beautiful, even.

The school band keeps playing, mostly in tune, and the music floats across the field and is echoed by the birds wheeling in the sky. It's like something lifts in that moment, some huge pressure or divide, and before I know what's happening all my classmates are crushing together in a huge hug, jumping up and down and screaming, 'We did it! We did it! We did it!' And none of the parents or teachers try to separate us. As we start to break away I see them encircling us, watching with patient expressions, hands folded. I catch my aunt's gaze and my stomach does a weird twist and I know that she, like everyone else, is giving us this moment – our last moment together, before things change for good and forever.

And things will change – *are* changing, even at that second. As the group dissolves into clumps of students, and the clumps dissolve into individuals, I notice Theresa Grass and Morgan Dell already starting across the lawn toward the street. They are each walking with their families, heads down, without once looking back. They haven't been celebrating with us, I realize, and it occurs to me I haven't seen Eleanor Rana or Annie Hahn or the other cureds either. They must have already gone home. A curious ache throbs in the back of my throat, even though, of course, this is how things are: everything ends, people move on, they don't look back. It's how they *should* be.

I catch sight of Rachel through the crowd and go running up to her, suddenly eager to be next to her, wishing she would reach down and ruffle my hair like she used to when I was very little, and say, 'Good job, Loony,' her old nickname for me.

'Rachel!' I'm breathless for no reason, and I have trouble squeezing the words out. I'm so happy to see her I feel like I could burst into tears. I don't though, obviously. 'You came.'

'Of course I came.' She smiles at me. 'You're my only sister, remember?' She passes me a bouquet of daisies she has brought with her, loosely wrapped in brown paper. 'Congratulations, Lena.'

I stick my face in the flowers and inhale, trying to fight down the urge to reach out and hug her. For a second we just stand there, blinking at each other, and then she reaches out to me. I'm sure she's going to put her arms around me for old times' sake, or at the very least give me a one-armed squeeze.

Instead she just flicks a bang off my forehead. 'Gross,' she says, still smiling. 'You're all sweaty.'

It's stupid and immature to feel disappointed, but I do. 'It's the gown,' I say, and realize that yes, that must be the problem: the gown is what's choking me, stifling me, making it hard to breathe.

'Come on,' she says. 'Aunt Carol will want to congratulate you.'

Aunt Carol is standing at the field's periphery with my uncle, Grace, and Jenny, talking to Mrs. Springer, my history teacher. I fall into step beside Rachel. She is only a few inches taller than I am and we walk together, in sync, but separated by three feet of space. She is quiet. I can tell she's already wondering when she can go home and get on with her life.

I let myself look back once. I can't help it. I watch the girls circulating in their orange gowns like flames. Everything seems to zoom back, recede away at once. All the voices intermingle and become indistinguishable from one another – like the constant white noise of the ocean running underneath the rhythm of the Portland streets, so constant you hardly notice it. Everything looks stark and vivid and frozen, as though drawn precisely and outlined in ink – parents' smiles frozen, camera flashes blinding, mouths open and white teeth glistening, dark glossy hair and deep-blue sky and unrelenting light, everyone drowning in light – everything so clear and perfect I'm sure it must already be a memory, or a dream.

eight

H is for hydrogen, a weight of one;
When fission's split, as brightly lit
As hot as any sun.

He is for helium, a weight of two;
The noble gas, the ghostly pass
That lifts the world anew.

Li is for lithium, a weight of three;
A funeral pyre, when touched with fire –
And deadly sleep for me.

Be is for beryllium, a weight of four . . .

– From the Elemental Prayers
('Prayer and Study,' *The Book of Shhh*)

During the summers I have to help my uncle at the Stop-N-Save on Mondays, Wednesdays, and Saturdays, mostly stocking shelves and working behind the deli counter and occasionally helping with filing and accounting in the little office behind the cereal and dry goods aisle. Thankfully, in late June, Andrew Marcus gets cured and reassigned to a permanent position at another grocery store.

On the Fourth of July I head to Hana's house in the morning. Every year we go to see the fireworks at the Eastern Promenade. A band is always playing and vendors set up their carts, selling fried meat on skewers and corn on the cob and apple pie floating in a puddle of ice cream, served in little paper boats. The Fourth of July – the day of our independence, the day we commemorate the closing of our nation's border forever – is one of my favourite holidays. I love the music that pipes through the streets, love the way the steam rising thick from the grills makes the streets look cloudy, the people shadowy and unclear. I especially love the temporary extension of curfew: instead of being home at nine o'clock, all uncureds are allowed to stay out until eleven. In recent years Hana and I have made it a kind of game to stay out until the last possible second, cutting it closer and closer every year. Last year I stepped into the house at 10:58 exactly, heart hammering in my chest, shaking with exhaustion – I'd had to sprint home. But as I lay in bed I couldn't stop grinning. I felt like I'd gotten away with something.

I type in Hana's four-digit gate code – she gave it to me in eighth grade, saying it was 'a sign of trust' and also that she'd slit me 'from the top of the head to the heels' if I shared it with anyone else – and slip in through the front door. I never bother knocking. Her parents are hardly ever home, and Hana never answers the door. I'm pretty much the only person who comes over to see her. It's weird. Hana was always really popular in school – people looked up to her and wanted to be like her – but even though she was really friendly with everybody, she never really got *close* close with anyone besides me.

Sometimes I wonder whether she wishes she'd been

assigned a different desk partner in Mrs. Jablonski's second-grade class, which is how we first became friends. Hana's last name is Tate, and we were linked up by alphabetical order (by then I was already going by my aunt's last name, Tiddle). I wonder whether she wishes she'd been placed with Rebecca Tralawny, or Katie Scarp, or even Melissa Portofino. Sometimes I feel like she deserves a best friend who is just a little more *special*. Once Hana told me that she likes me because I'm for real – because I really feel things. But that's the whole problem: how much I feel things.

'Hello?' I call out, as soon as I'm inside Hana's house. The front hall is dark and cool as always. Goose bumps prick up over my arms. No matter how many times I come to Hana's house I'm always shocked by the power of the air-conditioning, which hums somewhere deep inside the walls. For a moment I just stand there, inhaling the clean smells of furniture polish and Windex and fresh-cut flowers. Music is pulsing from Hana's room upstairs. I try to identify the song but can't make out any words, just bass throbbing through the floorboards.

At the top of the stairs I pause. Hana's bedroom door is closed. I definitely don't recognize the song she's playing – or blasting, really, so loud I have to remind myself that Hana's house is shielded on four sides by trees and lawn, and no one will sick the regulators on her. It's not like any music I've ever heard. It's a shrieky, shrill, fierce kind of music: I can't even tell whether the singer is male or female. Little fingers of electricity creep up my spine, a feeling I used to have when I was a tiny child, when I would creep into the kitchen and try to sneak an extra cookie from the pantry – the feeling right before the creak and squeak of my mom's footsteps in the kitchen behind me, when I would whirl around, my hands and face coated in crumbs, guilty.

I shake off the feeling and push open Hana's door. She's sitting at her computer, feet propped up on her desk, bobbing her head and tapping out a rhythm on her thighs. As soon as she sees me she swings forward and hits a key on her keyboard. The music cuts off instantly. Strangely, the silence that follows seems just as loud.

She flips her hair over one shoulder and scoots away from the desk. Something flickers over her face, an expression that passes too quickly for me to identify it. 'Hi,' she chirrups, a little too cheerfully. 'Didn't hear you come in.'

'I doubt you would have heard me *break* in.' I go over to her bed and collapse on top of it. Hana has a queen-size bed, with three down pillows. It's like heaven. 'What was that?'

'What was what?' She lifts her knees to her chest and swivels a full circle in her chair. I sit up on my elbows and watch her. Hana only acts this dumb when she's hiding something.

'The music.' She still stares at me blankly. 'The song you were blasting when I came in. The one that almost burst my eardrums.'

'Oh – *that*.' Hana blows her bangs out of her face. This is another one of her tells. Whenever she's bluffing in poker she won't stop fussing with her bangs. 'Just some new band I found online.'

'On LAMM?' I press. Hana's music-obsessed and used to spend hours surfing LAMM, the Library of Authorized Music and Movies, when we were in middle school.

Hana looks away. 'Not exactly.'

'What do you mean, "not exactly"?' The intranet, like everything else in the United States, is controlled and monitored for our protection. All the websites, all the content, is written by government agencies, including the List of Authorized Entertainment, which gets updated biannually. Digital books go into the LAB, the Library of Approved Books, movies and music go into LAMM, and for a small fee you can download them to your computer. If you have one, that is. I don't.

Hana sighs, keeping her eyes averted. Finally she looks at me. 'Can you keep a secret?'

Now I sit up all the way, scooting to the edge of the bed. I don't like the way she's looking at me. I don't trust it. 'What is this about, Hana?'

'Can you keep a secret?' she repeats.

I think of standing with her in front of the labs on Evaluation Day, the sun beating down on us, the way she forced her mouth close to my ear to whisper about happiness, and unhappiness. I'm suddenly afraid for her, *of* her. But I nod and say, 'Yeah, of course.'

'Okay.' She looks down, fiddles with the hem of her shorts for a second, takes a deep breath. 'So last week I met this guy—'

'*What?*' I nearly fall off the bed.

'Relax.' She holds up a hand. 'He's cured, okay? He works for the city. He's a censor, actually.'

My heartbeat slows and I settle back against her pillows again. 'Okay. So?'

'*So,*' Hana says, drawing the word out, 'he was waiting at the doctor's with me. When I went to have my PT, you know?' Hana sprained her ankle in the fall and still has to do physical therapy once a week, to keep it strong. 'And we started talking.'

She pauses. I don't really see where the story is going, or how it relates to the music she was playing, so I just wait for her to go on.

Finally she does. 'Anyway, I was telling him about boards, and how I really want to go to USM, and he was telling me about his job – what he does, you know, day to day. He codes the online access restrictions, so people can't just write whatever, or post things themselves, or write up false information or "inflammatory opinions"' – she puts this in quotes, rolling her eyes – 'and other stuff like that. He's, like, an intranet security guard.'

'Okay,' I say again. I want to tell Hana to get to the point – I know all about online security restrictions, everybody does – but that would just make her clam up.

She sucks in a deep breath. 'But he doesn't just code the security. He checks for lapses – like, break-ins. Hackers, basically, who jump through all the security hoops and manage to post their own stuff. The government calls them floaters – websites that might be up for an hour, or a day, or two days before they're discovered, websites full of unauthorized stuff – opinions and message boards and video clips and music.'

'And you found one.' A sick feeling has settled in my stomach. Words keep flashing in my brain, like a neon sign going in and out: *illegal, interrogation, surveillance. Hana.*

She doesn't seem to notice that I've gone totally still. Her face is suddenly animated, as alive and energetic as I've ever seen it, and she leans forward on her knees, talking in a rush. 'Not just one. Dozens. There are tons of them out there, if you know how to look. If you know *where* to look. It's incredible, Lena. All these people – they must be all over the country – sneaking in through the loops and the holes. You should see some of the things people write. About – about the cure. It's not just the Invalids who don't believe in it. There are people here, all over the place, who don't think . . .' I'm staring at her so hard she drops her eyes and switches topics. 'And you should *hear* the music. Incredible, amazing music, like nothing you've ever heard, music that almost takes your head off, you know? That makes you want to scream and jump up and down and break stuff and cry . . .'

Hana's room is big – almost twice as big as my room at home – but I feel as though the walls are pressing down around me. If the air-conditioning's still working, I can no longer feel it. The air feels hot and heavy, like a wet breath, and I stand up and move to the window. Hana breaks off, finally. I try to shove open her window, but it won't budge. I push and strain against the windowsill.

'Lena,' Hana says timidly, after a minute.

'It won't open.' All I can think is: I need air. The rest of my thoughts are a blur of radio static and fluorescent lights and lab coats and steel tables and surgical knives – an image of Willow Marks getting dragged off to the labs, screaming, her house defaced with marker and paint.

'Lena,' Hana says, louder now. 'Come on.'

'It's stuck. Wood must be warped from the heat. If it would just *open*.' I heave and the window flies upward, finally. There's a popping sound, and the latch that's been keeping it in place snaps off and skitters to the middle of the floor. For a second Hana and I both stand there, staring at it. The air coming in the open window doesn't make me feel better. It's even hotter outside.

'Sorry,' I mumble. I can't look at her. 'I didn't mean to – I didn't know it was locked. The windows at my house don't lock.'

'Don't worry about the window. I don't care about the stupid window.'

'One time Grace got out of her crib when she was little, almost made it onto the roof. Just slid the window right open and started climbing.'

'Lena.' Hana reaches out and grabs my shoulders. I don't know if I have a fever or what, going hot and cold every five seconds, but her touch makes a chill go through me and I pull away quickly. 'You're mad at me.'

'I'm not mad. I'm worried about you.' But that's only half-true. I *am* mad – furious, in fact. All this time I've been blindly coasting along, the idiot sidekick, thinking about our last real summer together, stressing about the matches I'll get and evaluations and boards and normal stuff and she's been nodding and smiling and saying, 'Uh-huh, yeah, me too,' and 'I'm sure things will be fine,' and meanwhile, behind my back, she's been turning into someone I don't know – someone with secrets and weird habits and opinions about things we're not even supposed to *think* about. Now I know why I was so startled on Evaluation Day, when she turned back to whisper to me, eyes huge and glowing. It was like she had dropped away for a second – my best friend, my only real friend – and in her place was a stranger.

That's what's been happening all this time: Hana has been morphing into a stranger.

I turn back to the window.

A sharp blade of sadness goes through me, deep and quick. I guess it was bound to happen eventually. I've always known it would. Everyone you trust, everyone you think you can count on, will eventually disappoint you. When left to their own devices, people lie and keep secrets and change and disappear, some behind a different face or personality, some behind a dense early morning fog, beyond a cliff. That's why the cure is so important. That's why we need it.

'Listen, I'm not going to get arrested just for looking at some websites. Or listening to music, or whatever.'

'You could. People have been arrested for less.' She knows this too. She knows, and doesn't care.

'Yeah, well, I'm sick of it.' Hana's voice trembles a little, which throws me. I've never heard her sound less than certain.

'We shouldn't even be talking about this. Someone could be—'

'Someone could be listening?' She cuts me off, finishes my sentence for me. 'God, Lena. I'm sick of that, too. Aren't you? Sick of always checking your back, looking behind you, watching what you say, think, do. I can't – I can't breathe, I can't sleep, I can't *move*. I feel like there are walls everywhere. Everywhere I go – *bam!* There's a wall. Everything I want – *bam!* Another wall.'

She rakes a hand through her hair. For once, she doesn't look pretty and in control. She looks pale and unhappy, and her expression reminds me of something, but I can't place it right away.

'It's for our own protection,' I say, wishing I sounded more confident. I've never been good in a fight. 'Everything will get better once we're—'

Again, she jumps in. 'Once we're cured?' She laughs, a short barking sound with no humour in it, but at least she doesn't contradict me directly. 'Right. That's what everybody says.'

All of a sudden it hits me: she reminds me of the animals we saw once on a class trip to the slaughterhouse. All the cows were lined up, packed in their stalls, staring at us mutely as we walked by, with that same look in their eyes, fear and resignation and something else. Desperation. I'm really scared, then, truly terrified for her.

But when she speaks again, she sounds a little bit calmer. 'Maybe it will. Get better, I mean, once we're cured. But until then . . . This is our last chance, Lena. Our last chance to do *anything*. Our last chance to choose.'

There's the word from Evaluation Day again – *choose* – but I nod because I don't want to set her off again. 'So what are you going to do?'

She looks away, biting her lip, and I can tell she's debating whether or not to trust me. 'There's this party tonight . . .'

'*What?*' Zoom. The fear floods back in.

She rushes on. 'It's something I found on one of the floaters – it's a music thing, a few bands playing out by the border in Stroudwater, on one of the farms.'

'You can't be serious. You're not – you're not actually going, right? You're not even *thinking* about it.'

'It's safe, okay? I promise. These websites . . . it's really amazing, Lena, I swear you'd be into it if you looked. They're hidden. Links, usually, embedded on normal pages, approved government stuff, but I don't know, somehow you can tell they don't feel right, you know? They don't belong.'

I grasp at a single word. 'Safe? How can it be safe? That guy you met – the censor – his whole job is to track down people who are stupid enough to post these things—'

'They're not *stupid*, they're incredibly smart, actually—'

'Not to mention the regulators and patrols and the youth

guard and curfew and segregation and just about everything else that makes this one of the worst ideas—'

'Fine.' Hana raises her arms and brings them slapping down against her thighs. The noise is so loud it makes me jump. 'Fine. So it's a bad idea. So it's risky. You know what? *I don't care.*'

For a second there's silence. We're glaring at each other, and the air between us feels charged and dangerous, a thin electrical coil, ready to explode.

'What about me?' I say finally, struggling to keep my voice from shaking.

'You're welcome to come. Ten thirty, Roaring Brook Farms, Stroudwater. Music. Dancing. You know – *fun*. The stuff we're supposed to be having, before they cut out half of our brain.'

I ignore the last part of her comment. 'I don't think so, Hana. In case you've forgotten, we have other plans for tonight. Have had plans for tonight for, oh, the past fifteen years.'

'Yeah, well, things change.' She turns her back to me, but I feel like she's reached out and punched me in the stomach.

'Fine.' My throat is squeezing up. This time I know it's the real deal, and I'm on the verge of crying. I go over to her bed and start gathering up my stuff. Of course my bag has spilled over on its side, and now her comforter is covered with little scraps of paper and gum wrappers and coins and pens. I start stuffing these back into my bag, fighting back the tears. 'Go ahead. Do whatever you want tonight. I don't care.'

Maybe Hana feels bad, because her voice softens a little bit. 'Seriously, Lena. You should think about coming. We won't get in any trouble, I promise.'

'You can't promise that.' I take a deep breath, wishing my

voice would stop quivering. 'You don't know that. You can't be positive.'

'And *you* can't go on being so scared all the time.'

That's it: that does it. I whirl around, furious, something deep and black and old rising inside of me. 'Of *course* I'm scared. And I'm *right* to be scared. And if you're not scared it's just because you have the perfect little life, and the perfect little family, and for you everything is perfect, perfect, perfect. You don't *see*. You don't *know*.'

'Perfect? That's what you think? You think my life is perfect?' Her voice is quiet but full of anger.

I'm tempted to move away from her but force myself to stay put. 'Yeah. I do.'

Again she lets out a barking laugh, a quick explosion. 'So you think this is it, huh? As good as it gets?' She turns a full circle, arms extended, like she's embracing the room, the house, everything.

Her question startles me. 'What else is there?'

'*Everything*, Lena.' She shakes her head. 'Listen, I'm not going to apologize. I know you have your reasons for being scared. What happened to your mom was terrible—'

'Don't bring my mom into this.' My body goes tight, electric.

'But you can't go on *blaming* her for everything. She died more than *ten years ago*.'

Anger swallows me, a thick fog. My mind careens wildly like wheels over ice, bumping up against random words: *Fear. Blame. Don't forget. Mom. I love you*. And now I see that Hana *is a snake* – has been waiting a long time to say this to me, has been waiting to squirm her way in, as deep and painful as she can go, and bite.

'Fuck you.' In the end, these are the two words that come.

She holds up both hands. 'Listen, Lena, I'm just saying you have to let it go. You're *nothing* like her. And you're not going to end up like her. You don't have it in you.'

'Fuck you.' She's trying to be nice, but my mind is closed up and the words come out on their own, cascading over one another, and I wish every single one was a punch so that I could hit her in the face, *bambambambam*. 'You don't know a single thing about her. And you don't know me. You don't know *anything*.'

'Lena.' She reaches for me.

'Don't touch me.' I'm stumbling backward, grabbing my bag, bumping against her desk as I move toward the door. My vision is cloudy. I can barely make out the banisters. I'm tripping, half falling down the stairs, finding the front door by touch. I think Hana might be calling to me, but everything is lost to a roaring, rushing in my ears, inside my head. Sunshine, brilliant, brilliant white light – cool biting iron under my fingers, the gate – ocean smells, gasoline. Wailing, growing louder. A punctuated shriek: *beep, beep, beep*.

My head clears all at once and I jump out of the middle of the street just before I'm squashed by a police car, which barrels past me, horn still blaring, siren whirling, leaving me coughing up dirt and dust. The ache in my throat gets so bad it feels like I'm gagging, and when I finally let the tears come it's a huge relief, like dropping something heavy after you've been carrying it for a long time. Once I start crying I can't stop, and all the way home I have to keep mashing my palm into my eyes every few seconds, smearing away the tears just so I can see where I'm going. I comfort myself by thinking that in less than two months this will seem like nothing to me. All of it will fall away and I'll rise up new and free, like a bird winging up into the air.

That's what Hana doesn't understand, has never understood. For some of us, it's about more than the *deliria*. Some of us, the lucky ones, will get the chance to be reborn: newer, fresher, better. Healed and whole and perfect again, like a misshapen slab of iron that comes out of the fire glowing, glittering, razor sharp.

That is all I want – all I have ever wanted. That is the promise of the cure.

nine

That night, even after I'm in bed, Hana's words replay themselves endlessly in my head. *You won't end up like her. You don't have it in you.* She only said it to comfort me, I know – it should be reassuring – but for some reason it isn't. For some reason it makes me upset; there's a deep aching in my chest, as though something large and cold and sharp is lodged there.

Here's another thing Hana doesn't understand: thinking about the disease, and worrying about it, and stressing about whether I've inherited some predisposition for it – that's all I have of my mom. The disease is what I know about her. It is the link.

Otherwise, I have nothing.

It's not that I don't have memories of her. I do – lots of them, considering how young I was when she died. I remember that when there was fresh snow she would send me outside to pack pans with handfuls of it. Once inside we would drizzle maple syrup into the snow-filled pans, watching it harden into amber candy almost instantly, all loops and fragile, sugared filigree, like edible lace. I remember how much she loved to sing to us as she bounced me in the water at the beach off Eastern Prom. I didn't know how strange this was at the time. Other mothers teach their children to swim. Other mothers bounce their babies in the water, and apply sunscreen to make sure their babies don't burn, and do all the things that a mother is supposed to do, as outlined in the Parenting section of *The Book of Shhh*.

But they don't sing.

I remember that she brought me trays of buttered toast when I was sick and kissed my bruises when I fell, and I remember once when she lifted me to my feet after I fell off my bike and began to rock me in her arms, a woman gasped and said to her, 'You should be ashamed of yourself,' and I didn't understand why, which made me cry harder. After that she comforted me only in private. In public she would just frown and say, 'You're okay, Lena. Get up.'

We used to have dance parties too. My mother called them 'sock jams,' because we would roll up the carpets in the living room and put on our thickest socks, and slip and slide along the wooden hallways. Even Rachel joined in, though she always claimed to be too old for baby games. My mom would draw the curtains and wedge pillows under the front and back doors and turn up the music. We laughed so hard I always went to bed with a stomachache.

Eventually, I understood that on our sock-jam nights she'd closed the curtains to prevent us from being seen by passing patrols, that she'd stopped up the doors with pillows so that the neighbors would not report us for playing music and laughing too much, both potential warning signs of the *deliria*. I understood that she used to tuck my father's military pin – a silver dagger he had inherited from his own father, which she wore every day on a chain around her neck – beneath the collar of her shirt whenever we left the house, so no one would see it and become suspicious. I understood that all the happiest moments of my childhood were a lie. They were wrong and unsafe and illegal. They were freakish. My *mother* was freakish, and I'd probably inherited the freakishness from her.

For the first time, really, I wonder what she must have been feeling, thinking, the night she walked out to the cliffs and kept walking, feet pedaling the air. I wonder whether she was scared. I wonder whether she thought of me or Rachel. I wonder whether she was sorry for leaving us behind.

I start thinking about my father, too. I don't remember him at all, though I have some dim, ancient impression of two warm, rough hands and a large looming face floating above mine, but I think that's just because my mother kept a framed portrait in her bedroom of my father and me. I was only a few months old and he was holding me, smiling, looking at the camera. But there's no way I'm remembering for *real* real. I wasn't even a year old when he died. Cancer.

The heat is horrible, thick, clotting on the walls. Jenny is rolled over on her back, arms and legs flung open on top of her comforter, breathing silently with her mouth gaping open. Even Grace is fast asleep, murmuring soundlessly into her pillow. The whole room smells like a wet exhalation, skin and tongues and warm milk.

I ease out of bed, already dressed in black jeans and a T-shirt. I didn't even bother to change into my pajamas. I knew I would never be able to sleep tonight. And earlier in the evening, I'd come to a decision. I was sitting at the dinner table with Carol and Uncle William and Jenny and Grace, while everyone chewed and swallowed in silence, staring blankly at one another, feeling as though the air was weighing down on me, constricting my breath, like two fists squeezing tighter and tighter around a water balloon, when I realized something.

Hana said I didn't have it in me, but she was wrong.

My heart is beating so loudly I can hear it, and I'm positive that everyone else will too – that it will make my aunt sit bolt upright in her bed, ready to catch me and accuse me of trying to sneak out. Which is, of course, exactly what I *am* trying to do. I didn't even know a heart could beat so loudly, and it reminds me of an Edgar Allan Poe story we had to read in one of our social studies classes, about this guy who kills this other guy and then gives himself up to the police because he's convinced he can hear the dead guy's heart beating up from beneath his floorboards. It's supposed to be a story about guilt and the dangers of civil disobedience, but when I first read it I thought it seemed kind of lame and melodramatic. Now I get it, though. Poe must have snuck out a lot when he was young.

I ease open the bedroom door, holding my breath, praying

it doesn't squeak. At one point Jenny lets out a shout and my heart freezes. But then she rolls over, flinging one arm across her pillow, and I exhale slowly, realizing she's just fussing in her sleep.

The hall is totally dark. The room my aunt and uncle share is dark too, and the only sound comes from the whispering of the trees outside and the low ticks and groans from the walls, the usual old-house arthritic noises. I finally work up the courage to slip out into the hall and slide the bedroom door shut behind me. I go so slowly that it almost feels like I'm not moving at all, feeling my way by the bumps and ripples in the wallpaper over to the stairs, then sliding my hand inch by inch over the banister, walking on my very tiptoes. Even so, it seems like the house is fighting me, like it's just screaming for me to be caught. Every step seems to creak, or shriek, or moan. Every single floorboard quivers and shudders under my feet, and I start mentally bargaining with the house: *If I make it to the front door without waking up Aunt Carol, I swear to God I'll never slam another door. I'll never call you 'an old piece of turd' again, not even in my head, and I'll never curse the basement when it floods, and I will never, ever, ever kick the bedroom wall when I'm annoyed at Jenny.*

Maybe the house hears me, because, miraculously, I *do* make it to the front door. I pause for a second longer, listening for the sounds of footsteps upstairs, whispered voices, anything – but other than my heart, which is still going strong and loud, it's silent. Even the house seems to hesitate and take a breath, because the front door swings open with barely a whisper, and in the last second before I slip out into the night the rooms behind me are as dark and still as a grave.

Outside, I hesitate on the front stoop. The fireworks stopped an hour ago – I heard the last stuttering explosions, like distant gunfire, just as I was getting ready for bed – and now the streets are strangely silent, and totally empty. It's a little after eleven o'clock. Some cureds must be lingering at the Eastern Prom. Everyone else is home by now. Not a single light is burning on the street. All the streetlamps were disabled years ago, except in the richest parts of Portland, and they look to me like blinded eyes. Thank God the moon is so bright.

I strain to detect the sounds of passing patrols or groups of regulators – I almost hope I do, because then I'll have to go back inside, to my bed, to safety, and already the panic is starting to drill through me again. But everything is perfectly still and quiet, almost like it's frozen. Everything rational, right, and good is screaming for me to turn around and go upstairs, but some stubborn inner center keeps me moving forward.

I go down the walk and unchain my bike from the gate.

It rattles a little bit, particularly when you first start pedaling, so I walk it a ways down the street. The wheels tick reassuringly over the pavement. I've never been out this late on my own in my life. I've *never* broken curfew. But alongside the fear – which is always there, of course, that constant crushing weight – is a small, flickering feeling of excitement that works its way up and underneath the fear, pushing it back some. Like, *It's okay, I'm all right, I can do this.* I'm just a girl – an in-between girl, five-two, nothing special – but I can do this, and all the curfews and the patrols in the world aren't stopping me. It's amazing how much comfort this thought gives me. It's amazing how it breaks up the fear, like a tiny candle lit in the middle of the night, lighting up the shapes of things, burning away the dark.

When I reach the end of my street I hop up on my bike, feeling the gears shudder into place. The breeze feels good as I start pedaling, careful not to go too quickly, staying alert in case there are regulators nearby. Fortunately, Stroudwater and Roaring Brook Farms are in the exact opposite direction from the Fourth of July celebrations at Eastern Prom. Once I get to the broad swath of farmland that surrounds Portland like a belt, I should be okay. The farms and slaughterhouses rarely get patrolled. But first I have to make it through the West End, where rich people like Hana live, through Libby-town, and over the Fore River at the Congress Street Bridge. Thankfully, each street I turn down is empty.

Stroudwater is a good thirty minutes away, even if I'm biking quickly. As I get off-peninsula – moving away from the buildings and businesses of downtown Portland and onto the more suburban mainland – the houses get smaller and farther apart, set back on weedy, patchy yards. This isn't rural Portland yet, but there are signs of the countryside creeping in: plants poking up through half-rotted porches, an owl hooting mournfully in the dark, a black scythe of bats cutting suddenly across the sky. Almost all these houses have cars in front of them – just like the richer houses in West End – but these have obviously been salvaged from the junkyards. They're mounted on cinder blocks and covered in rust. I pass one that has a tree growing straight through its sunroof, like the car has just dropped out of the sky and been impaled there, and another one, hood open, missing its engine. As I go past, a cat startles up out of its black cavity, meowing, blinking at me.

After I cross the Fore River the houses fall away altogether, and it's just field after field and farm after farm, with names like Meadow Lane and Sheepsbay and Willow Creek, which make them sound all homey and nice: places where someone might be baking muffins and skimming fresh cream for butter. But most of the farms are owned by big corporations, packed with livestock and often staffed by orphans.

I've always liked it out here, but it's kind of freaky in the dark, open and totally empty, and I can't help but think that if I did come across a patrol there would be no place to hide, no alley to turn down. Across the fields I see the low, dark silhouettes of barns and silos, some of them brand new, some of them barely standing, clinging to the earth like teeth digging into something. The air smells slightly sweet, like growing things and manure.

Roaring Brook Farms is right next to the southwestern border. It's been abandoned for years, since half the main building and both grain silos were destroyed in a fire. About five minutes before I get there, I think I can make out a rhythm drumming almost imperceptibly under the throaty song of the crickets, but for a while I'm not sure if I'm just imagining it or only hearing my heart, which has started pounding again. Farther on, though, and I'm sure. Even before I reach the little dirt road that leads down to the barn – or at least, the portion of the barn that's still standing – strains of music spring up, crystallizing in the night air like rain turning suddenly to snow, drifting to earth.

Now I'm scared again. All I can think is: *wrong, wrong, wrong*, a word that drums in my head. Aunt Carol would kill me if she knew what I was doing. Kill me, or have me thrown into the Crypts or taken to the labs for an early procedure, Willow Marks-style.

I hop off my bike when I see the turnoff to Roaring Brook, and the big metal sign staked in the ground that reads PROPERTY OF PORTLAND, NO TRESPASSING. I wheel my bike a little ways into the woods at the side of the road. The actual farmhouse and the old barn are still five or six hundred feet down the road, but I don't want to bring my bike any farther. I don't lock it up, though. I don't even want to think about what would happen if there was a raid, but if there is, I'm not going to want to be fumbling with a lock in the half dark. I'll need *speed*.

I step around the NO TRESPASSING sign. I'm getting to be quite the expert at ignoring them, I realize, remembering how Hana and I hopped the gate at the labs. It's the first time I've thought about that afternoon in a while, and right then a vision of Alex rises up in front of me, a memory of seeing him on the observation deck, head tilted back and laughing.

I have to focus on the land around me, the brightness of the moon, the wildflowers on the road. It helps me beat back the feeling that I'm going to be sick at any second. I don't really know what compelled me out of the house, why I felt like I had to prove Hana wrong about something, and I'm trying to ignore the idea – way more disturbing than anything else – that my argument with Hana was just an excuse.

That maybe, deep down, I was just curious.

I'm not feeling curious now. I'm feeling scared. And very, very stupid.

The farmhouse and the old barn are positioned in a dip of land between two hills, a mini valley, like the buildings are sitting right in the middle of somebody's pursed lips.

Because of the way the land slopes I can't see the farmhouse yet, but as I get closer to the top of the hill the music gets clearer, louder. It's like nothing I've ever heard before. It's definitely not like the authorized music you can download off LAMM, prim and harmonious and structured, the kind of music that gets played in the band shell in Deering Oaks Park during official summer concerts.

Someone is singing: a beautiful voice as thick and heavy as warm honey, spilling up and down a scale so quickly I feel dizzy just listening. The music that's playing underneath the voice is strange and clashing and wild – but nothing like the wailing and scratching that I heard Hana playing on her computer earlier today, though I recognize certain similarities, certain patterns of melody and rhythm. That music was metallic and awful, fuzzy through the speakers. This music ebbs and flows, irregular, sad. It reminds me, weirdly, of watching the ocean during a bad storm, the lashing, crashing waves and the spray of sea foam against the docks; the way it takes your breath away, the power and the hugeness of it.

That's exactly what happens as I listen to the music, as I come up over the final crest of hill, and the half-ruined barn and collapsing farmhouse fan out in front of me, just as the music swells, a wave about to break. The breath leaves my body all at once, and I'm struck dumb by the beauty of it. For a second it seems to me like I really am looking down at the ocean – a sea of people, writhing and dancing in the light spilling down from the barn like shadows twisting up around a flame.

The barn is completely gutted: split open and blackened by the fire, exposed to the elements. Only half of it is left standing – fragments of three walls, a portion of the roof, part of an elevated platform that must once have been used to store hay. That's where the band is playing. Thin, stalky trees have begun pushing up in the fields. Older trees, seared completely white from the fire and totally bald of branches and leaves, point like ghostly fingers to the sky.

Fifty feet beyond the barn, I see the low fringe of blackness where the unregulated land begins. The Wilds. I can't make out the border fence from this distance, but I imagine I can feel it, can sense the electricity buzzing through the air. I've only been close to the border fence a few times. Once with my mother years ago, when she made me listen to the zipping of the electricity – a current so strong the air seems to hum with it; you can get a shock just from standing four feet away – and promise never, ever, ever to touch it. She told me that when the cure was first made mandatory, some people tried to escape over the border. They never put more than a hand on the fence before being fried like bacon – I remember that's exactly what she said, like bacon. Since then I've run alongside it with Hana a few times, always careful to stay a good ten feet away.

In the barn, someone has set up speakers and amps and even two enormous, industrial-sized lamps, which make everyone close to the stage look starkly white and hyper-real, and everyone else dark and indistinct, blurry. A song ends and the crowd roars together, an ocean sound. I think, *They must be mooching power from a grid on one of the other farms.* I think, *This is stupid, I'll never find Hana, there are too many people* – and then a new song starts, this one just as wild and beautiful, and it's like the music reaches across all that black space and pulls at something at the very heart and root of me, plucking me like a string. I head down the hill toward the barn. The weird thing is I don't choose to do it. My feet just go on their own, as though they've happened on some invisible track and it's all just slide, slide, slide.

For a moment I forget that I'm supposed to be looking for Hana. I feel as though I'm in a dream, where strange things are happening but they don't feel strange. Everything is cloudy – everything is wrapped in a fog – and I'm filled from head to toe with the single, burning desire to get closer to the music, to hear the music better, for the music to go on and on and on.

'Lena! Oh my God, Lena!'

Hearing my name snaps me out of my daze, and I'm suddenly aware that I'm standing in a huge crush of people.

No. Not just people. Boys. And girls. Uncureds, all of them, without a hint of a blemish on their necks – at least the ones standing close enough for me to scope out. Boys and girls talking. Boys and girls laughing. Boys and girls sharing sips from the same cup. All of a sudden, I think I might faint.

Hana is barreling toward me, elbowing people out of the way, and before I can even open my mouth she's jumping on top of me like she did at graduation, squeezing me in a hug. I'm so startled I stumble backward, nearly falling over.

'You're here.' She pulls away and stares at me, keeping her hands on my shoulders. 'You're actually *here*.'

Another song ends and the lead singer – a tiny girl with long black hair – calls out something about a break. As my brain slowly reboots, I have the dumbest thought: *She's even shorter than I am, and she's singing in front of five hundred people.*

Then I think, *Five hundred people, five hundred people, what am I doing here with five hundred people?*

'I can't stay,' I say quickly. The moment the words are out

of my mouth I feel relieved. Whatever I came here to prove has been proven; now I can go. I need to get out of this crowd, the babble of voices, a shifting wall of chests and shoulders all around me. I was too wrapped up in the music earlier to look around, but now I have the sensation of colours and perfumes and hands twisting and turning around us.

Hana opens her mouth – maybe to object – but at that second we're interrupted. A boy with dirty blond hair falling into his eyes pushes his way over to us, carrying two big plastic cups.

The boy passes a cup to Hana. She takes it, thanks him, and then turns back to me.

'Lena,' she says, 'this is my friend Drew.' I think she looks guilty for just a second, but then the smile is back on her face, as wide as ever, like we're standing in the middle of St. Anne's talking about a bio quiz.

I open my mouth but no words come out, which is probably a good thing, considering that there's a giant fire alarm going off in my head. It may sound stupid and naive, but not once when I was heading to the farms did I even consider that the party would be coed. It didn't even *occur* to me.

Breaking curfew is one thing; listening to unapproved music is even worse. But breaking segregation laws is one of the worst offenses there is. Thus Willow Marks's early procedure, and the graffiti scrawled on her house; thus the fact that Chelsea Bronson was kicked out of school after allegedly being found breaking curfew with a boy from Spencer, and her parents were mysteriously fired, and her whole family was forced to vacate their house. And – at least in Chelsea Bronson's case – there wasn't even any *proof*. Just a rumor going around.

Drew gives me a half wave. 'Hey, Lena.'

My mouth opens and closes. Still no sound. For a second we stand there in awkward silence. Then he extends a cup to me, a sudden, jerky gesture. 'Whiskey?'

'Whiskey?' I squeak back. I've only had alcohol a few times. At Christmas, when Aunt Carol pours me a quarter glass of wine, and once at Hana's house, when we stole some blackberry liqueur from her parents' liquor cabinet and drank until the ceiling started spinning overhead. Hana was laughing and giggling, but I didn't like it, didn't like the sweet sick taste in my mouth or the way my thoughts seemed to break apart like a mist in the sun. Out of control – that's what it was, that's what I hated.

Drew shrugs. 'It's all they had. Vodka always goes first at these things.' *At these things* – as in, *these things happen*, as in, *more than once*.

'No.' I try to shove the cup back at him. 'Take it.'

He waves me away, obviously misunderstanding. 'It's cool. I'll just get another.'

Drew smiles quickly at Hana before disappearing into the crowd. I like his smile, the way it rises crookedly toward his left ear – but as I realize I'm thinking about liking his smile, I feel the panic winging its way through me, beating through my blood, a lifetime of whispers and accusations.

Control. It's all about control.

'I have to go,' I manage to say to Hana. Progress.

'Go?' She wrinkles her forehead. 'You walk all the way out here—'

'I biked.'

'Whatever. You bike all the way out here and then you're just going to go?' Hana reaches for my hand, but I cross my arms quickly to avoid her. She looks momentarily hurt. I pretend to shiver so she doesn't feel bad, wondering why it feels so awkward to talk to her. This is my best friend, the girl I've known since second grade, the girl who used to split her cookies with me at lunch, and once put her fist in Jillian Dawson's face after Jillian said my family was diseased.

'I'm tired,' I say. 'And I shouldn't be here.' I want to say, *You shouldn't be here either*, but I stop myself.

'Did you hear the band? They're amazing, aren't they?' Hana's being way too nice, totally un-Hana, and I feel a deep, sharp pain under my ribs. She's trying to be polite. She's acting like we're strangers. She feels the awkwardness too.

'I – I wasn't listening.' For some reason I don't want Hana to know that yes, I heard, and yes, I thought they were amazing, better than amazing. It's too private – embarrassing even, something to be ashamed of, and despite the fact that I came all the way to Roaring Brook Farms and broke curfew and everything, just to see her and apologize, the feeling I had earlier today returns to me: I don't know Hana anymore, and she doesn't really know me.

I'm used to a feeling of doubleness, of thinking one thing and having to do another, a constant tug of war. But somehow Hana has fallen cleanly away into the double half, the other world, the world of unmentionable thoughts and things and people.

Is it possible that all this time I've been living my life, studying for tests, taking long runs with Hana – and this other world has just *existed*, running alongside and underneath mine, alive, ready to sneak out of the shadows and the alleyways as soon as the sun goes down? Illegal parties, unapproved music, people touching one another with no fear of the disease, with no fear for themselves.

A world without fear. Impossible.

And even though I'm standing in the middle of the biggest crowd I've ever seen in my life, I suddenly feel very alone.

'Stay,' Hana says quietly. Even though it's a command, there's a hesitation in her voice, like she's asking a question. 'You can catch the second set.'

I shake my head. I wish I hadn't come. I wish I hadn't seen this. I wish I didn't know what I know now, could wake up tomorrow and ride over to Hana's house, could lie out at Eastern Prom with her and complain about how boring summers are, like we always do. Could believe that nothing had changed. 'I'm going to go,' I say, wishing my voice didn't come out shaky. 'It's all right, though. You can stay.'

The second I say it, I realize she never offered to come back with me. She's looking at me with the weirdest mixture of regret and pity.

'I can come back with you if you want,' she says, but I can tell she's only offering now to make me feel better.

'No, no. I'll be fine.' My cheeks are burning and I take a step back, desperate to get out of there. I bump against someone – a boy – who turns and smiles at me. I step quickly away from him.

'Lena, wait.' Hana goes to grab me again. Even though she already has a drink, I shove my cup in her free hand so she has to pause, momentarily frowning as she tries to juggle both drinks into the crook of an elbow, and in that second I dance backward out of her reach.

'I'll be fine, I promise. I'll talk to you tomorrow.' Then I'm slipping through a narrow space between two people – that's the only benefit of being five-two, you have a good vantage point on all the in-between spaces – and before I know it, Hana has dropped behind me, swallowed up by the crowd. I weave a path away from the barn, keeping my eyes down, hoping my cheeks cool off fast.

Images swirl by, a blur, making me feel like I'm dreaming again. Boy. Girl. Boy. Girl. Laughing, shoving each other, touching each other's hair. I've never, not once in my whole life, felt so different and out of place. There's a high, mechanized shriek, and then the band starts playing again, but this time the music does nothing for me. I don't even pause. I just keep walking, heading for the hill, imagining the cool silence of the starlit fields, the familiar dark streets of Portland, the regular rhythm of the patrols, marching quietly in sync, the feedback from the regulators' walkie-talkies – regular, normal, familiar, mine.

Finally the crowd starts thinning. It was hot, pressed up against so many people, and the breeze stings my skin, cools my cheeks. I've started to calm down a little, and at the edge of the crowd I allow myself one look back at the stage. The barn, open to the sky and the night and glowing white with light, reminds me of a palm cupping a small bit of fire.

'Lena!'

It's strange how I instantly recognize the voice even though I've heard it only once before, for ten minutes, fifteen tops – it's the laughter that runs underneath it, like someone leaning in to let you in on a really good secret in the middle of a really boring class. Everything freezes. The blood stops flowing in my veins. My breath stops coming. For a second even the music falls away and all I hear is something steady and quiet and pretty, like the distant beat of a drum, and I think, *I'm hearing my heart,* except I know that's impossible, because my heart has stopped too. My vision does its camera-zoom focus again and all I see is Alex, shouldering his way out of the crowd toward me.

'Lena! Wait.'

A brief flash of terror zips through me – for a wild second I think he must be here as part of a patrol, as a raiding group or something – but then I see he's dressed normally, in jeans and his scuffed-up sneakers with the ink-blue laces and a faded T-shirt.

'What are you doing here?' I stammer out as he catches up to me.

He grins. 'Nice to see you too.'

He has left a few feet of distance between us, and I'm glad. In the half-light I can't make out the colour of his eyes and I don't need to be distracted right now, don't need to feel the way I did at the labs when he leaned in to whisper to me – the total awareness of the bare inch that separated his mouth from my ear, terror and guilt and excitement all at once.

'I'm serious.' I do my best to scowl at him.

His smile falters, though it doesn't disappear entirely. He blows air out of his lips. 'I came to hear the music,' he says. 'Like everybody else.'

'But you can't—' I'm struggling to find words, not quite sure how to say what I want to say. 'But this is—'

'Illegal?' He shrugs. One strand of hair curls down over his left eye, and when he turns to scan the party it catches the light from the stage and winks that crazy golden-brown colour. 'It's okay,' he says, quieter, so that I have to lean forward to hear him over the music. 'Nobody's hurting anybody.'

You don't know that, I start to say, but the way his words are just edged with sadness stops me. Alex runs a hand through his hair and I make out the small, dark, three-pronged scar behind his left ear, perfectly symmetrical. Maybe he's only regretful for the things he lost after the cure. Music doesn't move people the same way, for example, and while he should have been cured of feelings of regret, too, the procedure works differently for everybody, and it isn't always perfect. That's why my aunt and uncle sometimes still dream. That's why my cousin Marcia used to find herself crying hysterically, with no warning or apparent cause.

'So what about you?' He turns back to me and the smile is on again, and the teasing, winking quality of his voice. 'What's your excuse?'

'I didn't want to come,' I say quickly. 'I had to—' I break off, realizing I'm not *sure* why I had to come. 'I had to give something to someone,' I say finally.

He raises his eyebrows, clearly unimpressed. I rush on, 'To Hana. My friend. You met her the other day.'

'I remember,' he says. I've never seen anyone maintain a smile for so long. It's like his face is naturally molded that way. 'You haven't said you're sorry yet, by the way.'

'For what?' The crowd has continued to press closer to the stage, so Alex and I are no longer surrounded by people. Occasionally someone walks by, swinging a bottle of something or singing along, slightly off-key, but for the most part we're alone.

'For standing me up.' One corner of his mouth hitches higher, and again I have the feeling that he's sharing some delicious secret with me, that he's trying to tell me something. 'You were a no-show at Back Cove that day.'

I feel a burst of triumph – he *was* waiting for me at Back Cove! He did want me to meet him! At the same time the anxiety blooms inside of me. He wants something from me. I'm not sure what it is, but I can sense it, and it makes me afraid.

'So?' He folds his arms and rocks back on his heels, still smiling. 'Are you going to apologize, or what?'

His easiness and self-assurance aggravate me, just like they did at the labs. It's so unfair, so different from how I feel, like I'm about to have a heart attack, or melt into a puddle.

'I don't apologize to liars,' I say, surprised by how steady my voice sounds.

He winces. 'What's that supposed to mean?'

'Come on.' I roll my eyes, feeling more and more confident by the second. 'You lied about seeing me at evaluations. You lied about recognizing me.' I'm ticking his lies off on my fingers. 'You lied about even being *inside* the labs on Evaluation Day.'

'Okay, okay.' He holds up both hands. 'I'm sorry, okay? Look, I'm the one who should apologize.' He stares at me for a second and then sighs. 'I told you, security isn't allowed in the labs during evaluations. To keep the process "pure" or something, I don't know. But I really needed a cup of coffee, and there's this machine on the second floor of the C complex that has the good kind, with real milk and everything, so I used my code to get in. That's it. End of story. And afterward I had to lie about it. I could lose my job. And I only work at the stupid labs to subsidize my school . . .' He trails off. For once he doesn't look confident. He looks worried, like he's scared I might actually tell on him.

'So why were you on the observation deck?' I press on. 'Why were you watching me?'

'I didn't even make it to the second floor,' he says. He is staring at me closely, as though judging my reaction. 'I came inside and – and I just heard this crazy noise. That rushing, roaring sound. And something else, too. Screaming or something.'

I close my eyes briefly, recalling the feeling of the burning white lights, my impression of hearing the ocean pounding outside the labs, of hearing my mother scream across the distance of a decade. When I open them again, Alex is still watching me.

'Anyway, I had no idea what was going on. I thought – I don't know, it's stupid – but I thought maybe the labs were under attack or something. And then as I'm standing there, all of a sudden there's, like, a hundred cows charging me . . .' He shrugs. 'There was a staircase to my left. I freaked out and booked it. Figured cows don't climb stairs.' A smile appears again, this time fleeting, tentative. 'I ended up on the observation deck.'

A perfectly normal, reasonable explanation. I feel relieved, and less frightened of him now. At the same time there's something working under my chest, a dull feeling, a disappointment. And some stubbornness, a part of me that still doubts him. I remember the way he looked on the observation deck, head tilted back, laughing; the way he winked at me. The way he looked – amused, confident, happy. Totally unafraid.

A world without fear . . .

'So you don't know anything about how . . . how it happened?' I can't believe I'm being so bold. I ball up my fists and squeeze, hoping he doesn't notice the sudden strangled sound of my voice.

'The mix-up in the deliveries, you mean?' He says it smoothly, without a pause or a break in his voice, and the last of my doubts vanish. Just like any cured, he doesn't question the official story. 'I wasn't in charge of signing for deliveries that day. The guy who was – Sal – was fired. You're supposed to check the cargo. I guess he skipped that step.' He cocks his head to one side, spreads his hands. 'Satisfied now?'

'Satisfied,' I say. But the pressure in my chest is still there. Even though earlier I was desperate to be out of the house, now I just wish I could blink and be home, sit up in bed, pushing the covers off of my legs, realizing that everything – the party, seeing Alex – was a dream.

'So . . . ?' He tilts his head back toward the barn. The band is playing something loud and fast-paced. I don't know why the music appealed to me before. It just seems like noise now – rushing noise. 'Think we can get closer without getting trampled?'

I ignore the fact that he has just said 'we,' a word that for some reason sounds amazingly appealing when pronounced with his lilting, laughing accent. 'Actually, I was just heading home.' I realize I'm angry at him without knowing why – for not being what I thought he was, I guess, even though I should be grateful that he's normal, and cured, and safe.

'Heading home?' he repeats disbelievingly. 'You can't go home.'

I've always been careful not to let myself give in to feelings of anger or irritation. I can't afford to at Carol's house. I owe her too much – and besides, after the few tantrums I threw as a child, I hated the way she looked at me sideways for days, as though analysing me, measuring me. I knew she was thinking, *Just like her mother*. But now I give in, let the anger surge. I'm sick of people acting like this world, this other world, is the normal one, while I'm the freak. It's not fair, like all the rules have suddenly been changed and somebody forgot to tell me.

'I can, and I am.' I turn around and start heading up the hill, figuring he'll leave me alone. To my surprise, he doesn't.

'Wait!' He comes bounding up the hill after me.

'What are you doing?' I whirl around to face him – again, surprised by how confident I sound, considering that my heart is rushing, tumbling. Maybe this is the secret to talking to boys – maybe you just have to be angry all the time.

'What do you mean?' We're both slightly out of breath from hoofing it up the hill, but he still manages a smile. 'I just want to talk to you.'

'You're following me.' I cross my arms, which helps me feel as though I'm closing off the space between us. 'You're following me *again*.'

There it is. He starts backward, and I get a momentary, sick twinge of pleasure that I've surprised him. 'Again?' he repeats. I'm glad that for once I'm not the one stuttering, or struggling to find words.

The words fly out: 'I think it's a little bit strange that I go pretty much my whole life without seeing you, and then all of a sudden I start seeing you everywhere.' I hadn't planned on saying this – it actually hadn't struck me as strange – but the second the words are out of my mouth I realize they're true.

I think he's going to be angry, but to my surprise he tips

his head back and laughs, long and loud, moonlight turning
the curve of his cheeks and chin and nose silver. I'm so
surprised by his reaction I just stand there, staring at him.
Finally he looks at me. Even though I still can't make out
his eyes – the moon draws everything starkly, highlighting
it in bright, crystalline silver or leaving it in blackness – I
have the impression of heat, and light, the same impression
I had that day at the labs.

'Maybe you just haven't been paying attention,' he says
quietly, rocking forward slightly on his toes.

I take an unconscious, half-shuffling step backward. I find
myself frightened by his closeness, by the fact that even
though our bodies are separated by several inches I feel as
though we're touching.

'What – what do you mean?'

'I mean that you're wrong.' He pauses, watching me, and
I struggle to keep my face composed, even though I can feel
my left eye straining and fluttering. Hopefully in the darkness he can't tell. 'We've seen each other plenty.'

'I would remember if we'd met before.'

'I didn't say that we'd *met*.' He doesn't try to close the new
distance between us and I'm grateful, at least, for that. He
chews on the corner of his lip – a gesture that makes him
look younger. 'Let me ask you a question,' he goes on. 'How
come you don't run past the Governor anymore?'

Without meaning to I gasp a little. 'How do you know
about the Governor?'

'I take classes at UP,' he says. University of Portland – I
remember now, the afternoon we walked up to see the ocean
from the back of the lab complex, hearing bits of his conversation floating back to me on the wind. He *did* say he was

a student. 'I worked at the Grind last semester, in Monument Square. I used to see you all the time.'

My mouth opens and shuts. No words come out; my brain goes on lockdown whenever I need it the most. Of course I know the Grind; Hana and I used to run past it two, maybe three times a week, watching the college students float in and out like drifting snowflakes, blowing the steam from the top of their cups. The Grind looks out onto a small square, all cobblestone, called Monument Square: it marked the halfway point of one of the six-mile routes I used to do all the time.

In its center is a statue of a man, half-eroded from snow and weather and scrawled over with a few looping curls of graffiti. He is striding forward, one hand holding his hat on his head so that it looks like he is walking through a horrible storm, or a headwind. His other fist is extended in front of him. It's obvious that he was, in the distant past, holding something – probably a torch – but at some point that portion of the statue was broken or stolen. So now the Governor strides forward with an empty fist, a circular hole cut in his hand, a perfect hiding place for notes and secret stuff. Hana and I used to check his fist sometimes, to see if there was anything good inside. But there wasn't – just a few pieces of wadded-up chewing gum and some coins.

I don't actually know when Hana and I started calling him the Governor, or why. The wind and rain has rubbed the plaque at the base of the statue indecipherable. No one else calls him that. Everyone else just says, 'The statue at Monument Square.' Alex must have overheard us talking about the Governor one day.

Alex is still looking at me, waiting, and I realize I never

answered his question. 'I have to switch my routes up,' I say. I probably haven't run past the Governor since March or April. 'It gets boring.' And then, because I can't help it, I squeak out, 'You remember me?'

He laughs. 'You were pretty hard to miss. You used to run around the statue and do this jumping, whooping thing.'

Heat creeps up my neck and cheeks. I must be going a deep red again, and I thank God for the fact that we've moved away from the stage lights. I completely forgot; I used to jump up and try to high-five the Governor as Hana and I ran past, a way of psyching myself up for the run back to school. Sometimes we would even scream out, 'Halena!' We must have looked completely crazy.

'I don't . . .' I lick my lips, fumbling for an explanation that won't sound ridiculous. 'When you run you sometimes do weird things. Because of the endorphins and stuff. It's kind of like a drug, you know? Messes with your brain.'

'I liked it,' he says. 'You looked . . .' He trails off for a moment. His face contracts slightly, a tiny shift I can barely make out in the dark, but in that second he looks so still and sad it almost takes my breath away, like *he's* a statue, or a different person. I'm afraid he won't finish his sentence, but then he says, 'You looked happy.'

For a second we just stand there in silence. Then, suddenly, Alex is back, easy and smiling again. 'I left a note for you one time. In the Governor's fist, you know?'

I left a note for you one time. It's impossible, too crazy to think about, and I hear myself repeating, 'You left a note for *me*?'

'I'm pretty sure it said something stupid. Just hi, and a smiley face, and my name. But then you stopped coming.'

He shrugs. 'It's probably still there. The note, I mean. Probably just a bit of paper pulp by now.'

He left me a note. He left *me* a note. For me. The idea – the fact of it, the fact that he even noticed and thought about me for more than one second – is huge and overwhelming, makes my legs go tingly and my hands feel numb.

And then I'm frightened. This is how it starts. Even if he *is* cured, even if he *is* safe – the fact is, I'm not safe, and this is how it starts. *Phase One: preoccupation; difficulty focusing; dry mouth; perspiration, sweaty palms; dizziness and disorientation.* I feel a rushing blend of sickness and relief, a feeling like finding out that everyone actually knows your worst secret, has known all along. All this time Aunt Carol was right, my teachers were right, my cousins were right. I'm just like my mother, after all. And the *thing*, the disease, is inside of me, ready at any moment to start working on my insides, to start poisoning me.

'I have to go.' I start up the hill again, nearly sprinting now, but again he comes after me.

'Hey. Not so fast.' At the top of the hill he reaches out and puts a hand on my wrist to stop me. His touch burns, and I jerk away quickly. 'Lena. Hold on a second.'

Even though I know I shouldn't, I stop. It's the way he says my name, like music.

'You don't have to be worried, okay? You don't have to be scared.' His voice is twinkling again. 'I'm not flirting with you.'

Embarrassment sweeps through me. *Flirting.* A dirty word. He thinks I think he's flirting. 'I'm not – I don't think you were – I would never think that you—' The words collide in my mouth, and now I know there's no amount of darkness that can cover the rush of red to my face.

He cocks his head to the side. 'Are *you* flirting with *me*, then?'

'What? No,' I splutter. My mind is spinning blindly in a panic, and I realize I don't even know what flirting is. I just know about it from textbooks; I just know that it's bad. Is it possible to flirt without knowing you're flirting? *Is* he flirting? My left eye goes full flutter.

'Relax,' he says, holding up both hands, a gesture like, *Don't be mad at me*. 'I was kidding.' He turns just slightly to the left, watching me the whole time. The moon lights up his three-pronged scar vividly: a perfect white triangle, a scar that makes you think of order and regularity. 'I'm safe, remember? I can't hurt you.'

He says it quietly, evenly, and I believe him. And yet my heart won't stop its frantic winging in my chest, spinning higher and higher, until I'm sure it's going to carry me off. I feel the way I do whenever I get to the top of the Hill and can see back down Congress Street, with the whole of Portland lying behind me, the streets a shimmer of greens and greys – from a distance, both beautiful and unfamiliar – just before I spread my arms and let go, trip and skip and run down the hill, wind whipping in my face, not even trying to move, just letting gravity pull me.

Breathless; excited; waiting for the drop.

I suddenly realize how quiet it is. The band has stopped playing, and the crowd has gone silent too. The only sound is the wind shushing over the grass. From where we are, fifty feet past the crest of the hill, the barn and the party are invisible. I have a brief fantasy that we're the only two people out in the darkness – that we are the only two people awake and alive in the city, in the world.

Then soft strands of music begin to weave themselves up in the air, gentle, sighing, so quiet at first I confuse the sounds for the wind. This music is totally different from the music that was playing earlier – soft, and fragile, as though each note is spun glass, or silken thread, looping up and back into the night air. Once again I'm struck by how absolutely beautiful it is, like nothing I've ever heard, and out of nowhere I'm overwhelmed by the dual desire to laugh and cry.

'This song is my favourite.' A cloud skitters across the moon, and shadows dance over Alex's face. He's still staring at me, and I wish I knew what he was thinking. 'Have you ever danced?'

'No,' I say, a little too forcefully.

He laughs softly. 'It's okay. I won't tell.'

Images of my mother: the softness of her hands as she spun me down the long polished wood floors of our house, as though we were ice-skaters; the fluted quality of her voice as she sang along to the songs piping from the speakers, laughing. 'My mother used to dance,' I say. The words slip out, and I regret them almost instantly.

But Alex doesn't question me or laugh. He keeps watching me steadily. For a moment he seems on the verge of saying something. But then he just holds out his hand to me across the space, across the dark.

'Would you like to?' he says. His voice is hardly audible above the wind – so low it's barely a whisper.

'Would I like to what?' My heart is roaring, rushing in my ears, and though there are still several inches between his hand and mine, there's a zipping, humming energy that connects us, and from the heat flooding my body you would think we were pressed together, palm to palm, face to face.

'Dance,' he says, at the same time closing those last few inches and finding my hand and pulling me closer, and at that second the song hits a high note and I confuse the two impressions, of his hand and the soaring, the lifting of the music.

We dance.

Most things, even the greatest movements on earth, have their beginnings in something small. An earthquake that shatters a city might begin with a tremor, a tremble, a breath. Music begins with a vibration. The flood that rushed into Portland twenty years ago after nearly two months of straight rain, that hurtled up beyond the labs and damaged more than a thousand houses, swept up tires and trash bags and old, smelly shoes and floated them through the streets like prizes, that left a thin film of green mold behind, a stench of rotting and decay that didn't go away for months, began with a trickle of water, no wider than a finger, lapping up onto the docks.

And God created the whole universe from an atom no bigger than a thought.

Grace's life fell apart because of a single word: *sympathizer.* My world exploded because of a different word: *suicide.*

Correction: that was the *first* time my world exploded.

The second time my world exploded, it was also because of a word. A word that worked its way out of my throat and danced onto and out of my lips before I could think about it, or stop it.

The question was: *Will you meet me tomorrow?*

And the word was: *Yes.*

ten

Symptoms of Amor Deliria Nervosa

PHASE ONE

> *preoccupation; difficulty focusing*
> *dry mouth*
> *perspiration, sweaty palms*
> *fits of dizziness and disorientation*
> *reduced mental awareness; racing thoughts; impaired*
>   *reasoning skills*

PHASE TWO

> *periods of euphoria; hysterical laughter and heightened*
>   *energy*
> *periods of despair; lethargy*
> *changes in appetite; rapid weight loss or weight gain*
> *fixation; loss of other interests*
> *compromised reasoning skills; distortion of reality*
> *disruption of sleep patterns; insomnia or constant fatigue*
> *obsessive thoughts and actions*
> *paranoia; insecurity*

PHASE THREE (CRITICAL)

> *difficulty breathing*
> *pain in the chest, throat, or stomach*
> *difficulty swallowing; refusal to eat*
> *complete breakdown of rational faculties; erratic behaviour;*
>   *violent thoughts and fantasies; hallucinations and*
>   *delusions*

PHASE FOUR (FATAL)
> *emotional or physical paralysis (partial or total)*
> *death*

If you fear that you or someone you know may have contracted deliria, please call the emergency line toll-free at 1-800-PREVENT to discuss immediate intake and treatment.

I'd never understood how Hana could lie so often and so easily. But just like anything else, lying becomes easier the more you do it.

Which is why, when I get home from work the next day and Carol asks me whether I don't mind having hot dogs for the fourth straight night in a row (the result of a shipment surplus at the Stop-N-Save; we once went a whole two weeks having baked beans every day), I say that actually, Sophia Hennerson from St. Anne's invited me and some other girls over for dinner. I don't even have to think about it. The lie just comes. And even though I still feel sweat pricking up under my palms, my voice stays calm, and I'm pretty sure my face keeps its normal colour, because Carol just gives me one of her flitting smiles and says that that sounds nice.

At six thirty I get on my bike and head to East End Beach, where Alex and I agreed to meet.

There are plenty of beaches in Portland. East End Beach is probably one of the least popular – which of course made it one of my mother's favourites. The current is stronger there than it is at Willard Beach or Sunset Park. I'm not exactly sure why. I don't mind. I've always been a strong swimmer. After that first time – when my mother released her arms from around my waist and I felt both the surging panic and the thrill, the excitement – I learned pretty quickly, and by four I was paddling out by myself all the way past the breaks.

There are other reasons why most people avoid East End Beach, even though it's only a short walk down the hill from Eastern Prom, one of the most popular parks. The beach is nothing more than a short strip of rocky, gravel-flecked sand. It backs up against the far side of the lab complex, where the storage and waste sheds are, which doesn't make for particularly pretty scenery. And when you swim out at East End Beach you get a clear view of Tukey's Bridge and the wedge of unregulated land between Portland and Yarmouth. A lot of people don't like being so close to the Wilds. It makes them nervous.

It makes me nervous too, except that there's a part of me – a tiny, little flick of a part – that likes it. For a while after my mom died I used to have these fantasies that she wasn't dead, really, and that my father wasn't dead either – that they had escaped to the Wilds to be together. He had gone five years before her, to prepare everything, to build a little house with a woodstove and furniture hewed from tree branches. At some point, I imagined, they would come back and get me. I even imagined my room down to the smallest detail: a dark red carpet, a little red and green patchwork quilt, a red chair.

I had the fantasy only a few times before I realized how wrong it was. If my parents had escaped to the Wilds it would make them sympathizers, resisters. It was better that they were dead. Besides, I learned pretty quickly that my fantasies about the Wilds were just that – make-believe, little kiddie stuff. The Invalids have nothing, no way of trading or getting red patchwork quilts or chairs, or anything else for that matter. Rachel once told me that they must live like animals: filthy, hungry, desperate. She says that's why the government doesn't bother doing anything about them, doesn't even acknowledge their existence. They'll die out soon enough, all of them, freeze or starve or just let the disease run its course, turn them against each other, have them raging and fighting and clawing one another's eyes out.

She said as far as we know that's already happened – she said the Wilds might be empty now, dark and dead, full of only the rustle and whispers of animals.

She's probably right about the other stuff – about the Invalids living like animals – but she's obviously wrong about them being dead. They're alive, and out there, and they don't want us to forget it. That's why they stage the demonstrations. That's why they let the cows loose in the labs.

I'm not nervous until I get to East End Beach. Even though the sun is sinking behind me, it lights the water white and makes everything shimmer. I shield my eyes against the glare and spot Alex down by the water, a long black brushstroke against all that blue. I flash back to last night, to the fingers of one of his hands just pressed against my lower back, so lightly it was like I was only dreaming them – the other hand cupping mine, dry and reassuring as a piece of wood warmed by the sun. We really danced, too, the kind of dancing that people do at their wedding after the pairing has been formalized, but better somehow, looser and less unnatural.

He has his back toward me, facing the ocean, and I'm glad. I feel self-conscious as I plod down the rickety, salt-warped stairs that lead from the parking lot to the beach, pausing to unlace and kick off my sneakers, which I carry in one hand. The sand is warm on my bare feet as I set off toward him.

An old man is coming up from the water, carrying a fishing pole. He shoots me a suspicious glance, then turns to stare at Alex, then looks at me again and frowns. I open my mouth to say, 'He's cured,' but the man just grunts at me as he walks past, and I can't imagine he'd bother to call the regulators, so I don't say anything. Not that we'd get in *trouble* trouble if we were caught – that's what Alex meant when he said, 'I'm safe' – but I don't want to answer a lot of questions and have my ID number run through SVS and all of that. Besides, if the regulators *did* haul ass all the way out to East End Beach to check out 'suspicious behaviour,' only to discover it was some cured taking pity on a seventeen-year-old nobody, they'd definitely be annoyed – and guaranteed to take it out on someone.

Taking pity. I push the words out of my mind quickly, surprised by how difficult it is to even think them. All day I tried not to worry about why on earth Alex would be so nice to me. I even imagined – for one brief, stupid second – that maybe after my evaluation I'd get matched with him. I'd had to shunt that thought aside too. Alex has already received his printed sheet, his recommended matches – he would have gotten it even before his cure, directly after the evaluations. He's not married yet because he's still in school, end of story. But he will be, as soon as he finishes.

Of course, then I started wondering about the kind of girl

he's been matched with – someone like Hana, I decided, with bright blonde hair and an irritating ability to make even pulling her hair into a ponytail look graceful, like a choreographed dance.

There are four other people on the beach: a mother and a child, one hundred feet away, the mother sitting in a faded fabric folding chair, staring blankly toward the horizon, while the child – who is probably no more than three – toddles in the waves, gets knocked over, lets out a shriek (of pain? pleasure?) and struggles back to her feet. Beyond them a couple is walking, a man and a woman, not touching. They must be married. Both have their hands clasped in front of them, and both look straight ahead, not talking – and not smiling, either, but calm, as though they are each surrounded by an invisible protective bubble.

Then I'm coming up behind Alex and he turns and sees me, smiles. The sun catches his hair, turns it momentarily white. Then it smolders back to its normal golden-brown colour.

'Hi,' he says. 'I'm glad you came.'

I feel shy again, stupid, holding my ratty shoes in one hand. I can feel my cheeks getting hot, so I look down, drop my shoes, turn them over once in the sand with my toe. 'I said I would, didn't I?' I don't mean for the words to come out so harshly and I wince, mentally cursing myself. It's like there's a filter set up in my brain, except instead of making things better, it twists everything around so what comes out of my mouth is totally wrong, totally different from what I was thinking.

Thankfully, Alex laughs. 'I just meant that you stood me up last time,' he says. He nods toward the sand. 'Sit?'

'Sure,' I say, relieved. I feel much less awkward once we're both settled in the sand. There's less chance of falling over or doing something dumb. I draw my legs up to my chest, resting my chin on my knees. Alex leaves a good two or three feet of space between us.

We sit in silence for a few minutes. At first I'm searching frantically for something to say. Every beat of silence seems to stretch into an infinity, and I'm pretty sure Alex must think I'm a mute. But then he flicks a half-buried seashell out of the sand and hurls it into the ocean, and I realize he's not uncomfortable at all. After that I relax. I'm even glad for the silence.

Sometimes I feel like if you just watch things, just sit still and let the world exist in front of you – sometimes I swear that just for a second time freezes and the world pauses in its tilt. Just for a second. And if you somehow found a way to live in that second, then you would live forever.

'Tide's going out,' Alex says. He chucks another seashell in a high arc, and it just hits the break.

'I know.' The ocean is leaving a litter of pulpy green seaweed, twigs, and scrabbling hermit crabs in its wake, and the air smells tangy with salt and fish. A seagull pecks its way across the beach, blinking, leaving tiny thatched claw prints. 'My mom used to bring me here when I was little. We'd walk out a little bit at low tide – as far as you can go, anyway. Crazy stuff gets stranded on the sand – horseshoe crabs and giant clams and sea anemone. Just gets left behind when the water goes out. She taught me to swim here too.' I'm not sure why the words bubble out of me then, why I have the sudden urge to talk. 'My sister used to stay on the shore and build sand castles, and we would pretend that they were real cities, like we'd swum all the way to the other side of the world, to the uncured places. Except in our games they weren't diseased at all, or destroyed, or horrible. They were beautiful and peaceful, and built of glass and light and things.'

Alex stays silent, tracing shapes in the sand with a finger. But I can tell he's listening.

The words tumble on: 'I remember my mom would bounce me in the water on her hip. And then one time she just let me go. I mean, not for *real* real. I had those little inflatable thingies on my arms. But I was so scared I started bawling my head off. I was only a few years old but I remember it, I swear I do. I was so relieved when she scooped me back up. But – but disappointed, too. Like I'd lost the chance at something great, you know?'

'So what happened?' Alex tips his head to look at me. 'You don't come here anymore? Your mom lose her taste for the ocean?'

I look away, toward the horizon. The bay is relatively calm today. Flat, all shades of blue and purple as it draws away from the beach with a low sucking sound. Harmless. 'She died,' I say, surprised by how difficult it is to say. Alex is quiet next to me and I rush on, 'She killed herself. When I was six.'

'I'm sorry,' he says, so low and quiet I almost miss it.

'My dad died when I was eight months old. I don't remember him at all. I think – I think it kind of broke her, you know? My mom, I mean. She wasn't cured. It didn't work. I don't know why. She had the procedure three separate times, but it didn't . . . it didn't fix her.' I pause, sucking in a breath, afraid to look at Alex, who is as still and silent next to me as a statue, as a carved piece of shadow. Still, I can't stop speaking. I realize, strangely, that I've never told the story of my mother before. I've never had to. Everyone around me, everyone in school, all my neighbors and my aunts' friends – they all knew about my family already, and my family's shameful secrets. That's why they always looked at me pityingly, from the corner of their eyes. That's why for years I rode a wave of whispering into every room, was slapped with sudden silence when I entered – silence and guilty, startled faces. Even Hana knew before she and I were desk partners in second grade. I remember because she found me in the bathroom stall, crying into a piece of paper towel, stuffing my mouth with it so no one would hear, and she kicked the door right open with a foot and stood there staring. *Is it because of your mom?* she said, the first words she ever spoke to me.

'I didn't know there was something wrong with her. I didn't know she was sick. I was too young to understand.' I keep my eyes focused on the horizon, a solid thin line, taut as a tightrope. The bay edges farther from us, and as always I have the same fantasy I did as a child: that maybe it won't come back, maybe the whole ocean will disappear forever, drawn back across the surface of the earth like lips retracting over teeth, revealing the cool, white hardness underneath, the bleached bone. 'If I had known, maybe I could have . . .'

At the last second my voice falters and I can't say any more, can't finish the sentence. *Maybe I could have stopped it.* It's a sentence I've never spoken before, never even allowed myself to think. But the idea is there, looming up solid and unavoidable, a sheer rock face: I could have stopped it. I should have stopped it.

We sit in silence. At some point during my story the mother

and child must have packed up and gone home; Alex and I are all alone on the beach. Now that the words aren't bubbling, rushing out of me, I can't believe how much I've shared with a next-to-perfect stranger – and a boy, no less. I'm suddenly, itchingly, squirmingly embarrassed. I'm desperate for something else to say – something harmless, about the tide or the weather – but as usual my mind goes totally blank now that I actually need it to function. I'm afraid to look at Alex. When I finally work up the courage to shoot him a tiny sidelong glance, he's sitting, staring out at the bay. His face is completely unreadable except for a tiny muscle, which flutters in and out at the base of his jaw. My heart sinks. Just like I feared – he's ashamed of me now, disgusted by my family's history, by the disease that runs in my blood. At any second he'll stand up and tell me it's better if he doesn't speak to me anymore. It's weird. I don't even really know Alex, and there's an impassable divide between us, but the idea upsets me anyway.

I'm two seconds away from jumping up and running away, just so I won't have to nod and pretend to understand when he turns to me and says, *Listen, Lena. I'm sorry, but* . . . and gives me that all-too-familiar look. (Last year there was a rabid dog loose on the Hill, biting and snapping at everyone, frothing at the mouth. It was half-starved, mangy, flea-riddled, and missing one leg, but still it took two cops to shoot it down. A crowd gathered to watch, and I was there. I stopped on the way back from my run. For the first time in my life I understood the look that people had been giving me forever, the same curl of the lip whenever they hear the name *Haloway*. Pity, yes – but disgust, also, and fear of contamination. It was the same way they were looking at the dog while he circled and snapped and spit; and then a mass exhalation of relief when the third bullet finally took him down and he stopped twitching.)

Just when I think I can't take it anymore, Alex reaches over and barely skims my elbow with one finger. 'I'll race you,' he says, standing up and beating the sand off his shorts. He reaches a hand out to me and helps me up, a smile flickering back on his face. I'm endlessly grateful to him in that second. He's not going to hold my family's past against me. He doesn't think I'm dirty or damaged. He pulls me to my feet, and I think he squeezes my hand once I'm standing, a quick pulse, and I'm startled and happy, thinking of my secret sign with Hana.

'Only if you've got a thing for total humiliation,' I say.

He raises his eyebrows. 'So you think you can beat me?'

'I don't think. I *know*.'

'We'll see about that.' He cocks his head to the side. 'First one to the buoys, then?'

That throws me. The tide doesn't go out too far in the bay; the buoys are still floating on at least four feet of water. 'You want to race *into* the bay?'

'Scared?' he asks, grinning.

'I'm not *scared*, I'm just—'

'Good.' He reaches out and brushes my shoulder with two fingers. 'Then how about a little less conversation, and a little more – *Go!*'

He screams out the last word and takes off at full speed. It takes me two whole seconds to launch myself after him, and I'm calling out, 'No fair! I wasn't ready!' and both of us are laughing as we splash through the shallows in our clothes, the little ripples and dips of the ocean floor now exposed

by the tide's retreat. Shells crunch under my feet. I get my
toe caught in a tangle of red and purple seaweed and nearly
do a face-plant. I push myself off the wet sand with a palm
and get my balance again, have almost caught up to Alex,
when he ducks down and scoops up a handful of wet sand,
whirling around to peg me with it. I shriek and duck out of
the way, but a bit of it still catches me on the cheek, dribbling down my neck.

'You are such a cheater!' I manage to gasp, out of breath
from running and laughing.

'You can't cheat if there are no rules,' Alex shoots back over
his shoulder.

'No rules, huh?' We're splashing shin deep now and I start
palming water at him, making a splatter pattern over his
back and shoulders. He turns around, sweeping his arm
across the surface of the water, a glittering arc. I twist to
avoid it and end up slipping and falling elbow deep, soaking
my shorts and the bottom half of my T-shirt, the sudden
cold making me gasp. He's still slogging forward, his head
craned back, his smile dazzling, his laugh rolling off and
away so loud I imagine it dipping past Great Diamond Island
and over the horizon, reaching all the way to other parts of
the world. I scramble up and haul after him. The buoys are
bobbing twenty feet ahead of us and the water is at my knees,
and then my thighs, and then all the way to my waist, until
both of us are half running and half swimming, frantically
paddling forward with our arms. I can't breathe or think or
do anything but laugh and splash and focus on the bright
red bobbing buoys, focus on winning, winning, I have to
win, and when we're only a few feet away and he's still in
the lead and my shoes are leaden and filled with water, my

clothes dragging me down like my pockets have been weighted with stones, without thinking I leap forward and tackle him, wrestling down into the water, feeling my foot connect with his thigh as I rocket off of him and reach out to slap the nearest buoy, the plastic shooting away from my hand when I hit it. We must be a quarter mile off the beach, but the tide's still going out so I can stand, the water hitting me at my chest. I raise my arms triumphantly as Alex comes up spluttering water, shaking his head so water pinwheels from his hair.

'I won,' I pant out.

'You cheated,' he says, pushing forward a few more steps and collapsing with both arms behind him, looped over the rope stringing along the buoys. He arches his back so his face is tilted up toward the sky. His T-shirt is completely soaked, and water beads off his eyelashes, trickles down his cheeks.

'No rules,' I say, 'so no cheating.'

He turns to me, grinning. 'I let you win, then.'

'Yeah, right.' I splash him a little and he holds up his hands, surrendering. 'You're just a sore loser.'

'I don't have much practice at it.' There's that confidence again, that semi-infuriating easiness of his, the tilt of his head and the smile. But today it's not infuriating. Today I like it, feel like it's somehow rubbing off on me, like if I was around him enough I would never feel awkward or frightened or insecure.

'Whatever.' I roll my eyes and hook one arm over the buoys next to him, enjoying the feel of the currents swishing around my chest, enjoying the strangeness of being in the bay with my clothes on, the stickiness of my T-shirt and the sucking of my shoes on my feet. Soon the tide will turn and the water will come in again. Then it will be a slow, exhausting swim back to the beach.

But I don't care. I don't care about *anything* – I'm not worried about how in a million years I'll explain to Carol why I've come home soaking wet, with seaweed clinging to my back and the smell of salt in my hair, not worried about how long I have until curfew or why Alex is even being nice to me. I'm just *happy*, a pure, bubbly feeling. Beyond the buoys the bay is dark purple, the waves brushed over with whitecaps. It is illegal to go beyond the buoys – beyond the buoys are the islands and the lookout points, and beyond them is open ocean, ocean that leads to unregulated places, places of disease and fear – but for that moment I fantasize about ducking underneath the rope and swimming out.

To our left we can see the bright white silhouette of the lab complex and beyond it, distantly, Old Port, all the docks like gigantic wooden centipedes. To our right is Tukey's Bridge, and the long string of guard huts that runs its length and continues up along the border. Alex catches me looking.

'Pretty, isn't it?' he says.

The bridge is mottled grey-green, all coated in backsplash and algae, and it looks like it's keening slightly into the wind. I wrinkle my nose. 'It looks kind of like it's rotting, doesn't it? My sister always said that someday it would fall into the ocean, just topple right over.'

Alex laughs. 'I wasn't talking about the bridge.' He tilts his chin just slightly, gesturing. 'I meant past the bridge.' He pauses for just a fraction of a second. 'I meant the Wilds.'

Beyond Tukey's Bridge is the northern border, located along the far side of Back Cove. As we're standing there the lights in the guard huts click on, one after another, shining out against the deepening blue sky – a sign that it's getting late and I should be going home soon. Still, I can't force myself to leave, even as I feel the water around my chest start to bubble and eddy, the tide turning. Beyond the bridge the lush greens of the Wilds move together in the wind like an endlessly rearranging wall, a thick wedge of green cutting down toward the bay and separating Portland from Yarmouth. From here we can just make out the barest section of it, an empty place marked with no lights, no boats, no buildings: impenetrable and strange and black. But I know that the Wilds extend back, go on for miles and miles and miles all through the mainland, all across the country, like a monster reaching its tentacles around the civilized parts of the world.

Maybe it was the race, or beating him to the buoys, or the fact that he didn't criticize me or my family when I told him about my mother, but in that moment the giddiness and happiness is still flowing strong and I feel like I could tell Alex anything, ask him anything. So I say, 'Can I tell you a secret?' I don't wait for him to answer; I don't have to, and knowing that makes me feel dizzy and careless. 'I used to think about it a lot. The Wilds, I mean, and what they were like . . . and the Invalids, whether they really existed.' Out of the corner of my eye I think I see him flinch slightly, so I press on, 'I used to sometimes think . . . I used to pretend that maybe my mom didn't die, you know? That maybe she'd only run away to the Wilds. Not that that would be any better. I guess I just didn't want her to be gone for good. It was better to imagine her out there somewhere, singing . . .' I break off, shaking my head, amazed that I feel so comfortable talking to Alex. Amazed, and grateful. 'What about you?' I say.

'What about me?' Alex is watching me with an expression I can't read. Like I've hurt him, almost, but that doesn't make any sense.

'Did you used to think about going to the Wilds when you were little? Just for fun, I mean, like a game.'

Alex squints, looks away from me, and grimaces. 'Yeah, sure. A lot.' He reaches out and slaps the buoys. 'None of these. No walls to run into. No eyes. Freedom and space, places to stretch out. I still think about the Wilds.'

I stare at him. Nobody uses words like that anymore: *freedom*, *space*. Old words. 'Still? Even after this?'

Without meaning to or thinking about it I reach out and brush my fingers, once, against the three-pronged scar on his neck.

He jerks away from my touch as though I've scalded him, and I drop my hand, embarrassed.

'Lena . . . ,' he says, in the strangest voice: like my name is a sour thing, a word that tastes bad in his mouth.

I know I shouldn't have touched him like that. I've overstepped my boundaries, and he's going to remind me of it, of what it means to be uncured. I think I will die of humiliation if he starts to lecture me, so to cover my discomfort I start babbling. 'Most cureds don't think about that kind of stuff. Carol – that's my aunt – she always said it was a waste of time. She always said there was nothing out there but animals and land and bugs, that all the talk of Invalids was make-believe stuff, kid stuff. She said believing in Invalids is the same thing as believing in werewolves or vampires. Remember how people used to say there were vampires in the Wilds?'

Alex smiles, but it's more like a wince. 'Lena, I have to tell you something.' His voice is a little stronger now, but something about his tone makes me afraid to let him speak.

Now I can't *stop* talking. 'Did it hurt? The procedure, I mean. My sister said it was no big deal, not with all the painkillers they give you, but my cousin Marcia used to say it was worse than anything, worse than having a baby, even though her second kid took, like, fifteen hours to deliver—' I break off, blushing, mentally cursing myself for the ridiculous conversational turn. I wish I could rewind back to last night's party, when my brain was coming up empty; it's like I've been saving up for a case of verbal vomit. 'I'm not scared, though,' I nearly scream, as Alex again opens his mouth to speak. I'm desperate to salvage the situation somehow. 'My procedure's coming up. Sixty days. It's dorky, huh? That I count. But I can't wait.'

'Lena.' Alex's voice is stronger, more forceful now, and it finally stops me. He turns so that we're face-to-face. At that moment my shoes skim off the sand bottom, and I realize that the water is lapping up to my neck. The tide is coming in fast. 'Listen to me. I'm not who – I'm not who you think I am.'

I have to fight to stand. All of a sudden the currents tug and pull at me. It's always seemed this way. The tide goes out a slow drain, comes back in a rush. 'What do you mean?'

His eyes – shifting gold, amber, an animal's eyes – search my face, and without knowing why, I'm scared again. 'I was never cured,' he says. For a moment I close my eyes and imagine I've misheard him, imagine I've only confused the shushing of the waves for his voice. But when I open my eyes he's still standing there, staring at me, looking guilty and something else – sad, maybe? – and I know I heard correctly. He says, 'I never had the procedure.'

'You mean it didn't work?' I say. My body is tingling, going numb, and I realize then how cold it is. 'You had the procedure and it didn't work? Like what happened to my mom?'

'No, Lena. I—' He looks away, squinting, says under his breath, 'I don't know how to explain.'

Everything from the tips of my fingers through the roots of my hair now feels as if it's encased in ice. Disconnected images run through my head, a skipping movie reel: Alex standing on the observation deck, his hair like a crown of leaves; turning his head, showing the neat three-pronged scar just beneath his left ear; reaching out to me and saying, *I'm safe. I won't hurt you.* The words start rattling out of me again but I don't feel them, hardly feel anything. 'It didn't work and you've been lying about it. Lying so you could still go to school, still get a job, still get paired and matched and everything. But really you're not – you're still – you might still be—' I can't bring myself to say the word. Diseased. Uncured. Sick. I feel like *I'll* be sick.

'No.' Alex's voice is so loud it startles me. I take a step back, sneakers slipping on the slick and uneven bottom of the ocean floor, and nearly go under, but when Alex makes a move to touch me I jerk backward, out of his reach. Something hardens in his face, like he's made a decision. 'I'm telling you I was never cured. Never paired or matched or anything. I was never even evaluated.'

'Impossible.' The word barely squeezes itself out, a whisper. The sky is whirling above me, all blues and pinks and reds swirling together until it looks like parts of the sky are bleeding. 'Impossible. You have the scars.'

'Scars,' he corrects me, a little more gently. 'Just scars. Not *the* scars.' He looks away then, giving me a view of his neck.

'Three tiny scars, an inverted triangle. Easy to replicate. With a scalpel, a penknife, anything.'

I close my eyes again. The waves swell around me and the motion, the lift and the drop, convinces me I really will throw up, right here in the water. I choke down the feeling, trying to hold back the realization that is battering at the back of my mind, threatening to overwhelm me – fighting back the feeling of drowning. I open my eyes and croak out, 'How . . . ?'

'You have to understand. Lena, I'm *trusting* you. Do you see that?' He's staring at me so intently I can feel his eyes like a touch, and I keep my eyes averted. 'I didn't mean to – I didn't want to lie to you.'

'How?' I repeat, louder now. Somehow my brain gets stuck on the word *lie* and makes an endless loop: *No way to avoid evaluations unless you lie. No way to avoid procedure unless you lie. You must lie.*

For a moment Alex is silent, and I think he's going to chicken out, refuse to tell me anything more. I almost *wish* he would. I'm desperate to rewind time, go back to the moment before he said my name in that strange tone of voice, go back to the triumphant, surging feeling of beating him to the buoys. We'll race back to the beach. We'll meet up tomorrow, try to wheedle some fresh crabs from the fishermen at the dock.

But then he speaks. 'I'm not from here,' he says. 'I mean, I wasn't born in Portland. Not exactly.' He's speaking in the tone of voice that everyone uses when they're about to break you apart. Gentle – kind, even – like they can make the news sound better just by speaking in a lullaby voice. *I'm sorry, Lena, but your mother was a troubled woman.* Like you won't somehow hear the violence underneath.

'Where are you from?' I don't have to ask. I know already. The realization has broken, spilled, overrun me. But a little part of me believes that as long as he doesn't say it, it's not true.

His eyes are steady on mine, but he tilts his head back — back toward the border, beyond the bridge, to that endlessly moving arrangement of branches and leaves and vines and tangled, growing things. 'There,' he says, or maybe I just think he says it. His lips barely move. But the meaning is clear.

He comes from the Wilds.

'An Invalid,' I say. The word feels like it's grating against my throat. 'You're an Invalid.' I'm giving him a final chance to deny it.

But he doesn't. He just winces slightly and says, 'I've always hated that word.'

Standing there, I realize something else: that it wasn't a coincidence whenever Carol made fun of me for still believing in the Invalids, whenever she would shake her head without bothering to look up from her knitting needles — tic, tic, tic, they went together, flashing metal — and say, 'I suppose you believe in vampires and werewolves, too?'

Vampires and werewolves and Invalids: things that will rip into you, tear you to shreds. Deadly things.

I'm suddenly so frightened a desperate pressure starts pushing down in the bottom of my stomach and between my legs, and for one wild and ridiculous second I'm positive that I'm about to pee. The lighthouse on Little Diamond Island clicks on, cuts a wide swath across the water, an enormous, accusatory finger: I'm terrified I'll get caught up in its beam, terrified it will point in my direction and then

I'll hear the whirling of the state helicopters and the mega-phone voices of the regulators shouting, 'Illegal activity! Illegal activity!' The beach looks hopelessly and impossibly remote. I can't imagine how we got out so far. My arms feel heavy and useless, and I think of my mother, and her jacket filling slowly with water.

I take deep breaths, trying to keep my mind from spinning, trying to focus. There's no way for anyone to know that Alex is an Invalid. I didn't know. He looks normal, has the scar in the right place. There's no way anyone could have heard us talking.

A wave lifts and breaks against my back. I stumble forward. Alex reaches out and grabs my arm to steady me, but I twist away from him just as a second round of waves surges over us. I get a mouthful of seawater, feel the salt stinging my eyes and am momentarily blinded.

'Don't,' I stutter. 'Don't you dare touch me.'

'Lena, I swear. I didn't mean to hurt you. I didn't want to lie to you.'

'Why are you doing this?' I can't think straight, can hardly even breathe. 'What do you want from me?'

'Want . . . ?' Alex shakes his head. He looks genuinely confused – and hurt, too, as though *I'm* the one who did something wrong. For a second I feel a flash of sympathy for him. Maybe he sees it on my face, that fraction of a second when I let my guard down, because in that moment his expression softens and his eyes go bright as flame and even though I barely see him move, suddenly he has closed the space between us and he's wrapping his warm hands over my shoulders – fingers so warm and strong I almost cry out – and saying, 'Lena. I like you, okay? That's it. That's all. I

like you.' His voice is so low and hypnotic it reminds me
of a song. I think of predators dropping silently from trees:
I think of enormous cats with glowing amber eyes, just
like his.

And then I'm stumbling backward, paddling away from
him, my shirt and shoes heavy with water, my heart
hammering painfully against my chest and my breath rasping
in my throat. I'm kicking off the ground and sweeping forward
with my arms, half running, half swimming, as the tide lifts
and drags at me so I feel like I can only creep forward an
inch at a time, so I feel like I'm moving through molasses.
Alex calls my name, but I'm too afraid to turn my head and
see if he's coming after me. It's like one of those nightmares
where something's chasing you but you're too afraid to look
and see what it is. All you hear is its breath, getting closer
and closer. You feel its shadow looming up behind you but
you're paralysed: You know that any second you'll feel its icy
fingers closing on your neck.

I'll never make it, I think. *I'll never make it back*. Something
scrapes across my shin and I begin to imagine that the bay
around me is full of horrible underwater things, sharks and
jellyfish and poisonous eels, and even though I know I'm
panicking I feel like falling backward and giving up. The
beach is still so far, and my arms and legs feel so heavy.

Alex's voice gets whipped away by the wind, sounding
fainter and fainter, and when I finally work up the courage
to look over my shoulder I see him bobbing up and down
by the buoys. I realize I've gone farther than I thought, and
at the very least Alex isn't following me. My fear eases up,
and the knot in my chest loosens. The next wave is so
strong it helps skim me over a steep underwater ridge, drops

me to my knees into soft sand. When I struggle to my feet the water hits me just at the waist, and I slosh the rest of the way to shore, shivering, grateful, exhausted.

My thighs are shaking. I collapse onto the beach, gasping and coughing. From the flames of colour licking across the sky over Back Cove – orange, reds, pinks – I'm guessing it's close to sunset, probably around eight o'clock. Part of me wants to just lie down, spread my arms and stretch out and sleep all through the night. I feel like I've swallowed half my weight in salt water. My skin stings and there's sand everywhere, in my bra and underwear and between my toes and under my fingernails. Whatever scraped my shin in the water left its mark: a long trickle of blood snakes around my calf.

I look up, and for one panicked second I can't find Alex by the buoys. My heart stops. Then I see him, a dark spot cutting quickly through the water. His arms pinwheel gracefully as he swims. He's fast. I haul myself to my feet, grab my shoes, and limp up to my bike. My legs are so weak it takes me a minute to find my balance, and at first I weave crazily up and down the road like a toddler just learning to ride.

I don't look back, not once, until I'm at my gate. By then the streets are empty and quiet, night about to fall, curfew about to come down like a giant warm embrace, keeping us all in our places, keeping us all safe.

eleven

Think of it this way: when it's cold outside and your teeth are chattering, you bundle up in a winter coat, and scarves, and mittens, to keep from catching the flu. Well, the borders are like hats and scarves and winter coats for the whole country! They keep the very worst disease away, so we can all stay healthy!

After the borders went up, the president and the Consortium had one last thing to take care of before we could all be safe and happy. The Great Sanitation* (sometimes called 'the blitz') lasted less than a month, but afterward all the wild spaces were cleared of the disease. We went in there with some old-fashioned elbow grease and scrubbed the problem spots away, just like when your mom wipes the kitchen counters down with a sponge, easy as one, two, three . . .

*Sanitation
1. The application of sanitary measures for the sake of cleanliness or protecting health
2. The disposal of sewage and waste

– Excerpt from *Dr. Richard's History Primer for Children*, Chapter One

Here is a secret about my family: my sister contracted the *deliria* several months before her scheduled procedure. She fell in love with a boy named Thomas, who was also uncured. During the day, she and Thomas spent all their time lying in a field of wildflowers, shielding their eyes against the sun, whispering promises to each other that could never be kept. She cried all the time, and once she confessed to me that Thomas liked to kiss away her tears. Still, now, when I think of those days—I was only eight at the time—I think of the taste of salt.

The disease slowly worked its way deeper and deeper inside of her, an animal chewing her from within. My sister couldn't eat. What little we could convince her to swallow came up just as quickly, and I was afraid for her life.

Thomas broke her heart, of course, to nobody's surprise. *The Book of Shhh* says: 'Amor deliria nervosa produces shifts in the prefrontal cortex of the brain, which result in fantasies and delusions that, once revealed, lead in turn to psychic devastation' (See 'Effects,' p. 36). Then my sister did nothing but lie in bed and watch the shadows shift slowly across the walls, her ribs rising up under her pale skin like wood rising through water.

Even then she refused the procedure and the comfort it would give her, and on the day the cure was to be administered it took four scientists and several needles full of tranquilizer before she would submit, before she would stop scratching with her long, sharp nails, which had gone uncut for weeks, and screaming and cursing and calling for Thomas. I watched them come for her, to bring her to the labs; I sat in a corner, terrified, while she spit and hissed and kicked, and I thought of my mom and dad.

That afternoon, though I was still more then a decade away from safety, I began to count the months until my procedure.

In the end my sister *was* cured. She came back to me gentle and content, her nails spotless and round, her hair pulled back in a long, thick braid. Several months later she was pledged to an IT tech, roughly her age, and several weeks after she graduated from college they married, their hands linked loosely under the canopy, both of them staring straight ahead as though at a future of days unmarred by worry or discontent or disagreement, a future of identical days, like a series of neatly blown bubbles.

Thomas was cured too. He was married to Ella, once my sister's best friend, and now everybody is happy. Rachel told me a few months ago that the two couples often see each other at picnics and neighborhood events, since they live fairly close to each other in the East End. The four of them sit, making polite and quiet conversation, with not a sole flicker of the past to disturb the stillness and completeness of the present.

That's the beauty of the cure. No one mentions those lost, hot days in the field, when Thomas kissed Rachel's tears away and invented worlds just so he could promise them to her, when she tore the skin off her own arms at the thought of living without him. I'm sure she's embarrassed by those days, if she remembers them at all. True, I don't see her that often now – just once every couple of months, when she remembers she is supposed to stop by – and in that way I guess you could say that even *with* the procedure I lost a little bit of her. But that's not the point. The point is that she's protected. The point is that she's safe.

I'll tell you another secret, this one for your own good. You may think the past has something to tell you. You may think that you should listen, should strain to make out its whispers, should bend over backward, stoop down low to hear its voice breathed up from the ground, from the dead places. You may think there's something in it for you, something to understand or make sense of.

But I know the truth: I know from the nights of Coldness. I know the past will drag you backward and down, have you snatching at whispers of wind and the gibberish of trees rubbing together, trying to decipher some code, trying to piece together what was broken. It's hopeless. The past is nothing but a weight. It will build inside of you like a stone.

Take it from me: if you hear the past speaking to you, feel it tugging at your back and running its fingers up your spine, the best thing to do – the only thing – is run.

In the days that follow Alex's confession, I check constantly for symptoms of the disease. When I'm manning the register at my uncle's store I lean forward on my elbow, keep my hand resting on my cheek so I can crook my fingers back toward my neck and count my pulse, make sure it's normal. In the mornings I take long, slow breaths, listening for rasping or hitches in my lungs. I wash my hands constantly. I know the *deliria* isn't like a cold—you can't get it from being sneezed on—but still, it's contagious, and when I woke up the day after our meeting at East End with my limbs still heavy and my head as light as a bubble and an ache in my throat that refused to go away, my first thought was that I'd been infected.

After a few days I feel better. The only weird thing is the way my senses seem to have dulled. Everything looks washed out, like a bad colour copy. I have to load my food with salt before I can taste it, and every time my aunt speaks to me it seems like her voice has been muted a few degrees. But I read through *The Book of Shhh*, and all the recognized symptoms of *deliria*, and don't see anything that matches up, so in the end I figure I'm safe.

Still, I take precautions, determined not to make one false

step, determined to prove to myself that I'm not like my mother – that the thing with Alex was a fluke, a mistake, a horrible, horrible accident. I can't ignore how close I was to danger. I don't even want to think about what would happen if anyone found out what Alex was, if anyone knew that we had stood together shivering in the water, that we had talked, laughed, *touched*. It makes me feel sick. I have to keep repeating to myself that my procedure is less than two months away now. All I have to do is keep my head down and make it through the next seven weeks and I'll be fine.

I come home every evening a full two hours before curfew. I volunteer to spend extra days at the store, and I don't even ask for my usual eight-dollar-an-hour wage. Hana doesn't call me. I don't call her, either. I help my aunt cook dinner, and I clear and wash the dishes unprompted. Gracie is in summer school – she's only in first grade and they're already talking about holding her back – and every night I pull her onto my lap and help her sludge through her work, whispering in her ear, begging her to speak, to focus, to listen, cajoling her, finally, into writing at least half of the answers down in her workbook. After a week my aunt stops looking at me suspiciously whenever I walk into the house, stops demanding to know where I've been, and another weight eases off me: she trusts me again. It wasn't easy to explain why on earth Sophia Hennerson and I would decide on an impromptu swim in the ocean – in our clothes, no less – just after a big family dinner, even harder to explain why I came home pale and shaking, and I could tell my aunt didn't buy it. But after a while she relaxes around me again, stops looking at me distrustfully, like I'm some caged-up animal she's worried will go feral.

Days pass, time ticks away, seconds click forward like

dominoes toppling in a line. Every day the heat gets worse and worse. It creeps through the streets of Portland, festers in the Dumpsters, makes the city smell like a giant armpit. The walls sweat and the trolleys cough and shudder, and every day people gather in front of the municipal buildings, praying for a brief blast of cold air whenever the mechanized doors swoosh open because a regulator or politician or guard has to go in and out.

I have to give up my runs. The last time I do a full loop outside I find that my feet carry me down to Monument Square, past the Governor.' The sun is a high white haze, all the buildings cut sharply against the sky like a series of metal teeth. By the time I make it to the statue I'm panting, exhausted, and my head is spinning. When I grab the Governor's arm and swing myself up onto the statue's base, the metal burns underneath my hand and the world seesaws crazily, light zigzagging everywhere. I'm dimly aware that I should go inside, out of the heat, but my brain is all foggy and so there I go, poking my fingers around the hole in the Governor's cupped fist. I don't know what I'm looking for. Alex already told me that the note he'd left for me months ago must have turned to pulp by now. My fingers come out sticky, pieces of melting gum stringing between my thumb and forefinger, but still I root around. And then I feel it slide between my fingers, cool and crisp, folded in a square: a note.

I'm half-delirious as I open it, but still I don't really expect it to be from him. My hands begin to shake as I read:

Lena,
I'm so sorry. Please forgive me.
Alex

I don't remember the run home, and my aunt finds me later half passed out in the hallway, murmuring to myself. She has to put me in a bathtub full of ice to get my temperature down. When I finally come to I can't find the note anywhere. I realize I must have dropped it, and feel half-relieved and half-disappointed. That evening we read that the Time and Temperature Building registered 102 degrees: the hottest day on record for the summer so far.

My aunt forbids me to run outside for the rest of the summer. I don't put up a fight. I don't trust myself, can't be sure my feet won't lead me back down to the Governor, to East End Beach, to the labs.

I receive a new date for the evaluations and spend my evenings in front of the mirror rehearsing my answers. My aunt insists on accompanying me to the labs again, but this time I don't see Hana. I don't see anyone I recognize. Even the four evaluators are different: floating oval faces, different shades of brown and pink, two-dimensional, like shaded drawings. I am not afraid this time. I don't feel anything.

I answer all the questions exactly as I should. When I am asked to give my favourite colour, for just the briefest, tiniest of seconds my mind flashes on a sky the colour of polished silver, and I think I hear a word – *grey* – whispered quietly into my ear.

I say, 'Blue,' and everyone smiles.

I say, 'I'd like to study psychology and social regulation.' I say, 'I like to listen to music, but not too loudly.' I say, 'The definition of happiness is security.' Smiles, smiles, smiles all around, a room full of teeth.

After I'm done, as I am leaving, I think I see a shifting

shadow, a flicker in my peripheral vision. I glance up quickly at the observation deck. Of course, it's empty.

Two days later we receive the results of my boards – all passes – and my final score: eight. My aunt hugs me, the first time she has hugged me in years. My uncle pats me on the shoulder awkwardly and gives me the largest piece of chicken at dinner. Even Jenny looks impressed. Gracie rams the top of her head into my leg, one, two, three times, and I step away from her, tell her to stop fussing. I know she's upset that I'll be leaving her.

But that's life, and the sooner she gets used to it, the better.

I receive my 'Approved Matches' too, a list of four names and statistics – age, scores, interests, recommended career path, salary projections – printed neatly on a white sheet of paper with the Portland city crest at its top. At least Andrew Marcus isn't on it. I recognize only one name: Chris McDonnell. He has bright red hair and teeth that stick out like a rabbit's. I only know him because once when I was playing outside last year with Gracie, he started chanting, 'There goes the retard and the orphan,' and without really thinking about what I was doing, I scooped up a rock from the ground and turned around and hurled it in his direction. It caught him on the temple. For a second his eyes crossed and uncrossed. He lifted his fingers to his head, and when he pulled them away they were dark with blood. For days afterward I was terrified to go out, terrified I'd be arrested and thrown in the Crypts. Mr. McDonnell owned a tech services firm, and was a volunteer regulator besides. I was convinced he would come after me for what I'd done to his son.

Chris McDonnell. Phinneas Jonston. Edward Wung. Brian

Scharff. I stare at the names for so long that the letters re-arrange themselves into nonsense words, into baby babble. *Gone Crap, Just Fine, Won't Spill, Pick Chris, Sharp Things.*

In mid-July, when my procedure is only seven weeks away, it's time to make my decision. I rank my choices arbitrarily, inserting numbers next to names: Phinneas Jonston (1), Chris McDonnell (2), Brian Scharff (3), Edward Wung (4). The boys will be submitting their rankings too; the evaluators will do their best to match preferences.

Two days later I receive the official notification: I'll be spending the rest of my life with Brian Scharff, whose hobbies are 'watching the news' and 'fantasy baseball,' and who plans to work 'in the electricians' guild,' and who can 'someday expect to make $45,000,' a salary that 'should support two to three kids.' I'll be pledged to him before I begin Regional College of Portland in the fall. When I graduate we'll be married.

At night I sleep dreamlessly. In the mornings I wake to fog.

twelve

In the decades before the development of the cure, the disease had become so virulent and widespread it was extraordinarily rare for a person to reach adulthood without having contracted a significant case of amor deliria nervosa *(please see 'Statistics, Pre–Border Era') . . . Many historians have argued that pre-cure society was itself a reflection of the disease, characterized by fracture, chaos, and instability . . . Almost half of all marriages ended in dissolution . . . Incidence of drug use skyrocketed, as did alcohol-related deaths.*

People were so desperate for relief and protection from the disease they began widespread experimentation with makeshift folk remedies that were in themselves deadly, consuming concoctions of drugs assembled from common cold medications and synthesized into an extremely addictive and often fatal compound (please see 'Folk Cures Through the Ages') . . .

The discovery of the procedure to cure deliria *is typically credited to Cormac T. Holmes, a neuroscientist who was a member of the initial Consortium of New Scientists and one of the first disciples of the New Religion, which teaches the Holy Trinity of God, Science, and Order. Holmes was canonized several years after his death, and his body was preserved and displayed in the All-Saints' Monument in Washington, DC (see photographs on pp. 210–212).*

– From "Before the Border," *A Brief History of the United States of America,* by E. D. Thompson, p. 121

O ne hot evening toward the end of July I'm walking home from the Stop-N-Save when I hear someone call my name. I turn around and see Hana jogging up the hill toward me.

'So what?' she says as she gets closer, panting a little. 'You're just going to walk by me now?'

The obvious hurt in her voice surprises me. 'I didn't see you,' I say, which is the truth. I'm tired. Today we did inventory at the store, unshelving and reshelving packages of diapers, canned goods, rolls of paper towels, counting and recounting everything. My arms are aching, and whenever I close my eyes I see bar codes. I'm so tired I'm not even embarrassed to be out in public wearing my paint-spotted Stop-N-Save T-shirt, which is about ten sizes too big for me.

Hana looks away, biting her lip. I haven't spoken to her since that night at the party and I'm searching desperately for something to say, something casual and normal. It suddenly seems incredible to me that this was my best friend, that we could hang out for days and never run out of things to talk about, that I would come home from her house with my throat sore from laughing. It's like there's a glass wall between us now, invisible but impenetrable.

I finally come up with, 'I got my matches,' at the same time that Hana blurts out, 'Why didn't you call me back?'

Both of us pause, startled, and then again start up at the same time. I say, 'You called?' and Hana says, 'Did you accept yet?'

'You first,' I say.

Hana actually seems uncomfortable. She looks at the sky, at a small child standing across the street in a baggy swimsuit, at the two men loading buckets of something into a truck down the street – everywhere but at me. 'I left you, like, three messages.'

'I never got any messages,' I say quickly, my heart speeding up. For weeks I've been pissed that Hana didn't try to reach out to me after the party – pissed, and hurt. But I told myself it was better this way. I told myself Hana had changed, and she probably wouldn't have much to say to me anymore.

Hana is looking at me like she's trying to judge whether I'm telling the truth. 'Carol didn't tell you that I called?'

'No, I swear.' I'm so relieved I laugh. In that second, it hits me just how much I've missed Hana. Even when she's mad at me, she's the only person who's ever really looked out for me by choice, not because of family obligation and duty and responsibility and all the other stuff that *The Book of Shhh* says is so important. Everyone else in my life – Carol and all my cousins, the other girls at St. Anne's, even Rachel – have only spent time with me because they had to. 'I had no idea.'

Hana doesn't laugh, though. She frowns. 'No worries. It's no big deal.'

'Listen, Hana—'

She cuts me off. 'Like I said, it's no big deal.' She crosses her arms and shrugs. I don't know whether she believes me or not but it's clear that, after all, things *are* different. This isn't going to be some big, happy reunion. 'So you got matched?'

Her voice is polite now, and slightly formal, so I take on the same tone. 'Brian Scharff. I accepted. You?'

She nods. A muscle flexes at the corner of her mouth, almost imperceptible. 'Fred Hargrove.'

'Hargrove? Like the mayor?'

'His son.' Hana nods, looks away again.

'Wow. Congratulations.' I can't help sounding impressed. Hana must have killed at the evaluations. Not that that's any surprise, really.

'Yeah. Lucky me.' Hana's voice is completely toneless. I can't tell if she's being sarcastic. But she is lucky, whether she knows it or not.

And there it is: even though we're standing in the same patch of sun-drenched pavement, we might as well be a hundred thousand miles apart.

You came from different starts and you'll come to different ends: that's an old saying, something Carol used to repeat a lot. I never really understood how true it was until now.

This must be why Carol didn't tell me Hana called. Three phone calls is a lot of phone calls to forget, and Carol's pretty careful about stuff like that. Maybe she was trying to hurry up the inevitable, skip us both to the ending, the part where Hana and I aren't friends anymore. She knows that after the procedure – once the past and all our shared history has loosened its grip on us, once we don't feel our memories so much – we won't have anything in common. Carol was probably trying to protect me, in her own way.

There's no point in confronting her about it. She won't try and deny it. She'll just give me one of her blank looks and rattle off a proverb from *The Book of Shhh. Feelings aren't forever. Time waits for no man, but progress waits for man to enact it.*

'You walking home?' Hana is still looking at me like I'm a stranger.

'Yeah,' I say. I gesture to my T-shirt. 'I figured I should probably get inside before I blind someone with this.'

A smile flits over Hana's face. 'I'll walk with you,' she says, which surprises me.

For a while we walk in silence. We're not that far from my house, and I'm worried we'll go the whole way back without speaking at all. I've never seen Hana so quiet, and it's making me nervous.

'Where are you coming from?' I say, just to say something.

Hana starts next to me, as though I've woken her from a dream. 'East End,' she says. 'I'm on a strict tanning schedule.'

She presses her arm next to mine. It's at least seven shades darker than mine, which is still pale, maybe a little more freckled than it is in the winter. 'Not you, huh?' This time she smiles for real.

'Um, no. Haven't gotten down to the beach very much.' I will away a blush.

Thankfully, Hana doesn't notice, or if she does she doesn't say anything. 'I know. I was looking for you.'

'You were?' I shoot her a look from the corner of my eye.

She rolls her eyes. I'm glad to see her attitude is coming back online. 'I mean, not actively. But I've been down there a few times, yeah. Haven't seen you.'

'I've been working a lot,' I say. I don't add, *to avoid East End, actually.*

'You still running?'

'No. Too hot.'

'Yeah, me too. Figured I'd give it a rest until fall.' We walk a few more paces in silence and then Hana squints at me, tilting her head. 'So what else?'

Her question catches me off guard. 'What do you mean, *what else?*'

'That *is* what I mean. I mean, what else? Come on, Lena. It's the last summer, remember? The last summer of no responsibilities and all that good stuff. So what have you been doing? Where have you been?'

'I – nothing. I haven't done anything.' This was the whole point – to stay out of trouble, to do as little as possible – but saying the words makes me feel kind of sad. The summer seems to be narrowing rapidly, shrinking down to a fine point before I've even had a chance to enjoy it. It's already almost August. We'll have another five weeks of this weather before the wind starts cutting in at night and the leaves get trimmed with edges of gold. 'What about you?' I say. 'Good summer so far?'

'The usual.' Hana shrugs. 'I've been going to the beach a lot, like I said. Been babysitting for the Farrels some.'

'Really?' I wrinkle my nose. Hana's always had a thing against children. She's always saying they're too sticky and clingy, like Jolly Ranchers that have been left too long in a hot pocket.

She makes a face. 'Yeah, unfortunately. My parents decided I needed to "practice managing a household," or some crap like that. You know they're actually making me work out a budget? Like figuring out how to spend sixty dollars a week is going to teach me about paying bills, or responsibility or something.'

'Why? It's not like you'll even *have* a budget.' I don't mean to sound bitter but there it is, the difference in our futures cutting between us again.

We go silent after that. Hana looks away, squinting slightly against the sunlight. Maybe I'm just feeling depressed about how quickly the summer is cycling by, but memories start coming thick and fast, like a deck of cards being reshuffled in my head: Hana swinging open the bathroom door that first day in second grade, folding her arms as she blurted out, *Is it because of your mom?*; staying up past midnight one of the few times we were ever allowed to have a sleepover, giggling and imagining amazing and impossible people for our matches some day, like the president of the United States or the stars of our favourite movies; running side by side, legs beating in tandem on the pavement, like the rhythm of a single heartbeat; bodysurfing at the beach and buying triple cones of ice cream on the way home, arguing about whether vanilla or chocolate was better.

Best friends for more than ten years and in the end it all comes down to the edge of a scalpel, to the motion of a laser beam through the brain and a flashing surgical knife. All that history and its importance gets detached, floats away like a severed balloon. In two years – in two *months* – Hana and I will pass each other on the streets with nothing more than a nod – different people, different worlds, two stars revolving silently, separated by thousands of miles of dark space.

Segregation has it all wrong. We should be protected from the people who will leave us in the end, from all the people who will disappear or forget us.

Maybe Hana's feeling nostalgic too, because she suddenly comes out with, 'Remember all our plans for this summer? All the things we said we'd finally do?'

I don't even skip a beat. 'Break into the Spencer Prep pool—'

'—and go swimming in our underwear,' Hana finishes.

I crack a smile. 'Hop the fence at Cherryhill Farms—'

'—and eat the maple syrup straight out of the barrels.'

'Run all the way from the Hill to the old airport.'

'Ride our bikes down Suicide Point.'

'Try and find that rope swing Sarah Miller told us about. The one above Fore River.'

'Sneak into the movie theater and see four movies back to back.'

'Finish off the Hobgoblin Sundae at Mae's.' I'm fully smiling now and Hana is too. I start quoting, '"A gargantuan sundae for enormous appetites only, featuring thirteen scoops, whipped cream, hot fudge—"'

Hana jumps in, '"And all the toppings your little monsters can handle!"'

Both of us laugh. We've probably read that sign a thousand times. We've been debating making a second attack on the Hobgoblin since fourth grade: that's when we tried the first time. Hana insisted on going there for her birthday and took me along. Both of us spent the rest of the night rolling around on the floor of her bathroom, and we'd only made it through *seven* of the thirteen scoops.

We've reached my street. A few kids are playing in the middle of the road. It's a makeshift game of soccer: they're kicking a can around and shouting, bodies brown and shiny with sweat. I see Jenny among them. As I'm watching, a girl tries to elbow her out of the way, and Jenny turns around and pushes her to the ground. The younger girl starts to wail. No one comes out of any of the houses, even as the girl's voice crescendos to a high-pitched scream, like a siren going off. A curtain or a dish towel flutters in a window: other than that, the street is silent, motionless.

I'm desperate to keep riding the wave of good feeling, to fix things between Hana and me, even if it's only for a month. 'Listen, Hana' – I feel like I'm working the words past an enormous lump in my throat; I'm almost as nervous as I was before the evaluations – 'they're playing *The Defective Detective* in the park tonight. Double feature, Michael Wynn. We could go if you want.' *The Defective Detective* is this film franchise Hana and I used to love when we were little, about a famous detective who's actually incompetent, and his dog sidekick: the dog always ends up solving the crimes. A lot of actors have played the lead role, but our favourite was Michael Wynn. When we were kids, we used to pray to get matched with him.

'Tonight?' Hana's smile falters, and my stomach sinks. *Stupid, stupid*, I think. *It doesn't matter anyway.*

'It's okay if you can't. No worries. Just an idea,' I say quickly, looking away so she won't see how disappointed I am.

'No – I mean, I *want* to, but—' Hana sucks in a breath. I hate this, hate how awkward we both are. 'I kind of have this party' – she corrects herself quickly – 'this *thing* I'm supposed to go to with Angelica Marston.'

My stomach gets that hollowed-out feeling. It's amazing how words can do that, just shred your insides apart. Sticks and stones may break my bones, but words can never hurt me – *such* bullshit. 'Since when do you hang out with Angelica Marston?'

Again, I'm not trying to sound bitter, but I realize I sound like someone's whiny little sister, complaining about being left out of a game. I bite my lip and turn away, furious with myself.

'She's actually not that bad,' Hana says mildly. I can hear it in her voice; she feels sorry for me. This is worse than anything. I almost wish we were screaming at each other again, like we did the day at her house – even that would be better than her careful tone of voice, the way we're dancing around each other's feelings. 'She's not really stuck-up. Just shy, I guess.'

Angelica Marston was a junior last year. Hana made fun of her for the way she wore her uniform. It was always perfectly pressed and spotless, the collar of her button-down turned down exactly, her skirt hitting exactly at the knee. Hana said Angelica Marston had a stick up her butt because her father was a big scientist at the labs. And she *did* kind of walk that way, all constipated and careful.

'You used to hate her,' I squeak out. My words don't seem to be asking my brain for permission before popping out of my mouth.

'I didn't *hate* her,' Hana says, like she's trying to explain algebra to a two-year-old. 'I didn't *know* her. I always thought she was a bitch, you know? Because of her clothes and stuff. But that's all her parents. They're super strict, really protective and stuff.' Hana shakes her head. 'She's not like that at all. She's . . . different.'

That word seems to vibrate in the air for a second: *different*. For a second I have an image of Hana and Angelica, arms linked, trying not to laugh, sneaking through the streets after curfew: Angelica fearless and beautiful and fun, just like Hana. I push the image out of my head. Down the street one of the kids kicks the can, hard. It skitters between two dented silver garbage cans that have been set out in the road, a makeshift goal. Half of the kids start jumping up and down, pumping their fists; the others, Jenny included, gesticulate and yell something about offsides. It occurs to me for the first time how ugly my street must look to Hana, all the houses squished together, half of them missing windowpanes, porches sagging in the middle like old beaten-down mattresses. It's so different from the clean, quiet streets in West End, from the silent, gleaming cars and the gates and the green hedges.

'You could come tonight,' Hana says quietly.

A rush of hatred overwhelms me. Hatred for my life, for its narrowness and cramped spaces; hatred for Angelica Marston, with her secretive smile and rich parents; hatred for Hana, for being so stupid and careless and stubborn, first and foremost, and for leaving me behind before I was ready to be left; and underneath all those layers something else, too, some white-hot blade of unhappiness flashing in the very deepest part of me. I can't name it, or even focus on it clearly, but somehow I understand that this – this other thing – makes me the angriest of all.

'Thanks for the invitation,' I say, not even bothering to keep the sarcasm out of my voice. 'Sounds like a blast. Will there be boys there too?'

Either Hana doesn't notice the tone of my voice – which is doubtful – or she chooses to ignore it. 'That's kind of the whole point,' she says, deadpan. 'Well, and the music.'

'Music?' I say. I can't help but sound interested. 'Like the last time?'

Hana's face lights up. 'Yeah. I mean, no. Different band. But these guys are supposed to be amazing – even better than last time.' She pauses, then repeats quietly, 'You could come with us.'

Despite everything, this gives me pause. In the days after the party at Roaring Brook Farms, snatches of music seemed to follow me everywhere: I heard it winging in and out of the wind, I heard it singing off the ocean and moaning through the walls of the house. Sometimes I woke up in the middle of the night, drenched in sweat, my heart pounding, with the notes sounding in my ears. But every time I was awake and trying to remember the melodies consciously, hum a few notes or recall any of the chords, I couldn't.

Hana's staring at me hopefully, waiting for my response. For a second I actually feel bad for her. I want to make her happy, like I always did, want to see her give a whoop and put her fist in the air and flash me one of her famous smiles. But then I remember she has Angelica Marston now, and something hardens in my throat, and knowing that I'm going to disappoint her gives me a kind of dull satisfaction.

'I think I'll pass,' I say. 'But thanks anyway.'

Hana shrugs, and I can tell she's fighting to look like it's no big deal. 'If you change your mind . . .' She tries to smile but can't keep it up for longer than a second. 'Tanglewild Lane. Deering Highlands. You know where to find me.'

Deering Highlands. Of course. The Highlands is an abandoned subdivision off-peninsula. A decade ago the government discovered sympathizers – and, if the rumours are true, even some Invalids – living together in one of the big mansions out there. It was a huge scandal, and the bust the result of a yearlong sting operation. When all was said and done, forty-two people had been executed and another hundred thrown in the Crypts. Since then Deering Highlands has been a ghost town: avoided, forgotten, condemned.

'Yeah, well. You know where to find me.' I gesture lamely down the street.

'Yeah.' Hana looks down at her feet, hops from one to the other. There's nothing else to say, but I can't stand to turn around and just walk away. I have a terrible feeling this is the last time I'll see Hana before we're cured. Fear seizes me all at once, and I wish I could backpedal through our conversation, take back all the sarcastic or mean things that I said, tell her I miss her and I want to be best friends again.

But just when I'm about to blurt this out, she gives me a quick wave and says, 'Okay, then. See you around,' and the moment collapses in on itself and with it, my chance to speak.

'Okay. See you.'

Hana starts off down the road. I'm tempted to watch her go. I get the urge to memorize her walk – to imprint her in my brain somehow, just as she is – but as I'm watching her waver in and out of the fierce sunlight, her silhouette gets confused with another one in my head, a shadow weaving in and out of darkness, about to walk off the cliff, and I don't know who I'm looking at anymore. Suddenly the edges of the world are blurring and there's a sharp pain in my throat, so I turn around and walk quickly toward the house.

'Lena!' she calls out to me, just before I reach the gate.

I spin around, heart leaping, thinking maybe she'll be the one to say it. *I miss you. Let's go back.*

Even from a distance of fifty feet, I can see Hana hesitating. Then she makes this fluttering gesture with her hand and calls out, 'Never mind.' This time when she turns around she doesn't waver. She walks straight and quickly, turns a corner, and is gone.

But what did I expect?

That's the whole point, after all: there's no going back.

thirteen

In the years before the cure was perfected, it was offered on a trial basis only. The risks attached to it were great. At the time one out of every hundred patients suffered a fatal loss of brain function after the procedure.

Nonetheless, people swarmed the hospitals in record number, demanding to be cured; they camped outside the laboratories for days at a time, hoping to secure a procedural slot.

These years are also known as the Miracle Years because of the quantity of lives that were healed and made whole, and the number of souls brought out of sickness.

And if there were people who died on the operating table, they died for a good cause, and no one can lament them . . .

– From 'The Miracle Years: The Early Science of the Cure,' *A Brief History of the United States of America*, by E. D. Thompson, p. 87

When I get into the house it's even hotter than usual: a wet, suffocating wall of heat. Carol must be cooking. The house smells like browned meat and spices – mixed with the normal summer smells of sweat and mildew, it's kind of nauseating. For the past few weeks we've been eating dinner out on the porch: runny macaroni salads, cold cuts, and sandwiches from my uncle's deli counter.

Carol pokes her head out of the kitchen as I go by. Her face is red and she's sweating big-time. Dark swaths of sweat have left pit stains on her pale blue blouse, navy crescents.

'Better get changed,' she says. 'Rachel and David will be here any second.'

I'd completely forgotten my sister and her husband were coming over for dinner. Normally I see Rachel four or five times a year, tops. When I was younger, especially after Rachel had first moved out of Carol's house, I used to count the days until she would come and see me. I don't think I fully understood then about the procedure and what it meant for her – for me – for us. I knew that she'd been saved from Thomas, and from the disease, but that was it. I think I thought that otherwise things would be exactly the same. I thought that as soon as she came to see me it would be like old times again, that we would bust out our socks to have a dance party, or she would pull me onto her lap and start braiding my hair, launch into one of her stories – of distant places and witches who could change into animals.

But she only skimmed a hand over my head as she came through the door, and applauded politely when Carol made me recite my multiplication and division tables.

'She's grown up now,' Carol told me, when I asked her why Rachel didn't like to play anymore. 'Someday you'll see.'

After that I stopped paying attention to the notation that appeared every few months on the kitchen wall calendar: *R to visit.*

At dinner the big topics of conversation are Brian Scharff – Rachel's husband, David, works with Brian's cousin's friend, so David feels like he's an expert on the family – and Regional College of Portland, where I'll be starting in the fall. It's the first time in my life I'll be in class with members of the opposite sex, but Rachel tells me not to worry.

'You won't even notice,' she says. 'You'll be so busy with work and studying.'

'There are safeguards,' says Aunt Carol. 'All the students are vetted.' Code for: all the students are cured.

I think of Alex and almost say, *Not all of them.*

Dinner drags on well past curfew. By the time my aunt helps me clear the plates it's almost eleven o'clock, and still Rachel and her husband make no sign to leave. That's another thing I'm excited about: in thirty-six days, I won't have to worry about curfew anymore.

After dinner my uncle and David go out onto the porch. David has brought two cigars – cheap ones, but still – and the smell of the smoke, sweet and spicy and just a little bit oily, floats in through the windows, intermingles with the sound of their voices, fills the house with blue haze. Rachel and Aunt Carol stay in the dining room, drinking cups of watered-down boiled coffee, the dirty pale colour of old dishwater. From upstairs I hear the sound of scampering feet. Jenny will tease Grace until she's bored, until she climbs into bed, sour and dissatisfied, letting the dullness and sameness of another day lull her to sleep.

I wash the dishes – many more of them than usual, since Carol insisted on having a soup (hot carrot, which we all choked down, sweating) and a pot roast slathered in garlic and limp asparagus, probably rescued from the very bottom of the vegetable bin, and some stale cookies. I'm full, and the warmth of the dishwater on my wrists and elbows – plus the familiar rhythms of conversation, the pitter-patter of feet upstairs, the heavy blue smoke – make me feel very sleepy.

Carol has finally remembered to ask about Rachel's children; Rachel goes over their accomplishments as though reciting a list she has only memorized recently, and with difficulty – Sara is reading already; Andrew said his first word at only thirteen months.

'Raid, raid. This is a raid. Please do as you are commanded and do not try and resist . . .'

The voice booming from outside makes me jump. Rachel and Carol have paused momentarily in their conversation, are listening to the commotion in the street. I can't hear David and Uncle William, either. Even Jenny and Grace have stopped fooling around upstairs.

Patchy interference from the street; the sounds of hundreds and hundreds of boots, clicking away in time; and that awful voice, amplified through a bullhorn: *'This is a raid. Attention, this is a raid. Please be ready with your identification papers . . .'*

A raid night. Instantly I think of Hana and the party. The room starts spinning. I reach out, grabbing on to the counter.

'Seems pretty early for a raid,' Carol says mildly from the dining room. 'We had one just a few months ago, I think.'

'February eighteenth,' Rachel says. 'I remember. David and I had to come out with the kids. There was some problem with SVS that night. We stood in the snow for half an hour before we could be verified. Afterward Andrew had pneumonia for two weeks.' She relates this story as though she's talking about some minor inconvenience at the laundromat, like she's misplaced a sock.

'Has it been that long?' Carol shrugs, takes a sip of her coffee.

The voices, the feet, the static – it's all coming closer. The raiding parties move as one, from house to house – sometimes hitting every house on a street, sometimes skipping whole blocks, sometimes going every other. It's random. Or at least, it's supposed to be random. Certain houses always get targeted more than others.

But even if you're not on a watch list you can end up standing in the snow, like Rachel and her husband, while the regulators and police try to prove your validity. Or – even worse – while the raiders come inside your house, tear the walls down, and look for signs of suspicious activity. Private property laws are suspended on raid nights. Pretty much every law is suspended on raid nights.

We've all heard horror stories: pregnant women stripped down and probed in front of everybody, people thrown in jail for two or three years just for looking at a policeman the wrong way, or for trying to prevent a regulator from entering a certain room.

'This is a raid. If you are asked to step out of the house, please make sure you have all your identification papers in hand, including the papers of any children over the age of six months . . . Anyone who resists will be detained and questioned . . . Anyone who delays will be charged with obstruction . . .'

At the end of the street. Then a few houses away . . . Then two houses away . . . No. Next door. I hear the Richardsons' dog start barking furiously. Then Mrs. Richardson, apologizing. More barking – then someone (a regulator?) mutters something, and I hear a few heavy thuds and a whimper, then someone else saying, 'You don't have to kill the damn thing,' and someone else saying, 'Why not? Probably has fleas, anyway.'

Then for a while there's quiet: just the occasional cackle of walkie-talkies, someone reciting identification numbers into a phone, the shuffling of papers.

Then: 'All right. You're in the clear.' And the boots start up again.

For all their nonchalance, even Rachel and Carol tense up as the boots clomp by our house. I can see Carol gripping her coffee cup tightly, knuckles white. My heart is jumping and skipping, a grasshopper in my chest.

But the boots pass us by. Rachel heaves out an audible sigh of relief as we hear the regulators pound on a door farther down the street. 'Open up . . . This is a raid.'

Carol's teacup clatters in its saucer, making me jump. 'Silly, isn't it?' she says, forcing a laugh. 'Even when you haven't done anything wrong, it still makes you jumpy.'

I feel a dull pain in my hand and realize I'm still holding on to the counter as though it's going to save my life. I can't relax, can't calm down, even as the sounds of the footsteps grow fainter, the bullhorn voice more and more distorted, until it is completely unintelligible. All I can picture are the raiding parties – sometimes as many as fifty in a single night – swirling around Portland, swarming it, surrounding it like water cascading around a whirlpool, sweeping up anyone and everyone they can find and accuse of misbehaviour or disobedience, and even people they can't.

Somewhere out there Hana is dancing, spinning, blonde hair fanning out behind her, smiling – while around her boys are pressing close and unapproved music pumps through the speakers. I fight a feeling of incredible nausea. I don't even want to think about what will happen to her – to all of them – if they're caught.

All I can do is hope she hasn't made it to the party yet. Maybe she took too long to get ready – it seems possible, Hana's always late – and was still at home when the raids started. Even Hana would never venture outside during raids. It's suicide.

But Angelica Marston and everyone else . . . Every single person there . . . Everyone who just wanted to hear some music . . .

I think about what Alex said the night I ran into him at Roaring Brook Farms: *I came to hear the music, like everybody else.*

I will the image out of my mind and tell myself it's not my problem. I should be happy if the party is raided and everyone there is busted. What they're doing is dangerous, not just for them but for all of us: that's how the disease gets in.

But the underneath part of me, the stubborn part that said *grey* at my first evaluation, keeps pressing and nagging at me. *So what?* it says. So they wanted to hear some music. Some real music – not the dinky little songs that get tooted out at the Portland Concert Series, all boring rhythms and bright, chipper notes. They're not doing anything *that* bad.

Then I remember the other thing Alex said: *Nobody's hurting anybody.*

Besides, there's always the possibility that Hana didn't run late tonight, and she's out there, oblivious, as the raids circle closer and closer. I have to squeeze my eyes shut against the thought, and against the thought of dozens of glittering blades descending on her. If she's not thrown in jail she'll be carted directly to the labs – she'll be cured before dawn, regardless of the dangers or risks.

Somehow, despite my racing thoughts and the fact that the

room continues its frantic spinning, I've managed to clean all the dishes. I've also come to a decision.

I have to go. I have to warn her.

I have to warn all of them.

By the time Rachel and David leave and everyone is settled in bed it's midnight. Every second that passes feels like agony. I can only hope the door-to-door on peninsula is taking longer than usual, and it will be a while before the raiders make it to Deering Highlands. Maybe they've decided to skip the Highlands altogether. Given the fact that the majority of the houses up there are vacant, it's always a possibility. Still, since Deering Highlands used to be the hotbed of resistance in Portland, it seems doubtful.

I slip out of bed, not bothering to change out of my sleep pants and T-shirt, both of which are black. Then I put on black flats, and, even though it's about a thousand degrees, pull a black ski hat out of the closet. Can't be too careful tonight.

Just as I'm about to crack open the bedroom door I hear a small noise behind me, like the mewing of a cat. I whip around. Grace is sitting up in bed, watching me.

For a second we just stare at each other. If Grace makes a noise, or gets out of bed, or does anything, she's bound to wake Jenny, and then I'm done, finished, kaput. I'm trying to think of what I can say to reassure her, trying to fabricate a lie, but then, miracle of miracles, she just lies back down in bed and closes her eyes. And even though it's very dark, I would swear that there's the smallest smile on her face.

I feel a quick rush of relief. One good thing about the fact that Gracie refuses to speak? I know she won't tell on me.

I slip out into the street without any other problems, even

remembering to skip the third-to-last stair, which last time let out such an awful squeak I thought for sure Carol would wake up.

After the noise and the commotion of the raids, the street is freakily still and quiet. Every single window is dark, all the blinds drawn, like the houses are trying to turn away from the street, or put up their shoulders against prying eyes. A stray piece of red paper sweeps by me, turning on the wind like the tumbleweed you see in old cowboy movies. I recognize it as a raider's notice, a proclamation filled with impossible-to-pronounce words explaining the legality of suspending everyone's rights for the evening. Other than that, it could be any other night – any other quiet, dead, ordinary night.

Except that on the wind, just faintly, you can hear the distant murmur of footsteps, and a high wail as if someone is crying. The sounds are so quiet you might almost mistake them for ocean and wind sounds. Almost.

The raiders have moved on.

I start off quickly in the direction of Deering Highlands. I'm too afraid to take my bike. I'm worried the little reflective patch on the wheels will attract too much attention. I can't think about what I'm doing, can't think about the consequences if I'm caught. I don't know where I even got this rush of resolution. I never would have thought I'd have the courage to leave the house on a raid night, not in a million years.

I guess Hana was wrong about me. I guess I'm not scared *all* the time.

I'm passing a black trash bag heaped on the sidewalk when a low whimper stops me short. I spin around, my whole body on high alert in an instant. Nothing. The sound is repeated:

an eerie, crooning sound that makes the hair on my arms stand up. Then the garbage bag by my feet shakes itself.

No. Not a garbage bag. It's Riley, the Richardsons' black mutt.

I take a few shaky steps toward him. I need only one glance to know that he's dying. He's completely coated with a sticky, shiny, black substance – blood, I realize as I get closer. That's the reason I mistook his fur, in the dark, for the slick black surface of a plastic bag. One of his eyes is pressed to the pavement; the other is open. His head has been clubbed in. Blood is flowing freely from his nose, black and viscous.

I think of the voice I heard – *Probably has fleas, anyway,* the regulator said – and the swift thudding sound that followed.

Riley is staring at me with a look so mournful and accusatory I swear for a second it's like he's a human and he's trying to tell me something – trying to say, *You did this to me*. A wave of nausea overtakes me and I'm tempted to get down on my knees and scoop him up in my arms, or strip off my clothes and start soaking the blood off him. But at the same time I feel paralysed. I can't move.

As I'm standing there, frozen, he gives a long, shuddering jerk, from the tip of his tail to his nose. Then he goes still.

Instantly my arms and legs unfreeze. I stumble backward, bile pushing itself up into my mouth. I careen in a full circle, feeling like I did the day I got drunk with Hana, totally out of control of my own body. Anger and disgust are shredding through me, making me want to scream.

I find a flattened cardboard box sitting behind a Dumpster and drag it over to Riley's body, covering him completely. I try not to think of the insects that will tear into him by morning. I'm surprised to feel tears prick at my eyes. I wipe them away with the back of my arm. But as I start off toward Deering all I can think is, *I'm sorry, I'm sorry, I'm sorry*, like a mantra, or a prayer.

One good thing about raids: they're loud. All I have to do is pause in the shadows and listen for the footsteps, the static, the bullhorn voices. I switch directions, choose the side streets, the ones that have been skipped over or raided already. Evidence of the raids is everywhere: overturned garbage cans and Dumpsters, trash picked through and spilled out onto the street, mountains of old receipts and shredded letters and rotting vegetables and foul-smelling goop I don't even want to identify, red notices coating everything like a dust. My shoes get slick from clomping over it, and in the worst places I have to keep my arms out like a tightrope walker just to stay on my feet. I pass a few houses marked with a big *X*, black paint splashed across their walls and windows like a black gash, and my stomach sinks. The people who live in these houses have been identified as troublemakers or resisters. The hot wind whistling through the streets carries sounds of yelling and crying, dogs barking. I do my best not to think about Riley.

I stick to the shadows, slipping in and out of alleys and darting from one Dumpster to the next. Sweat is pooling at the base of my neck and under my arms, and it's not just from the heat. Everything looks strange and grotesque and distorted, certain streets glittering with glass from smashed windows, the smell of burning in the air.

At one point, I come around a corner onto Forest Avenue just as a group of regulators turns onto it from the other end. I whip back around, pressing flat against the wall of a hardware store and inching back in the direction I've come. The chances any of the regulators saw me are slim – I was a block away and it's pitch-black – but still, my heart never goes back to its normal pace. I feel like I'm playing some giant video game, or trying to solve a really complicated math equation. *One girl is trying to avoid forty raiding parties of between fifteen and twenty people each, spread out across a radius of seven miles. If she has to make it 2.7 miles through the center, what is the probability she will wake up tomorrow morning in a jail cell? Please feel free to round pi to 3.14.*

Before the shakedown, Deering Highlands was a nicer part of Portland. The houses were big and new – at least for Maine, which means they were built within the past hundred years – and set back behind gates and hedges, on streets with names like Lilac Way and Timber Road. There are a few families still clinging on in some of the houses, dirt-poor ones who can't afford to move anywhere else, or haven't gotten permission for a new residence, but for the most part it's totally empty. Nobody wanted to stay on; nobody wanted to be associated with the resistance.

The weirdest thing about Deering Highlands is how quickly it was abandoned. There are still rusting toys scattered among the grass and cars parked in some of the driveways, though most of them have been picked apart, cleaned of metal and plastic like corpses scavenged by enormous buzzards. The whole area has the forlorn look of an abandoned animal: houses drooping slowly into the overgrown lawns.

Normally I get freaked out just being in the vicinity of the Highlands. A lot of people say it's bad luck, like passing a graveyard without holding your breath. But tonight, when I finally make it there, I feel like I could dance a jig on the sidewalk. Everything is dark and quiet and undisturbed, not a single raider's notice to be seen, not a whisper of conversation or the brush of a heel on a sidewalk. The raiders haven't come yet. Maybe they won't come at all.

I speed quickly through the streets, picking up the pace now that I don't have to worry so much about sticking to the shadows and moving soundlessly. Deering Highlands is pretty big, a maze of winding streets that all look weirdly similar, houses looming out of the darkness like ships run aground. The lawns have all gone wild over the years, trees stretching their gnarled branches to the sky and casting crazy zigzag shadows on the moonlit pavement. I get lost on Lilac Way – somehow I manage to make a complete circle and wind up hitting the same intersection twice – but when I turn onto Tanglewild Lane I see a dull light burning dimly in the distance, behind a knotted mass of trees, and I know I've found the place.

An old mailbox is staked crookedly in the ground next to the driveway. A black *X* is still faintly visible on one of its sides. 42 Tanglewild Lane.

I can see why they've chosen this house for the party. It's set back pretty far from the road, and surrounded on all sides by trees so dense I can't help but think of the dark and whispering woods on the far side of the border. Walking up the driveway is creepy. I keep my eyes focused on the fuzzy pale light of the house, which expands and brightens slowly as I get closer, eventually resolving into two lit windows. The windows have been covered with some kind of fabric, maybe to hide the fact that there are people inside. It isn't working. I can see shadow-people moving back and forth inside the house. The music is very quiet. It's not until I make it onto the porch that I hear it at all – faint, muffled strains that seem to vibrate up from the floorboards. There must be a basement.

I've been rushing to arrive, but I hesitate with my hand on the front door, my palm slick with sweat. I haven't given much thought to how I'll get everyone out. If I just start screaming about a raid it will cause a panic. Everyone will stream into the streets at once, and then the chances of getting home undetected go to zero. *Someone* will hear something; the raiders will catch on, and then we'll all be screwed.

I do a mental correction. *They'll* be screwed. I am not like these people on the other side of the door. I'm not them.

But then I think of Riley shuddering, going limp. I am not those people either, the ones who did that, the ones who watched. Even the Richardsons didn't bother trying to save him, their own dog. They didn't even cover him up as he was dying.

I would never do that. Never ever ever. Not even if I had a million procedures. He was alive. He had a heartbeat and blood and breath, and they left him there like trash.

They. Me. Us. Them. The words ricochet in my head. I palm my hands on the back of my pants and open the door.

Hana said this party would be smaller, but to me it seems even more crowded than the last one, maybe because the rooms are tiny and totally packed. They are filled with a choking curtain of cigarette smoke, which shimmers over everything and makes it look as though everyone is swimming underwater. It's deathly hot in here, at least ten degrees hotter than it was outside – people move slowly and have rolled up their short sleeves above the shoulders, tugged their jeans to their knees, and wherever there is skin, there is a glistening sheen on it. For a moment I can only stand there and watch. I think, *I wish I had a camera.* If I ignore the fact that there are hands touching hands and bodies bumping together and a thousand things that are terrible and wrong, I can see that it's kind of beautiful.

Then I realize I'm wasting time.

There's a girl standing directly in front of me, blocking my way. She has her back to me. I reach out and put a hand on her arm. Her skin is so hot it burns. She turns to me, face red and flushed, craning her head backward to hear.

'It's a raid night,' I say to her, surprised that my voice comes out so steady.

The music is soft but insistent – it's definitely coming up from a basement of some kind – not as crazy as the last time but just as strange and just as gorgeous. It reminds me of warm, dripping things, honey and sunlight and red leaves swirling down on the wind. But the layers of conversation, the creakings of footsteps and floorboards, make it difficult to hear.

'What?' She sweeps her hair away from her ear.

I open my mouth to say *raid* but instead of my voice it's someone else's that comes out: an enormous, mechanical voice bellowing from outside, a voice that seems to shake and rattle from all sides at once, a voice that cuts through the warmth and the music like a cold razor edge through skin. At the same time the room starts spinning, a swirling mass of red and white lights revolving over terrified, stunned faces.

'*Attention. This is a raid. Do not try to run. Do not try to resist. This is a raid.*'

A few seconds later, the door explodes inward and a spotlight as bright as the sun turns everything white and motionless, turns everything to dust and statue.

Then they let the dogs loose.

fourteen

*Human beings, in their natural state, are unpredictable,
erratic, and unhappy. It is only once their animal instincts are
controlled that they can be responsible, dependable, and content.*

— The Book of Shhh, p.31

I once saw a news report about a brown bear that had
accidentally been punctured by its trainer at the Portland
circus during routine training. I was really young, but
I'll never forget the way the bear looked, an enormous dark
blob, tearing around its circle with a ridiculous red paper
hat still flopping crazily from its head, ripping into whatever
it could get its jaws around: paper streamers, folding chairs,
balloons. Its trainer, too: the bear mauled him, turned his
face into hamburger meat.

The worst part – the part I've never forgotten – was its panicked roaring: a horrible, continuous, enraged bellow that sounded somehow human.

That's what I remember as the raiders start flooding the house, pouring in through the shattered door, battering on the windows. That's what I think of as the music cuts off suddenly and instead the air is full of barking and screaming and shattering glass, as hot hands push me from the front and from the side and I catch an elbow under my chin and another one in my ribs. I remember the bear.

Somehow I've surged forward in the panicked crowd that is flowing and scrabbling toward the back of the house. Behind me I hear dogs snapping their jaws and regulators swinging heavy clubs. People are screaming – so many people it sounds like a single voice. A girl falls behind me, stumbling forward and reaching for me as one of the regulator's batons catches her on the back of the head with a sickening crack. I feel her fingers tighten momentarily on the cotton of my shirt, and I shake her off and keep running, pushing, squeezing forward. I have no time to be sorry, and no time to be scared. I have no time to do anything but move, push, *go*, can't think of anything but *escape, escape, escape.*

The strange thing is that for a minute in the middle of all that noise and confusion, I see things super clearly, in slow motion, like I'm watching a film from a distance: I see a guard dog make a leap for a guy to my left; I see his knees buckle as he topples forward with the barest, tiniest noise, like a breath or a sigh, a crescent of blood spattering up from his neck, where the dog's teeth tear into him. A girl with flashing blonde hair goes down under the raiders' clubs, and as I see the arc of her hair, for a second my heart goes totally still and I think I've died; I think it's all over. Then she twists her head my way, shouting, as the regulators get her with pepper spray, and I see that she isn't Hana, and relief rushes through me, a wave.

More snapshots. A movie – only a movie. Not happening, could never really happen. A boy and a girl, fighting to make it into one of the side rooms, maybe thinking there's an exit that way. The door is too small for both of them to enter at once. He is wearing a blue shirt that reads PORTLAND NAVAL CONSERVATORY, and she has long red hair, bright as a flame. Only five minutes ago they were talking and laughing together, standing so close that if one of them had even tipped forward accidentally they might have kissed. Now they wrestle, but she is too small. She locks her teeth on his arm like a dog, like a wild thing; he roars, rages, grabs her by the shoulders, and slams her back against the wall, out of the way. She stumbles, falls, slipping, trying to stand up; one of the raiders, an enormous man with the reddest face I've ever seen, reaches down, knots his fingers around her ponytail, and hauls her to her feet. Naval Conservatory doesn't get away either. Two raiders follow him, and as I run by I hear the thud of their clubs, the mangled sound of screaming.

Animals, I think. *We're animals.*

People are shoving, pulling, using one another as shields as the raiders keep gaining, surging forward, swinging at us, dogs at our heels, batons whirling so close to my head I can feel the air whooshing on my neck as the wood twirls, twirls near the back of my skull. I think of searing pain, I think of red. The crowd is thinning around me as the raiders advance. One by one people are screaming next to me – *crack!*

– and dropping, getting wrestled to the ground by three, four, five dogs. Screaming, screaming. Everyone screaming.

Somehow I've managed to avoid being caught, and I'm still rocketing through the narrow, creaking hallways, passing a blur of rooms, a blur of people and raiders, more lights, more shattered windows, the sound of engines. They've got the place surrounded. And then the open back door rises up in front of me – and beyond it dark trees, the cool and whispering woods behind the house. If I can make it outside . . . if I can hide from the lights for long enough . . .

I hear a dog barking behind me, and behind that, a raider's pounding footsteps, gaining, gaining, a sharp voice yelling, 'Stop!' and I suddenly realize I'm alone in the hallway. Fifteen more steps . . . then ten. If I can make it into the darkness . . .

Five feet from the door and sudden, shooting pain rips through my leg. The dog has got its jaws around my calf, and I turn and that's when I see him, the regulator with the massive red face, eyes glittering, smiling – *oh, God, he's smiling, he actually enjoys this* – club raised, ready to swing. I close my eyes, think of pain as big as the ocean, think of a blood-red sea. Think of my mother.

Then I'm being jerked to the side, and I hear a crack and a yelp, the regulator saying, 'Shit.' The fire in my leg stops and the weight of the dog falls off, and there's an arm around my waist and a voice in my ear – a voice so familiar in that moment it's like I've been waiting for it all along, like I've been hearing it forever in my dreams – breathing out, 'This way.'

Alex keeps one arm around my waist, half carrying me. We're in a different hallway now, this one smaller and totally empty. Every time I put weight on my right leg the pain flares up again, searing all the way into my head. The raider is still behind us and *pissed* – Alex must have pulled me to safety at just the right second, so the raider cracked down on his dog instead of my skull – and I know I must be slowing Alex down, but he doesn't let me go, not for a second.

'In here,' he says, and then we're ducking into another room. We must be in a part of the house that wasn't being used for the party. This room is pitch-black, although Alex doesn't slow down at all, just keeps going through the dark. I let the pressure of his fingertips guide me – left, right, left, right. It smells like mold in here, and something else – fresh paint, almost, and something smoky, like someone's been cooking here. But that's impossible. These houses have been empty for years.

Behind us the raider is struggling in the dark. He bumps up against something and curses. A second later something crashes to the ground; glass shatters; more cursing. From the sound of his voice I can tell that he's falling behind.

'Up,' Alex whispers, so quiet and so close it's like I've only imagined it, and just like that he is lifting me and I realize I'm going out a window, feel the rough wood of the windowsill grate against my back, land on my good foot on the soft, damp grass outside.

A second later Alex follows soundlessly, materializing beside me in the dark. Though the air is hot, a breeze has picked up, and as it sweeps across my skin I could cry from gratitude and relief.

But we're not safe yet – far from it. The darkness is mobile, twisting, alive with paths of light. Flashlights cut through the woods to our right and left, and in their glare I see fleeing figures, lit up like ghosts, frozen for a moment in the beams. The screams continue, some only a few feet away, some so distant and forlorn you could mistake them for something else – for owls, maybe, hooting peacefully in their trees. Then Alex has taken my hand and we're running again. Every step on my right foot is a fire, a blade. I bite the inside of my cheeks to keep from crying out, and taste blood.

Chaos. Scenes from hell: floodlights from the road, shadows falling, bone cracking, voices shattering apart, dissolving into silence.

'In here.'

I do what he says without hesitating. A tiny wooden shed has appeared miraculously in the dark. It's falling apart, and so overgrown with moss and climbing vines that even from a distance of only a few feet it appeared to be a tangle of bushes and trees. I have to stoop to get inside, and when I do the smell of animal urine and wet dog is so strong I almost gag. Alex comes in behind me and shuts the door. I hear a rustling and see him kneeling, stuffing a blanket in the gap between the door and the ground. The blanket must be the source of the smell. It absolutely reeks.

'God,' I whisper, the first thing I've said to him, cupping my hand over my mouth and nose.

'This way the dogs won't pick up our scent,' he whispers back matter-of-factly.

I've never met someone so calm in my life. I think fleetingly that maybe the stories I heard when I was little were true – maybe Invalids really are monsters, freaks.

Then I feel ashamed. He just saved my life.

He *saved* my *life* – from the raiders. From the people who are supposed to protect us and keep us safe. From the people who are supposed to keep us safe from the people like Alex.

Nothing makes sense anymore. My head is spinning, and

I feel dizzy. I stumble, bumping against the wall behind me, and Alex reaches up to steady me.

'Sit down,' he says, in that same commanding voice he has been using all along. It's comforting to listen to his low, forceful directives, to let myself go. I lower myself to the ground. The floor is damp and rough underneath me. The moon must have broken through the clouds; gaps in the walls and roof let in little spots of silvery light. I can just make out some shelves beyond Alex's head, a set of cans – paint, maybe? – piled in one corner. Now that Alex and I are both sitting there's hardly any room left to maneuver – the whole structure is only a few feet wide.

'I'm going to take a look at your leg now, okay?' He's still whispering. I nod okay. Even when I'm sitting down, the dizziness doesn't subside.

He sits up on his knees and draws my leg into his lap. It's not until he begins rolling up my pant leg that I feel how wet the fabric is against my skin. I must be bleeding. I bite my lip and press my back up hard against the wall, expecting it to hurt, but the feeling of his hands against my skin – cool and strong – somehow dampens everything, sliding across the pain like an eclipse blotting the moon dark.

Once he has my pants rolled up to the knee he tilts me gently, so he can see the back of my calf. I lean one elbow on the floor, feeling the room sway. I must be bleeding *a lot*.

He exhales sharply, a quick sound between his teeth.

'Is it bad?' I say, too afraid to look.

'Hold still,' he says. And I know that it is bad, but he won't tell me so, and in that moment I'm so flooded with gratitude for him and hatred for the people outside – hunters, primitives, with their sharp teeth and heavy sticks – the air goes out of me and I have to struggle to breathe.

Alex reaches into a corner of the shed without removing my leg from his lap. He fiddles with a box of some kind and metal latches creak open. A second later he's hovering over my leg with a bottle.

'This is going to burn for a second,' he says. Liquid splatters my skin, and the astringent smell of alcohol makes my nostrils flare. Flames lick up my leg and I nearly scream. Alex reaches out a hand, and without thinking I take it and squeeze.

'What is that?' I force out through gritted teeth.

'Rubbing alcohol,' he says. 'Prevents infection.'

'How did you know it was here?' I ask, but he doesn't answer.

He draws his hand away from mine and I realize I've been grabbing on to him, hard. But I don't have the energy to be embarrassed or afraid: the room seems to be pulsing, the half darkness growing fuzzier.

'Shit,' Alex mutters. 'You're really bleeding.'

'It doesn't hurt that much,' I whisper, which is a lie. But he's so calm, so together, it makes me want to act brave too.

Everything has taken on a strange, distant quality – the sounds of running and shouting outside get warped and weird like they're being filtered through water, and Alex looks miles away. I start to think I might be dreaming, or about to pass out.

And then I decide I'm *definitely* dreaming, because as I'm watching, Alex starts peeling his shirt off over his head.

What are you doing? I almost scream. Alex finishes shaking loose the shirt and begins tearing the fabric into long strips, shooting a nervous glance at the door and pausing to listen every time the cloth goes *rriiip.*

I've never in my whole life seen a guy without a shirt on, except for really little kids or from a distance on the beach, when I've been too afraid to look for fear of getting in trouble.

Now I can't stop staring. The moonlight just touches his shoulder blades so they glow slightly, like wing tips, like pictures of angels I've seen in textbooks. He's thin but muscular, too: when he moves I can make out the lines of his arms and chest, so strangely, incredibly, beautifully different from a girl's, a body that makes me think of running and being outside, of warmth and sweating. Heat starts beating through me, a thrumming feeling like a thousand tiny birds have been released in my chest. I'm not sure if it's from the bleeding, but the room feels like it's spinning so fast we're in danger of flying out of it, both of us, getting thrown out into the night. Before, Alex seemed far away. Now the room is full of him: he is so close I can't breathe, can't move or speak or think. Every time he brushes me with his fingers, time seems to teeter for a second, like it is in danger of dissolving. The whole world is dissolving, I decide, except for us. Us.

'Hey.' He reaches out and touches my shoulder, just for a second, but in that second my body shrinks down to that single point of pressure under his hand, and glows with warmth. I've never felt like this, so calm and peaceful. Maybe I'm dying. The idea doesn't really upset me, for some reason. In fact, it seems kind of funny. 'You okay?'

'Fine.' I start to giggle softly. 'You're naked.'

'What?' Even in the dark I can tell he's squinting at me.

'I've never seen a boy like – like that. With no shirt on. Not up close.'

He begins wrapping the shredded T-shirt around my leg carefully, tying it tight. 'The dog got you good,' he says. 'But this should stop the bleeding.'

The phrase *stop the bleeding* sounds so clinical and scary it snaps me awake and helps me to focus. Alex finishes tying off the makeshift bandage. Now the searing pain in my leg has been replaced by a dull, throbbing pressure.

Alex lifts my leg carefully out of his lap and rests it on the ground. 'Okay?' he says, and I nod. Then he scoots around next to me, leaning back against the wall like I am so we're sitting side by side, arms just touching at the elbows. I can feel the heat coming off his bare skin, and it makes me feel hot. I close my eyes and try not to think about how close we are, or what it would feel like to run my hands over his shoulders and chest.

Outside, the sounds of the raid grow more and more distant, the screams fewer, the voices fainter. The raiders must be passing on. I say a silent prayer that Hana managed to escape; the possibility that she didn't is too terrible to contemplate.

Still, Alex and I don't move. I'm so tired I feel like I could sleep forever. Home seems impossibly, incomprehensibly far away, and I don't see how I'll ever make it back.

Alex starts speaking all at once, his voice a low, urgent rush. 'Listen, Lena. What happened at the beach – I'm really sorry. I should have told you sooner, but I didn't want to frighten you away.'

'You don't have to explain,' I say.

'But I want to explain. I want you to know that I didn't mean to—'

'Listen,' I cut him off. 'I'm not going to tell anyone, okay? I'm not going to get you in trouble or anything.'

He pauses. I feel him turn to look at me, but I keep my eyes fixed on the darkness in front of us.

'I don't care about that,' he says, lower. Another pause, and then, 'I just don't want you to hate me.'

Again the room seems to be shrinking, closing in around us. I can feel his eyes on me like the hot pressure of touch, but I'm too afraid to look at him. I'm afraid that if I do I'll lose myself in his eyes, forget all the things I'm supposed to say. Outside, the woods have fallen silent. The raiders must have left. After a second the crickets begin singing all at once, warbling throatily, a great swelling of sound.

'Why do you care?' I say, barely a whisper.

'I told you,' he whispers back. I can feel his breath just tickling the space behind my ear, making the hair prick up on my neck. 'I like you.'

'You don't know me,' I say quickly.

'I want to, though.'

The room is spinning more and more quickly. I press up more firmly against the wall, trying to steady myself against the feeling of dizzying movement. It's impossible: he has an answer for everything. It's too quick. It must be a trick. I press my palms against the damp floor, taking comfort in the solidity of the rough wood.

'Why me?' I don't mean to ask it, but the words slide out. 'I'm nobody . . .' I want to say, *I'm nobody special*, but the words dry up in my mouth. This is what I imagine it feels like to climb to the top of a mountain, where the air is so thin you can inhale and inhale and inhale and still feel like you can't take a breath.

Alex doesn't answer and I realize he doesn't have an answer, just like I suspected – there's no reason for it at all. He's picked me at random, as a joke, or because he knew I'd be too scared to tell on him.

But then he starts speaking. His story is so rapid and fluid you can tell he has thought about it a lot, the kind of story you tell over and over to yourself until the edges get all smoothed over. 'I was born in the Wilds. My mother died right afterward; my father's dead. He never knew he had a son. I lived there for the first part of my life, just kind of bouncing around. All the other' – he hesitates slightly, and I can hear the grimace in his voice – '*Invalids* took care of me together. Like a community thing.'

Outside, the crickets pause temporarily in their song. For a second it's like nothing bad has happened, like nothing out of the ordinary at all has happened tonight – just another hot and lazy summer night, waiting for morning to peel it back. Pain knifes through me in that moment, but it has nothing to do with my leg. It strikes me how small everything is, our whole world, everything with meaning – our stores and our raids and our jobs and our lives, even. Meanwhile, the world just goes on the same as always, night cycling into day and back into night, an endless circle; seasons shifting and reforming like a monster shaking off its skin and growing it again.

Alex keeps talking. 'I came into Portland when I was ten, to join up with the resistance here. I won't tell you how. It was complicated. I got an ID number; I got a new last name, a new home address. There are more of us than you think – Invalids, and sympathizers, too – more of us than anybody knows. We have people in the police force, and all the municipal departments. We have people in the labs, even.'

Goosebumps pop up all over my arms when he says this. 'My point is that it's *possible* to get in and out. Difficult, but possible. I moved in with two strangers – sympathizers, both of them – and was told to call them my aunt and uncle.' He shrugs ever so slightly next to me. 'I didn't care. I'd never known my real parents, and I'd been raised by dozens of different aunts and uncles. It didn't make a difference to me.'

His voice has gotten super quiet, and he seems almost to have forgotten that I'm there. I'm not exactly sure where his story is going but I hold my breath, afraid that if I even so much as exhale he'll stop speaking entirely.

'I hated it here. I hated it here so much you can't even imagine. All the buildings and the people looking so dazed and the smells and the closeness of everything and the rules – rules everywhere you turned, rules and walls, rules and walls. I wasn't used to it. I felt like I was in a cage. We *are* in a cage: a bordered cage.'

A little shock pulses through me. In all the seventeen years and eleven months of my life I have never, not once, thought of it that way. I've been so used to thinking of what the borders are keeping *out* that I haven't considered that they're also penning us *in*. Now I see it through Alex's eyes, see what it must have been like for him.

'At first I was angry. I used to light things on fire. Paper, handbooks, school primers. It made me feel better somehow.' He laughs softly. 'I even burned my copy of *The Book of Shhh*.'

Another shock pulses through me: defacing or destroying *The Book of Shhh* is sacrilege.

'I used to walk along the borders for hours every day. Sometimes I cried.' He squirms next to me, and I can tell he's embarrassed. It's the first sign he has given in a while that he knows I'm still there, that he's talking to me, and the urge to reach out and grab his hand, to squeeze him or give him some kind of reassurance, is almost overwhelming. But I keep my hands glued to the floor. 'After a while, though, I would just walk. I liked to watch the birds. They would lift off from our side and soar over into the Wilds, as easily as anything. Back and forth, back and forth, lifting and curling through the air. I could watch them for hours at a time. Free. They were totally free. I'd thought that nothing and nobody was free in Portland, but I was wrong. There were always the birds.'

He falls silent for a while, and I think maybe he's done with his story. I wonder if he's forgotten about my original question – *why me?* – but I'm too embarrassed to remind him, so I just sit there and imagine him standing at the border, motionless, watching the birds swoop above his head. It calms me down.

After what seems like forever he starts talking again, this time in a voice so quiet I have to shift nearer to him just to hear. 'The first time I saw you, at the Governor, I hadn't been to watch the birds at the border in years. But that's what you reminded me of. You were jumping up, and you were yelling something, and your hair was coming loose from your ponytail, and you were so *fast* . . .' He shakes his head. 'Just a flash, and then you were gone. Exactly like a bird.'

I don't know how – I hadn't intended to move and hadn't noticed moving – but somehow we've ended up face-to-face in the dark, only inches apart.

'Everyone is asleep. They've been asleep for years. You seemed . . . awake.' Alex is whispering now. He closes his eyes, opens them again. 'I'm tired of sleeping.'

My insides are lifting and fluttering like they've done what he said and been transformed into swooping, soaring birds;

the rest of my body seems to be floating away on massive currents of warmth, as though a hot wind is pushing through me, breaking me apart, turning me to air.

This is wrong, a voice says inside of me, but it isn't my voice. It's someone else's – some composite of my aunt, and Rachel, and all my teachers, and the pinchy evaluator who asked most of the questions the second time around.

Out loud I squeak, 'No,' even though another word is rising and lifting inside of me, bubbling up like fresh water sprung from the earth. *Yes, yes, yes.*

'Why?' He's barely whispering. His hands find my face, his fingertips barely skim my forehead, the top of my ears, the hollows of my cheeks. Everywhere he touches is fire. My whole body is burning up, the two of us becoming twin points of the same bright white flame. 'What are you afraid of?'

'You have to understand. I just want to be happy.' I can barely get the words out. My mind is a haze, full of smoke – nothing exists but his fingers dancing and skating over my skin, through my hair. I wish it would stop. I want it to go on forever. 'I just want to be normal, like everybody else.'

'Are you sure that being like everybody else will make you happy?' The barest whisper; his breath on my ear and neck, his mouth grazing my skin. And I think then I might really have died. Maybe the dog bit me and I got clubbed on the head and this is all just a dream – the rest of the world has dissolved. Only him. Only me. Only us.

'I don't know any other way.' I can't feel my mouth open, don't feel the words come, but there they are, floating on the dark.

He says, 'Let me show you.'

And then we're kissing. Or at least, I think we're kissing –

I've only seen it done a couple of times, quick closed-mouth pecks at weddings or on formal occasions. But this isn't like anything I've ever seen, or imagined, or even dreamed: this is like music or dancing but better than both. His mouth is slightly open so I open mine, too. His lips are soft, the same soft pressure as the quietly insistent voice in my head that keeps saying *yes*.

The warmth is only growing inside of me, waves of light swelling and breaking and making me feel like I'm floating. His fingers lace my hair, cup my neck and the back of my head, skim over my shoulders, and without thinking about it or meaning to, my hands find his chest, move over the heat of his skin, the bones of his shoulder blades like wing tips, the curve of his jaw, just stubbled with hair – all of it strange and unfamiliar and gloriously, deliciously new. My heart is drumming in my chest so hard it aches, but it's the good kind of ache, like the feeling you get on the first day of real autumn, when the air is crisp and the leaves are all flaring at the edges and the wind smells just vaguely of smoke – like the end and the beginning of something all at once. Under my hand I swear I can feel his heart beating out a response, an immediate echo of mine, as though our bodies are speaking to each other.

And suddenly it's all so ridiculously and stupidly clear I feel like laughing. This is what I want. This is the only thing I've ever wanted. Everything else – every single second of every single day that has come before this very moment, this kiss – has meant nothing.

When he finally pulls away it's like a blanket has come down over my brain, quieting all my buzzing thoughts and questions, filling me with a calm and happiness as deep and cool as snow. The only word left there is *yes*. Yes to everything.

I really like you, Lena. Do you believe me now?

Yes.

Can I walk you home?

Yes.

Can I see you tomorrow?

Yes, yes, yes.

The streets are empty by now. The whole city is silent and still. The whole city might have wound down into nothing, burned away while we were in the shed, and I wouldn't have noticed or cared. The walk home is fuzzy, a dream. He holds my hand the whole way and we stop to kiss twice again in the longest, deepest shadows we can find. Both times I wish the shadows were solid, had weight, and they would fold down around us and bury us there so we could stay like that forever, chest to chest, lip to lip. Both times I feel my chest seize up when he pulls away and takes my hand and we have to start walking again, *not* kissing, like suddenly I can only breathe correctly when we are.

Somehow – too soon – I'm home, and whispering good-bye to him and feeling his lips brush mine one last time, as light as wind.

Then I'm sneaking into the house and up the stairs and into the bedroom, and it's not until I've been lying in bed for a long time, shivering, aching, missing him already, that I realize my aunt and my teachers and the scientists are right about the *deliria*. As I lie there with the hurt driving through my chest and the sick, anxious feeling churning through me and the desire for Alex so strong inside of me it's like a razor blade edging its way through my organs, shredding me, all I can think is: *It will kill me, it will kill me, it will kill me. And I don't care.*

fifteen

Last, God created Adam and Eve, to live together happily as husband and wife: eternal partners. They lived peacefully for years in a beautiful garden full of tall, straight plants that grew in neat rows, and well-behaved animals to serve as pets. Their minds were as clear and untroubled as the pale and cloudless blue sky, which hung like a canopy over their heads. They were untouched by illness, pain, or desire. They did not dream. They did not ask questions. Each morning they woke as refreshed as newborns. Everything was always the same, but it always felt new and good.

– From *Genesis: A Complete History of the World and the Known Universe*, by Steven Horace, PhD, Harvard University

The next day, a Saturday, I wake up thinking of Alex. Then I try to stand up, and pain shoots through my leg. Hitching up my pajamas, I see a small spot of blood has seeped through the T-shirt Alex wrapped around my calf. I know I should wash it or change the bandage or do something, but I'm too scared to see how bad the damage is. The details from the party – of screaming and shoving and dogs and batons whirling through the air, deadly – come flooding back, and for a moment I'm sure I'm going to be sick. Then the dizziness subsides and I think of Hana.

Our phone is in the kitchen. My aunt is at the sink, washing dishes, and gives me a small look of surprise when I come downstairs. I catch a glimpse of myself in the hallway mirror. I look terrible – hair sticking up all over my head, big bags under my eyes – and it strikes me as unbelievable that anyone could ever find me pretty.

But someone does. Thinking of Alex makes a golden glow spread through me.

'Better hurry,' Carol says. 'You'll be late for work. I was just about to wake you.'

'I just have to call Hana,' I say. I snake the cord as far as it will go and back up into the pantry, so at least I'll have some privacy.

I try Hana's house first. One, two, three, four, five rings. Then the answering machine clicks on. *'You've reached the Tate residence. Please leave a message of no more than two minutes . . .'*

I hang up quickly. My fingers have begun to tremble, and I have trouble punching in Hana's cell phone number. Straight to voice mail.

Her greeting is exactly the same as it's always been (*'Hey, sorry I couldn't get to the phone. Or maybe I'm not sorry I couldn't get to the phone – it depends on who's calling.'*), her voice coming in fuzzy, bubbling with suppressed laughter. Hearing it – the normalcy of it – after last night gives me a jolt, like suddenly dreaming yourself back into a place you haven't thought about for a while. I remember the day she recorded it. It was after school and we were in her room, and she went through about a million greetings before she settled on that one. I was bored and kept whacking her with a pillow whenever she wanted to try *just one more*.

'Hana, you need to call me,' I say into the phone, keeping my voice as low as possible. I'm far too aware that my aunt is listening. 'I'm working today. You can reach me at the store.'

I hang up, feeling dissatisfied and guilty. While I was in the shed last night with Alex, she could have been hurt or in trouble; I should have done more to find her.

'Lena.' My aunt calls me sharply back into the kitchen just as I'm headed upstairs to get ready.

'Yes?'

She comes forward a few steps. Something in her expression makes me anxious.

'Are you limping?' she asks. I've been trying as hard as possible to walk normally.

I look away. It's easier to lie when I'm not staring in her eyes. 'I don't think so.'

'Don't lie to me.' Her voice turns cold. 'You think I don't know what this is about, but I do.' For one terrified second I think she's going to ask me to roll up my pajama pants, or tell me she knows about the party. But then she says, 'You've been running again, haven't you? Even though I told you not to.'

'Only once,' I blurt out, relieved. 'I think I may have twisted my ankle.'

Carol shakes her head and looks disappointed. 'Honestly, Lena. I don't know when you started disobeying me. I thought that you of all people—' She breaks off. 'Oh, well. Only five weeks to go, right? Then all of this will be worked out.'

'Right.' I force myself to smile.

All morning, I oscillate between worrying about Hana and thinking of Alex. I ring up the wrong charge for customers twice and have to call for Jed, my uncle's general manager, to come override it. Then I knock down a whole shelf of frozen pasta dinners, and mislabel a dozen cartons of cottage cheese. Thank God my uncle's not in the store today; he's out doing deliveries, so it's just Jed and me. And Jed hardly looks at me or speaks to me except in grunts, so I'm pretty sure he's not going to notice that I've suddenly turned into a clumsy, incompetent mess.

I know part of the problem, of course. The disorientation, the distraction, the difficulty focusing – all classic Phase One signs of *deliria*. But I don't care. If pneumonia felt this good I'd stand out in the snow in the winter with bare feet and no coat on, or march into the hospital and kiss pneumonia patients.

I've told Alex about my work schedule and we've agreed to meet up at Back Cove directly after my shift, at six o'clock. The minutes crawl toward noon. I swear I've never seen time go more slowly. It's like every second needs encouragement just to click forward into the next. I keep willing the clock to go faster, but it seems to be resisting me deliberately. I see a customer picking her nose in the tiny aisle of (kind of) fresh produce; I look at the clock; look back at the customer; look back at the clock – and the second hand *still* hasn't moved. I have this terrible fear that time will stop completely, while this woman has her pinkie finger buried up her right nostril, right in front of the tray of wilted lettuce.

At noon I get a fifteen-minute break, and I go outside and sit on the sidewalk and choke down a few bites of a sandwich, even though I'm not hungry. The anticipation of seeing Alex again is messing with my appetite big-time. Another sign of the *deliria*.

Bring it.

At one o'clock Jed starts restocking the shelves, and I'm still stuck behind the counter. It's wickedly hot, and there's a fly trapped in the store that keeps buzzing around and bumping up against the overhanging shelf above my head, where we keep a few packs of cigarettes and bottles of Mylanta and things like that. The droning of the fly and the tiny fan whirring behind my back and the heat all make me want to sleep. If I could, I would rest my head on the counter and dream, and dream, and dream. I would dream I was back in the shed with Alex. I would dream of the firmness of his chest pressed against mine and the strength of his hands and his voice saying, 'Let me show you.'

The bell above the door chimes once and I snap out of my reverie.

And there he is, walking through the door with his hands stuffed in the pockets of a pair of raggedy board shorts, and his hair sticking up all crazy around his head like it really is made out of leaves and twigs. Alex.

I nearly topple off my stool.

He shoots me a quick sideways grin and then starts walking the aisles lazily, picking up really random things – like a bag of pork skin cracklings and a can of really gross cauliflower soup – and making exaggerated noises of interest, like 'This looks *delicious*,' so it's all I can do to keep from cracking up laughing. He has to squeeze by Jed at one point – the aisles at the store are pretty narrow, and Jed's not exactly a light-weight – and when Jed barely glances at him, a thrill shoots through me. He doesn't know. He doesn't know that I can still taste Alex's lips against mine, can still feel his hand sliding over my shoulders.

For the first time in my life I've done something for me and by choice and not because somebody told me it was good or bad. As Alex walks through the store, I think that there's an invisible thread tethering us together, and somehow it makes me feel more powerful than ever before.

Finally Alex comes up to the counter with a pack of gum, a bag of chips, and a root beer.

'Will that be all?' I say, careful to keep my voice steady. But I can feel the colour rising to my cheeks. His eyes are amazing today, almost pure gold.

He nods. 'That's all.'

I ring him up, my hands shaking, desperate to say something more to him but worried that Jed will hear. At that moment another customer comes in, an older man who has the look of a regulator. So I count out Alex's change as slowly and carefully as I can, trying to keep him standing in front of me for as long as possible.

But there are only so many ways you can count change for a five-dollar bill. Eventually I pass him his change. Our hands connect as I place the bills in his palm, and a shock of electricity goes through me. I want to grab him, pull him toward me, kiss him right there.

'Have a great day.' My voice sounds high-pitched, strangled. I'm surprised I can even get the words out.

'Oh, I will.' He shoots me his amazing, crooked smile as he backs up toward the door. 'I'm going to the Cove.'

And then he's gone, pivoting out into the street. I try to watch him go, but the sun blinds me as soon as he's out the door and he turns into a winking, blurry shadow, wavering and disappearing.

I can't stand it. I hate thinking of him weaving through the streets, getting farther and farther away. And I have five more hours to get through before I'm supposed to meet him. I'll never make it. Before I can think about what I'm doing, I duck around the counter, peeling off the apron I've been wearing since dealing with a leak in one of the freezer cases.

'Jed, grab the register for a second, okay?' I call.

He blinks at me confusedly. 'Where are you going?'

'Customer,' I say. 'I gave him the wrong change.'

'But—,' Jed starts to say. I don't stop to hear his objections. I can imagine what they'll be, anyway. *But you counted his change for five minutes.* Oh well. So Jed will think I'm stupid. I can live with it.

Down the street Alex is paused on the corner, waiting for a city truck to grumble past.

'Hey!' I shout out, and he turns. A woman pushing a stroller on the other side of the street stops, raises her hand to shield her eyes, and follows my progress down the street. I'm going as fast as I can, but the pain in my leg makes it difficult to do more than hobble along. I can feel the woman's gaze pricking up and down my body like a series of needles.

'I gave you the wrong change,' I call out again, even though I'm close enough to him now to speak normally. Hopefully it will get the woman off my back. But she keeps watching us.

'You shouldn't have come,' I whisper, when I catch up to him. I pretend to press something into his hand. 'I told you I'd meet you later.'

He moves his hand easily to his pocket, picking up

seamlessly on our little charade, and whispers back, 'I couldn't wait.'

Alex waggles his hand in my face and looks stern, like he's scolding me for being careless. But his voice is soft and sweet. Again I have the sensation that nothing else is real – not the sun, or the buildings, or the woman across the street, still staring at us.

'There's a blue door around the corner, in the alley,' I say quietly as I back away, raising my hands like I'm apologizing. 'Meet me there in five. Knock four times.' Then, more loudly, I say, 'Listen, I'm really sorry. Like I said, it was an honest mistake.'

Then I turn and limp back to the store. I can't believe what I've just done. I can't believe the risks I'm taking. But I need to see him. I need to *kiss* him. I need it as much as I've ever needed anything. I have that same pressing feeling in my chest like when I'm at the very end of one of my sprints and I'm just dying, screaming to stop, to catch my breath.

'Thanks,' I say to Jed, taking my spot behind the counter. He mumbles something unintelligible to me and shuffles back toward his clipboard and pen, which he has left lying on the floor in aisle three: CANDY, SODA, CHIPS.

The guy I made for a regulator has his nose buried in one of the freezer compartments. I'm not sure whether he's looking for a frozen dinner or just taking advantage of the free cold air. Either way, as I look at him I have a flashback to last night, to the whistling of the air as the clubs came down like scythes, and I feel a rush of hatred for him – for all of them. I fantasize about pushing the old guy inside the freezers and bolting the door over his head.

Thinking about the raids makes me anxious about Hana

again. News of the raids is in all the papers. Apparently hundreds of people all over Portland were taken last night to be interrogated, or summarily shipped off to the Crypts, though I didn't hear anyone reference the party in the Highlands specifically.

I tell myself if Hana hasn't called me back by this evening, I'll go to her house. I tell myself that in the meantime there's no *point* in worrying, but all the same the guilty feeling keeps worming around in my stomach.

The old guy is still hovering over the freezer compartments and paying me absolutely no attention. Good. I slip on the apron again, and then, after checking to see that Jed isn't watching, reach up and grab all the bottles of ibuprofen – about a dozen of them – and slide them into the apron pocket.

Then I sigh loudly. 'Jed, I need you to cover for me again.'

He looks up with those watery blue eyes. Blink, blink. 'I'm reshelving.'

'Well, we're totally out of painkillers back here. Didn't you notice?'

He stares at me for several long seconds. I keep my hands clasped tightly behind my back. Otherwise I'm sure their trembling would give me away. Finally he shakes his head.

'I'm going to see if I can dig some up in the supply room. Grab the register, okay?' I slip out from behind the counter slowly, so I don't rattle, keeping my body angled slightly away from him. Hopefully he won't notice the bulge in my apron. This is one symptom of the *deliria* no one ever tells you about: apparently the disease turns you into a world-class liar.

I slip around a teetering pile of sagging cardboard boxes stacked at the back of the store and shoulder my way into the supply room, shutting the door behind me. Unfortunately it doesn't lock, so I drag a crate of applesauce in front of the door, just in case Jed decides to come investigate when my search for the ibuprofen takes longer than usual.

A moment later there's a quiet tap on the door that leads out into the alley. *Tap, tap, tap, tap, tap.*

The door feels heavier than usual. It takes all my strength just to yank it open.

'I said to knock *four* times—' I'm saying, as the sun cuts into the room, temporarily dazzling me. And then the words dry up in my throat and I nearly choke.

'Hey,' Hana says. She's standing in the alley, shifting from foot to foot, looking pale and worried. 'I was hoping you'd be here.'

For a second I can't even answer her. I'm overwhelmed with relief – Hana is here, intact, whole, fine – and at the same time anxiety starts drumming through me. I scan the alley quickly: no sign of Alex. Maybe he saw Hana and got scared off.

'Um.' Hana wrinkles her forehead. 'Are you going to let me in, or what?'

'Oh, sorry. Yeah, come in.' She scoots past me, and I shoot one last look up and down the alley before closing the door behind me. I'm happy to see Hana but nervous, too. If Alex shows up while she's here . . .

But he won't, I tell myself. *He must have seen her. He must know it's not safe to come now.* Not that I'm worried that Hana would tell on me, but still. After all the lectures I gave her about safety and being reckless, I wouldn't *blame* her for wanting to bust me.

'Hot in here,' Hana says, lifting her shirt away from her

back. She's wearing a white billowy shirt and loose-fitting jeans with a thin gold belt that picks up the colour of her hair. But she looks worried, and tired, and thin. As she turns a circle, checking out the storeroom, I notice tiny scratches crisscrossing the backs of her arms. 'Remember when I used to come and hang out with you here? I'd bring magazines and that stupid old radio I used to have? And you'd steal—'

'Chips and soda from the cooler,' I finish. 'Yeah, I remember.' That was how we got through summers in middle school, when I first started logging time at the store. I used to fabricate reasons to come back here all the time, and Hana would show up at some point in the early afternoon and knock on the door five times, really soft. Five times. I should have known.

'I got your message this morning,' Hana says, turning toward me. Her eyes look even bigger than usual. Maybe it's that the rest of her face looks smaller, drawn inward somehow. 'I walked by and didn't see you at the register, so I figured I'd come around this way. I wasn't in the mood to deal with your uncle.'

'He's not here today.' I'm beginning to relax. Alex would have been here already if he was planning on coming. 'It's just me and Jed.'

I'm not sure if Hana hears me. She's chewing on her thumbnail – a nervous habit I thought she'd kicked years ago – and staring down at the floor like it's the most fascinating bit of linoleum she's ever seen.

'Hana?' I say. 'Are you okay?'

An enormous shudder goes through her all at once, and her shoulders cave forward and she starts to sob. I've seen Hana cry only twice in my life – once when someone pegged her directly in the stomach during dodgeball in second grade, and once last year, after we saw a diseased girl getting wrestled to the street by police in front of the labs, and they accidentally cracked her head so hard against the pavement we heard it all the way up where we were standing, two hundred feet away – and for a moment I'm totally frozen and unsure of what to do. She doesn't bring her hands to her face or try to wipe her tears or anything. She just stands there, shaking so hard I'm worried she'll fall over, her hands clenched at her sides.

I reach out and skim her shoulder with one hand. 'Shhh, Hana. It's okay.'

She jerks away from me. 'It's not okay.' She draws a long, shaky breath and starts speaking in a rush: 'You were right, Lena. You were right about everything. Last night – it was horrible. There was a raid . . . The party got broken up. Oh God. There were people screaming, and dogs – Lena, there was blood. They were beating people, just cracking them over the head with their nightsticks like nothing. People were dropping right and left and it was – oh, Lena. It was so awful, so awful.' Hana wraps her arms around her stomach and doubles forward like she's about to be sick.

She starts to say something else, but the rest of her words get lost: huge, shuddering sobs run through her whole body. I step forward and wrap her in a hug. For a second she tenses up – it's very rare for us to hug, since it has always been discouraged – but then she relaxes and presses her face into my shoulder and lets herself cry. It's kind of awkward, since she's so much taller than I am; she has to hunch over. It would be funny if it weren't so awful.

'Shhh,' I say. 'Shhh. It's going to be okay.' But the words

seem stupid even as I say them. I think of holding Grace in my arms and rocking her to sleep, saying the same thing, as she screamed silently into my pillow. *It's going to be okay.* Words that mean nothing, really, just sounds intoned into vastness and darkness, little scrabbling attempts to latch on to something when we're falling.

Hana says something else I don't understand. Her face is mashed into my shoulder blade and her words are garbled.

And then the knocking begins. Four soft but deliberate knocks, one right after the other.

Hana and I step away from each other immediately. She draws an arm across her face, leaving a slick of tears from wrist to elbow.

'What's that?' she says. Her voice is trembling.

'What?' My first thought is to pretend I haven't heard anything – and pray to God that Alex goes away.

Knock, knock, knock. Pause. *Knock.* Again.

'*That.*' Irritation creeps into Hana's voice. I guess I should be happy she's not crying anymore. 'The knocking.' She narrows her eyes, staring at me suspiciously. 'I thought nobody comes in this way.'

'They don't. I mean – sometimes – I mean, the delivery guys—' I'm stumbling over my words, praying for Alex to go away, grasping for a lie that isn't coming. So much for my newfound skills.

Then Alex pokes his head in the door and calls out, 'Lena?' He catches sight of Hana first and freezes, half-in and half-out of the alley.

For a minute nobody speaks. Hana's mouth literally falls open. She whips around from Alex to me and then back to Alex, so quickly it looks like her head is going to fly off her neck. Alex doesn't know what to do either. He just stands completely still, like he can go invisible if he doesn't move.

And it's the stupidest thing in the world, but all I can blurt out is, 'You're late.'

Hana and Alex both speak at once. 'You told him to meet you?' she says, as he says, 'I got stopped by patrol. Had to show my cards.'

Hana gets businesslike all at once. This is why I admire her: one second she's sobbing hysterically, the next second she's completely in control.

'Come inside,' she says, 'and shut the door.'

He does. Then he stands there awkwardly, shuffling his feet. His hair is sticking up all weirdly, and in that second he looks so young and cute and nervous I have a crazy urge to walk right up to him, in front of Hana, and kiss him.

But she quashes that urge really quickly. She turns to me and folds her arms and gives me a look I swear she stole from Mrs. McIntosh, the principal of St. Anne's.

'Lena Ella Haloway Tiddle,' she says. 'You have some explaining to do.'

'Your middle name is Ella?' Alex blurts.

Hana and I both shoot him a death stare, and he takes a step backward and ducks his head.

'Um.' Words still aren't coming very easily. 'Hana, you remember Alex.'

She keeps her arms locked in place and narrows her eyes. 'Oh, I *remember* Alex. What I don't remember is why Alex is *here*.'

'He . . . well, he was going to drop off . . .' I'm still searching for a convincing explanation but, as usual, my brain picks that second to conveniently die on me. I look at Alex helplessly.

He gives a minute shrug of his shoulders, and for a moment we just stare at each other. I'm still not used to seeing him, to being around him, and again I have the sensation of falling into his eyes. But this time it's not dizzying. It's the opposite – grounding, like he's whispering to me wordlessly, saying he's there and he's with me and we're fine.

'Tell her,' he says.

Hana leans up against the shelves stocked with toilet paper and canned beans, relaxing her arms just enough so I know she isn't mad, and gives me a look like, *You* better *tell me*.

So I do. I'm not sure how long we have until Jed gets tired of manning the register by himself, so I try to keep it short. I tell her about running into Alex at Roaring Brook Farms; I tell her about swimming out to the buoys with him at East End Beach and what he told me when we were there. I choke a little bit on the word *Invalid* and Hana's eyes widen – just for a second I see a look of alarm flash across her face – but she keeps it together pretty well. I finish by telling her about last night, and going to find her to warn her about the raids, and the dog and how Alex saved me. When I describe hiding out in the shed I get nervous again – I don't tell her about the kissing, but I can't help but think about it – but Hana is openmouthed again at that point, and obviously in shock, so I don't think she notices.

The only thing she says at the end of my story is: 'So you were there? You were there last night?' Her voice is weird and trembly, and I'm worried she's going to start crying again. At the same time I feel a tremendous rush of relief. She's not going to freak out about Alex, or be mad that I didn't tell her.

I nod.

She shakes her head, staring at me like she's never seen me before. 'I can't believe that. I can't believe you snuck out during a raid – for me.'

'Yeah, well.' I shift uncomfortably. It feels like I've been talking for ages, and Hana and Alex have both been staring at me the whole time. My cheeks are flaming hot.

Just then there's a sharp knock on the door that opens to the store, and Jed calls out, 'Lena? Are you in there?'

I gesture frantically to Alex. Hana shoves him behind the door just as Jed starts pushing at it from the other side. He manages to get the door open only a few inches before it collides with the crate of applesauce.

In those few inches of space, I can see one of Jed's eyes blinking at me disapprovingly.

'What are you doing in there?'

Hana pops her head around the door and waves. 'Hi, Jed,' she says cheerfully, once again switching effortlessly into cheerful public mode. 'I just came by to give Lena something. And we started gossiping.'

'We have customers,' Jed says sullenly.

'I'll be out in a second,' I say, trying to match Hana's tone. The fact that Jed and Alex are separated by only a few inches of plywood is terrifying.

Jed grunts and retreats, closing the door again. Hana, Alex, and I look at one another in silence. All three of us exhale at the same time, a collective sigh of relief.

When Alex speaks again, he keeps his voice to a whisper. 'I brought some things for your leg,' he says. He takes the backpack off and sets it on the ground, then starts pulling out peroxide, Bacitracin, bandages, adhesive tape, cotton balls. He kneels in front of me. 'Can I?' he says. I roll up my jeans, and he starts unwinding the strips of T-shirt. I can't believe Hana is standing there watching a boy – an Invalid – touch my skin. I know she would never in a million years have expected it, and I look away, embarrassed and proud at the same time.

Hana inhales sharply once the makeshift bandages come off my leg. Without meaning to I've been squeezing my eyes shut.

'Damn, Lena,' she says. 'That dog got you good.'

'She'll be fine,' Alex says, and the quiet confidence in his voice makes warmth spread through my whole body. I crack open an eye and sneak a look at the back of my calf. My stomach does a flop. It looks like an enormous chunk has been torn out of my leg. A few square inches of skin are just plain missing.

'Maybe you should go to the hospital,' Hana says doubtfully.

'And tell them what?' Alex uncaps the tube of peroxide and begins wetting cotton balls. 'That she got hurt during a raid on an underground party?'

Hana doesn't answer. She knows I can't actually go to the doctor. I'd be strapped down in the labs, or thrown in the Crypts, before I could finish giving my name.

'It doesn't hurt that bad,' I say, which is a lie. Hana again gives me that look, like we've never met before, and I realize that she's actually – and possibly for the first time in our lives – impressed with me. In awe of me, even.

Alex dabs on a thick coat of antibacterial cream and then starts wrestling with the gauze and the adhesive tape. I don't have to ask where he got so many supplies. Another benefit to having security access to the labs, I assume.

Hana drops to her knees. 'You're doing it wrong,' she says, and it's a relief to hear her normal, bossy tone. I almost laugh. 'My cousin's a nurse. Let me.'

She practically elbows him out of the way. Alex shuffles over and raises his hands in surrender. 'Yes, ma'am,' he says, and then winks at me.

Then I do start laughing. Fits of giggling overtake me, and I have to clamp my hands over my mouth to keep from shrieking and gasping and totally blowing our cover. For a second Hana and Alex just stare at me, amazed, but then they look at each other and start grinning stupidly.

I know we're all thinking the same thing.

It's crazy. It's stupid. It's dangerous. But somehow, standing in the sweltering storeroom surrounded by boxes of mac 'n' cheese and canned beets and baby powder, the three of us have become a team.

It's us against them, three against countless thousands. But for some reason, and even though it's absurd, at that moment I feel pretty damn good about our odds.

sixteen

Unhappiness is bondage; therefore, happiness is freedom.
The way to find happiness is through the cure.
Therefore, it is only through the cure that one finds freedom.

– From *Will It Hurt? Common Questions and Answers About the Procedure*, 9th edition, Association of American Scientists, Official USA Government Agency Pamphlet

After that I find a way to see Alex almost every day, even on days I have to work at the store. Sometimes Hana comes along with us. We spend a lot of time at Back Cove, mostly in the evenings after everyone has left. Since Alex is on the books as cured, it's not technically illegal for us to spend time together, but if anyone knew how *much* time we spent together – or saw us laughing and dunking and having water fights or racing down by the marshes – they'd definitely get suspicious. So when we walk through the city we're careful to stand apart, Hana and I on one sidewalk, Alex on the other. Plus, we look for the emptiest streets, the run-down parks, the abandoned houses – places where we won't be seen.

We return to the houses in Deering Highlands. I finally understand how Alex knew how to find the toolshed during the raid night, and how he navigated the halls so perfectly in the pitch-dark. For years he has spent a few nights a month squatting in the abandoned houses; he likes to take a break from the noise and the bustle of Portland. He doesn't say so, but I know squatting must remind him of the Wilds.

One house in particular becomes our favourite: 37 Brooks Street, an old colonial that used to be home to a family of sympathizers. Like many of the other houses in Deering Highlands, the property has been boarded up and fenced off ever since the great rout that emptied the area, but Alex shows us a way to sneak in through a loosened plank covering one of the first-floor windows. It's strange: even though the place has been looted, some of the bigger furniture and the books are still there, and if it weren't for the smoke stains creeping up the walls and ceilings, you might expect the owners to come home any moment.

The first time we go, Hana walks ahead of us calling, 'Hello! Hello!' into the darkened rooms. I shiver in the sudden dark and coolness. After the blinding sunshine outside, it comes as a shock. Alex pulls me closer to him. I'm finally getting used to letting him touch me, and I don't flinch or whip around to look over my shoulder every time he leans in for a kiss.

'Want to dance?' he teases.

'Come on.' I slap him away. It feels weird to talk loudly in such a quiet place. Hana's voice rolls back to us, sounding distant, and I wonder how big the house is, how many rooms there are, all covered in the same thick layer of dust, all draped in shadow.

'I'm serious,' he says. He spreads his arms. 'It's the perfect place for it.'

We're standing in the middle of what must once have been a beautiful living room. It's enormous – bigger than the whole ground floor of Carol and William's apartment. The ceiling stretches up into darkness and a gigantic chandelier hangs above us, winking dully in the limited shafts of light that sneak through the boarded-up windows. If you listen hard, you can hear mice moving quietly in the walls. But somehow it's not gross or frightening. Somehow it's kind of nice, and it makes me think of woods and endless cycles of growth and death and regrowth – like what we're really hearing is the house folding down around us, centimeter by centimeter.

'There's no music,' I say.

He shrugs, winks, holds out his hand. 'Music is overrated,' he says.

I let him draw me toward him so we're standing chest to chest. He's so much taller than I am, my head barely reaches his shoulder, and I can feel his heart drumming through his chest, and it gives us all the rhythm we need.

The best part of 37 Brooks is the garden in the back. An enormous overgrown lawn winds between ancient trees, so thick and gnarled and knotted their arms twist overhead and form a canopy. The sunlight filters through the trees and spots the grass a pale white. The whole garden feels as cool and quiet as the library at school. Alex brings a blanket and leaves it inside the house. Whenever we come we take it and shake it out on the grass, and all three of us lie there, sometimes for hours, talking and laughing about nothing in particular. Sometimes Hana or Alex buys some food for a picnic, and one time I manage to swipe three cans of soda and a whole carton of candy bars from my uncle's store, and we get totally crazy on a sugar high and play games like we did when we were little – hide-and-seek and tag and leapfrog.

Some of the tree trunks are as wide as four garbage pails mashed together, and I take a picture of Hana, laughing, trying to fit her arms around one of them. Alex says the trees must have been here for hundreds of years, which makes Hana and me go silent. That means they were here *before* – before the borders were shut down, before the walls were put up, before the disease was driven into the Wilds. When he says it, something aches in my throat. I wish I could know what it was like then.

Most of the time, though, Alex and I spend time alone and Hana covers for us. After weeks and weeks of not seeing her at all, suddenly I'm going to Hana's every single day – and sometimes twice in one day (when I see Alex; and then when I *actually* see Hana). Fortunately, my aunt doesn't pry. I think she assumes we had a fight and are making up for lost time now, which is kind of true anyway and suits me fine. I'm happier than I can ever remember being. I'm happier than I can ever remember even dreaming of being, and when I tell Hana I can never in a million years repay her for covering for me, she just crooks her mouth into a smile and says, 'You've already repaid me.' I'm not sure what she means by that, but I'm just glad to have her back on my side.

When Alex and I are alone we don't do much – just sit and talk – but still time seems to shrivel away, fast as paper catching on fire. One minute it's three o'clock in the afternoon. The next minute, I swear, the light is draining from the sky and it's almost curfew.

Alex tells me stories about his life: about his 'aunt' and 'uncle,' and some of the work they do, although he's still pretty vague about what the sympathizers and the Invalids are aiming for and how they're working to achieve it. That's okay. I'm not sure I want to know. When he mentions the need for resistance, there is a tightness to his voice, and anger coiling underneath his words. At those times, and only for a few seconds, I'm still afraid of him, still hear the word *Invalid* drumming in my ear.

But mostly Alex tells me normal stuff, about his aunt's Frito pie and how whenever they get together his uncle gets a little too tipsy and tells the same stories about the past over and over. They're both cured, and when I ask him whether they aren't happier now, he shrugs and says, 'They miss the pain, too.'

This seems incredible to me, and he looks at me out of the corner of his eye and says, 'That's when you really lose people, you know. When the pain passes.'

Mostly, though, he talks about the Wilds and the people who live there, and I lay my head on his chest and close my eyes and dream of it: of a woman everyone calls Crazy Caitlin, who makes enormous wind chimes out of scrap metal and crushed soda cans; of Grandpa Jones, who must be at least ninety but still hikes through the woods every day, foraging for berries and wild animals to eat; of campfires outside and sleeping under the stars and staying up late to sing and talk and eat, while the night sky goes smudgy with smoke.

I know that he still goes back there sometimes, and I know

he still considers it his real home. He nearly says as much when I tell him one time that I'm sorry I can't go home with him to check out his studio on Forsyth Street, where he has lived since starting at the university – if any of his neighbors saw me going into the building with him, we'd be finished. But he corrects me really quickly, 'That's not home.'

He admits that he and the other Invalids have found a way to get in and out of the Wilds, but when I press him for details he clams up.

'Someday maybe you'll see,' is all he says, and I'm equal parts terrified and thrilled.

I ask him about my uncle, who escaped before he could stand trial, and Alex frowns and shakes his head.

'Hardly anybody goes by a real name in the Wilds,' he says, shrugging. 'He doesn't sound familiar, though.' But he explains that there are thousands and thousands of settlements all around the country. My uncle could have gone anywhere – north or south or west. At least we know he didn't go east; he would have ended up in the ocean. Alex tells me that there are at least as many square miles of wilderness in the USA as there are recognized cities. This is so incredible to me that for a while I can't believe it, and when I tell Hana she can't believe it either.

Alex is a good listener, too, and can stay silent for hours while I tell him about growing up in Carol's house, and how everybody thinks Grace can't speak and only I know the truth. He laughs out loud when I describe Jenny, and her pinched look and old-lady face and habit of looking down her nose at me like *I'm* the nine-year-old.

I feel comfortable talking about my mother with him too, and how it used to be when she was alive and it was just the three of us – me, her, and Rachel. I tell him about the sock hops and the way my mom used to sing us lullabies, even though I can only remember a few snatches of the songs. Maybe it's the way he listens so quietly, and stares at me steadily with his eyes bright and warm, and never judges me. One time I even tell him about the last thing my mom ever said to me, and he just sits and rubs my back when suddenly I feel like I'm about to cry. The feeling passes. The warmth of his hands draws it out of me.

And, of course, we kiss. We kiss so much that when we're not kissing it feels weird, like I get used to breathing through his lips and into his mouth.

Slowly, as we get more comfortable, I start to explore other parts of his body too. The delicate structure of his ribs under his skin, his chest and shoulders like chiseled stone, the soft curls of pale hair on his legs, the way his skin always smells a little bit like the ocean – all beautiful and strange. Even crazier is that I let him look at me, too. First I'll only let him pull my shirt aside and kiss my collarbone and shoulders. Then I let him draw my whole shirt over my head and lie me down in the bright sunshine and just stare at me. The first time I'm shaking. I keep having the urge to cross my hands over my chest, to cover up my breasts, to hide. I'm suddenly aware of how pale I look in the sunshine, and how many moles I have spotting up and down my chest, and I just know he's looking at me thinking I'm wrong or deformed.

But then he breathes, 'Beautiful,' and when his eyes meet mine I know that he really, truly means it.

That night, for the first time in my life, I stand in front of the bathroom mirror and don't see an in-between girl. For the first time, with my hair swept back and my nightgown slipping off one shoulder and my eyes glowing, I believe what Alex said. I am beautiful.

But it's not just me. *Everything* looks beautiful. *The Book of Shhh* says that *deliria* alters your perception, disables your ability to reason clearly, impairs you from making sound judgments. But it does not tell you this: that love will turn the whole world into something greater than itself. Even the dump, shimmering in the heat, an enormous mound of scrap metal and melting plastic and stinking things, seems strange and miraculous, like some alien world transported to earth. In the morning light the seagulls perched on the roof of city hall look like they've been coated in thick white paint; as they light up against the pale blue sky I think I've never seen anything so sharp and clear and pretty in my life. Rainstorms are incredible: falling shards of glass, the air full of diamonds. The wind whispers Alex's name and the ocean repeats it; the swaying trees make me think of dancing. Everything I see and touch reminds me of him, and so everything I see and touch is perfect.

The Book of Shhh also doesn't mention the way that time will start to run away from you.

Time jumps. It leaps. It pours away like water through fingers. Every time I come down to the kitchen and see that the calendar has flipped forward yet another day I refuse to believe it. A sick feeling grows in my stomach, a leaden sensation that gets heavier every day.

Thirty-three days until the procedure.

Thirty-two days.

Thirty days.

And in-between, snapshots, moments, mere seconds; Alex smearing chocolate ice cream on my nose after I've complained

I'm too hot; the heavy drone of bees circling above us in the garden; a neat line of ants marching quietly over the remains of our picnic; Alex's fingers in my hair; the curve of his elbow under my head; Alex whispering, 'I wish you could stay with me,' while another day bleeds out on the horizon, red and pink and gold; staring up at the sky, inventing shapes for the clouds: a turtle wearing a hat, a mole carrying a zucchini, a goldfish chasing a rabbit that is running for its life.

Snapshots, moments, mere seconds: as fragile and beautiful and hopeless as a single butterfly, flapping on against a gathering wind.

seventeen

There has been significant debate in the scientific community about whether desire is a symptom of a system infected with amor deliria nervosa, or a precondition of the disease itself. It is unanimously agreed, however, that love and desire enjoy a symbiotic relationship, meaning that one cannot exist without the other. Desire is enemy to contentment; desire is illness, a feverish brain. Who can be considered healthy who wants? The very word want suggests a lack, an impoverishment, and that is what desire is: an impoverishment of the brain, a flaw, a mistake. Fortunately, that can now be corrected.

– From *The Roots and Repercussions of* Amor Deliria Nervosa *on Cognitive Functioning*, 4th edition, by Dr. Phillip Berryman

August makes itself comfortable in Portland, breathes its hot and stinking breath over everything. The streets are unbearable during the day, the sun unrelenting, and people rush the parks and beaches, desperate for shade or breeze. It gets harder to see Alex. East End Beach – normally unpopular – is packed most of the time, even in the evenings after I get off work. Twice I show up to meet him and it's too dangerous for us to talk or make a sign to each other, except for the quick nod that might pass between two strangers. Instead we lay out beach towels fifteen feet apart on the sand. He slips on his headphones and I pretend to read. Whenever our eyes meet my whole body lights up like he's lying right next to me, rubbing his hand on my back, and even though he keeps a straight face, I can tell by his eyes that he's smiling. Nothing has ever been so painful or delicious as being so close to him and being unable to do anything about it: like eating ice cream so fast on a hot day you get a splitting headache. I start to understand what Alex said about his "aunt" and "uncle" – about how they even missed the pain after their procedures. Somehow, the pain only makes it better, more intense, more worth it.

Since the beaches are out, we stick to 37 Brooks. The garden is suffering from the heat. It hasn't rained in more than a week, and the sunlight filtering through the trees – which in July fell softly, like the lightest footstep – now slices daggerlike through the canopy of trees, turning the grass brown. Even the bees seem drunk in the heat, circling slowly, colliding, hitting up against the withering flowers before thudding to the ground, then starting dazedly back into the air.

One afternoon Alex and I are lying on the blanket. I'm on my back; the sky above me seems to break apart into shifting patterns of blue and green and white. Alex is lying on his stomach and seems nervous about something. He keeps lighting matches, watching them flare, and blowing them out only when they're almost at his fingertips. I think about what he told me that time in the shed: his anger about coming to Portland, the fact that he used to burn things.

There is so much about him I don't know – so much past and history buried somewhere inside of him. He has had to learn to hide it, even more than most of us. Somewhere, I think, there is a center to him. It glows like a coal being slowly crushed into diamond, weighed down by layers and layers of surface.

So much I haven't asked him, and so much we never talk about. Yet in other ways I feel like I *do* know him, and have always known him, without having to be told anything at all.

'It must be nice to be in the Wilds right now,' I blurt out, just for something to say. Alex turns to look at me, and I stammer quickly, 'I mean – it must be cooler there. Because of all the trees and shade.'

'It is.' He props himself up on one elbow. I close my eyes and see spots of colour and light dancing behind my lids. For a second Alex doesn't say anything, but I can feel him watching me. 'We could go there,' he says at last.

I think he must be joking, so I start to laugh. He stays quiet, though, and when I open my eyes I see his face is totally composed.

'You're not serious,' I say, but already a deep well of fear has opened inside of me and I know that he is. Somehow I know, too, that this is why he's been acting strange all day: he misses the Wilds.

'We could go if you want to.' He looks at me for a beat longer and then rolls onto his back. 'We could go tomorrow. After your shift.'

'But how would we—' I start to say. He cuts me off.

'Leave that to me.' For a moment his eyes look deeper and darker than I've ever seen them, like tunnels. 'Do you want to?'

It feels wrong to talk about it so casually, lying on the blanket, so I sit up. Crossing the border is a capital offense, punishable by death. And even though I know that Alex still does it sometimes, the enormity of the risk hasn't really hit me until now. 'There's no way,' I say, almost in a whisper. 'It's impossible. The fence – and the guards – and the *guns . . .*'

'I told you. Leave that to me.' He sits up too, reaches out and cups my face quickly, smiling. 'Anything's possible, Lena,' he says, one of his favourite expressions. The fear recedes. I feel so safe with him. I can't believe that anything bad can happen when we're together. 'A few hours,' he says. 'Just to see.'

I look away. 'I don't know.' My throat feels parched; the words tear at my throat as they come out.

Alex leans forward, gives me a quick kiss on the shoulder, and lies down again. 'No big deal,' he says, throwing one arm over his eyes to shield them from the sun. 'I just thought you might be curious, that's all.'

'I am curious. But . . .'

'Lena, it's fine if you don't want to go. Seriously. It was just an idea.'

I nod. Even though my legs are sticky with sweat, I hug them to my chest. I feel incredibly relieved but also disappointed. I have a sudden memory of the time Rachel dared me to do a back dive off the pier at Willard Beach and I stood trembling at its edge, too scared to jump. Eventually she let me off the hook, bending down to whisper, 'It's okay, Lena-Loo. You're not ready.' All I'd wanted was to get away from the edge of the pier, but as we walked back onto the beach I felt sick and ashamed.

That's when I realize: 'I do want to go,' I burst out.

Alex removes his arm. 'For real?'

I nod, too afraid to say the words again. I'm worried if I open my mouth I'll take it back.

Alex sits up slowly. I thought he'd be more excited, but he doesn't smile. He just chews on the inside of his lip and looks away. 'It means breaking curfew.'

'It means breaking a *lot* of rules.'

He looks at me then, and his face is so full of concern it makes something ache deep inside of me. 'Listen, Lena.' He looks down and rearranges the pile of matches he has made, placing them neatly side by side. 'Maybe it's not such a good idea. If we get caught – I mean, if *you* got caught—' He sucks in a deep breath. 'I mean, if anything ever happened to you, I could never forgive myself.'

'I trust you,' I say, and mean it 150 percent.

He still won't look at me. 'Yeah, but . . . the penalty for crossing over . . .' He takes another deep breath. 'The penalty for crossing over is . . .' At the last second he can't say *death*.

'Hey.' I nudge him gently. It's an incredible thing, how you can feel so taken care of by someone and yet feel, also, like you would die or do anything just for the chance to protect him back. 'I know the rules. I've been living here longer than you have.'

He cracks a smile then. He nudges me back. 'Hardly.'

'Born and raised. You're a transplant.' I nudge him again, a little harder, and he laughs and tries to catch hold of my arm. I squirm away, giggling, and he stretches out to tickle my stomach. 'Country bumpkin!' I squeal, as he grabs out and wrestles me back onto the blanket, laughing.

'City slicker,' he says, rolling over on top of me, and then kisses me. Everything dissolves: heat, explosions of colour, floating.

We agree to meet at Back Cove the next evening, a Wednesday; since I won't be working again until Saturday, it should be relatively easy to get Carol to allow me to sleep over at Hana's. Alex walks me through some of the major points of the plan. Crossing over isn't *impossible*, but hardly anyone risks it. I guess the whole punishable-by-death thing isn't really a big attraction.

I don't see how we'll ever make it past the electrified fence, but Alex explains that only certain portions of it are actually electrified. Pumping electricity through miles and miles of fence is too expensive, so relatively few stretches of the fence are actually 'online': the remainder of the fence is no more dangerous than the one that encircles the playground at Deering Oaks Park. But as long as everyone *believes* that the whole thing is juiced up with enough kilowattage to fry a person like an egg in a pan, the fence is serving its purpose just fine.

'Smoke and mirrors, all of it,' Alex says, waving his hand vaguely. I assume he means Portland, the laws, maybe all of the USA. When he gets serious a little crease forms between his eyebrows, a tiny comma, and it's the cutest thing I've ever seen. I try to stay focused.

'I still don't see how you know all this,' I say. 'I mean, how did you guys figure it out? Did you just keep running people at the fence, to see whether they got fried in certain places?'

Alex cracks a tiny smile. 'Trade secrets. But I can tell you there were some observational experiments involving wild animals.' He raises his eyebrows. 'Ever eaten fried beaver?'

'Ew.'

'Or fried skunk?'

'Now you're just *trying* to gross me out.'

There are more of us than you think: that's another one of Alex's favourite expressions, his constant refrain. Sympathizers everywhere, uncured *and* cured, positioned as regulators, police officers, government officials, scientists. That's how we'll get past the guard huts, he tells me. One of the most active sympathizers in Portland is matched with the guard who works the night shift at the northern tip of Tukey's Bridge, right where we'll be crossing. She and Alex have developed a sign. On nights he wants to cross over, he leaves a certain flyer in her mailbox, the stupid photocopied kind that takeout delis and dry cleaners give out. This one advertises for a free eye exam with Dr. Swild (which seems pretty obvious to me, but Alex says that resisters and sympathizers live with so much stress they need to be allowed their little private jokes) and whenever she finds it she makes sure to put an extra-large dose of Valium in the coffee she makes for her husband to drink during his shift.

'Poor guy,' Alex says, grinning. 'No matter how much coffee he drinks, he just can't seem to stay awake.' I can tell how much the resistance means to him, and how proud he is of the fact that it is there, healthy, thriving, shooting its arms through Portland. I try to smile, but my cheeks feel stiff. It still blows my mind that everything I've been taught is so wrong, and it's still hard for me to think of the sympathizers and resisters as allies and not enemies.

But sneaking over the border will make me one of them beyond a shadow of a doubt. At the same time, I can't seriously consider backing out now. I *want* to go; and if I'm honest with myself, I became a sympathizer a long time ago, when Alex asked me whether I wanted to meet him at Back Cove and I said yes. I seem to have only hazy memories of the girl I was before then – the girl who always did what she was told and never lied and counted the days until her procedure with feelings of excitement, not horror and dread. The girl who was afraid of everyone and everything. The girl who was afraid of herself.

When I get home from the store the next day, I make a big point of asking Carol if I can borrow her cell phone. Then I text Hana: *Sleepover 2nite w A?* This has been our code recently whenever I need her to cover for me. We've told Carol we've been spending a lot of time with Allison Doveney, who recently graduated with us. The Doveneys are even richer than Hana's family, and Allison is a stuck-up bitch. Hana originally protested against using her as the mysterious 'A,' on the grounds that she didn't even like to think about pretend hanging out with her, but I convinced her in the end. Carol would never call the Doveneys to check up on me. She'd be too intimidated, and probably embarrassed – my family is impure, tainted by Marcia's husband's defection and, of course, by my mother, and Mr. Doveney is the president and founder of the Portland chapter of the DFA, Deliria-Free America. Allison Doveney could hardly stand to look at me when we were in school together, and way back in elementary school, after my mother died, she asked to switch desks to be farther away from me, telling the teacher that I smelled like something dying.

Hana's response comes almost immediately. *U got it. C u tonight.*

I wonder what Allison would think if she knew I'd been

using her as cover for my boyfriend. She would freak out for sure, and the thought makes me smile.

A little before eight o'clock I come downstairs with my overnight bag slung conspicuously over my shoulder. I've even let a little bit of my pajamas poke out. I've packed the whole bag exactly as I would have if I were really going to Hana's. When Carol gives me a flitting smile and tells me to have a good time, I feel a brief pang of guilt. I lie so often and so easily now.

But it's not enough to stop me. Once outside I head toward the West End, just in case Jenny or Carol is watching from the windows. Only after I reach Spring Street do I double back toward Deering Avenue and head for 37 Brooks. The walk is long, and I make it to Deering Highlands just as the last of the light is swirling out of the sky. As always, the streets here are deserted. I push through the rusted metal gate that surrounds the property, slide aside the loose slats covering one first-floor window, and hoist myself into the house.

The darkness surprises me, and for a moment I stand there, blinking, until my eyes adjust to the low light. The air feels sticky, and stale, and the house smells like mildew. Various shapes begin to emerge, and I make my way into the living room, and to the mold-spotted couch. Its springs are busted and half of its stuffing has been torn out, probably by mice, but you can tell that once it must have been pretty – elegant, even.

I fish my clock out from my bag and set the alarm for eleven thirty. It's going to be a long night. Then I stretch out on the bumpy couch, balling my backpack underneath my head. It's not the world's most comfortable pillow, but it will do.

I close my eyes and let the sounds of the mice scrabbling, and the low groans and mysterious tickings of the walls, lull me to sleep.

I wake up in the darkness from a nightmare about my mother. I sit up straight, and for one panicked second don't know where I am. The faulty springs squeal underneath me and then I remember: 37 Brooks. I fumble for my alarm clock and see that it's already 11:20. I know I should get up but I still feel groggy from the heat and the dream, and for a few more moments I just sit there, taking deep breaths. I'm sweating; the hair is sticking to the back of my neck.

My dream was the one I usually have but this time reversed: I was floating in the ocean, treading water, watching my mother perched on a crumbling ledge hundreds and hundreds of feet above me – so far I couldn't make out any of her features, just the blurry lines of her silhouette, framed against the sun. I was trying to call out a warning to her, trying to lift my arms and wave at her to go back, away from the edge, but the more I struggled the more the water seemed to drag at me and hold me back, the consistency of glue, suctioning my arms in place and oozing in my throat to freeze the words there. And all the time sand was drifting around me like snow, and I knew at any second she would fall and smash her head on the jagged rocks, which poked up through the water like sharpened fingernails.

Then she was falling, flailing, a black spot growing bigger and bigger against the blazing sun, and I was trying to scream but I couldn't, and as the figure grew larger I realized it wasn't my mother headed for the rocks.

It was Alex.

That's when I woke up.

I finally stand, slightly dizzy, trying to ignore a feeling of dread. I go slowly, gropingly, to the window, and am relieved once I'm outside, even though I'm in more danger on the streets. But at least there's a bit of a breeze. The atmosphere in the house was stifling.

Alex is already waiting for me when I arrive at Back Cove, crouching in the shadows cast by a group of trees that stand near the old parking lot. He is so perfectly concealed that I almost trip over him. He reaches up and draws me down into a crouch. In the moonlight his eyes seem to glow, like a cat's.

He gestures silently across Back Cove, to the line of twinkling lights just before the border: the guard huts. From a distance they look like a line of bright white lanterns strung up for a nighttime picnic – cheerful, almost. Twenty feet beyond the security points is the actual fence, and beyond the fence, the Wilds. They've never looked quite so strange to me as they do now, dancing and swaying in the wind. I'm glad Alex and I agreed not to speak until we crossed over. The lump in my throat is making it difficult to breathe, much less say anything.

We'll be crossing over at the tip of Tukey's Bridge, on the northeast point of the cove: if we were swimming, a direct diagonal from our meet-up point. Alex pumps my hand three times. That's our signal to move.

I follow him as we skirt the perimeter of the cove, being careful to avoid the marshland; it looks deceptively like grass, especially in the dark, but you can get sucked down almost knee deep before you realize the difference. Alex darts from shadow to shadow, moving noiselessly on the grass. In places he seems to vanish completely before my eyes, to melt into darkness.

As we loop around to the north side of the cove, the guard stations begin to outline themselves more clearly – becoming actual buildings, one-room huts made of concrete and bullet-proof glass.

Sweat pricks up on my palms and the lump in my throat seems to quadruple in size, until I feel like I'm being strangled. I suddenly see how stupid our plan is. A hundred – a thousand! – things could go wrong. The guard in number twenty-one might not have had his coffee yet – or he might have had it, but not enough to knock him out – or the Valium might not have kicked in. And even if he is asleep, Alex could have been wrong about the parts of the fence that aren't electrified; or the city might have pumped on the power, just for the night.

I'm so scared I feel like I might faint. I want to get Alex's attention and scream that we have to turn around, call the whole thing off, but he's still moving swiftly up ahead of me, and screaming anything or making any noise at all will bring the guards down on us for sure. And guards make the regulators look like little kids playing cops and robbers. Regulators and raiders have nightsticks and dogs; guards have rifles and tear gas.

We finally reach the northern arm of the cove. Alex drops down behind one of the larger trees and waits for me to catch up. I go into a crouch next to him. This is my last opportunity to tell him I want to go back. But I can't speak, and when I try to shake my head no, nothing happens. I feel like I'm back in my dream, getting slurped into the dark, floundering like an insect stuck in a bowl of honey.

Maybe Alex can tell how frightened I am. He leans forward and fumbles for a moment, trying to find my ear. His mouth bumps once on my neck and grazes my cheek lightly – which despite my panic makes me shiver with pleasure – and then skims my earlobe. 'It's going to be okay,' he whispers, and I feel slightly better. Nothing bad will happen when I'm with Alex.

Then we're up again. We dart forward at intervals, sprinting silently from one tree to the next and then pausing while Alex listens and makes sure there has been no change, no shouts or sounds of approaching footsteps. The moments of exposure – of dashing from cover to cover – grow longer as the trees begin to thin out, and the whole time we're getting closer and closer to the line where the fringe of grass and growth disappears altogether and we will have to move out in the open, completely vulnerable. It is a distance of only about fifty feet from the last bush to the fence, but as far as I'm concerned it might as well be a lake of burning fire.

Beyond the torn-up remains of a road that existed before Portland was enclosed is the fence itself: looming, silver in the moonlight, like some enormous spiderweb. A place where things stick, get caught, are eaten. Alex has told me to take my time, to focus when I pick my way over the barbed wire at the top, but I can't help but picture myself impaled on all of those sharp, spiny barbs.

And then, suddenly, we are out – past the limited protection offered by the trees, moving quickly over the loose gravel and shale of the old road. Alex moves ahead of me, bent nearly double, and I stoop as low as I can, but it doesn't make me feel any less exposed. Fear screams, slams into me from all sides at once; I have never known anything like it.

I'm not sure whether the wind picks up at that second or whether it's just the terror cutting through me, but my whole body feels like ice.

The darkness seems to come alive on all sides of us, full of darting shadows and malicious, looming shapes, ready to turn into a guard any second, and I picture the silence suddenly punctuated by screams, sighs, horns, bullets. I picture blooming pain, and bright lights. The world seems to transform into a series of disconnected images: a bright white circle of light surrounding guard hut twenty-one, which expands ever outward, as though hungry and ready to swallow us; inside, a guard slumped backward in his chair, mouth open, sleeping; Alex turning to me, smiling – is it possible he's *smiling*? – stones dancing underneath my feet. Everything feels far away, as unreal and insubstantial as a shadow cast by a flame. Even *I* don't feel real, can't feel myself breathing or moving, though I must be doing both.

And then just like that we're at the fence. Alex springs into the air, and for a second he pauses there. I want to scream *Stop! Stop!* I picture the crack and sizzle as his body connects with fifty thousand volts of electricity, but then he lands on the fence and the fence sways silently: dead and cold, just like he said.

I should be climbing up after him, but I can't. Not immediately. A feeling of wonder creeps over me, slowly pushing out the fear. I've been terrified of the border fence since I was a baby. I've never gotten within five feet of the fence. We've been warned not to, had it drilled into us. They told us we would fry; told us it would make our hearts go haywire, kill us instantly. Now I reach out and lace my hand through the chain-link, run my fingers over it. Dead and cold and harmless, the same kind of fence the city uses for playgrounds and schoolyards. In that second it really hits me how deep and complex the lies are, how they run through Portland like sewers, backing up into everything, filling the city with stench: the whole city built and constructed within a perimeter of lies.

Alex is a fast climber; he's made it halfway up the fence. He looks over his shoulder and sees that I'm still standing there like an idiot, not moving. He jerks his head at me like, *What are you doing?*

I put my hand out to the fence again and then immediately jerk it back: A shock runs through me all at once, but it has nothing to do with the voltage that should be pumping there. Something has just occurred to me.

They've lied about everything – about the fence, and the existence of the Invalids, about a million other things besides. They told us the raids were carried out for our own protection. They told us the regulators were only interested in keeping the peace.

They told us that love was a disease. They told us it would kill us in the end.

For the very first time I realize that this, too, might be a lie.

Alex rocks carefully back and forth on the fence so that it sways a little. I glance up, and he gestures to me again. We're not safe. It's time to move. I reach up and hoist myself onto the fence and start climbing. Being on the fence is even worse, in some ways, than being out in the open on the gravel. At least there we had more control – we could have seen if a guard was patrolling, could have hurried back to the cove and hoped to lose him in the darkness and the trees. A small hope, but hope nonetheless. Here we have our backs turned to the guard huts, and I feel like I'm a gigantic moving target with a big sign on my back saying SHOOT ME.

Alex reaches the top before me, and I watch him pick his way slowly, painstakingly, around the loops of barbed wire. He makes it over and lowers himself carefully down the other side, climbing backward a few feet and pausing to wait for me. I follow his motions exactly. I'm shaking by this point, from fear and exertion, but I manage to pass over the top of the fence and then I'm climbing down the other side. My feet hit the ground. Alex takes my hand and pulls me quickly into the woods, away from the border.

Into the Wilds.

eighteen

Mary bring out your umbrella –
The sun shines down on this fine, fine day
But the ashes raining down forever
Are going to turn your hair to grey.

Mary keep your oars a-steady
Sail away on the rising flood
Keep your candle at the ready
Red tides can't be told from blood.

– 'Miss Mary' (a common child's clapping game,
dating from the time of the blitz), from
Pattycake and Beyond: A History of Play

The lights from the guard hut get suctioned away all at once like they've been sealed back behind a vault. Trees close in around us, leaves and bushes press on me from all sides, brushing my face and shins and shoulders like thousands of dark hands, and from all around me a strange cacophony starts up, of fluttering things and owls hooting and animals scrabbling in the underbrush. The air smells so thickly of flowers and life it feels textured, like a curtain you could pull apart. It's pitch-black. I can't even see Alex in front of me now, can just feel his hand in mine, pulling.

I think I might be even more frightened now than I was making the crossing, and I tug on Alex's hand, willing him to understand me and stop.

'A little farther,' comes his voice, from the darkness ahead of me. He tugs me on. We go slowly, though, and I hear twigs snapping and the rustle of tree branches, and I know that Alex is feeling his way, trying to clear a path for us. It seems that we move forward by inches, but it's amazing how quickly we've lost sight of the border and everything on the other side of it, as though they've never existed at all. Behind me is blackness. It's like being underground.

'Alex—' I start to say. My voice comes out strange and strangled-sounding.

'Stop,' he says. 'Wait.' He lets go of my hand, and I let out a little shriek without meaning to. Then his hands are fumbling on my arms, and his mouth bumps against my nose as he kisses me.

'It's okay,' he says. He's speaking almost at a normal volume now, so I guess we're safe. 'I'm not going anywhere. I just have to find this damn flashlight, okay?'

'Yeah, okay.' I struggle to breathe normally, feeling stupid. I wonder if Alex regrets bringing me. I haven't exactly been Miss Courageous.

As though he can read my mind, Alex gives me a second small peck, this time near the corner of my lips. I guess his eyes haven't adjusted to the dark either. 'You're doing great,' he says.

Then I hear him rustling in the branches all around us, muttering little curses under his breath, a monologue I don't quite follow. A minute later he lets out a quick, excited yelp, and a second after that a broad beam of light cuts upward, illuminating the densely packed trees and growth all around us.

'Found it,' Alex says, grinning, showing off the flashlight to me. He directs the light down to a rusty toolbox half buried in the ground. 'We leave it there, for the crossers,' he explains. 'Ready?'

I nod. I feel much better now that we can see where we're going. The branches above us form a canopy that reminds me of the vaulted ceiling of St. Paul's Cathedral, where I used to sit in Sunday school to hear lectures about atoms and probabilities and God's order. The leaves rustle and shake all around us, a constantly shifting pattern of greens and blacks, set dancing as countless unseen things hurry and skip from branch to branch. Every so often Alex's flashlight is reflected for a brief second in a pair of bright wide blinking eyes, which watch us solemnly from within the mass of foliage before vanishing once again into the dark. It's incredible. I've never seen anything like it – all this life pushing everywhere, growing, as though at every second it's expanding and thrusting upward, and I can't really explain it but it makes me feel small and kind of silly, like I'm trespassing on property owned by someone way older and more important than myself.

Alex walks more surely now, occasionally sweeping a branch out of the way so I can pass underneath it, or swatting at the branches blocking our way, but we're not following any path that I can see, and after fifteen minutes I begin to fear that we're just turning in circles, or going deeper and deeper into the woods without any real destination. I'm about to ask him how he knows where we're going when I notice that every so often he hesitates and sweeps his flashlight over the tree trunks that surround us like tall, ghostly silhouettes. Some of them, I see, are marked with a swath of blue paint.

'The paint . . . ,' I say.

Alex shoots me a look over his shoulder. 'Our road map,' he says, pressing on, and then adds, 'you don't want to get lost in here, trust me.'

And then, abruptly, the trees just peter out. One second we're in the middle of the forest, penned in on all sides, and the next we're stepping out onto a paved road, a ribbon of concrete lit silver by the moonlight like a ribbed tongue.

The road is filled with holes, and cracked and buckled in places, so we have to step around enormous piles of concrete rubble. It winds up a long, low hill, and then disappears over the hill's crest, where another black fringe of trees begins.

'Give me your hand,' Alex says. He's whispering again and without knowing why, I'm glad of it. For some reason, I feel as though I've just entered a cemetery. On either side of the road are gigantic clearings, covered in waist-high grasses that sing and whisper against one another, and some thin, young trees, which look frail and exposed in the middle of all of that openness. There seem to be some beams, too – enormous beams of timber piled on top of one another, and twists of things that look metallic, gleaming and glinting in the grass.

'What is this?' I whisper to Alex, but just after I ask the question a little scream builds in my throat and I see, and I know.

In the middle of one of the fields of whispering grass is a large blue truck, perfectly intact, like someone might have driven up just to have a picnic.

'This *was* a street,' Alex says. His voice has turned tense. 'Destroyed during the blitz. There are thousands and thousands of them, all across the country. Bombed out, totally destroyed.'

I shiver. No wonder I felt like I was walking through a graveyard. I am, in a way. The blitz was a yearlong campaign that happened long before my birth, when my mom was still a baby. It was supposed to have gotten rid of all the Invalids, and any resisters who didn't want to leave their homes and move into an approved community. My mother once said that her earliest memories were all clouded by the sound of bombs and the smell of smoke. She said for years the smell of fire continued to drift over the city, and every time the wind blew it would bring with it a covering of ash.

We go on walking. I feel like I could cry. Being here, seeing this, it's nothing like what I was taught in my history classes: smiling pilots giving the thumbs-up, people cheering at the borders because we were at last safe, houses incinerated neatly, with no mess, as though they were just blipped off a computer screen. In the history books there were no people, really, who lived in these houses; they were shadows, wraiths, unreal. But as Alex and I walk hand in hand down the bombed-out road, I understand that it wasn't like that at all. There was mess and stink and blood and the smell of skin burning. There were people: people standing and eating, talking on the phone, frying eggs or singing in the shower. I'm overwhelmed with sadness for everything that was lost, and filled with anger toward the people who took it away.

My people – or at least, my *old* people. I don't know who I am anymore, or where I belong.

That's not totally true. Alex. I know I belong with Alex.

A little farther up the hill we come across a trim white house standing in the middle of a field. Somehow it escaped the blitz unscathed, and other than a shutter that has become detached and is now hanging at a crazy angle, tapping lightly in the wind, it could be any house in Portland. It looks so strange standing there in the middle of all of that emptiness, surrounded by the shrapnel of disintegrated neighbors. It looks tiny all on its own, like a single lamb that has gotten lost in the wrong pasture.

'Does anyone stay there now?' I ask Alex.

'Sometimes people squat, when it's rainy or freezing. Only the roamers, though – the Invalids who always move around.' Again he pauses for a fraction of a second before he says *Invalids*, grimacing like the word tastes bad in his mouth. 'We pretty much stay away from here. People say the bombers might come back and finish off the job. But mostly it's just superstition. People think the house is bad luck.' He gives me a tight smile. 'It's been totally cleaned out, though. Beds, blankets, clothes – everything. I got my dishes there.'

Earlier, Alex told me he had his own special place in the Wilds, but when I pressed him for details he clammed up and told me I'd have to wait and see. It's still weird to think of people living out here, in the middle of all this vastness, needing dishes and blankets and normal things like that.

'This way.'

Alex pulls me off the road and draws me toward the woods again. I'm actually happy to be back in the trees. There was a heaviness to that strange, open space, with its single house and rusting truck and splintered buildings, a gash cut in the surface of the world.

This time we follow a fairly well-worn path. The trees are still splattered with blue paint at intervals, but it doesn't seem as though Alex needs to consult them. We go quickly, single file. The trees have been shoved away here, and much of the underbrush has been cleared so the walk is much easier. Beneath my feet the dirt has been tamped down over time by the pressure of dozens of feet. My heart starts thumping heavily against my ribs. I can tell we're getting close.

Alex turns around to face me, so abruptly I almost slam into him. He clicks the flashlight off, and in the sudden darkness strange shapes seem to rise up, take form, swirl away.

'Close your eyes,' he says, and I can tell he's smiling.

'Why bother? I can't see anything.'

I can practically hear him roll his eyes. 'Come on, Lena.'

'Fine.' I close my eyes and he takes my hands in both of his. Then he pulls me forward another twenty feet, murmuring things like, 'Step up. There's a rock,' or 'A little to the left.' The whole time a fluttery, nervous feeling builds inside of me. We stop, finally, and Alex drops my hands.

'We're here,' he says. I can hear the excitement in his voice. 'Open up.'

I do, and for a moment can't speak. I open my mouth several times and have to shut it again after all that emerges is a high-pitched squeak.

'Well?' Alex fidgets next to me. 'What do you think?'

Finally I stutter out, 'It's – it's *real*.'

Alex snorts. 'Of course it's real.'

'I mean, it's amazing.' I take a few steps forward. Now that

I'm here I'm not sure what, exactly, I was imagining the Wilds would be like – but whatever it was, it wasn't this. A long, broad clearing cuts through the woods, although in places the trees have begun to crowd in again, pushing slender stalks toward the sky, which stretches above us, a vast and glittering canopy, the moon sitting bright and huge and swollen at its center. Wild roses encircle a dented sign, faded nearly to illegibility. I can just make out the words CREST VILLAGE MOBILE PARK. The clearing is full of dozens of trailers, as well as more creative residences: tarps stretched between trees, with blankets and shower curtains to serve as front doors; rusting trucks with tents pitched in the back of their cabs; old vans with fabric stretched over their windows for privacy. The clearing is pitted with holes where campfires have been lit over the course of the day – now, well past midnight, they are smoldering still, letting up ribbons of smoke and the smell of charred wood.

'See?' Alex grins and spreads his arms. 'The blitz didn't get everything.'

'You didn't tell me.' I start walking forward down the center of the clearing, stepping around a series of logs that have been arranged in a circle, like an outdoor living room. 'You didn't tell me it was like this.'

He shrugs, trotting next to me like a happy dog. 'It's the kind of thing you need to see for yourself.' He toes a bit of dirt over a dying campfire. 'Looks like we came too late for the party tonight.'

As we progress through the clearing, Alex points out every 'house' and tells me a little bit about the people who live there, speaking all the time in a whisper, so we won't wake anybody. Some stories I've heard before; others are totally new.

I'm not even fully concentrating, but I'm grateful for the sound of his voice, low and steady and familiar and reassuring. Even though the settlement isn't that big – maybe an eighth of a mile long – I feel as though the world has suddenly split open, revealing layers and depths I could never have imagined.

No walls. No walls anywhere. Portland, by comparison, seems tiny, a blip.

Alex stops in front of a dingy grey trailer. Its windows are missing and have been replaced by squares of multicoloured fabric, pulled taut.

'And, um, this is me.' Alex gestures awkwardly. It's the first time he has seemed nervous all night, which makes me nervous. I swallow back the sudden and totally inappropriate urge to laugh hysterically.

'Wow. It's – it's—'

'It's not much, from the outside,' Alex jumps in. He looks away, chewing on a corner of his lip. 'Do you want to, um, come in?'

I nod, pretty sure that if I tried to speak right now I would only squeak again. I've been alone with him countless times, but this feels different. Here there are no eyes waiting to catch us, no voices waiting to shout at us, no hands ready to tear us apart – just miles and miles of space. It's exciting and terrifying at the same time. Anything could happen here, and when he bends down to kiss me it's as though the weight of the velvety darkness around us, the soft flutters of the trees, the pitter-patter of the unseen animals, come beating into my chest, making me feel as though I'm dissolving and expanding into the night. When he pulls away it takes me a few seconds to catch my breath.

'Come on,' he says. He leans a shoulder against the door of the trailer until it pops open.

Inside it's very dark. I can make out only a few rough outlines, and when Alex shuts the door behind us even those vanish, sucked up into black.

'There's no electricity out here,' Alex says. He's moving around, bumping up against things, cursing every so often under his breath.

'Do you have candles?' I ask. The trailer smells strange, like autumn leaves that have fallen off their branches. It's nice. There are other smells too – the sharp citrus sting of cleaning fluid, and very faintly, the tang of gasoline.

'Even better.' I hear rustling, and a spray of water descends on me from above. I let out a small shriek and Alex says, 'Sorry, sorry. I haven't been here in a while. Watch out.' More rustling. And then, slowly, the ceiling above my head trembles and folds back on itself, and all of a sudden the sky is revealed in its enormity. The moon sits almost directly above us, streaming light into the trailer and crowning everything in silver. I see now that the 'ceiling' is, in fact, one enormous plastic tarp, a bigger version of the kind of thing you'd use to cover a grill. Alex is standing on a chair, rolling it back, and with every inch more of the sky is revealed and everything inside only seems to glow brighter.

My breath catches in my throat. 'It's beautiful.'

Alex shoots me a look over his shoulder and grins. He continues folding back the tarp, pausing every few minutes to stop, scoot his chair forward, and begin again. 'One day a storm took out half the roof. I wasn't here, fortunately.' He, too, is glowing, his arms and shoulders touched with silver. Just as I did on the night of the raids, I think of the portraits in church of the angels with their sprouting wings. 'I decided I might as well get rid of the whole thing.' He finishes with the tarp and jumps lightly off the chair, turning to face me, smiling. 'It's my own convertible house.'

'It's incredible,' I say, and really mean it. The sky looks so close. I feel like I could reach up and slap my fingers on the moon.

'Now I'll get the candles.' Alex scoots past me toward the kitchen area and starts rummaging. I can see the big stuff now, though details are still lost in darkness. There's a small woodstove in one corner. At the opposite end is a twin bed. My stomach does a tiny flip when I see it, and a thousand memories flood me at once – Carol sitting on my bed and telling me, in her measured voice, about the expectations of husband and wife; Jenny sticking her hand on her hip and telling me I won't know what to do when the time comes; whispered stories of Willow Marks; Hana wondering out loud in the locker room what sex feels like, while I hissed at her to be quiet, checking over my shoulder to make sure no one was listening.

Alex finds a bunch of candles and starts lighting them one by one, and corners of the room flare into focus as he sets the candles carefully around the trailer. What strikes me most are the books: lumpy shapes that in the half dark appeared to be a part of the furniture now resolve into towering stacks of books – more books than I've seen anywhere except for at the library. There are three book-shelves mashed against one wall. Even the refrigerator, whose door has come unhinged, is filled with books.

I take a candle and scan the titles. I don't recognize any of them.

'What are these?' Some of the books look so old and cracked I'm afraid if I touch them they'll crumble to bits. I mouth the names I read off the spines, at least the ones I can make out: Emily Dickinson, Walt Whitman, William Wordsworth.

Alex glances at me. 'That's poetry,' he says.

'What's poetry?' I've never heard the word before, but I like the sound of it. It sounds elegant and easy, somehow, like a beautiful woman turning in a long dress.

Alex lights the last candle. Now the trailer is filled with warm, flickering light. He joins me by the bookshelf and squats, looking for something. He removes a book and stands, passes it to me for inspection.

Famous Love Poetry. My stomach flips as I see that word – *Love* – printed so brazenly on a book cover. Alex is watching me closely, so to cover up my discomfort I open the book and scan the list of featured authors, printed on the first few pages.

'Shakespeare?' This name I do recognize from health class. 'The guy who wrote *Romeo and Juliet*? The cautionary tale?'

Alex snorts. 'It's not a cautionary tale,' he says. 'It's a great love story.'

I think about that first day at the labs: the first time I ever saw Alex. It seems like a lifetime ago. I remember my mind churning out the word *beautiful*. I remember thinking something about sacrifice.

'They banned poetry years ago, right after they discovered a cure.' He takes the book back from me and opens it. 'Would you like to hear a poem?'

I nod. He coughs, then clears his throat, then squares his shoulders and rolls his neck like he's about to be let into a soccer game.

'Go on,' I say, laughing. 'You're stalling.'

He clears his throat again and begins to read: "'Shall I compare thee to a summer's day?'"

I close my eyes and listen. The feeling I had before of being surrounded by warmth swells and crests inside of me like a wave. Poetry isn't like any writing I've ever heard before. I don't understand all of it, just bits of images, sentences that appear half-finished, all fluttering together like brightly coloured ribbons in the wind. It reminds me, I realize, of the music that struck me dumb nearly two months ago at the farmhouse. It has the same effect, and makes me feel exhilarated and sad at the same time.

Alex finishes reading. When I open my eyes, he's staring at me.

'What?' I ask. The intensity of his gaze nearly knocks the breath out of me – as though he's staring straight *into* me.

He doesn't answer me directly. He flips forward a few pages in the book, but he doesn't glance down at it. He keeps his eyes on me the whole time. 'You want to hear a different one?' He doesn't wait for me to answer before beginning to recite, "'How do I love thee? Let me count the ways.'"

There's that word again: *love*. My heart stops when he says it, then stutters into a frantic rhythm.

"'I love thee to the depth and breadth and height my soul can reach . . .'"

I know he's only speaking someone else's words, but they seem to come from him anyway. His eyes are dancing with light; in each of them I see a bright point of candlelight reflected.

He takes a step forward and kisses my forehead softly. "'I love thee to the level of every day's most quiet need . . .'"

It feels as though the floor is swinging – like I'm falling.

'Alex—' I start to say, but the word gets tangled in my throat.

He kisses each cheekbone – a delicious, skimming kiss, barely grazing my skin. '"I love thee freely . . ."'

'Alex,' I say, a little louder. My heart is beating so fast I'm afraid it will burst from my ribs.

He pulls back and gives me a small, crooked smile. 'Elizabeth Barrett Browning,' he says, then traces a finger over the bridge of my nose. 'You don't like it?'

The way he says it, so low and serious, still staring into my eyes, makes me feel as though he's actually asking something else.

'No. I mean, yes. I mean, I do, but . . .' The truth is, I'm not sure what I mean. I can't think or speak clearly. A single word is swirling around inside me – a storm, a hurricane – and I have to squeeze my lips together to keep it from swelling up to my tongue and fighting its way out into the open. *Love, love, love, love.* A word I've never pronounced, not to anyone, a word I've never even really let myself think.

'You don't have to explain.' Alex takes another step backward. Again I have the sense, confusedly, that we're actually talking about something else. I've disappointed him somehow. Whatever has just passed between us – and something did, even if I'm not sure what or how or why – has made him sad. I can see it in his eyes, even though he's still smiling, and it makes me want to apologize, or throw my arms around him and ask him to kiss me. But I'm still afraid to open my mouth – afraid that the word will come shooting out, and terrified about what comes afterward.

'Come here.' Alex sets the book down and offers me his hand. 'I want to show you something.'

He leads me over to the bed, and again a wave of shyness overtakes me. I'm not sure what he expects, and when he sits down I hang back, feeling self-conscious.

'It's okay, Lena,' he says. As always, hearing him say my name relaxes me. He scoots backward on the bed and lies down on his back and I do the same, so we're lying side by side. The bed is narrow. There's just enough room for the two of us.

'See?' Alex says, tilting his chin upward.

Above our heads, the stars flare and glitter and flash: thousands and thousands of them, so many thousands they look like snowflakes whirling away into the inky dark. I can't help it; I gasp. I don't think I've ever seen so many stars in my life. The sky looks so close – strung so taut above our heads, beyond the roofless trailer – it feels as though we're falling into it, as though we could jump off the bed and the sky would catch us, hold us, bounce us like a trampoline.

'What do you think?' Alex asks.

'I love it.' The word pops out, and instantly the weight on my chest dissipates. 'I love it,' I say again, testing it. An easy word to say, once you say it. Short. To the point. Rolls off the tongue. It's amazing I've never said it before.

I can tell Alex is pleased. The smile in his voice grows bigger. 'The no-plumbing thing is kind of a bummer,' he says. 'But you have to admit the view is killer.'

'I wish we could stay here,' I blurt out, and then quickly stutter, 'I mean, not really. Not for good, but . . . *You* know what I mean.'

Alex moves his arm under my neck, so I inch over and

lay my head in the spot where his shoulder meets his chest, where it fits perfectly. 'I'm glad you got to see it,' he says.

For a while we just lie there in silence. His chest rises and falls with his breathing, and after a while the motion starts to lull me to sleep. My limbs feel impossibly heavy, and the stars seem to be rearranging themselves into words. I want to keep looking, to read out their meaning, but my lids are heavy too: impossible, impossible to keep my eyes open.

'Alex?'

'Yeah?'

'Tell me that poem again.' My voice doesn't sound like my own; my words seem to come from a distance.

'Which one?' Alex whispers.

'The one you know by heart.' Drifting; I'm drifting.

'I know a lot of them by heart.'

'Any one, then.'

He takes a deep breath and begins: '"I carry your heart with me. I carry it in my heart. I am never without it . . ."'

He speaks on, words washing over me, the way that sunlight skips over the surface of water and filters into the depths below, lighting up the darkness. I keep my eyes closed. Amazingly, I can still see the stars: whole galaxies blooming from nothing – pink and purple suns, vast silver oceans, a thousand white moons.

It seems like I've only been asleep five minutes when Alex is gently shaking me awake. The sky is still inky black, the moon high and bright, but I can tell by the way the candles are pooling around us that I must have been out for at least an hour or so.

'Time to go,' he says, brushing the hair off my forehead.

'What time is it?' My voice is thick with sleep.

'A little before three.' Alex sits up and scoots off the bed, then reaches out a hand and pulls me to my feet. 'We've got to cross before Sleeping Beauty wakes up.'

'Sleeping Beauty?' I shake my head confusedly.

Alex laughs softly. 'After poetry,' he says, leaning down to kiss me, 'we move on to fairy tales.'

Then it's back through the woods; down the broken path that leads past the bombed-out houses; through the woods again. The whole time I feel as though I haven't quite woken up. I'm not even scared or nervous when we climb the fence. Getting over the barbed wire is infinitely easier the second time around, and I feel as though the shadows have texture, and shield us like a cloak. The guard at hut number twenty-one is still in the exact same position – head tilted back, feet on his desk, mouth open – and soon we're weaving our way around the cove. Then we're slipping silently through the streets toward Deering Highlands, and it's then I have the strangest thought, half dread and half wish: that maybe all of this is a dream, and when I wake up I will find myself in the Wilds. Maybe I'll wake up and find I've *always* been there, and that all of Portland – and the labs, and the curfew, and the procedure – was some long, twisted nightmare.

37 Brooks: in through the window, and the heat and the smell of mildew slams us, a wall. I only spent a few hours there and I miss the Wilds already – the wind through the trees that sounds just like the ocean, the incredible smells of blooming plants, the invisible scurrying things – all that life, pushing and extending in every direction, on and on and on . . .

No walls . . .

Then Alex is leading me to the sofa and shaking out a blanket over me, kissing me and wishing me good night. He has the morning shift at the labs, and has just barely enough time to go home, shower, and make it to work on time. I hear his footsteps melting away into the darkness.

Then I sleep.

Love: a single word, a wispy thing, a word no bigger or longer than an edge. That's what it is: an edge; a razor. It draws up through the center of your life, cutting everything in two. Before and after. The rest of the world falls away on either side.

Before and *after* – and *during*, a moment no bigger or longer than an edge.

nineteen

Live free or die.

– Ancient saying, provenance unknown, listed in the
Comprehensive Compilation of Dangerous Words and Ideas,
www.ccdwi.gov.org

One of the strangest things about life is that it will
chug on, blind and oblivious, even as your private
world – your little carved-out sphere – is twisting
and morphing, even breaking apart. One day you have parents;
the next day you're an orphan. One day you have a place and
a path; the next day you're lost in a wilderness.

And still the sun rises and clouds mass and drift and people
shop for groceries and toilets flush and blinds go up and
down. That's when you realize that most of it – life, the
relentless mechanism of existing – isn't about you. It doesn't
include you at all. It will thrust onward even after you've
jumped the edge. Even after you're dead.

When I make my way back into downtown Portland in the morning, that's what surprises me the most – how normal everything looks. I don't know what I was expecting. I didn't really think that buildings would have tumbled down overnight, that the streets would have melted into rubble, but it's still a shock to see a stream of people carrying briefcases, and shop owners unlocking their front doors, and a single car trying to push through a crowded street.

It seems absurd that they don't *know*, haven't felt any change or tremor, even as my life has been completely turned upside down. As I head home I keep feeling paranoid, like someone will be able to smell the Wilds on me, will be able to tell just from seeing my face that I've crossed over. The back of my neck itches as though it's being poked with branches, and I keep whipping off my backpack to make sure there aren't any leaves or burrs clinging to it – not that it matters, since it's not like Portland is treeless. But no one even glances in my direction. It's a little before nine o'clock, and most people are rushing to get to work on time. An endless blur of normal people doing normal things, eyes straight ahead of them, paying no attention to the short, nondescript girl with a lumpy backpack pushing past them.

The short, nondescript girl with a secret burning inside of her like a fire.

It's as though my night in the Wilds has sharpened my vision around the edges. Even though everything looks superficially the same, it seems somehow different – flimsy, almost, as though you could put your hand through the buildings and sky and even the people. I remember being very young and watching Rachel build a sand castle at the beach. She must have worked on it for hours, using different cups and containers to shape towers and turrets. When it was done it looked perfect, like it could have been made out of stone. But when the tide came in, it didn't take more than two or three waves to dissolve its shape entirely. I remember I burst into tears, and my mother bought me an ice cream cone and made me share it with Rachel.

That's what Portland looks like this morning: like something in danger of dissolving.

I keep thinking about what Alex always says: *There are more of us than you think*. I sneak a glance at everyone who goes by, thinking maybe I'll be able to read some secret sign on their faces, some mark of resistance, but everyone looks the same as always: harried, hurried, annoyed, zoned out.

When I get home, Carol's in the kitchen washing dishes. I try to scoot past her, but she calls out to me. I pause with one foot on the stairs. She comes into the hallway, wiping her hands on a dish towel.

'How was Hana's?' she asks. She flicks her eyes all over my face, searchingly, as though checking for signs of something. I try to will back another bout of paranoia. She couldn't possibly know where I've been.

'It was fine,' I say, shrugging, trying to sound casual. 'Didn't get a lot of sleep, though.'

'Mmm.' Carol keeps looking at me intensely. 'What did you girls do together?'

She never asks about Hana's house, and hasn't for years. *Something's wrong*, I think.

'You know, the usual. Watched some TV. Hana gets, like, seven channels.' I can't tell if my voice sounds weird and high-pitched, or if I'm just imagining it.

Carol looks away, twisting her mouth up like she's

accidentally gotten a mouthful of sour milk. I can tell she's trying to work out a way to say something unpleasant; she gets her sour-milk face whenever she has to give out bad news. *She knows about Alex, she knows, she knows.* The walls press closer and the heat is stifling.

Then, to my surprise, she curls her mouth into a smile, reaches out, and places a hand on my arm. 'You know, Lena . . . it won't be like this for very much longer.'

I've successfully avoided thinking about the procedure for twenty-four hours, but now that awful, looming number pops back into my head, throwing a shadow over everything. Seventeen days.

'I know,' I squeeze out. Now my voice *definitely* sounds weird.

Carol nods, and keeps the strange half smile plastered to her face. 'I know it's hard to believe, but you won't miss her once it's over.'

'I know.' Like there's a dying frog caught in my throat.

Carol keeps nodding at me really vigorously. It looks as though her head is connected to a yo-yo. I get the feeling she wants to say something more, something that will reassure me, but she obviously can't think of anything because we just stand there, frozen like that, for almost a minute.

Finally I say, 'I'm going upstairs. Shower.' It takes all my willpower just to get out the words. *Seventeen days* keeps tearing through my mind, like an alarm.

Carol seems relieved that I've broken the silence. 'Okay,' she says. 'Okay.'

I start up the stairs two at a time. I can't wait to lock myself in the bathroom. Even though it must be more than eighty degrees in the house, I want to stand under a stream of beating hot water, melt myself into vapour.

'Oh, Lena.' Carol calls out to me almost as an afterthought. I turn around and she's not looking at me. She's inspecting the fraying border of one of her dish towels. 'You should put on something nice. A dress – or those pretty white slacks you got last year. And do your hair. Don't just leave it to air-dry.'

'Why?' I don't like the way she won't look at me, especially since her mouth is going all screwy again.

'I invited Brian Scharff to come over today,' she says casually, as though it's an everyday, normal thing.

'Brian Scharff?' I repeat dumbly. The name feels strange in my mouth, and brings with it the taste of metal.

Carol snaps her head up and looks at me. 'Not *alone*,' she says quickly. 'Of course not alone. His mother will be coming with him. And I'll be here too, obviously. Besides, Brian had his procedure last month.' As though *that's* what's bothering me.

'He's coming here? Today?' I have to reach out and place one hand on the wall. Somehow I've managed to completely forget about Brian Scharff, that neat printed name on a page.

Carol must think I'm nervous about meeting him, because she smiles at me. 'Don't worry, Lena. You'll be fine. We'll do most of the talking. I just thought you two should meet, since . . .' She doesn't finish her sentence. She doesn't have to.

Since we're paired. Since we'll be married. Since I'll share my bed with him, and wake up every day of my life next to him, and have to let him put his hands on me, and have to sit across from him at dinner eating canned asparagus and listening to him rattle on about plumbing or carpentry or whatever it is he's going to get assigned to do.

'No!' I burst out.

Carol looks startled. She's not used to hearing that word, certainly not from me. 'What do you mean, *no*?'

I lick my lips. I know refusing her is dangerous, and I know that it's wrong. But I can't meet Brian Scharff. I won't. I won't sit there and pretend to like him, or listen to Carol talk about where we'll live in a few years, while Alex is out there somewhere – waiting for me to meet up with him, or tapping his fingers against his desk while he listens to music, or breathing, or doing anything at all. 'I mean . . .' I struggle for an excuse. 'I mean – I mean, couldn't we do it some other time? I don't really feel good.' This, at least, is true.

Carol frowns at me. 'It's an hour, Lena. If you can manage to sleep over at Hana's house, you can manage that.'

'But – but—' I ball one fist up, squeezing my fingernails into my palm until pain starts blooming there, which gives me something to focus on. 'But I want it to be a surprise.'

Carol's voice takes on an edge. 'There's nothing *surprising* about this, Lena. This is the order of things. This is your life. He is your pair. You will meet him, and you will like him, and that's that. Now go upstairs and get in the shower. They'll be coming at one o'clock.'

One. Alex gets off work at noon today; I was supposed to meet him. We were going to have a picnic at 37 Brooks, like we always do whenever he comes off the morning shift, and enjoy the whole afternoon together. 'But—' I start to protest, not even sure what else I can say.

'No buts.' Carol crosses her arms and glares at me fiercely. 'Upstairs.'

I don't know how I make it up the stairs; I'm so angry I can barely see. Jenny's standing on the landing, chewing gum, dressed in one of Rachel's old bathing suits. It's too big for her. 'What's wrong with you?' she says, as I push past her.

I don't answer. I make a beeline for the bathroom and turn the water on as high as it can go. Carol hates it when we waste water, and normally I make my showers as quick as I can, but today I don't care. I sit on the toilet and stuff my fingers in my mouth, biting down to keep from screaming. This is all my fault. I've been ignoring the date of the procedure, and I've avoided even *thinking* Brian Scharff's name. And Carol is absolutely right: this is my life, and the order of things. There's no changing it. I take a deep breath and tell myself to stop being such a baby. Everyone has to grow up sometime; my time is on September 3.

I go to stand up, but an image of Alex last night – standing so close to me, speaking those weird, wonderful words, *I love thee to the depth and breadth and height my soul can reach* – knocks me down again, and I thud back onto the toilet.

Alex laughing, breathing, living – separately, unknown to me. Waves of nausea overtake me, and I double over with my head between my knees, fighting it.

The disease, I tell myself. *The disease is progressing. It will all be better after the procedure. That's the* point.

But it's no use. When I finally manage to get into the shower, I try to lose myself in the rhythm of the water pounding on the porcelain, but images of Alex flicker through my mind – kissing me, stroking my hair, dancing his fingers over my skin – dancing, flashing, like light from a candle, about to be snuffed out.

*

The worst is that I can't even let Alex know I won't be able to meet him. It's too dangerous to call him. My plan was to go to the labs and tell him in person, but when I come downstairs, showered and dressed, and head for the door, Carol stops me.

'Where do you think you're going?' she says sharply. I can tell she's still angry that I was arguing with her earlier – angry, and probably offended. She no doubt thinks I should be turning cartwheels because I've finally been paired. She has a right to think it – a few months ago, I *would* have been turning cartwheels.

I turn my eyes to the ground, attempting to sound as sweet and meek as possible. 'I just thought I'd take a walk before Brian comes.' I try to conjure up a blush. 'I'm kind of nervous.'

'You've been spending enough time out of the house as it is,' Carol snaps back. 'And you'll only get sweaty and dirty again. If you want something to do, you can help me organize the linen closet.'

There's no way I can disobey my aunt, so I follow her back upstairs and sit on the floor as she passes ratty towel after ratty towel down to me, and I inspect them for holes and stains and damage, fold and refold, count napkins. I'm so angry and frustrated I'm shaking. Alex won't know what has happened to me. He'll worry. Or even worse, he'll think I'm deliberately avoiding him. Maybe he'll think going to the Wilds freaked me out.

It frightens me, how violent I'm feeling – crazy, almost, and capable of anything. I want to climb up the walls, burn down the house, *something*. Several times I have the fantasy of taking one of Carol's stupid dish towels and strangling her with it. This is what all the textbooks and *The Book of*

Shhh and parents and teachers have always warned me about. I don't know whether they're right or whether Alex is. I don't know whether these feelings – this *thing* growing inside of me – is something horrible and sick or the best thing that's ever happened to me.

Either way, I can't stop it. I've lost control. And the *truly* sick thing is that despite everything, I'm glad.

At twelve thirty Carol moves me downstairs to the living room, which I can tell has been straightened and cleaned. My uncle's shipping orders, which are usually scattered everywhere, have been stacked in a neat pile, and none of the old schoolbooks and broken toys that usually litter the floor are visible. She plops me down on a sofa and begins messing with my hair. I feel like a prize pig, but I know better than to say anything about it. If I do everything she tells me – if everything goes smoothly – maybe I'll still have time to go to 37 Brooks once Brian leaves.

'There,' Carol says, stepping away and squinting at me critically. 'That's as good as it's going to get.'

I bite my lip and turn away. I don't want her to notice, but her words have sent a sharp pain through me. Amazingly, I'd actually forgotten that I'm supposed to be plain. I'm so used to Alex telling me I'm beautiful. I'm so used to *feeling* beautiful around him. A hollow opens up in my chest. This is what life will be like without him: everything will become ordinary again. *I'll* become ordinary again.

At a few minutes after one I hear the front gate squeak open and footsteps on the path. I've been so focused on Alex I haven't had time to get nervous about Brian Scharff's arrival. But now I have the wild urge to make a run for the back door, or hurtle through the open window. Thinking about what Carol would do if I went belly flopping through the screen brings on an uncontrollable fit of giggling.

'Lena,' she hisses at me, just as Brian and his mother start knocking on the front door. 'Control yourself.'

Why? I'm tempted to fire back. It's not like he can do anything about it, even if he hates me. He's stuck with me and I'm stuck with him. We're stuck.

That's what growing up is all about, I guess.

In my imagination Brian Scharff was tall and fat, a hulking figure. In reality he's only a few inches taller than I am – which is impressively short, for a guy – and so thin I'm worried about breaking his wrist bone when we shake. His palms are damp with sweat, and he barely squeezes my hand. It feels like holding on to a damp tissue. Afterward, when we all take our seats, I surreptitiously wipe my hands against my pants.

'Thank you for coming,' Carol says, and there's a long, awkward pause. In the silence I can hear Brian wheezing through his nose. It sounds like there's a dying animal trapped in his nasal canal.

I must be staring, because Mrs. Scharff explains, 'Brian has asthma.'

'Oh,' I say.

'The allergies make it worse.'

'Um . . . what is he allergic to?' I ask, because she seems to be expecting it.

'Dust,' she says emphatically, like she's been waiting to break out that word since she sailed through the door. She looks witheringly around the room – which is not dusty – and Carol blushes. 'And pollen. Cats and dogs, of course, and peanuts, seafood, wheat, dairy, and garlic.'

'I didn't know you could be allergic to garlic,' I say. I can't help it: it just pops out.

'His face puffs up like an accordion.' Mrs. Scharff turns a disdainful eye toward me, as though I'm somehow responsible for this fact.

'Oh,' I say again, and then another uncomfortable silence descends on us. Brian doesn't say anything, but he wheezes louder than ever.

This time Carol comes to the rescue. 'Lena,' she says, 'perhaps Brian and Mrs. Scharff would like some water.'

I've never been so grateful for an excuse to leave a room in my life. I jump out of my seat, nearly taking down a lamp with my knee by accident. 'Of course. I'll get it.'

'Make sure it's filtered,' Mrs. Scharff calls after me, as I tear out of the room. 'And not too much ice.'

In the kitchen I take my time filling up the glasses – from the tap, obviously – and letting the cold air from the freezer blast my face. From the living room I can hear the low murmur of conversation, but I can't make out who is speaking or what is being said. Maybe Mrs. Scharff decided to reprise her list of Brian's allergies.

I know I have to go back into the living room eventually, but my feet just won't move toward the hallway. When I finally force them into action, they feel like they've been transformed into lead; still, they carry me far too quickly toward the living room. I keep seeing an endless series of bland days, days the colour of pale yellow and white pills, days that have the same bitter aftertaste as medicine. Mornings and evenings filled with a quietly whirring humidifier, with Brian's steady wheezing breath, with the *drip, drip, drip* from a leaking faucet.

There's no stopping it. The hallway doesn't last forever, and I step into the living room just in time to hear Brian say, 'She's not as pretty as in the pictures.'

Brian and his mom have their backs to me, but Carol's mouth falls open when she sees me standing there, and both of the Scharffs whip around to face me. At least they have the grace to look embarrassed. He drops his eyes quickly, and she flushes.

I've never felt so ashamed or exposed. This is worse, even, than standing in the translucent hospital gown at the evaluations, under the glare of the fluorescent lights. My hands are trembling so badly the water jumps over the lip of the glasses.

'Here's your water.' I don't know where I find the strength to come around the sofa and place the glasses down on the coffee table. 'Not too much ice.'

'Lena—' My aunt starts to say something, but I interrupt her.

'I'm sorry.' Miraculously, I even manage a smile. I can only hold it for a fraction of a second, though. My jaw is trembling too, and I know that at any moment I might cry. 'I'm not feeling very well. I think I might step outside for a bit.'

I don't wait to be given permission. I turn around and rush the front door. As I push out into the sun I hear Carol apologizing for me.

'The procedure is still several weeks away,' she's saying. 'So you'll have to forgive her for being so sensitive. I'm sure it will all work out . . .'

The tears come hot and fast as soon as I'm outside. The world begins to melt, colours and shapes bleeding together. The day is perfectly still. The sun has just inched past the middle of the sky, a flat white disk, like a circle of heated metal. A red balloon is caught in a tree. It must have been there for a while. It is going limp, bobbing listlessly, half-deflated, at the end of its string.

I don't know how I'll face Brian when I have to go back inside. I don't know how I'll face him *ever*. A thousand awful things race through my mind, insults I'd like to hurl at him. *At least I don't look like a tapeworm*, or, *Has it ever occurred to you that you're allergic to* life?

But I know I won't – can't – say any of those things. Besides, the problem isn't really that he wheezes, or is allergic to everything. The problem isn't even that he doesn't think I'm pretty.

The problem is that he isn't Alex.

Behind me the door squeaks open. Brian says, 'Lena?'

I mash my palms against my cheeks quickly, wiping away the tears. The absolute last thing in the world I want is for Brian to know that his stupid comment has upset me. 'I'm fine,' I call back, without turning, since I'm sure I look like a mess. 'I'll come inside in a second.'

He must be stupid or stubborn, because he doesn't leave me alone. Instead he closes the door behind him and comes down off the front stoop. I hear him wheezing a few feet behind me.

'Your mom said it was okay if I came out with you,' he says.

'She's not my mom,' I correct him quickly. I don't know why it seems so important to say. I used to like it when people confused Carol for my mom. It meant they didn't know the real story. Then again, I used to like a lot of things that seem ridiculous now.

'Oh, right.' Brian must know something about my real mom. It's on the record he would have seen. 'Sorry. I forgot.'

Of course you did, I think, but don't say anything. At least the fact that he's hovering over me has made me too angry to be sad anymore. The tears have stopped. I cross my arms and wait for him to take the hint – or get tired of staring at my back – and go inside. But the steady wheezing continues.

I've known him less than half an hour, and already I could kill him. Finally I get tired of standing there in silence, so I turn around and brush past him quickly.

'Feeling much better now,' I say. I don't look at him as I start toward the house. 'We should go in.'

'Wait, Lena.' He reaches out and grabs my wrist. I guess *grabs* isn't really the right word. More like *wipes sweat on*. But I stop anyway, though I still can't bring myself to meet his eyes. Instead I keep my eyes locked on the front door, noticing for the first time that the screen has three large holes in it, near the upper right corner. No wonder the house has been full of insects this summer. Grace found a ladybug in our bedroom the other day. She brought it to me, cupped in her tiny palm. I helped her carry it downstairs and release it outside.

I feel an overwhelming rush of sadness, unrelated to Alex or Brian or any of that. I'm just struck with a sense of time passing so quickly, rushing forward. One day I'll wake up and my whole life will be behind me, and it will seem to have gone as quickly as a dream.

'I didn't mean for you to hear what I said before,' he says. I wonder if his mom made him say this. The words seem to require a tremendous effort on his part. 'It was rude.'

As if I haven't already been completely humiliated – now

he has to *apologize* for calling me ugly. My cheeks feel like they're going to melt off, they're so hot.

'Don't worry about it,' I say, trying to extricate my wrist from his hand. Surprisingly, he won't let me go – even though technically he shouldn't be touching me at all.

'What I meant was—' His mouth works up and down for a second. He won't meet my eyes. He keeps scanning the street behind me, his eyes darting back and forth, like a cat watching a bird. 'What I meant was, you looked happier in the pictures.'

This is a surprise, and for a second I can't think of a response. 'I don't seem happy now?' I splutter out, and then feel even more embarrassed. It's so weird to be having this conversation with a stranger, knowing he won't be a stranger for very much longer.

But he doesn't seem freaked out by the question. He just shakes his head. 'I know you aren't,' he says. He drops my wrist, but I don't feel as desperate to go inside anymore. He's still staring off at the street behind me, and I sneak a closer look at his face. I guess he could be kind of good-looking. Not nearly so gorgeous as Alex, obviously – he's super pale and slightly feminine-looking, with a full, round mouth and a small, tapered nose – but his eyes are a clear, pale blue, like a morning sky, and he has a nice strong jawline. And now I start to feel guilty. He must know I'm unhappy because I've been paired with him. It's not his fault I've changed – seen the light or contracted the *deliria*, depending on who you ask. Maybe both.

'I'm sorry,' I say. 'It's not you. I'm just – I'm just scared about the procedure, that's all.' I think of how many nights I used to fantasize about stretching out on the operating table, waiting for the anesthesia to turn the world to fog, waiting to wake up renewed. Now I'll be waking up to a world without Alex: I'll be waking up *into* the fog, everything grey and blurry and unrecognizable.

Brian is looking at me, finally, with an expression I can't identify at first. Then I realize: pity. He feels sorry for me. He starts speaking all in a rush. 'Listen, I probably shouldn't tell you this, but before my procedure I was like you.' His eyes click back to the street. The wheezing has stopped. He speaks clearly, but low, so Carol and his mom can't hear through the open window. 'I didn't – I wasn't ready.' He licks his lips, drops his voice to a whisper. 'There was a girl I used to see sometimes at the park. She babysat for her cousins, used to bring them to the playground there. I was captain of the fencing team in high school – that's where we practiced.'

You would *be captain of the frigging fencing team*, I think. But I don't say this out loud; I can tell he's trying to be nice.

'Anyway, we used to talk sometimes. Nothing happened,' he qualifies quickly. 'Just a few conversations, here and there. She had a pretty smile. And I felt . . .' He trails off.

Wonder and fear sweep through me. He's trying to tell me that we're alike. He somehow knows about Alex – not about Alex specifically, but about *someone*. 'Wait a second.' My mind is churning. 'Are you trying to say that before the procedure you were . . . you got sick?'

'I'm just saying I understand.' His eyes flick to mine for barely a fraction of a second, but that's all I need. I'm positive now. He knows I've been infected. I'm both relieved and terrified – if he can see it, other people will see it too.

'My point is only that the cure works.' He places extra

emphasis on the last word. I know, now, that he's trying to be kind. 'I'm much happier now. You will be too, I promise.'

Something inside of me fractures when he says that, and I feel like I could cry again. His voice is so reassuring. There's nothing I want more in that moment than to believe him. Safety, happiness, stability: what I've wanted my whole life. And for that moment I think maybe the past few weeks really have just been some long, strange delirium. Maybe after the procedure I'll wake up as from a high fever, with only a vague recollection of my dreams and a sense of overwhelming relief.

'Friends?' Brian says, offering me his hand to shake, and this time I don't flinch when he touches me. I even let him hold my hand an extra few seconds.

He's still facing the street, and as we're standing there a frown flickers temporarily across his face. 'What does he want?' he mutters, and then calls out, 'It's okay. She's my pair.'

I turn around just in time to see a flash of burnt golden-brown hair – the colour of leaves in autumn – disappear around the corner. Alex. I wrench my hand away from Brian's, but it's too late. He's gone.

'Must have been a regulator,' Brian says. 'He was just standing there, staring.'

The feeling of calm and reassurance I'd had only a minute earlier vanishes in a rush. Alex saw me – he saw us, holding hands, heard Brian say I was his pair. And I was supposed to have met him an hour ago. He doesn't know that I couldn't get out of the house, couldn't get a message to him. I can't imagine what he must be thinking about me right now. Or actually, I *can* imagine.

'Are you okay?' Brian's eyes are so pale they're almost grey. A sickly colour, not like sky at all – like mold or rot. I can't believe I thought he could be attractive for even a second. 'You don't look too good.'

'I'm fine.' I try to take a step toward the house and stumble. Brian reaches out to steady me, but I twist away from him. 'I'm fine,' I repeat, even though everything around me is breaking, fracturing.

'It's hot out here,' he says. I can't stand to look at him. 'Let's go inside.'

He puts a hand on my elbow and propels me up the stairs, through the door, and into the living room, where Carol and Mrs. Scharff are waiting for us, smiling.

twenty

Ex rememdium salus.
'From the cure, salvation.'

– Printed on all American currency

By some miracle, I must make a good enough impression on Brian and Mrs. Scharff to satisfy Carol, even though I barely speak during the remainder of their visit (or maybe *because* I barely speak). It's midafternoon by the time they leave, and although Carol insists I help out with a few more chores and she makes me stick around for dinner – every minute that I can't run to Alex an agony, sixty seconds of pure, driving torture – she promises me I can go for a walk when I'm done eating, before curfew. I inhale my baked beans and frozen fish sticks so fast I almost puke, and practically sit bouncing in my chair until she releases me. She even lets me out of dishwashing duty, but I'm too angry at her for cooping me up in the first place to feel grateful.

I go to 37 Brooks first. I don't really think he'll be there waiting for me, but I'm hoping for it anyway. But the rooms are empty, the garden, too. I must be half delirious by that point because I check behind the trees and bushes, as though he might suddenly pop out, like he used to do a few weeks ago when he and Hana and I would play our epic games of hide-and-seek. Just thinking about it brings a sharp pain to my chest. Less than a month ago all of August still stretched before us – long and golden and reassuring, like an endless period of delicious sleep.

Well, now I've woken up.

I make my way back through the house. Seeing all our stuff scattered in the living room – blankets, a few magazines and books, a box of crackers and some cans of soda, old board games, including a half-completed game of Scrabble, abandoned when Alex began making up words like *quozz* and *yregg* – makes me overwhelmingly sad. It reminds me of that single house that survived the blitz, and that cracked and bombed-out street: a place where everybody went on stupidly doing everyday things, right up until the moment of disaster, and afterward everyone said, 'How could they not have known what was coming?'

Stupid, stupid – to be so careless with our time, to believe we had so much of it left.

I head into the streets, frantic and desperate now, but unsure of what to do next. He mentioned to me once that he lived on Forsyth – a long row of grey slab buildings owned by the university – so I go that way. But all the buildings look identical. There must be dozens of them, hundreds of individual apartments. I'm tempted to tear through each and every one until I find him, but that would be suicide. After a couple of students give me suspicious glances – I'm sure I look like a disaster, red-faced and wild-eyed and close to hysterical – I duck into a side street. To calm myself I start reciting the elemental prayers: 'H is for hydrogen, a weight of one; when fission's split, as brightly lit, as hot as any sun . . .'

I'm so distracted walking home that I get lost in the tangle of streets leading away from the U.P. campus. I end up on a narrow one-way street I've never seen before and have to backtrack to Monument Square. The Governor is standing there as always, his empty palm outstretched, looking sad and forlorn in the fading evening light, as though he's a beggar, forever condemned to ask for alms.

But seeing him gives me an idea. I dig in the bottom of my bag for a scrap of paper and a pen, and scrawl out, *Let me explain, please. Midnight at the house. 8/17.* Then, after checking to make sure that no one is watching me from the few remaining lit windows that overlook the square, I hop up onto the statue's base and stuff the note into the little cavity in the Governor's fist. The chance that Alex will think to check there is a million to one. But still, there's a chance.

That night, as I'm slipping out of the bedroom, I hear rustling behind me. When I turn around, Gracie's sitting up in bed again, blinking at me, her eyes as reflective as an animal's. I touch my finger to my lips. She does the same, an unconscious mimic, and I slip out the door.

When I'm on the street I look up once toward the window. For a second I think I see Gracie looking down at me, her face as pale as a moon. But maybe it's just a trick of the shadows skating silently over the side of the house. When I look again, she's gone.

*

The house at 37 Brooks is all dark when I push my way in through the window, and totally silent. *He's not here*, I think. *He didn't come* – but a piece of me refuses to believe it. He *must* have come.

I've brought a flashlight with me, and I begin a sweep of the house, my second of the day, refusing for superstitious reasons to call out for him. Somehow I can't stand it. If he doesn't answer, I'll be forced, finally, to accept that he never received my note – or, even worse, did receive it but has decided not to come.

In the living room I stop short.

All our things – the blankets, the games, the books – are gone. The warped wooden floor lies bare and exposed under the beam of my flashlight. The furniture sits cold and silent, stripped of all our personal touches, the discarded sweatshirts and half-used bottles of sunscreen. It has been a long time since I've been afraid of the house or frightened of walking into its rooms at night, but now a sense of the cavernous empty spaces around me comes back – room after room of tumbling-down things, rotting things, rodents blinking at you from dark spaces – and a deep chill runs through me. Alex must have been here after all, to clean up our stuff.

The message is as clear to me as any note. He's done with me.

For a moment I even forget to breathe. And then the Coldness comes, a surge of it so strong it hits me in the chest like a physical force, like walking straight into the breakers at the beach. My knees buckle and I go into a crouch, shivering uncontrollably.

He's gone. A strangled sound works its way out of my throat and breaks the silence around me all at once. Suddenly I'm sobbing loudly into the dark, letting the flashlight fall to the ground and blink out. I fantasize that I'll cry so much I'll fill the house and drown, or be carried away on a river of tears to some distant place.

Then I feel a warm hand on the back of my neck, working through a tangle of my hair.

'Lena.'

I turn around and Alex is there, bending over me. I can't really make out his expression, but in the limited light it looks hard to me, hard and immobile, as though it's made out of stone. For a second I'm worried that I'm only dreaming him, but then he touches me again and his hand is solid and warm and rough.

'Lena,' he says again, but he doesn't seem to know what else to say. I scramble to my feet, wiping my face on my forearm.

'You got my note.' I'm trying to gulp back the tears but just succeed in hiccuping several times.

'Note?' Alex repeats.

I wish I was still holding the flashlight so I could see his face more clearly. At the same time, I'm terrified of it, and of the distance I might find there. 'I left you a note at the Governor,' I said. 'I wanted you to meet me here.'

'I didn't get it,' he says. I think I hear a coldness in his voice. 'I just came to—'

'Stop.' I can't let him finish. I can't let him say that he came to pack up, that he doesn't want to see me again. It will kill me. *Love, the deadliest of all deadly things.* 'Listen,' I say, hiccuping through the words. 'Listen, about today . . . It wasn't my idea. Carol said I had to meet him, and I couldn't get a message to you. And then we were standing there and I was thinking about you, and the Wilds, and how everything is so changed and how there's no time, there's no more time for us, and for a second – a single second – I wished I could go back to how things were before.' I'm not really making any sense, and I know it. The explanation I'd reviewed so many times in my head is getting all screwed up, words leapfrogging over one another. The excuses seem irrelevant: as I'm speaking I realize there's only a single thing that really matters. Alex and I are out of time. 'But I swear I didn't really wish it. I would never have – if I'd never met you I could never have – I didn't know what anything *meant* before you, not really . . .'

Alex pulls me toward him and wraps his arms around me. I bury my face in his chest. I seem to fit so precisely, just exactly as though our bodies had been built for each other.

'Shhh,' he whispers into my hair. He's squeezing me so tightly it hurts a little, but I don't mind. It feels good, like if I wanted to I could lift my feet off the ground and stop trying at all and he'd still be holding me up. 'I'm not mad at you, Lena.'

I pull back just a fraction. I know that even in the dark I probably look horrible. My eyes are swelling up and my hair is sticking to my face. Thankfully, he keeps his arms around me. 'But you—' I swallow hard, take deep breaths in and out. 'You took everything away. All our stuff.'

He looks away for a second. His whole face is swallowed in shadow. When he speaks his voice is over-loud, as though he can only say the words by forcing them out. 'We always knew this would happen. We knew that we didn't have much time.'

'But – but—' I don't have to say that we've been pretending. We've been acting as if things would never change.

He places a hand on either side of my face, wipes the tears

away with his thumbs. 'Don't cry, okay? No more crying.' He kisses the tip of my nose lightly, then takes one of my hands. 'I want to show you something.' There's a small break in his voice, and I think of things coming unhinged, falling apart.

He leads me to the staircase. Far above us, the ceiling is rotted away in patches, so the stairs are outlined in silvery light. The staircase must have been magnificent at some point, sweeping upward majestically before splitting in two, leading to landings on either side.

I haven't been upstairs since the first time Alex brought me here with Hana, when we made it a point to explore every room of the house. I didn't even think to check the second floor earlier this afternoon. Here it's even darker than downstairs, if possible, and hotter too, a black and drifting mist.

Alex starts shuffling down the hall, past a row of identical wooden doors. 'This way.'

Above us, a frantic sound of fluttering: bats, disturbed by the sound of his voice. I let out a little squeak of fear. Mice? Fine. Flying mice? Not so fine. That's another reason I've been sticking to the ground floor. During our initial exploration we came into what must have been the master bedroom – an enormous room, with the half-collapsed beams of a four-poster bed still standing in the middle of it – and looked up into the gloom, and saw dozens and dozens of dark, silent shapes massed along the wooden beams, like horrible black buds dangling along a flower stem, ready to drop. When we moved, several of them opened their eyes and seemed to wink at me. The floor was streaked with bat shit; it smelled sickly sweet.

'In here,' he says, and though I can't be positive, I think he stops at the door to the master bedroom. I shiver. I have zero desire to see the inside of the Bat Room again. But Alex is emphatic, so I let him open the door and I pass inside in front of him.

As soon as we walk into the room I gasp and stop so suddenly he bumps into me. The room is incredible; it's transformed.

'Well?' There's a note of anxiety in Alex's voice. 'What do you think?'

I can't answer him immediately. Alex has shoved the old bed out of the way, into one of the corners, and swept the floor perfectly clean. The windows – or what windows remain – are flung open, so the air smells like gardenias and night-blooming jasmine, their scents drifting in on the wind from outside. He has arranged our blanket and books in the center of the room and unraveled a sleeping bag there too, surrounding the whole area with dozens and dozens of candles stuck in funny make-shift canisters, like old cups and mugs or discarded Coca-Cola cans, just like they were at his house in the Wilds.

But the best part is the ceiling: or rather, the lack of ceiling. He must have broken through the rotted wood to the roof, and now an enormous patch of sky is once again stretched above our heads. There are fewer stars visible in Portland than on the other side of the border, but it's still beautiful. Even better, the bats – disturbed from their roost – have gone. Far above us, outside, I see several dark shapes looping back and forth across the moon, but as long as they stay in the open air, they don't bother me.

All of a sudden it hits me: he did this for me. Even after what happened today, he came and did this for me. Gratitude overwhelms me, and another feeling too, bringing with it a twinge of pain. I don't deserve it. I don't deserve him. I turn back to him and can't even speak; his face is lit up with flame and he seems to be glowing, transforming into fire. He is the most beautiful thing I have ever seen.

'Alex—' I start to say, but can't finish. Suddenly I'm almost frightened of him, terrified of his absolute and utter perfection.

He leans forward and kisses me. And when he's pressed so close to me, with the softness of his T-shirt brushing my face and the smell of suntan lotion and grass coming off his skin, he feels less frightening.

'It's too dangerous to go back to the Wilds.' His voice is hoarse, as though he's been yelling for a very long time, and a muscle is working furiously in his jaw. 'So I brought the Wilds here. I thought you would like it.'

'I do. I – I love it.' I press my hands against my chest, wishing I could somehow be even closer to him. I hate skin; I hate bones and bodies. I want to curl up inside of him and be carried there forever.

'Lena.' Different expressions are passing over his face so quickly I can barely catch them all, and his jaw keeps twitching back and forth. 'I know we don't have much time, like you said. We hardly have any time at all . . .'

'No.' I bury my face in his chest, wrap my arms around him and squeeze. Unimaginable, incomprehensible: a life lived without him. The idea breaks me – the fact that he's almost crying breaks me – the fact that he did this for me, the fact that he believes I'm worth it – kills me. He is my world and my world is him and without him there is no world. 'I won't do it. I won't go through with it. I can't. I want to be with you. I *need* to be with you.'

Alex grasps my face, bends down to look in my eyes. His face is blazing now, full of hope.

'You don't have to go through with it,' he says. His words come tumbling out. He's obviously been thinking about this for a long time and only trying not to say it. 'Lena, you don't have to do anything. We could run away together. To the Wilds. Just go and never come back. Only – Lena, we *couldn't* ever come back. You know that, right? They'd kill us both, or lock us up forever . . . But Lena, we could do it.'

Kill us both. Of course, he's right. A lifetime of running: that's what I've just said I wanted. I take a quick step backward, feeling suddenly dizzy. 'Wait,' I say. 'Just hold on a second.'

He releases me. The hope dies in his face all at once, and for a moment we just stand there, looking at each other. 'You weren't serious,' he says finally. 'You didn't mean it.'

'No, I did mean it, it's just—'

'It's just that you're scared,' he says. He walks to the window and stares out at the night, refusing to look at me. His back is terrifying again: so solid and impenetrable, a wall.

'I'm not scared. I'm just . . .' I fight a murky feeling. I don't know what I am. I want Alex and I want my old life and I want peace and happiness and I know that I can't live without him, all at the same time.

'It's okay.' His voice is dull. 'You don't have to explain.'

'My mother,' I burst out. Alex turns then, looking startled. I'm as surprised as he is. I didn't even know I was going to say the words until I said them. 'I don't want to be like her. Don't you understand? I saw what it did to her, I saw how she was . . . It killed her, Alex. She left me, left my sister, left it all. All for this thing, this thing inside of her. I *won't* be like her.' I've never really spoken about this, and I'm surprised by how difficult it is. Now I have to turn away, feeling sick and ashamed that the tears have started again.

'Because she wasn't cured?' Alex asks softly.

For a moment I can't speak, and I just let myself cry, silently now, hoping he can't tell. When I have control of my voice, I say, 'It's not just that.'

Then all of it comes rushing out, the details, things I've never shared with anyone before: 'She was so different from everybody else. I knew that – that *she* was different, that we were different – but it wasn't scary at first. It just felt like our little, delicious secret. Mine, and hers, and Rachel's, too, like we were in a cocoon. It was . . . It was amazing. We kept all the curtains drawn so no one could see in. We used to play this game where she would hide in the hallway and we would try to run past her and she would leap out and grab us – playing goblin, she called it. It always ended in a tickle war. She was always laughing. We were all always laughing. Then every so often when we got too loud, she would clap her hands over our mouths and get all tense for a second, listening. I guess she was listening for the neighbors, to make sure none of them were alarmed. But no one ever came.

'Sometimes she would make us blueberry pancakes for dinner, as a treat. She picked the blueberries herself. And she was always singing. She had a beautiful voice, just gorgeous, like honey—'

My voice cracks, but I can't stop now. The words are pouring, tumbling out. 'She used to dance, too. I told you that. When I was little I would stand with my feet on top of hers. She would wrap her arms around me and we would move slowly around the room while she counted out the beat, tried to teach me about rhythm. I was terrible at it, clumsy, but she always told me I was beautiful.' Tears make the floorboards blur beneath my feet.

'It wasn't all good, not all the time. Sometimes I would get up in the middle of the night to go to the bathroom and I'd hear her crying. She always tried to muffle it by turning into her pillow, but I knew. It was terrifying when she cried. I'd never seen a grown-up cry before, you know? And the way she did it, the wailing . . . like some kind of animal. And there were days she didn't get out of bed at all. She called those her black days.'

Alex moves closer to me. I'm shaking so badly I can hardly stand. My whole body feels like it's trying to expel something, cough something up from deep in my chest. 'I used to pray that God would cure her of the black days. That he would keep her – keep her safe for me. I wanted us to stay together. Sometimes it seemed like the praying worked. It was good most of the time. It was more than good.' I can barely bring myself to say these words. I have to force them out in a low whisper. 'Don't you get it? She left all that. She gave it up – for, for that *thing*. Love. *Amor deliria nervosa* – whatever you want to call it. She gave *me* up.'

'I'm sorry, Lena,' Alex whispers, behind me. This time he does reach out. He starts drawing long, slow circles on my back. I lean into him.

But I'm not done yet. I swipe at the tears furiously, take a big breath. 'Everyone thinks she killed herself because she couldn't stand to have the procedure again. They were still trying to cure her, you know. It would have been her fourth time. After her second procedure they refused to put her under – they thought the anesthesia was interfering with the way the cure was taking. They cut into her *brain*, Alex, and she was *awake*.'

I feel his hand stiffen temporarily, and I know he's just as angry as I am. Then the circles start up again.

'But I know that's not really why.' I shake my head. 'My mom was brave. She wasn't afraid of pain. That was the whole problem, really. She wasn't afraid. She didn't want to be cured; she didn't want to stop loving my dad. I remember she told me that once, just before she died. "They're trying to take him from me," she said. She was smiling so sadly. "They're trying to take him, but they can't." She used to wear one of his pins around her neck, on a chain. She kept it hidden most of the time, but that night she had it out and was staring at it. It was this strange, long, silver dagger-thing, with two bright jewels in the hilt, like eyes. My dad used to wear it on his sleeve. After he died she wore it every day, never took it off even to bathe . . .'

I suddenly realize that Alex has removed his hand and taken two steps away from me. I turn around and he's staring at me, white-faced and shocked, as though he's just seen a ghost.

'What?' I wonder if it's possible I've offended him in some way. Something about the way he's staring makes fear start beating at my chest, a frantic flutter. 'Did I say something wrong?'

He shakes his head, an almost imperceptible motion. The rest of his body stays as straight and tense as a wire stretched between two posts. 'How big was it? The pin, I mean.' His voice sounds strangely high-pitched.

'The point isn't the pin, Alex, the point is—'

'How big was it?' Louder now, and forceful.

'I don't know. Like the size of a thumb, maybe.' I'm completely baffled by Alex's behaviour. He has the most pained look on his face, as though he's trying to swallow a whole porcupine. 'It was originally my grandfather's – made just for him, a reward for performing a special service for the government. Unique. That's what my dad always said, anyway.'

Alex doesn't say anything for a minute. He turns away, and with the moon shining down on him, and his profile so hard and straight, he could be built out of stone. I'm glad he's not staring at me anymore, though. He was starting to freak me out.

'What are you doing tomorrow?' he asks finally, slowly, as though every word is an effort.

It seems like a weird thing to ask in the middle of a completely unrelated conversation, and I start to get annoyed. 'Were you even *listening* to me?'

'Lena, please.' There it is: the strangled, choking note again. 'Just answer me. Are you working?'

'Not until Saturday.' I rub my arms. The wind blowing in has a chilly edge to it. It lifts the hair on my arms, makes goosebumps prick up on my legs. Autumn is coming. 'Why?'

'You have to meet me. I have – I have something to show you.' Alex turns back to me again, and his eyes are so wild and black, his face so unfamiliar-looking, I take a step backward.

'You'll have to do better than that.' I try to laugh, but what comes out is a little gurgling sound. *I'm scared*, I want to say. *You're scaring me.* 'Can you at least give me a hint?'

Alex takes a deep breath, and for a minute I think he won't answer me.

But he does.

'Lena,' he says at last. 'I think your mother is alive.'

twenty-one

LIBERTY IN ACCEPTANCE;
PEACE IN ENCLOSURE;
HAPPINESS IN RENUNCIATION

– Words carved above the gates
at the entrance to the Crypts

When I was in fourth grade, I went on a field trip to the Crypts. It's mandated that every child visit at least once in elementary school as part of the government's anti-crime, anti-resistance education. I don't remember much about my visit except for a feeling of utter terror, a dim impression of coldness, of blackened concrete hallways, slicked with mold and moisture, and heavy electronic doors. To be honest, I think I've successfully blocked out most of the memory. The whole purpose of the trip was to traumatize us into staying on the straight-and-narrow, and they definitely had the *traumatize* part right.

What I do remember is stepping out afterward into the bright sunshine of a beautiful spring day with a sense of overwhelming, overpowering relief – and also confusion, as I realized that in order to exit the Crypts we actually had to descend several staircases to the ground floor. The whole time we'd been inside, even as we climbed, I had the impression of being buried underground, locked several stories under the surface of the earth. That's how dark it was, how close and bad-smelling: like being encased in a coffin with rotting bodies. I also remember that as soon as we got outside Liz Billmun began to cry, just sobbed right there while a butterfly flapped around her shoulder, and we were all in shock because Liz Billmun was super tough, and kind of a bully, and hadn't even cried the time she broke her ankle in gym class.

I had sworn that day that I would never, ever return to the Crypts for any reason. But the morning after my conversation with Alex I'm standing outside its gates, pacing, one arm wrapped around my stomach. I wasn't able to force anything down this morning except the thick black sludge my uncle calls coffee, a decision I am now regretting. I feel like acid is eating my insides.

Alex is late.

Overhead, the sky is packed tight with enormous black storm clouds. It's supposed to thunderstorm later, which seems fitting. Beyond the gate, at the end of a short, paved road, the Crypts looms black and imposing. Silhouetted against the dark sky, it looks like something out of a nightmare. A dozen or so tiny windows – like the multiple staring eyes of a spider – are scattered across its stone façade. A short field surrounds the Crypts on this side, enclosed within the gates. I remember it from my childhood as a meadow, but it is actually just a lawn, closely tended and bare in patches. Still, the vivid green of the grass – where the grass is actually managing to assert itself through the dirt – seems out of place. This seems like a place where nothing should flourish or grow, where the sun should never shine: a place on the edge, at the limit, a place completely removed from time and happiness and life.

I guess, technically, it *is* on the edge, since the Crypts is sitting right on the eastern border, flanked on its rear by the Presumpscot River, and beyond that, the Wilds. The electrified (or not-so-electrified) fence runs directly into one side of the Crypts, and begins again on its other side, the building itself serving as a seamless connective bridge.

'Hey.'

Alex is coming down the sidewalk, his hair whipping up around his head. The wind is definitely chilly today. I should have worn a heavier sweatshirt. Alex looks cold too. He's keeping his arms folded across his chest. Of course, he's just wearing a thin linen shirt, the official guard uniform he wears at the labs. He has his badge swinging around his neck, too. I haven't seen him with it since the first day we spoke. He's even wearing a pair of nice jeans, crisp dark ones with cuffs that aren't totally ragged and stepped on. This was all part of the plan: to get us both in, he needs to convince the prison administrators that we're on official business. I take comfort in the fact that he's still wearing his scuffed-up sneakers with the ink-stained laces, though. Somehow that little familiar detail makes it possible to be here, with him, doing this. It gives me something to focus on and hold on to, a tiny flash of normalcy in a world that has suddenly become unrecognizable.

'Sorry I'm late,' he says. He stops several feet away from me. I can see the concern in his eyes, even if he manages to keep the rest of his face composed. There are guards circulating the yard and standing just beyond the gate. This is no place for us to touch or reveal any kind of familiarity with each other.

'That's okay.' My voice cracks. I feel like I might have a fever. Ever since Alex and I spoke last night my head has been spinning, and my body has been burning one second and icy the next. I can hardly think. It's a miracle I was able to get out of the house today. It's a miracle I'm even wearing pants, a double miracle I remembered to wear shoes.

My mother might be alive. My mother might be alive. That is the single idea in my mind, the one that has supplanted the possibility of all other rational thought.

'Are you ready to do this?' He keeps his voice low and toneless in case the guards will overhear us – but I can detect the note of worry running underneath it.

'I think so,' I say. I try to manage a smile, but my lips feel cracked and dry as stone. 'It might not even be her, right? You could be wrong.'

He nods, but I can tell he's sure he hasn't made a mistake. He's sure that my mom is in here – this *place*, this above-ground tomb – has been there all this time. The idea is overwhelming. I can't think too much about the possibility that Alex is right. I need to concentrate, focus all my energy on just staying on my feet.

'Come on,' he says. He walks in front of me, like he's leading me on official business. I keep my eyes trained on the ground. I'm almost glad that the presence of the guards requires Alex to ignore me. I'm not sure I could handle a conversation right now. A thousand feelings swirl through me, a thousand questions whip around my mind, a thousand suppressed hopes and desires, buried long ago – and yet I can't hold on to anything, not a single theory or explanation that makes any kind of sense.

Alex had refused to tell me more after his declaration last night. 'You have to see,' he kept repeating dumbly, as though it was the only thing he knew how to say. 'I don't want to get your hopes up for nothing.' And then he'd told me to meet him at the Crypts. I think I must have been in shock. The whole time I kept congratulating myself for not freaking out, for not screaming or crying or demanding an explanation, but when I got home later I realized I had no memory of the walk at all and hadn't been keeping an eye out for regulators or patrols. I must have just marched stiffly down the street, blind to everything.

But now I get the point of shock, of numbness. Without the numbness I probably wouldn't have been able to get up and dressed this morning. I wouldn't have been able to find my way here, and I wouldn't be taking careful steps forward now, pausing a respectful distance behind him as Alex shows his ID badge to a guard at a gate and begins gesturing to me.

Alex launches into an explanation he has obviously rehearsed. 'There was an . . . *incident* at her evaluation,' he says, his voice icy. He and the guard are both staring at me: the guard, suspiciously; Alex with as much detachment as he can muster. His eyes are steel, all the warmth drained out of them, and it makes me nervous to know that he can do that so successfully – become someone else, someone who doesn't have any attachment to me. 'Nothing too severe. But her parents and my superiors thought she might benefit from a little reminder about the dangers of disobedience.'

The guard flicks his eyes over me. His face is fat and red, the skin on either side of his eyes protruding and puffy, like he is a mound of dough in the middle of rising. Soon, I fantasize, his eyes will be concealed behind flesh altogether. 'What kind of incident?' he says, snapping his gum. He shifts the enormous automatic rifle he is carrying to his other shoulder.

Alex leans forward, so that he and the guard are separated through the gate by only a few inches. He drops his voice, but I can still hear him. 'Her favourite colour is the colour of sunrise,' he says.

The guard stares at me for a split second longer and then waves for us to pass through. 'Stand back while I get the gate,' he says. He disappears into a guard hut, similar to the one at the labs where Alex is stationed, and after a few seconds the electronic gates shudder inward. Alex and I start across the courtyard, toward the building entrance. With every step, the hulking silhouette of the Crypts looms a little larger. The wind picks up, whirling bits of dust across the bleak yard, sending a lone plastic bag tumbling and skipping across the grass, and the air is filled with the kind of electricity that always comes before a thunderstorm – the kind of crazed, vibrating energy that makes it seem like something huge could happen at any second, like the whole world could just dissolve into chaos. I would give anything to have Alex turn around, smile at me, and offer me his hand. Of course, he can't. He strides quickly ahead of me, spine stiff, eyes forward.

I'm not sure how many people are confined in the Crypts.

Alex estimated it to be about three thousand. There's hardly any crime at all in Portland – thanks to the cure – but occasionally people do steal things or vandalize or resist police procedurals. Then there are the resisters and sympathizers. If they aren't executed immediately, some of them are left to rot in the Crypts.

The Crypts also serves as Portland's mental institution, and while there may not be much crime, despite the cure we have our share of crazies just like anywhere else. Alex would say *because* of the cure we have our crazies, and it's true that early procedures or procedures gone wrong can lead to mental difficulties or a kind of mental fracture. Plus, some people are just never the same after the procedure. They go catatonic, all staring eyes and drool, and if their families can't afford to keep them they get shoved into the Crypts as well, to molder and die.

Two enormous double doors lead into the Crypts. Tiny panes of glass, probably bulletproof and webbed with dirt and the residue of smeared insect parts, give me a blurred view of the long, dark hallway beyond, and several flickering electric lights. A typed sign, warped from rain and wind, is taped to the door. It says ALL VISITORS PROCEED DIRECTLY TO CHECK-IN AND SECURITY.

Alex pauses for just a fraction of a second. 'Ready?' he says to me, without looking back.

'Yes,' I choke out.

The smell that hits us as we enter nearly jettisons me backward – out the door, through time, back to fourth grade. It's the smell of thousands of unwashed bodies packed closely together, underneath the stinging, burning scent of industrial-strength bleach and cleanser. Overlaying it all is the smell of *wet* – corridors that aren't ever truly dry, leaking pipes, mold growing behind walls and in all the little twisty places visitors are never allowed to see. Check-in is to our left, and the woman who is manning the desk behind another panel of bulletproof glass is wearing a medical mask. I don't blame her.

Strangely, as we approach her desk, she looks up and addresses Alex by name.

'Alex,' she says, nodding curtly. Her eyes flicker to me. 'Who's that?'

Alex repeats his story about the incident at the evaluations. He's obviously on pretty familiar terms with the guard, because he uses her first name a couple of times, and I can't see that she's wearing any kind of name tag. She logs our names into the ancient computer on her desk and waves us through to security. Alex says hello to the security personnel here too, and I admire him for his coolness. I'm having a pretty hard time just undoing my belt before the metal detector, my hands are shaking so badly. The guards at the Crypts seem to be about 50 percent larger than normal people, with hands like tennis rackets and chests as broad as boats. And they're all carrying guns. *Big* guns. I'm doing my best not to seem utterly terrified, but it's difficult to stay calm when you have to strip down practically to your underwear in front of giants equipped with automatic assault weapons.

Eventually we make it through security. Alex and I dress again in silence, and I'm surprised – and pleased – when I actually manage to tie my own shoelaces.

'Wards one through five only,' one of the guards calls out, as Alex gestures for me to follow him down the hall.

The walls are painted a sickly yellow colour. In a home, or a brightly lit nursery or office, it might be cheerful,' but illuminated only by the patchy fluorescent lights that keep buzzing on and off, and stained with years and years of water and handprints and squashed insects and I don't-want-to-know-what, it seems incredibly depressing – like getting a big smile from someone with blackened, rotting teeth.

'You got it,' Alex says. I'm assuming this means that certain areas are restricted from visitors.

I follow Alex down one narrow corridor, and then another. The hallways are empty, and so far we haven't passed any cells, although as we continue making twists and turns the sounds of moaning and shrieking begin to float to us, as well as strange animal sounds, bleating and mooing and cawing, like a bunch of people are imitating a barnyard. We must be near the mental ward. We don't pass any other people, though, no nurses or guards or patients. Everything is so still it's almost frightening; silent, too, except for those awful sounds, which seem to emanate from the walls.

It seems safe to talk, so I ask Alex, 'How does everybody know you here?'

'I come by a lot,' he says, as though this is a satisfactory answer. People don't 'come by' the Crypts. It's not exactly up there with the beach. It's not even up there with a public restroom.

I'm thinking he won't elaborate further, and I'm about to press him for a more detailed answer, when he blows air out of his cheeks and says, 'My father's here. That's why I come.'

I really didn't think that anything could further surprise me at this point, or penetrate the fog in my brain, but this does. 'I thought you said your father was dead.'

Alex told me a long time ago that his dad had died, but he'd refused to give any details. 'He never knew he had a son': that's the only thing Alex had said, and I figured it meant that his dad was dead before Alex was born.

Ahead of me, Alex's shoulders rise and fall: a small sigh. 'He is,' he says, and makes an abrupt right turn down a short hallway that ends at a heavy iron door. This is marked with another printed sign. It says LIFERS. Underneath the word, someone has written in pen, HA HA.

'What are you—' I'm more confused than ever, but I don't have time to finish formulating my question. Alex pushes his way out the door and the smell that greets us – of wind and grass and fresh things – is so unexpected and welcome that I stop speaking, taking long, grateful gulps of air. Without realizing it, I've been breathing through my mouth.

We're in a tiny courtyard, surrounded on all sides by the stained grey sides of the Crypts. The grass here is amazingly lush, reaching practically to my knees. A single tree twists upward to our left, and a bird is twittering in its branches. It's surprisingly nice out here, peaceful and pretty – strange to be standing in the middle of a little garden while enclosed by the massive stone walls of the prison, like being at the exact center of a hurricane, and finding peace and silence in the middle of so much shrieking damage.

Alex has moved several paces away. He is standing, head bowed, with his eyes on the ground. He must have a sense too of the peacefulness here, the stillness that seems to hang in the air like a veil, covering everything in softness and rest. The sky above us is darker than it was when we first entered the Crypts: against all the greyness and shadow, the grass stands vivid and electric, as though it is lit up from inside. It will rain at any second. It has to. I have the sensation of the world holding its breath before a giant exhale, balancing, teetering, about to let go.

'Here.' Alex's voice rings out, surprisingly loud, and it startles me. 'Right here.' He points to a shard of rock sticking up crookedly from the ground. 'That's where my father is.'

The grass is broken up by dozens of these rocks, which at first glance appeared to be naturally, haphazardly arranged. Then I realize that they've been deliberately tamped down into the earth. Some of them are covered in faded black markings, mostly illegible, although on one stone I recognize the word RICHARD and on another DIED.

Tombstones, I realize, as the purpose of the courtyard dawns on me. We're standing in the middle of a graveyard.

Alex is staring down at a large chunk of concrete, as flat as a tablet, pressed down into the earth in front of his feet. All the writing is visible here, the words neatly printed in what looks like black marker, their edges slightly blurred as though someone has been continuously retracing them over a long period of time. It says WARREN SHEATHES, R.I.P.

'Warren Sheathes,' I say. I want to reach out and slip my hand into Alex's, but I don't think we're safe. There are a few windows surrounding the courtyard on the ground floor, and even though they are thickly coated in grime, someone could walk by at any moment, look out, and see us. 'Your father?'

Alex nods, then shakes his shoulders, a sudden movement as though trying to jerk himself away from sleep. 'Yeah.'

'He was here?'

One side of Alex's mouth quirks up into a smile, but the

rest of his face remains stony. 'For fourteen years.' He draws a slow circle in the dirt with his toe, the first physical sign of discomfort or distraction he has given since we arrived. In that moment I am in awe of him: since I've known him he has done nothing but support me and give me comfort and listen to me, and all this time he has been carrying the weight of his own secrets too.

'What happened?' I ask quietly. 'I mean, what did he . . . ?' I trail off. I don't want to push the issue.

Alex glances at me quickly and looks away. 'What did he do?' he says. The hardness has returned to his voice. 'I don't know. What all the people who end up in Ward Six do. He thought for himself. Stood up for what he believed in. Refused to give in.'

'Ward Six?'

Alex avoids my eyes carefully. 'The dead ward,' he says quietly. 'For political prisoners, mostly. They're kept in solitary confinement. And no one ever gets released.' He gestures around him, to the other shards of stone poking up through the grass, dozens of makeshift graves. 'Ever,' he repeats, and I think of the sign on the door: LIFERS, HA HA.

'I'm so sorry, Alex.' I would give anything to touch him, but the best I can do is inch closer to him so that our skin is separated by only a few inches.

He looks at me then, shooting me a sad smile. 'He and my mom were only sixteen when they met. Can you believe that? She was only eighteen when she had me.' He drops into a squat and traces his father's name with his thumb. I suddenly understand that the reason he comes here so often is to continue darkening the letters as they fade, to keep some record of his father. 'They wanted to run away together, but he was caught before they could finalize a plan. I never knew he'd been taken into custody. I just thought he was dead. My mom thought it would be better for me, and nobody in the Wilds knew enough to correct her. I think for my mom it was easier to believe he *had* really died. She didn't want to think of him rotting in this place.' He continues looping a finger over the letters, back and forth. 'My aunt and uncle told me the truth when I turned fifteen. They wanted me to know. I came here to meet him, but . . .' I think I see Alex shudder, a sudden stiffening movement of his shoulders and back. 'Anyway, it was too late. He was dead, had been dead for a few months, and buried here, where his remains wouldn't *contaminate* anything.'

I feel sick. The walls appear to be pressing closer around us, growing taller and narrower, too, so the sky feels more and more remote, an ever-diminishing point. *We'll never get out*, I think, and then take a deep breath, trying to stay calm.

Alex straightens up. 'Ready?' he asks me, for the second time this morning. I nod, even though I'm not sure that I am. He allows himself the brief flicker of a smile, and I see, for a second, a bit of warmth spark up in his eyes. Then he's all business again.

I take one last look at the tombstone before we go in. I try to think of a prayer or something appropriate to say, but nothing comes to me. The lessons of the scientists aren't really clear about what happens when you die: supposedly you dissipate into the heavenly matter that is God, and get absorbed by him, although they also tell us that the cured go to heaven and live forever in perfect harmony and order.

'Your name.' I spin around to face Alex. He has already moved past me, headed back for the door. 'Alex Warren.'

He gives an almost imperceptible shake of his head. 'Assigned to me,' he says.

'Your real name is Alex Sheathes,' I say, and he nods. He has a secret name, just like me. We stand there for one more moment, looking at each other, and in that instant I feel our connection so strongly it's as though it achieves physical existence, becomes a hand all around us, cupping us together, protecting us. *This* is what people are always talking about when they talk about God: this feeling, of being held and understood and protected. Feeling this way seems about as close to saying a prayer as you could get, so I follow Alex back inside, holding my breath as we again encounter that awful stink.

I follow Alex down a series of serpentine hallways. The sensation of stillness and peace I had in the courtyard is replaced almost immediately by fear so sharp it is like a blade going straight into the core of me, driving down and deep, until I can hardly breathe or keep going. At points the wailing grows louder, almost to a fever pitch, and I have to cover my ears; then it ebbs away again. Once we pass a man wearing a long white lab coat, stained with what looks like blood; he is leading a patient on a leash. Neither one looks at us as we pass.

We make so many twists and turns I'm beginning to wonder if Alex is lost, especially as the hallways grow dirtier, and the lights above us become fewer in number, so that eventually we are walking through murk and obscurity, with a single functioning bulb to light up twenty feet of blackened stone corridor. At intervals various glowing neon signs appear in the darkness, as though they are rising out of the air itself: WARD ONE, WARD TWO, WARD THREE, WARD FOUR. Alex keeps going, though, and when we pass the hallway that leads to Ward Five I call out to him, convinced he has gotten confused or lost his way.

'Alex,' I say, but even as I say the word it strangles me, because just then we come up to a heavy set of double doors marked with a small sign, barely illuminated, so faint I can hardly read it. And yet it seems to burn as brightly as a thousand suns.

Alex turns around, and to my surprise his face isn't composed at all. His jaw is working and his eyes are full of pain, and I can tell he hates himself for being there, for being the one to say it, for being the one to show me.

'I'm sorry, Lena,' he says. Above him the sign smolders in the darkness: WARD SIX.

twenty-two

Humans, unregulated, are cruel and capricious; violent and selfish; miserable and quarrelsome. It is only after their instincts and basic emotions have been controlled that they can be happy, generous, and good.

— *The Book of Shhh*

I have a sudden dread of going any farther. That thing in the pit of my stomach squeezes up like a fist, making it hard to breathe. I can't go on. I don't want to know.

'Maybe we shouldn't,' I say. 'He said – he said we weren't allowed.'

Alex reaches out for me like he's thinking of touching me, then remembers where we are and forces his arms to his sides. 'Don't worry,' he says. 'I have friends here.'

'It's probably not even her.' My voice is rising a little, and I'm worried I might have a meltdown. I lick my lips, trying to keep it together. 'It was probably just a big mistake. We shouldn't have come in the first place. I want to go home.'

I know I must sound like a toddler throwing a tantrum, but I can't help it. Walking through those double doors seems absolutely impossible.

'Lena, come on. You have to trust me.' Then he does reach out, for just a second, skating one finger across my forearm. 'Okay? Trust me.'

'I do trust you, it's just . . .' The air, the stench, the darkness and the sensation of rot all around me: it makes me want to run. 'If she *isn't* here . . . Well, that's bad. But if she *is* . . . I think – I think it might be even worse.'

Alex watches me closely for a second. 'You have to know, Lena,' he says finally, firmly, and he's right. I nod. He gives me the barest flicker of a smile, then reaches forward and heaves open the doors to Ward Six.

We step into a vestibule that looks exactly like what I imagine a cell in the Crypts might be like: the walls and floor are concrete, and whatever colour they might once have been painted has now faded to a dingy, mossy grey. A single bulb is set high in the ceiling, and barely delivers enough light to illuminate the tiny space. There is a stool in the corner, occupied by a guard. This guard is actually normal-sized – skinny, even, with acne pockmarks and hair that reminds me of overcooked spaghetti. As soon as Alex and I step through the door, the guard makes a small, reflexive adjustment to his gun, drawing it closer toward his body and swiveling the barrel ever so slightly in our direction.

Alex stiffens beside me. All of a sudden, I feel very alert.

'Can't be in here,' the guard says. 'Restricted area.'

For the first time since entering the Crypts, Alex appears uncomfortable. He fiddles nervously with his badge. 'I – I thought Thomas would be here.'

The guard gets to his feet. Amazingly, he's not much taller than I am – he's certainly shorter than Alex – but of all the guards I've seen today, he frightens me the most. There's something strange about his eyes, a flatness and hardness that reminds me of a snake. I've never had a gun pointed at me before, and staring into the long black tunnel of its barrel makes me feel like I'm going to faint.

'Oh, he's here, all right. He's *always* here, nowadays.' The guard smiles humourlessly, and his fingers dance against the trigger. When he speaks his lips curl upward, revealing a mouth full of crooked yellow teeth. 'What do you know about Thomas?'

The room takes on the stillness and charge of the air outside, and reminds me of waiting for thunder to crack. Alex allows himself one small indication of nervousness: he curls and flexes his fingers against his thighs. I can almost see him thinking, trying to figure out what to say next. He must know that mentioning Thomas was a bad decision – even I heard the contempt and suspicion in the guard's voice as he pronounced the name.

After what seems like a terribly long time – but is probably only a few seconds – the blank, official look sweeps down over his face again.

'We heard there was some kind of problem, that's all.' The statement is sufficiently vague, and a decent assumption. Alex twirls his security badge idly between two fingers. The guard flicks his eyes to it, and I can tell he relaxes. Fortunately, he doesn't try to look at it more closely. Alex has only Level One security clearance in the labs, which means he barely has the right to visit the janitor's closet, much less parade around restricted areas, there or anywhere else in Portland, as though he owns them.

'Took you long enough,' the guard says flatly. 'Thomas has been out for months. All the better for CID, I guess. It's not the kind of thing we wanted to publicize.' The CID is the Controlled Information Department (or, if you're cynical like Hana, the Corrupt Idiots Department or the Censorship Implementation Department), and goosebumps prick up on my arms. Something went very wrong in Ward Six if the CID got involved.

'You know how it is,' Alex says. He has recovered from his temporary slip-up; the confidence and ease return to his voice. 'Impossible to get a straight answer from anyone over there.' Another vague statement, but the guard just nods.

'You're telling me.' Then he jerks his head in my direction. 'Who's she?'

I can feel him staring at the unmarred skin on my neck, noticing that I have no procedural mark. Like many people, he unconsciously recoils – just a few inches, but enough so that the old feeling of humiliation, the feeling of being somehow *wrong*, creeps over me. I turn my eyes to the ground.

'She's nobody,' Alex says, and even though I know he *has* to say it, it makes my chest ache dully. 'I'm supposed to be showing her the Crypts, that's all. A re-educational process, if you know what I mean.'

I hold my breath, certain that at any second he'll boot us out, almost wishing he would. And yet . . . Just beyond the guard's stool is a single door made out of a heavy, thick metal, and protected by an electronic keypad. It reminds me of the bank vault at Central Savings downtown. Through it I can just make out distant sounds – human sounds, I think, though it's hard to tell.

My mother could be beyond that door. She could be *in* there. Alex was right. I do have to know.

For the first time, I begin to understand, fully, what Alex told me last night: all this time, my mother might have been alive. While I was breathing, she was breathing too. While I was sleeping, she was sleeping elsewhere. When I was awake thinking of her, she might have been thinking of me, too. It's overwhelming, both miraculous and fiercely painful.

Alex and the guard eye each other for a minute. Alex continues spinning his badge around one finger, winding and unwinding the chain. It seems to put the guard at ease.

'I can't let you back there,' he says, but this time he sounds apologetic. He lowers his gun and sits down on the stool again. I exhale quickly; I've been holding my breath without meaning to.

'You're just doing your job,' Alex says, keeping his voice neutral. 'So you're Thomas's replacement?'

'That's right.' The guard flicks his eyes to me and again I can feel his gaze lingering on my unmarked neck. I have to stop myself from covering my skin with a hand. But he must decide that we aren't going to be trouble, because he looks back to Alex and says, 'Frank Dorset. Got reassigned from Three in February – after the incident.'

Something about the way he says *incident* sends chills up my spine.

'Tough breaks, huh?' Alex leans up against a wall, the picture of casualness. Only I can detect the edge in his voice. He's stalling. He doesn't know what to do from here, or how to get us inside.

Frank shrugs. 'Quieter up here, that's for sure. Nobody in or out. At least, *almost* nobody.' He smiles again, showing off

those awful teeth, but his eyes maintain their strange flatness, as though there's a curtain drawn over them. I wonder
if this, for him, was a side effect of the cure, or whether he
was always like that.

He tilts his head back, peering at Alex through narrowed
eyes, and his resemblance to a snake grows even stronger.
'So how'd you hear about Thomas?'

Alex keeps up the unconcerned act, smiling, twirling the
badge. 'Rumours floating here and there,' he says, shrugging.
'You know how it is.'

'I know how it is,' Frank says. 'But the CID wasn't too
happy about it. Had us on lock for a few months. What
exactly did you hear, anyway?'

I can tell the question is an important one, some kind of
test. *Be careful*, I think in Alex's direction, as though he might
somehow hear me.

Alex hesitates for only a second before saying, 'Heard he
might have sympathies on the other side.'

Suddenly, it all makes sense: the fact that Alex said, 'I have
friends here,' the fact that he has seemingly had access to
Ward Six in the past. One of the guards must have been a
sympathizer, maybe an active part of the resistance. Alex's
constant refrain plays in my head: *There are more of us than
you think.*

Frank relaxes visibly. Apparently that was the right answer.
He seems to decide that Alex is, after all, trustworthy. He
strokes the barrel of his gun – which has been resting casually between his knees – as though it is a pet. 'That's right.
Came as a total shock to me. 'Course, I hardly knew him –
saw him sometimes in the break room, once or twice in the
shitter, that's about it. Kept to himself, mostly. I guess

it makes sense. Must have been getting chatty with the Invalids.'

This is the first time I've heard anyone in an official capacity acknowledge the existence of the people in the Wilds, and I suck in a sharp breath. I know it must be painful for Alex to stand there, talking dismissively about a friend who has been caught for being a sympathizer. The punishment must have been swift and severe, especially since he was on the government payroll. Most likely he was hanged or shot or electrocuted, or thrown into one of the cells to rot – if the courts were merciful and decided against a verdict of death by torture. If he even *had* a trial.

Amazingly, Alex's voice doesn't falter. 'What was the tip-off?'

Frank keeps massaging his gun, and something about the motion – gentle, almost, like he's willing it to life – makes me feel sick. 'No tip-off, exactly.' He sweeps his hair off his face, revealing a splotchy red forehead, shiny with sweat. It's much hotter here than it was in the other wards. The air must get trapped in these walls, rotting and festering like everything else in this place. 'It figures he must have known something about the escape. He was in charge of cell inspections. And the tunnel didn't just sprout up overnight.'

'The escape?' The words fly out of my mouth before I can help it. My heart starts jolting painfully in my chest. Nobody has ever escaped the Crypts, not ever.

For a moment Frank's hand pauses on the gun, his fingers once again performing a dance on the trigger. 'Sure,' he says, keeping his eyes on Alex, as though I'm not even there. 'You must have heard about it.'

Alex shrugs. 'A little of this, a little of that. Nothing confirmed.'

Frank laughs. It's a terrible sound. It reminds me of the time I saw two seagulls fighting in midair over a scrap of food, screeching as they tumbled toward the ocean. 'Oh, it's confirmed,' he says. 'Happened back in February. We got the alarm from Thomas, as a matter of fact. 'Course, if he was in on it, she might have had a lead time of six, seven hours.'

When he says the word *she* the walls seem to collapse around me. I take a quick step backward, bumping up against a wall. *It could be her*, I think, and for one horrible, guilty second I'm disappointed. Then I remind myself that she might not be here at all – and in any case, it could have been anyone who escaped, any female sympathizer or agitator. Still, the dizziness does not subside. I'm filled with anxiety and fear and a desperate craving, all at once.

'What's wrong with her?' Frank asks. His voice sounds distant.

'Air,' I manage to force out. 'It's the air in here.'

Frank laughs again, that unpleasant cackling sound. 'You think it's bad out here,' he says. 'It's paradise compared to the cells.' He seems to take pleasure in this, and it reminds me of a debate I had a few weeks ago with Alex, when he was arguing against the usefulness of the cure. I said that without love, there could also be no hate; without hate, no violence. *Hate isn't the most dangerous thing*, he'd said. *Indifference is.*

Alex starts talking. His voice is low and still casual, but there's an undertone of force to it: the kind of voice street peddlers lapse into when they are trying to get you to buy a carton of bruised berries or a broken toy. *It's okay, I'll give you a deal, no problem, trust me.* 'Listen, just let us in for a minute. That's all it will take: a minute. You can tell she's already scared out of her mind. I had to come all the way out here for this, day off and everything. I was going to go to the pier, maybe try out some fishing. Point is, if I bring her home and she's not straightened out . . . well, you know, chances are I'll just have to haul out here again. And I only have a couple days off, and summer's almost over . . .'

'Why all the trouble?' Frank says, jerking his head in my direction. 'If she's causing problems, there's an easy way to fix her up.'

Alex smiles tightly. 'Her father's Steven Jones, commissioner at the labs. He doesn't want to do an early procedure, no trouble, no violence or mess. Looks bad, you know.'

It's a bold lie. Frank could easily ask to see my ID card, and then Alex and I are screwed. I'm not sure what the punishment would be for infiltrating the Crypts under false pretenses, but it can't be good.

Frank appears interested in me for the first time. He looks me up and down like I'm a grapefruit he's evaluating in the supermarket for ripeness, and for a moment he doesn't say anything.

Then, finally, he stands, slipping the gun onto his shoulder. 'Come on,' he says. 'Five minutes.'

As he's fiddling with the keypad, which requires both that he type a code and scan his hand on some kind of fingerprint-matching screen, Alex reaches out and takes my elbow.

'Let's go,' he says, making his voice gruff, like my little fit has left him impatient. But his touch is gentle, and his hand warm and reassuring. I wish he could keep it there, but after only a second he lets me go again. I can read a plea, loud and clear, in his eyes: *Be strong. We're almost there. Be strong for just a little while longer.*

The locks on the door release with a click. Frank leans his shoulder against it, straining, and it slides open just enough for us to squeeze by into the hallway beyond. Alex goes first, then me, then Frank. The passage is so narrow we have to go single file, and it's even darker than the rest of the Crypts.

But the smell is what really hits me: a horrible, rotting, festering stink, like the Dumpsters by the harbour, the place where all the fish intestines get discarded, on the hottest day. Even Alex curses and coughs, covering his nose with his hand.

Behind me, I can imagine Frank grinning. 'Ward Six has its own special perfume,' he says.

As we walk I can hear the barrel of his gun, slapping against his thigh. I'm worried I might faint, and I want to reach out and steady myself against the walls, but they are coated with fungus and moisture. On either side of us, bolted metal cell doors appear at intervals, each outfitted with a single grimy window the size of a dinner plate. Through the walls we can hear low moaning, a constant vibration. It's worse, somehow, than the screeches and screams of earlier: this is the sound people make when they've long ago given up hope that anyone is listening, a reflexive sound, meant just to fill the time and the space and the darkness.

I'm going to be sick. If Alex is correct, my mother is here, behind one of these terrible doors – so close that if I could rearrange the particles and make the stone melt away, I might put my hand out and touch her. Closer than I ever thought I would be to her again.

I am filled with competing thoughts and desires: *My mother cannot be here; I would rather she was dead; I want to see her alive.* And filled, too, with that other word, pressing itself underneath all my other thoughts: *escape, escape, escape.* A possibility too fantastic to contemplate. If my mother had been the one to break out, I would have known. She would have come for me.

Ward Six consists of just the one long hallway. As far as I can tell, there are about forty doors, forty separate cells.

'This is it,' Frank says. 'The grand tour.' He pounds on one of the very first doors. 'Here's your boy Thomas, if you want to say hello.' Then he laughs again, that awful cackling sound.

I think about what he said when we first entered the vestibule: *He's* always *here, nowadays.*

Ahead of us, Alex does not respond, but I think I see him shudder.

Frank nudges me sharply in the back with the barrel of his gun. 'So what do you think?'

'Awful,' I croak out. My throat feels like it has been encircled with barbed wire. Frank seems pleased.

'Better to listen and do as you're told,' he says. 'No use ending up like *this* guy.'

We've paused in front of one of the cells. Frank nods toward the tiny window, and I take a hesitant step forward, pressing my face up to the glass. It's so grimy it's practically opaque, but if I squint I can just make out a few shapes in the obscurity of the cell: a single bed with a flimsy, dirty mattress; a toilet; a bucket that looks like it might be the human equivalent of a dog's water bowl. At first I think there's a pile of old rags in the corner too, until I realize that this thing is the 'guy' Frank was pointing out: a filthy, crouching heap of skin and bones and crazy, tangled hair. He's motionless, and his skin is so dirty it blends in with the grey of the stone walls behind him. If it weren't for his eyes, rolling continuously back and forth as though he is checking the air for insects, you would never know he was alive. You would never even know he was *human*.

The thought flashes again: *I would rather she be dead*. Not in this place. Anywhere but here.

Alex has continued down the hall, and I hear him draw in his breath sharply. I look up. He is standing perfectly still, and the expression on his face makes me afraid.

'What?' I say.

For a moment he doesn't answer. He is staring at something I cannot see – some door, presumably, farther down the hall. Then he turns to me abruptly, a quick, convulsive shake.

'Don't,' he says, his voice a croak, and the fear surges, overwhelms me.

'What is it?' I ask again. I start down the hall toward him. It seems, all of a sudden, that he is very far away, and when Frank speaks up behind me, his voice too sounds distant.

'That's where she was,' he is saying. 'Number one-eighteen. Admin hasn't coughed up the dough to get the walls patched, yet, so for now we're just leaving it as is. Not a lot of money around here for improvements . . .'

Alex is watching me. All his control and confidence has vanished. His eyes are blazing with anger, or maybe pain; his mouth is twisted into a grimace. My head feels full of noise.

Alex holds up his hand like he's thinking of blocking my progress. Our eyes meet for just a second and something flashes between us – a warning, or an apology, maybe – and then I am pushing beyond him into cell 118.

In almost every way it is identical to the cells I've glimpsed through the tiny hallway windows: a rough cement floor; a rust-stained toilet, and a bucket full of water, in which several cockroaches are revolving slowly; a tiny iron bed with a paper-thin mattress, which someone has dragged into the very center of the room.

But the walls.

The walls are covered – *crammed* – with writing. No. Not writing. They are covered with a single four-letter word that has been inscribed over and over, on every available surface.

Love.

Looped huge and scratched, just barely, in the corners; inscribed in graceful script and solid block lettering; chipped, scratched, picked away, as though the walls are slowly melting into poetry.

And on the ground, lying curled up against one wall, is a dull silver chain with a charm still attached to it: a ruby-encrusted dagger whose blade has been worn down to a small nub. My father's charm. My mother's necklace.

My *mother.*

All this time, during every long second of my life when I believed her dead, she was here: scratching, burrowing, chipping away, encased in the stone walls like a long-buried secret.

I feel, suddenly, as though I am back in my dream, standing on a cliff as the solid ground disintegrates underneath me, transforms into the sand in an hourglass, running away under my feet. I feel the way I do in that moment when I realize that all the ground has vanished, and I am standing on a bare blade of air, ready to drop.

'It's terrible, you see? Look at what the disease did to her. Who knows how many hours she spent scrabbling along these walls like a rat.'

Frank and Alex are standing behind me. Frank's words seem to be muffled by a layer of cloth. I take a step forward into the cell, suddenly fixated on a shaft of light, extending like a long golden finger from a space in the wall that has been chipped clear away. The clouds must have begun to break apart outside: through the hole, on the other side of the stone fortress, I see the flashing blue of the Presumpscot River, and leaves shifting and tumbling over one another, an avalanche of green and sun and the perfume of wild, growing things. The Wilds.

So many hours, so many days, looping those same four letters over and over: that strange and terrifying word, the word that confined her here for over ten years.

And, ultimately, the word that helped her escape. In the lower half of one wall, she has traced the word so many times in such enormous script – LOVE, each letter the size of a child – and gouged so deeply into the stone that the *O* has formed a tunnel, and she has gotten out.

twenty-three

Food for the body, milk for your bones,
ice for the bleeding, a belly of stones.

– A folklore blessing

Even after the iron gates clang shut behind us and the Crypts recedes in the distance, the feeling of being penned in on all sides doesn't go away. There's still a terrible, squeezing pressure in my chest, and I have to struggle to suck in full breaths.

An ancient prison bus with a wheezing motor carries us away from the border, to Deering. From there Alex and I walk back toward the center of Portland, staying on opposite sides of the sidewalk. Every couple of feet he swivels his head to look at me, opening and closing his mouth, like he's pronouncing a series of inaudible words. I know he's worried about me, and probably waiting for me to break down, but I can't bring myself to meet his eyes or speak to him. I keep my eyes locked straight ahead of me, keep my feet cycling forward. Other than the terrible pain in my chest and stomach, my body feels numb. I can't feel the ground underneath me or the wind zipping through the trees, skating past my face; can't feel the warmth of the sun, which has, against all odds, broken through the terrible black clouds, lighting the world up a strange greenish colour, as though everything is submerged under water.

When I was little and my mother died – when I thought she'd died – I remember going out for my first-ever run and getting hopelessly lost at the end of Congress, a street I'd been playing on my whole life. I turned a corner and found myself in front of the Bubble and Soap Cleaners and had been suddenly unable to remember where I was, and whether home was to the left or to the right. Nothing looked the same. Everything looked like a painted replica of itself, fragile and distorted, like I was caught in a fun house hall of mirrors reflecting my regular world back to me.

That's how I feel now, again. Lost and found and lost again, all at once. And now I know somewhere in this world, in the wildness on the other side of the fence, my mother is alive and breathing and sweating and moving and thinking. I wonder if she is thinking about me, and the pain shoots deeper, makes me lose my breath completely so I have to stop walking and double up, one hand on my stomach.

We're still off-peninsula, not far from 37 Brooks, where the houses are separated by large tracts of torn-up grass and run-down gardens, full of litter. Still, there are people on the streets, including a man I take for a regulator right away: even now, just before noon, he has a bullhorn swinging from his neck and a wooden baton strapped to one thigh. Alex must see him too. He stays a couple of feet away from me, scanning the street, trying to appear unconcerned, but he murmurs in my direction, 'Can you move?'

I have to fight my way through the pain. It is radiating through my whole body now, throbbing up into my head. 'I think so,' I gasp out.

'Alley. On your left. Go.'

I straighten up as much as I can – enough, at least, to hobble into the alley between two larger buildings. Halfway down the alley there are a few metal Dumpsters, arranged parallel to one another, buzzing with flies. The smell is disgusting, like being back in the Crypts, but I sink down between them anyway, grateful for the concealment and the chance to sit. As soon as I'm resting, the throbbing in my head subsides. I tilt my head back against the brick, feel the world swaying, a ship cut loose from its mooring.

Alex joins me a few moments later, squatting in front of me, brushing the hair away from my face. It's the first time he's been able to touch me all day.

'I'm sorry, Lena,' he says, and I know he really means it. 'I thought you'd want to know.'

'Twelve years,' I say simply. 'I thought she was dead for twelve years.'

For a while we stay there in silence. Alex rubs circles on my shoulders, arms, and knees – anywhere he can reach, really, like he's desperate to maintain physical contact with me. I wish I could close my eyes and be blown into dust and nothingness, feel all my thoughts disperse like dandelion fluff drifting off on the wind. But his hands keep pulling me back: into the alley, and Portland, and a world that has suddenly stopped making sense.

She's out there somewhere, breathing, thirsty, eating, walking, swimming. Impossible, now, to contemplate going on with my life, impossible to imagine sleeping, and lacing up my shoes for a run, and helping Carol load the dishes, and even lying in the house with Alex, when I know that she exists: that she is out there, orbiting as far from me as a distant constellation.

Why didn't she come for me? The thought flashes as quickly and clearly as an electrical surge, bringing the pain searing back. I squeeze my eyes shut, drop my head forward, pray for it to pass. But I don't know who to pray to. All at once I can't remember any words, can't think of anything but being in church when I was little and watching the sun blaze up and then fade away beyond the stained-glass windows, watching all that light die, leaving nothing but dull panes of coloured glass, tinny and insubstantial-looking.

'Hey. Look at me.'

Opening my eyes takes a tremendous effort. Alex looks hazy, even though he's crouching no more than a foot away from me.

'You must be hungry,' he says gently. 'Let's get you home, okay? Are you okay to walk?' He shuffles back a little, giving me space to stand.

'No.' It comes out more emphatically than I'd intended, and Alex looks startled.

'You're not okay to walk?' A little crease appears between his eyebrows.

'No.' It's a struggle to keep my voice at a normal volume. 'I mean I can't go home. At all.'

Alex sighs and rubs his forehead. 'We could go over to Brooks for a while, hang out at the house for a bit. And when you feel better—'

I cut him off. 'You don't get it.' A scream is welling inside of me, a black insect scrabbling in my throat. All I can think is: *They knew.* They all knew – Carol and Uncle William and maybe even Rachel – and still they let me believe all along that she was dead. They let me believe she had left me. They let me believe I wasn't worth it. I'm filled, suddenly, with white-hot anger, a blaze: if I see them, if I go home, I won't be able to stop myself. I'll burn the house down, or tear it apart, plank by plank. 'I want to run away with you. To the Wilds. Like we talked about.'

I think Alex will be happy, but instead he just seems tired. He looks away, squinting. 'Listen, Lena, it's been a really long day. You're exhausted. You're hungry. You're not thinking clearly—'

'I *am* thinking clearly.' I haul myself to my feet so I don't look so helpless. I'm angry at Alex, too, even though I know this isn't his fault. But the fury is whipping around inside of me, undirected, gaining force. 'I can't stay here, Alex. Not anymore. Not after – not after that.' My throat spasms as I swallow back the scream again. 'They knew, Alex. They knew and they never told me.'

He climbs to his feet too – slowly, like it hurts him. 'You don't know that for sure,' he says.

'I *do* know,' I insist, and it's true. I do know, deep down. I think of my mother bent over me, the floating pale whiteness of her face breaking through my sleep, her voice – *I love you. Remember. They cannot take it.* – sung quietly in my ear, the sad little smile dancing on her lips. She knew too. She must have known they were coming for her, and would take her to that terrible place. And only a week later I sat in a scratchy black dress in front of an empty coffin with a pile of orange peels to suck on, trying to keep back tears, while everyone I believed in built around me a solid, smooth surface of lies ('She was sick'; 'This is what the disease does'; 'Suicide'). *I* was the one who was really buried that day. 'I can't go home and I won't. I'll go with you. We can make our home in the Wilds. Other people do it, don't they? Other people *have* done it. My mother—' I want to say, *My mother is going to do it*, but my voice breaks on the word.

Alex is watching me carefully. 'Lena, if you leave – really leave – it won't be like it is for me now. You get that, right? You won't be able to go back and forth. You won't be able to come back ever. Your number will be invalidated. Everyone will know you're a resister. Everyone will be looking for you. If anyone found you – if you were ever caught . . .' Alex doesn't finish his sentence.

'I don't care,' I snap back. I'm no longer able to control my temper. 'You were the one who suggested it, weren't you? So what? Now that I'm ready to go, you take it back?'

'I'm just trying to—'

I cut Alex off again, rattling on, coasting on the anger, the desire to shred and hurt and tear apart. 'You're just like everybody else. You're as bad as all the rest of them. Talk, talk, talk – it comes so easily to you. But when it's time to do anything, when it's time to *help* me—'

'I'm *trying* to help you,' Alex says sharply. 'It's a big deal. Do you understand that? It's a huge choice, and you're pissed, and you don't know what you're saying.' He's getting angry too. The tone of his voice makes something painful run through me, but I can't stop speaking. Destroy, destroy, destroy: I want to break everything – him, me, us, the whole city, the whole world.

'Don't treat me like a child,' I say.

'Then stop acting like one,' he fires back. The second the words are out of his mouth I can tell he regrets them. He turns partially away, inhales, and then says, in a normal tone of voice, 'Listen, Lena. I'm really sorry. I know you've had – I mean, with everything that happened today – I can't imagine how you must be feeling.'

It's too late. Tears are blurring my vision. I turn away from him and start chipping at the wall with a fingernail. A minuscule portion of brick crumbles away. Watching it tumble to the ground reminds me of my mother, and those strange and terrifying walls, and the tears come faster.

'If you cared about me, you would take me away,' I say. 'If you cared about me at all you would go right now.'

'I do care about you,' Alex says.

'You don't.' Now I know I *am* being childish, but I can't help it. 'She didn't either. She didn't care at all.'

'That's not true.'

'Why didn't she come for me, then?' I'm still turned away from him, pressing a palm against the wall, hard; feeling like it, too, might collapse at any second. 'Where is she now? Why didn't she come looking for me?'

'You know why,' he says, more firmly. 'You know what would have happened if she was caught again – if she was caught with you. It would have meant death for both of you.'

I know he's right, but that doesn't make it any better. I keep going stubbornly, unable to stop myself. 'It's not that. She doesn't care, and you don't care. Nobody cares.' I draw my forearm across my face, swiping at my nose.

'Lena.' Alex puts a hand on each of my elbows and guides me around to face him. When I refuse to meet his eyes, he tilts my chin upward, forcing me to look at him. 'Magdalena,' he repeats, the first time since we met that he has ever used my full name. 'Your mother loved you. Do you understand that? She loved you. She still loves you. She wanted you to be safe.'

Heat rushes through me. For the first time in my life I am not afraid of the word. Something seems to yawn open inside of me, to stretch out, like a cat trying to soak up the sun, and I'm desperate for him to say it again.

His voice is endlessly soft. His eyes are warm and flecked with light, the colour of the sun melting like butter through the trees on a warm autumn evening.

'And I love you too.' His fingers skate the edge of my jaw, dance briefly over my lips. 'You should know that. You have to know that.'

That's when it happens.

Standing there in-between two disgusting Dumpsters in some crappy alley with the whole world crumbling down around me, and hearing Alex say those words, all the fear I have carried with me since I learned to sit, stand, breathe – since I was told that at the very heart of me was something wrong, something rotten and diseased, something to be suppressed; since I was told that I was always just a heartbeat away from being damaged – all of it vanishes at once. That thing – the heart of hearts of me, the core of my core – stretches and unfurls even further, soaring like a flag, making me feel stronger than I ever have before.

I open my mouth and say, 'I love you too.'

It's strange, but after that moment in the alley I suddenly understand the meaning of my full name, the reason my mom named me Magdalena in the first place and the meaning of the old biblical story, of Joseph and his abandonment of Mary Magdalene. I understand that he gave her up for a reason. He gave her up so she could be saved, even though it killed him to let her go.

He gave her up for love.

I think, maybe, my mother had a sense even when I was born that she would someday have to do the same thing. I guess that's just part of loving people: you have to give things up. Sometimes you even have to give *them* up.

Alex and I talk about all the things I'll be leaving behind to go with him to the Wilds. He wants to be absolutely sure that I know what we're getting into. Stopping by Fat Cats Bakery after closing and buying the day-old bagels and cheddar buns for a dollar each; sitting out on the piers and watching the gulls shriek and circle overhead; long runs up by the farms when the dew glistens off every blade of grass as though they're encased in glass; the constant rhythm of the oceans, beating under Portland like a heartbeat; the narrow cobblestone streets of the old harbour, shops crowded with bright, pretty clothes I could never afford.

Hana and Grace are my only regrets. The rest of Portland can dissolve into nothing, for all I care: its shiny, spindly false towers and blind storefronts and staring, obedient people, bowing their heads to receive more lies, like animals offering themselves up to be slaughtered.

'If we go together, it's just you and me,' Alex keeps repeating, as though needing to make sure I understand – as though needing to be sure that *I'm* sure. 'No going back. Ever.'

And I say, 'That's all I want. Just you and me. Always.'

I mean it too. I'm not even afraid. Now that I know I'll

have him – that we have each other – I feel as though I'll never be afraid of anything ever again.

We decide to leave Portland in a week, exactly nine days before my scheduled procedure. I'm nervous about delaying our departure so long – I'm halfway tempted to make a straight run for the border fence and try to barge my way through in broad daylight – but as usual, Alex calms me down and explains the importance of waiting.

In the past few years he has made the crossing only a handful of times. It's too dangerous to go back and forth more often than that. But in the next week, Alex will cross twice before we make our final escape – an almost suicidal risk, but he convinces me it's necessary. Once he leaves with me and starts missing work and class, he'll be invalidated too – even though, technically, his identity was never really valid in the first place, since it was created by the resistance.

And once we're both invalidated, we'll be erased from the system. Gone. *Blip!* It will be as though we've never existed. At least we can count on the fact that we won't be pursued into the Wilds. There won't be any raiding parties. No one will come looking for us. If they wanted to hunt us down, they'd have to admit that we'd made it out of Portland, that it was possible, that the Invalids exist.

We'll be nothing more than ghosts, traces, memories – and soon, as the cureds keep their eyes firmly focused on the future, and the long procession of days to march through – we won't even be that.

Since Alex won't be able to cross into Portland any longer, we need to bring over as much food as we can, plus clothes for the winter and anything else we can't do without. Invalids in the settlements are pretty good about sharing supplies. Still, autumn and winter in the Wilds are always hard, and after years of living in Portland, Alex isn't exactly a master hunter-gatherer.

We agree to meet at the house at midnight to continue planning. I'll bring him the first collection of belongings I want to take with me: my photo album, a sheath of notes Hana and I passed back and forth sophomore year in math class, and whatever food I can smuggle from the storeroom at the Stop-N-Save.

It's almost three o'clock by the time Alex and I split up and I head home. The clouds have mostly broken up, and between them the sky is interwoven, a pale blue, like faded and tattered silk. The air is warm but the wind is edged with an autumn smell of cold and smoke. Soon all the lush greens of the landscape will burn away into fierce reds and oranges, and then those, too, will burn away, into the stark black brittleness of winter. And I'll be gone – out there somewhere among the skinny, shivering trees, encased in snow. But Alex will be with me, and we'll be safe. We'll walk together holding hands, and kiss in broad daylight, and love each other as much as we want to, and no one will ever try to keep us apart.

Despite everything that happened today, I feel calmer than I've ever been, as though the words Alex and I said to each other today have wrapped me up in a protective haze.

I haven't been running regularly for over a month. It has been too hot, and until recently Carol has forbidden it. But as soon as I get home I call Hana and ask her to meet me at the tracks, our regular starting point, and she only laughs.

'I was about to call and ask you the same thing,' she says.

'Great minds,' I say, her laughter getting lost for a second in the fuzz that blasts through the receiver, as a censor somewhere deep in Portland tunes into our conversation momentarily. The old revolving eye, ever-turning, ever-vigilant. Anger worms through me for a second, but it disappears quickly. Soon I'll be off the map completely and forever.

I was hoping to get out of the house without seeing Carol, but she intercepts me on my way out the door. As always, she's been in the kitchen, endlessly repeating her cycle of cooking and cleaning.

'Where have you been all day?' she asks.

'With Hana,' I answer automatically.

'And you're going out again?'

'Just for a run.' Earlier I thought if I ever saw her again I would tear at her face, or kill her. But now, looking at her, I feel completely numb, like she's a painted billboard or a stranger passing on a bus.

'Dinner's at seven thirty,' she says. 'I'd like you to be home to set the table.'

'I'll be home,' I say. It occurs to me that this numbness, this feeling of separation, must be what she and every cured experiences all the time, as though there is a thick, muffling pane of glass between you and everybody else. Hardly anything penetrates. Hardly anything matters. They say the cure is about happiness, but I understand now that it isn't, and it never was. It's about fear: fear of pain, fear of hurt, fear, fear, fear – a blind animal existence, bumping between walls, shuffling between ever-narrowing hallways, terrified and dull and stupid.

For the first time in my life I actually feel sorry for Carol. I'm only seventeen years old, and I already know something she doesn't know: I know that life isn't life if you just float through it. I know that the whole point – the only point – is to find the things that matter, and hold on to them, and fight for them, and refuse to let them go.

'Okay.' Carol stands there, kind of awkwardly, like she always does when she wants to say something meaningful but can't quite remember how to do it. 'Two weeks until your cure,' she says finally.

'Sixteen days,' I say, but in my head I'm counting seven days. Seven days until I'm free, and away from all these people and their sliding, superficial lives, brushing past one another, gliding, gliding, gliding, from life to death. For them, there's hardly a change between the two.

'It's okay to be nervous,' she says. This is the difficult thing she has been trying to say, the words of comfort it has cost her so much effort to remember. Poor Aunt Carol: a life of dishes and dented cans of green beans and days that bleed forever into one another. It occurs to me, then, how old she looks. Her face is deeply lined, and her hair has patches of grey. It's only her eyes that have convinced me she is ageless: those staring, filmy eyes that all cureds share, as though they're always looking off into some vast distance. She must have been pretty when she was young, before she was cured – as tall as my mother at least, and probably just as thin – and a mental image flashes of two teenage girls, both slender black parentheses separated by a span of silver ocean, kicking water at each other, laughing. These are the things you do not give up.

'Oh, I'm not nervous,' I tell her. 'Trust me. I can't wait.'

Only seven more days.

twenty-four

What is beauty? Beauty is no more than a trick; a delusion; the influence of excited particles and electrons colliding in your eyes, jostling in your brain like a bunch of overeager schoolchildren, about to be released on break. Will you let yourself be deluded? Will you let yourself be deceived?

– 'On Beauty and Falsehood,'
The New Philosophy, by Ellen Dorpshire

Hana's already there when I arrive, leaning up against the chain-link fence that encircles the track, head tilted back and eyes closed against the sun. Her hair is loose and spilling down her back, nearly white in the sun. I pause when I'm fifteen feet away from her, wishing I could memorize her exactly like that, hold that precise image in my mind forever.

Then she opens her eyes and sees me. 'We haven't even

started to run yet,' she says, pushing off the fence and making a big show of checking her watch, 'and you're already coming in second.'

'Is that a challenge?' I say, closing the last ten feet between us.

'Just a fact,' she says, grinning. Her smile flickers a little as I get closer. 'You look different.'

'I'm tired,' I say. It feels strange to greet each other with no hug or anything, even though this is how things have always been between us, how things have always *had* to be. It feels strange that I've never told her how much she means to me. 'Long day.'

'You want to talk about it?' She squints at me. The summer has made her tan. The sun-freckles on her nose bunch up like a constellation of stars collapsing. I really think she might be the most beautiful girl in Portland, maybe in the whole world, and I feel a sharp pain behind my ribs, thinking of how she'll grow older and forget me. Someday she'll hardly think of all the time we spent together – when she does, it will seem distant and faintly ridiculous, like the memory of a dream whose details have already started to ebb away.

'After we run, maybe,' I say, the only thing I can *think* to say. You have to go forward: it's the only way. You have to go forward no matter what happens. This is the universal law.

'After you eat dirt, you mean,' she says, bending forward to stretch out her hamstrings.

'You talk a big game for someone who's been lying on her ass all summer.'

'You're one to talk.' She tilts her head up to wink at me. 'I don't think what you and Alex have been doing really counts as exercise.'

'Shhh.'

'Relax, relax. No one's around. I checked.'

It all seems so normal – so deliciously, wonderfully normal – that I'm filled from head to toe with a joy that makes me dizzy. The streets are striped with golden sun and shadow, and the air smells like salt and the odour of frying things and, faintly, seaweed washed up onto the beaches. I want to hold this moment inside of me forever, keep it safe, like a shadow-heart: my old life, my secret.

'Tag,' I say to Hana, giving her a tap on the shoulder. 'You're it.'

And then I'm off and she's yelping and leaping to catch up, and we're rounding the track and heading down to the piers without hesitating or debating our route. My legs feel strong, steady; the bite I got on the night of the raids has healed well and completely, leaving just a thin red mark along the back of my calf, like a smile. The cool air pumps in and out of my lungs, aching, but it's the good kind of pain: the pain that reminds you how amazing it is to breathe, to ache, to be able to feel at all. Salt stings my eyes and I blink rapidly, not sure whether I'm sweating or crying.

It's not the fastest run we've ever been on, but I think it might be one of our best. We keep up the same exact rhythm, running almost shoulder to shoulder, drawing a loop from the old harbour all the way out to Eastern Prom.

We're slower than we were at the start of the summer, that's for sure. At about the three-mile mark both of us are starting to lag, and by silent agreement we both cut down the sloping lawn onto the beach, flinging ourselves onto the sand, starting to laugh.

'Two minutes,' Hana says, gasping. 'I just need two minutes.'

'Pathetic,' I say, even though I'm just as grateful for the pause.

'Right back at you,' she says, lobbing a handful of sand in my direction. Both of us flop onto our backs, arms and legs flung apart like we're about to make snow angels. The sand is surprisingly cool on my skin, and a little damp. It must have rained earlier after all, maybe when Alex and I were in the Crypts. Thinking again of that tiny cell and the words drilled straight through the wall, sun revolving through the O as though beamed through a telescope, makes that thing constrict in my chest again. Even now, this second, my mother is out there somewhere – moving, breathing, being.

Well, soon I'll be out there too.

There are only a few people on the beach, mostly families walking, and one old man, plodding slowly by the water, staking his cane into the sand. The sun is sinking farther beyond the clouds, and the bay is a hard grey, just barely tinged with green.

'I can't believe in only a few weeks we won't have to worry about curfew anymore,' Hana says, then swivels her head to look at me. 'Less than three weeks, for you. Sixteen days, right?'

'Yeah.' I don't like to lie to Hana so I sit up, wrapping my arms around my knees.

'I think on my first night cured I'm going to stay out all night. Just because I can.' Hana props herself up on her elbows. 'We can make a plan to do it together – you and me.' There's a pleading note in her voice. I know I should just say, *Yeah, sure*, or *That sounds great*. I know it would make her feel better – it would make me feel better – to pretend that life will go on as usual.

But I can't force the words out. Instead I start blotting bits of sand from my thighs with a thumb. 'Listen, Hana. I have to tell you something. About the procedure . . .'

'What about it?' She squints at me. She's heard some note of seriousness in my voice, and it has worried her.

'Promise you won't be mad, okay? I won't be able to—' I stop myself before I can say, *I won't be able to leave if you're mad at me.* I'm getting ahead of myself.

Hana sits up completely, holding up a hand, forcing a laugh. 'Let me guess. You're jumping ship with Alex, making a run for it, going all rogue and Invalid on me.' She says it jokingly but there's an edge to her voice, an undercurrent of neediness. She wants me to contradict her.

I don't say anything, though. For a minute we just stare at each other, and all the light and energy drains from her face at once.

'You're not serious,' she says finally. 'You can't be serious.'

'I have to, Hana,' I tell her quietly.

'When?' She bites her lip and looks away.

'We decided today. This morning.'

'No. I mean – *when*. When are you going?'

I hesitate for only a second. After this morning, I feel like I don't know very much about the world or anything in it. But I do know that Hana would never, ever betray me – not now, at least, not until they stick needles into her brain and pick her apart, tease her into pieces. I realize now that that's what the cure does, after all: it fractures people, cuts them off from themselves.

But by then – by the time they get to her – it will be too late. 'Friday,' I say. 'A week from now.'

She breathes out sharply, the air whistling between her teeth. 'You can't be serious,' she repeats.

'There's nothing for me here,' I say.

She looks back at me then. Her eyes are enormous, and I can tell I've hurt her. '*I'm* here.'

Suddenly the solution comes to me – simple, ridiculously simple. I almost laugh out loud. 'Come with us,' I burst out. Hana scans the beach anxiously, but everyone has dispersed: the old man has plodded on, halfway down the beach by now and out of earshot. 'I'm serious, Hana. You could come with us. You'd love it in the Wilds. It's incredible. There are whole settlements there—'

'You've been?' she cuts in sharply.

I blush, realizing I'd never told her about my night with Alex in the Wilds. I know she'll see this, too, as a betrayal. I used to tell her everything. 'Just once,' I say. 'And only for a couple of hours. It's amazing, Hana. It's not like we imagined it at all. And the crossing . . . The fact that you can cross at all . . . So much is different from what we've been told. They've been *lying* to us, Hana.'

I stop, temporarily overwhelmed. Hana looks down, picking at the seam of her running shorts.

'We could do it,' I say, more gently. 'The three of us together.'

For a long time Hana doesn't say anything. She looks out at the ocean, squinting. Finally she shakes her head, an almost imperceptible movement, shooting me a sad smile. 'I'll miss you, Lena,' she says, and my heart sinks.

'Hana—' I start to say, but she cuts me off.

'Or maybe I won't miss you.' She heaves herself to her feet, slapping the sand off her shorts. 'That's one of the promises of the cure, right? No pain. Not that kind of pain, anyway.'

'You don't have to go through with it.' I scramble to my feet. 'Come to the Wilds.'

She lets out a hollow laugh. 'And leave all this behind?' She gestures around her. I can tell she's half joking, but only half. In the end, despite all her talk, and the underground parties and forbidden music, Hana doesn't want to give up this life, this place: the only home we've ever known. Of course, she *has* a life here: family, a future, a good match. I have nothing.

The corners of Hana's mouth are trembling and she drops her head, kicking at the sand. I want to make her feel better but can't think of anything to say. There's a frantic aching in my chest. It seems like as we stand there I'm watching my whole life with Hana, our entire friendship, fall away: sleepover parties with forbidden midnight bowls of popcorn; all the times we rehearsed for Evaluation Day, when Hana would steal a pair of her father's old glasses, and bang on her desk with a ruler whenever I got an answer wrong, and we always started choking with laughter halfway through; the time she put a fist, hard, in Jillian Dawson's face because Jillian said my blood was diseased; eating ice cream on the pier and dreaming of being paired and living in identical houses, side by side. All of it is being sucked into nothing, like sand getting swept up by a current.

'You know it's not about you,' I say. I have to force the words out, past a lump in my throat. 'You and Grace are the only people who matter to me here. Nothing else—' I break off. 'Everything else is nothing.'

'I know,' she says, but she still won't look at me.

'They – they took my mother, Hana.' I wasn't planning to tell her, initially. I didn't want to talk about it. But the words rush out.

She glances up at me sharply. 'What are you talking about?'

I tell her the story of the Crypts then. Amazingly, I keep it together. I just tell her about everything in detail. Ward

Six and the escape, the cell, the words. Hana listens in frozen silence. I've never seen her so still and serious.

When I'm finished speaking, Hana's face is white. She looks exactly like she did when we were little and used to stay up at night, trying to freak each other out by telling ghost stories. In a way, I guess my mother's story *is* a ghost story. 'I'm sorry, Lena,' she says, her voice barely a whisper. 'I don't know what else to say. I'm so sorry.'

I nod, staring out at the ocean. I wonder whether what we learned about the other parts of the world – the uncured parts – is accurate, whether they're really as wild and ravaged and savage and full of pain as everyone has always said. I'm pretty sure this, too, is a lie. Easier, in many ways, to imagine a place like Portland – a place with its own walls and barriers and half-truths, a place where love still flickers into existence but imperfectly.

'You see why I have to leave,' I say. It's not really a question, but she nods.

'Yeah.' Hana gives her shoulders a tiny shake, as though trying to rouse herself from a dream. Then she turns to me. Even though her eyes are sad, she manages a smile. 'You, Lena Haloway,' she says, 'are a legend.'

'Yeah, right.' I roll my eyes. But I feel better. She has called me by my mother's name, so I know she understands. 'A cautionary tale, maybe.'

'I'm serious.' She brushes her hair out of her face, staring at me intently. 'I was wrong, you know. Remember what I said at the beginning of the summer? I thought you were afraid. I thought you were too scared to take any chances.' The sad smile tugs at her lips again. 'Turns out you're braver than I am.'

'Hana—'

'That's okay.' She waves a hand, cutting me off. 'You deserve it. You deserve *more*.'

I don't really know what to say to that. I want to hug her, but instead I wrap my arms around my waist, squeezing. The wind coming off the water is biting.

'I'll miss you, Hana,' I say after a minute.

She walks a couple of steps toward the water, kicks sand in an arc with the toe of her shoe. It seems to hang in the air for a fraction of a second before scattering. 'Well, you know where I'll be.'

We stand there for a while, listening to the tide sucking on the shore, the water heaving and tumbling with bits of rock, stone whittled to sand over thousands and thousands of years. Someday maybe this will all be water. Someday maybe it will all get sucked into dust.

Then Hana spins around and says, 'Come on. Race you back to the track,' and takes off, running, before I can say, *Okay*.

'No fair!' I call after her. But I don't try very hard to catch up. I let her stay a few feet ahead of me and try to memorize her exactly as she is: running, laughing, tan and happy and beautiful and mine; blonde hair flashing in the last rays of sun like a torch, like a beacon of good things to come, and better days ahead for us both.

Love, the deadliest of all deadly things: it kills you both when you have it and when you don't.

But that isn't it, exactly.

The condemner and the condemned. The executioner; the blade; the last-minute reprieve; the gasping breath and the rolling sky above you and the *thank you, thank you, thank you, God*.

Love: it will kill you and save you, both.

twenty-five

I must be gone and live, or stay and die.

– From the cautionary tale *Romeo and Juliet*
by William Shakespeare, reprinted in *100 Quotes to
Know for the Boards*, by The Princeton Review

It's cold when I make my way toward 37 Brooks sometime
after midnight, and I have to zip my nylon windbreaker
up all the way to my chin. The streets are as dark and
still as I've ever seen them. There isn't a whisper of movement anywhere, no curtains twitching in windows, no
shadows skating across walls and making me jump, no glittering alley cat eyes or scrabbling rats' feet or the distant
drumbeat of footsteps on the pavement, as the regulators
make their rounds. It's as though everyone is already braced
for winter – as though the whole city is in the middle of a
deep freeze. It's a little freaky, actually. I think again of the
house that somehow survived the blitz and now stands out

there in the Wilds, perfectly preserved but totally uninhabited, with wildflowers growing through all its rooms.

I'm relieved when I turn the corner and see the rusty iron fence that marks 37 Brooks's periphery, feel a tremendous rush of happiness when I think of Alex squatting in one of the dark rooms, solemnly packing a backpack with blankets and canned food. I haven't realized until now that at some point over the summer I began to think of 37 Brooks as home. I hitch my own backpack a little higher on my shoulder and jog to the gate.

But something's wrong with it: I rattle it a few times but it doesn't open. At first I think it's stuck. Then I notice that someone has looped a padlock through the gate. It looks new, too. It glitters sharply in the moonlight when I tug it.

37 Brooks is locked.

I'm so surprised, I can't even be frightened or suspicious. My only thought is of Alex, and where he is, and whether he's responsible for the lock. Maybe, I think, he locked the property to protect our stuff. Or maybe I'm early, or maybe I'm late. I'm just about to try to swing myself over the fence when Alex materializes from the darkness to my right, stepping silently out of the shadows.

'Alex!' Though we've only been apart for a few hours, I'm so happy to see him – soon he'll be mine, openly and totally – I forget to keep my voice down as I run to him.

'Shhh.' He wraps his arms around me as I practically leap on top of him, and staggers backward a little. But when I tilt my head up to look at him, he's smiling, and I can tell he's just as happy as I am. He kisses the tip of my nose. 'We're not safe yet.'

'Yeah, but soon.' I stand on my tiptoes and kiss him softly.

As always, the pressure of his lips on mine seems to blot out everything bad in the world. I have to wrench myself away from him, slapping his arm playfully as I do. 'Thanks for giving me a key, by the way.'

'A key?' Alex squints, confused.

'For the lock.' I try to squeeze him but he steps away from me, shaking his head, his face suddenly stark white and terrified – and in that second I get it, we both do, and Alex opens his mouth but it seems to take forever, and at the exact moment I realize why I can suddenly see him so clearly, framed in light, frozen like a deer caught in the beams of a truck (*the regulators are using floodlights tonight*), a voice booms out through the night: 'Freeze! Both of you! Hands on your head!' At the same time Alex's voice finally reaches me, urgent – 'Go, Lena, go!' He's already backpedaling through the darkness, but it takes my feet longer to move and by the time I do, running blindly and without aim down the first street I see, the night has come alive with mobile shadows – grabbing at me, shouting, tearing at my hair – hundreds of them, it seems, pouring down the hill, materializing out of the ground, from trees, from air.

'Get her! Get her!'

My heart is bursting in my chest and I can't breathe; I've never been so scared; I'll die from fright. More and more shadows turn to people: all of them grabbing, screaming, holding glittering metal weapons, guns and clubs, cans of Mace. I duck and spin past rough hands, make a break for the hill that cuts over to Brandon Road, but it's no use. A regulator grabs me roughly from behind. I barely shake off his grasp before I'm pinballing off someone wearing a guard's uniform, feeling another pair of hands snatching at me.

The fear is a shadow now, a blanket: smothering me, making it impossible to breathe.

A patrol car springs to life beside me, and the revolving lights illuminate everything starkly but only for a second, and the world around me pulses black, white, black, white, moving forward in bursts, in slow motion.

A face contorted into a terrible scream; a dog leaping from the left, teeth bared; someone shouting, 'Take her down! Take her down!'

Can't breathe, can't breathe, can't breathe.

A high whistling sound, a scream; a club frozen moment-arily in the air.

A club falling; a dog jumping, snarling; searing pain, straight through me, like heat.

Then blackness.

When I open my eyes the world seems to have broken apart into a thousand pieces. All I see are tiny shards of light, fuzzy and swirling like they've been shaken up by a kal-eidoscope. I blink several times, and slowly the shards resolve and rearrange themselves into a bell-shaped light and a cream-coloured ceiling, marred by a large water stain in the shape of an owl. My room. Home. I'm home.

For a second I feel relieved. My body is prickling, like I've been stuck with needles all over my skin, and all I want to do is lie back against the softness of my pillows and sink into the darkness and oblivion of sleep, wait for the sharp pain in my head to dissipate. Then I remember: the lock, the attack, the swarming shadows. And Alex.

I don't know what happened to Alex.

I flail, trying to sit up, but agonizing pain shoots from my head down to my neck and forces me back against the pillows, gasping. I close my eyes and hear the door to my room scrape open. Voices swell suddenly from downstairs. My aunt is talking to someone in the kitchen, a man whose voice I don't recognize. A regulator, probably.

Footsteps cross the room. I keep my eyes squeezed tight, pretending to sleep, as someone leans across me. I feel a warm breath tickle the side of my neck.

Then more footsteps coming up the stairs, and Jenny's voice, a hiss, at the door. 'What are *you* doing here? Aunt Carol told you to stay away. Now get downstairs before I tell.'

The weight eases off the bed, and light footsteps patter away, back into the hall. I crack my eyes open, the barest squint, just enough to make out Grace as she ducks around Jenny, who is standing in the doorway. She must have been checking on me. I squeeze my eyes shut again as Jenny takes several tentative steps toward the bed.

Then she pivots abruptly, as though she can't leave the room fast enough. I hear her call out, 'Still asleep!' The door scrapes closed again. But not before I hear, from the kitchen, very clearly, 'Who was it? Who infected her?'

This time, I force myself to sit, despite the pain knifing through my head and neck and the terrible sensation of swinging that accompanies every movement I make. I try to stand but find my legs won't hold me. Instead I sink to the ground and crawl over to the door. Even on my hands and knees the effort is exhausting, and I lie down on the ground, shaking, as the room continues to rock back and forth like some diabolical seesaw.

Fortunately, keeping my head to the ground makes it easier

to hear downstairs, and I catch my aunt saying, 'You must have at least seen him.' I've never heard her sound so hysterical.

'Don't worry,' the regulator says. 'We'll find him.'

This, at least, is a relief. Alex must have escaped. If the regulators had any idea who had been with me on the street – if they had even a suspicion – they would have him in custody already. I say a silent prayer of gratitude that Alex managed, miraculously, to make it to safety.

'We had no idea,' Carol says, still in that trembling, urgent voice so unlike her regular measured tone. And now I understand; she's not just hysterical. She's terrified. 'You have to believe that we had no idea she'd been infected. There were no signs. Her appetite was the same. She went to work on time. No mood swings . . .'

'She was probably trying her hardest to conceal the signs,' the regulator cuts in. 'The infected often do.' I can practically hear the disgust in his voice when he pronounces the word *infected*, like he's actually saying *cockroach*, or *terrorist*.

'What do we do now?' Carol's voice is fainter now. She and the regulator must be passing into the living room.

'We're putting in calls as fast as we can,' he replies. 'With any luck, before the end of the week . . .'

Their voices become indecipherable, a low hum. I rest my forehead on the door for a minute, focusing on inhaling and exhaling, breathing past the pain. Then I get to my feet, carefully. The dizziness is still intense, and I have to brace myself against the wall as soon as I'm standing, trying to sort out my options. I have to find out what, exactly, happened. I need to know how long the regulators had been watching 37 Brooks, and I have to make absolutely positive that Alex is safe. I need to talk to Hana. She'll help me. She'll know what to do. I tug on the door handle before realizing that it has been locked from the outside.

Of course. I'm a prisoner now.

As I'm standing there with my hand on the door handle, it begins to rattle and turn. I turn as quickly as I am able and dive back into the bed – even *that* hurts – just as the door swings open again and Jenny re-enters.

I don't shut my eyes fast enough. She calls back into the hallway, 'She's awake now.' She is carrying a glass of water but seems reluctant to come farther into the room. She stays near the doorway, watching me.

I don't particularly want to talk to Jenny, but I'm absolutely desperate to drink. My throat feels like I've been swallowing sandpaper.

'Is that for me?' I say, gesturing to the glass. My voice is a croak.

Jenny nods, her lips stretched into a fine white line. For once, she has nothing to say. She darts forward suddenly, places the glass on the little rickety table next to the bed, then darts away just as quickly. 'Aunt Carol said it would help.'

'Help what?' I take a long, grateful sip, and the burning in my throat and head seems to ease up.

Jenny shrugs. 'The infection, I guess.'

This explains why she's staying by the door and doesn't want to get too close to me. I'm diseased, infected, dirty. She's worried she's going to catch it. 'You can't get sick just by being around me, you know,' I tell her.

'I know,' she says quickly, defensively, but stays frozen where she is, watching me warily.

I feel impossibly tired. 'What time is it?' I ask Jenny.

'Two thirty,' she says.

This surprises me. Relatively little time has passed since I went to meet Alex. 'How long was I out?'

She shrugs again. 'You were unconscious when they brought you home,' she says matter-of-factly, as though this is a natural fact of life, or something *I* did – and not because a bunch of regulators clubbed me on the back of the head. That's the irony of it. She's looking at me like I'm the crazy one, the dangerous one. Meanwhile, the guy downstairs who nearly fractured my skull and bled my brains all over the pavement is the saviour.

I can't stand to look at her, so I turn toward the wall. 'Where's Grace?'

'Downstairs,' she says. Some of the normal whine returns to her voice. 'We had to set up sleeping bags in the living room.'

Of course, they'd want to keep Grace away from me: young, impressionable Grace, safely sheltered from her crazed, sick cousin. I *do* feel sick too, with anxiety and disgust. I think of the fantasy I had earlier, of burning the whole house down. It's lucky for Aunt Carol I don't have any matches. Otherwise I just might do it.

'So who was it?' Jenny's voice drops to a sinuous whisper, like a little snake forking its tongue in my ear. 'Who was it who infected you?'

'Jenny.'

I turn my head, surprised to hear Rachel's voice. She's standing in the doorway, watching us, her expression completely unreadable.

'Aunt Carol wants you downstairs,' she says to Jenny, and

Jenny scurries eagerly for the door, shooting one last look over her shoulder at me, her face a mixture of fear and fascination. I wonder if that's how I looked all those years ago when Rachel got the *deliria* and had to be pinned down on the floor by four regulators before she could be dragged to the labs.

Rachel comes over to the bed, still watching me with that same unreadable expression. 'How are you feeling?' she asks.

'Fabulous,' I say sarcastically, but she just blinks at me.

'Take these.' She lays out two white pills on the table.

'What are those? Tranquilizers?'

Her eyelids flutter. 'Advil.' Irritation has crept into her voice, and I'm glad of it. I don't like that she's standing there, composed and detached, evaluating me like I'm a taxidermy specimen.

'So . . . Carol called you?' I'm debating whether to trust her about the Advil, but decide to risk it. My head is killing me, and at this point I'm not sure how much more damaging a tranquilizer would be. It's not exactly like I can make a break for the door in this condition, anyway. I swallow the two pills with a large gulp of water.

'Yes. I came right away.' She sits on the bed. 'I was sleeping, you know.'

'Sorry to inconvenience you. I didn't exactly ask to get knocked out and dragged here.' I've never spoken to Rachel this way, and I can see it surprises her. She rubs her forehead tiredly, and for a second a glimpse of the Rachel I used to know – my older sister Rachel, the one who tortured me with tickles and braided my hair and complained that I always got bigger scoops of ice cream – flickers through.

Then the blankness is back, like a veil. It's amazing how

I've always just accepted it, the way that most cureds seem to walk through the world as though wrapped in a thick cloak of sleep. Maybe it's because I, too, was sleeping. It wasn't until Alex woke me up that I could see things clearly.

For a while Rachel doesn't say anything else. I have nothing to say to her, either, so we just sit there. I close my eyes, waiting for the pain to begin ebbing away, trying to sort out words from the tangle of voices downstairs and the sounds of footsteps and muffled exclamations and the television going in the kitchen, but I can't make out any specific conversations.

Finally Rachel says, 'What happened tonight, Lena?'

When I open my eyes, I see she's staring at me again. 'You think I'll tell you?'

She gives a minute shake of her head. 'I'm your sister.'

'As if that means something to you.'

She recoils slightly, just a fraction of an inch. When she speaks again her voice is flinty. 'Who was he? Who infected you?'

'That's the question of the evening, isn't it?' I roll away from her, facing the wall, feeling cold. 'If you came here to grill me, you're wasting your time. You might as well go home again.'

'I came here because I'm worried,' she says.

'About what? About the family? About our reputation?' I keep staring stubbornly at the wall, pulling the thin summer blanket all the way to my neck. 'Or maybe you're worried that everyone will think you knew? Maybe you think you'll get labeled a sympathizer?'

'Don't be difficult.' She sighs. 'I'm worried about you. I *care*, Lena. I want you to be safe. I want you to be *happy*.'

I swivel my head to look at her, feeling a rush of anger – and, deeper than that, hatred. I hate her; I hate her for lying to me. I hate her for pretending to care, for even using that word in my presence. 'You're a liar,' I spit out. Then, 'You knew about Mom.'

This time the veil drops. She jerks back. 'What are you talking about?'

'You knew that she didn't – that she didn't really kill herself. You knew that they took her.'

Rachel squints at me. 'I really have no idea what you're talking about, Lena.'

And I can tell, then, that at least I'm wrong about this. Rachel doesn't know. She never knew. I feel a twin flood of relief and regret.

'Rachel,' I say, more gently. 'She was in the Crypts. She's been in the Crypts this whole time.'

Rachel stares at me for one long second, her mouth falling open. Then she stands abruptly, smoothing down the front of her pants as though brushing away invisible crumbs. 'Listen, Lena . . . you got bumped on the head pretty badly.' Again, as though I've somehow done it myself. 'You're tired. You're confused.'

I don't correct her. There's no point. It's too late for Rachel, anyway. She will always exist behind the wall. She will always be asleep.

'You should try to get some sleep,' she says. 'I'll refill your water.' She takes the glass and then moves toward the door, switching off the overhead light as she goes. She pauses in the doorway for a bit with her back turned to me. The light from the hallway looks fuzzy around her, and makes her features blur to black so she looks like a shadow-person, a silhouette.

'You know, Lena,' she says at last, turning back around to face me, 'things are going to get better. I know you feel angry. I know you think we don't understand. But I *do* understand.' She breaks off, staring down into the empty glass. 'I was just like you. I remember: those feelings, that anger and passion, the sense that you can't live without it, that you'd rather die.' She sighs. 'But trust me, Lena. It's all part of the disease. It's a sickness. In a few days you'll see. This will all feel like a dream to you. It was like a dream to me.'

'And you're happier now? You're glad you did it?' I ask her.

Maybe she takes my question as a sign that I'm listening and paying attention. In any case, she smiles. 'Much,' she says.

'Then you're not just like me,' I whisper fiercely. 'You're not like me at all.'

Rachel opens her mouth to say something else, but at that moment Carol comes to the door. Her face is flushed and red and her hair is sticking up at strange angles, but when she speaks she sounds calm. 'Everything's all right,' she says in a low voice to Rachel. 'Everything's been settled.'

'Thank God,' Rachel says. Then, grimly, 'But she won't go willingly.'

'Do they ever?' Carol asks drily. Then she disappears again.

Carol's tone of voice has frightened me. I try to sit up on my elbows, but my arms feel like they've been turned to Jell-O. 'What's settled?' I ask, surprised to hear that my voice sounds slurry.

Rachel looks at me for a second. 'I told you, we just want you to be safe,' she says flatly.

'What did you settle?' Panic is filling me, made even worse

by the simultaneous heaviness that seems to be creeping over me. I have to struggle to keep my eyes open.

'Your procedure.' That's Carol. She has just stepped back into the room. 'We managed to get you in early. You'll have your cure on Sunday, first thing in the morning. After that, we hope, you'll be okay.'

'Impossible.' I'm choking. Sunday morning is less than forty-eight hours from now. No time to alert Alex – no time to plan our escape. No time to do anything. 'I won't do it.' My voice doesn't even sound like my own now: it's one long groan.

'Someday you'll understand,' Carol says. Both she and Rachel are advancing toward me, and then I see that they are holding, stretched between them, coils of nylon cord. 'Someday you'll thank us.'

I try to thrash out but my body is impossibly heavy and my vision starts to blur. Clouds roll through my mind; the world goes to fuzz. I think, *So she was lying about the Advil* – and then I think, *That hurts*, as something sharp digs deep into my wrists, and then I don't think anything at all.

twenty-six

here is the deepest secret nobody knows
(here is the root of the root and the bud of the bud
and the sky of the sky of a tree called life; which grows
higher than the soul can hope or mind can hide)
and this is the wonder that's keeping the stars apart

i carry your heart (i carry it in my heart)

– From 'i carry your heart with me (i carry it in)' a poem by
E. E. Cummings, banned, listed in the Comprehensive Compilation of
Dangerous Words and Ideas, www.ccdwi.gov.org

When I wake up again it's because someone is repeating my name. As I struggle into consciousness I see wisps of blonde hair, like a halo, and for a confused moment think maybe I've died. Maybe the scientists were wrong and heaven isn't just for the cured.

Then Hana's features sharpen, and I realize she's leaning over me. 'Are you awake?' she's saying. 'Can you hear me?'

I groan and she sits back a little, exhaling. 'Thank God,' she says. She's keeping her voice to a whisper and she looks frightened. 'You were so still I thought for a minute that you – that they—' She breaks off. 'How do you feel?'

'Shitty,' I croak loudly, and Hana winces and looks over her shoulder. I notice a shadow flitting just outside the bedroom door. Of course. Her visit is being monitored. Either that or someone is on 24/7 guard duty. Probably both.

My headache is slightly better, at least, although now there's a searing pain in both of my shoulders. I'm still pretty groggy, and I try to adjust my position before remembering Carol, and Rachel, and the nylon cord, and realizing that both of my arms are stretched above my head and secured to the headboard, like a real honest-to-God prisoner. The anger comes again, waves of it, followed by panic as I remember what Carol said: my procedure has been moved to Sunday morning.

I swivel my head to one side. Sunlight is streaming in through the thin plastic blinds, which have been drawn down over the windows, lighting up dust motes in the room.

'What time is it?' I struggle to sit up and yelp as the cords bite farther into my wrists. 'What day is it?'

'Shhh.' Hana presses me back against the bed, holding me there as I squirm underneath her. 'It's Saturday. Three o'clock.'

'You don't understand.' Every word grates against my throat. 'They're taking me to the labs tomorrow. They moved my procedure—'

'I know. I heard.' Hana is staring at me intently, like she's trying to communicate something important. 'I came as soon as I could.'

Even the brief struggle has left me exhausted. I sink back

against the pillows. My left arm has gone totally numb from being elevated all night and the numbness seeps through me, turning my insides to ice. Hopeless. The whole thing is hopeless. I've lost Alex forever.

'How did you hear?' I ask Hana.

'Everyone's talking about it.' She gets up, goes to her bag, and rummages around before pulling out a water bottle. Then she comes back and kneels by the bed so we're eye-to-eye. 'Drink this,' she says. 'It will make you feel better.' She has to hold the bottle to my lips like I'm an infant. Kind of embarrassing, but I'm long past caring.

The water kills some of the fire in my throat. She's right; it does make me feel slightly better. 'Do people know . . . are they saying . . . ?' I lick my lips and shoot a glance over Hana's shoulder. The shadow is there; as it shifts, I make out the flicker of a candy-striped apron. I drop my voice to a whisper. 'Are they saying who . . . ?'

Hana says, overly loud, 'Don't be stubborn, Lena. They'll find out who infected you sooner or later. You might as well just tell us who it was now.' This little speech is for Carol's benefit, obviously. As she speaks Hana gives me a little wink and a minute shake of her head. So Alex *is* safe. Maybe there's hope after all.

I mouth to Hana, *Alex*. Then I jut my chin at her, hoping she'll understand that I want her to go find him, and tell him what happened.

Her eyes flicker, and the little smile dies from her lips. I can tell she's about to give me bad news. Still enunciating her words loudly and clearly, she says, 'It's not just stubborn, Lena. It's selfish. If you tell them, maybe they'll realize I had nothing to do with it. I don't like being babysat twenty-four-seven.'

My heart sinks: of course they've put a tail on Hana. They must suspect her of being involved in some way, or at least of having information.

Maybe it's selfish, but at that moment I can't even feel sorry for her, or for the trouble I've caused. I can only feel bitterly disappointed. There's no way for her to get word to Alex without bringing the whole Portland police force down on his head. And if they find out he's been masquerading as a cured and helping the resistance . . . well, I doubt they'd bother with a trial. They'd skip straight to the execution.

Hana must read the despair on my face. 'I'm sorry, Lena,' she says, this time in a whisper. 'You know I would help if I could.'

'Yeah, well, you can't.' As soon as the words are out of my mouth, I regret them. Hana looks terrible, almost as bad as I feel. Her eyes are puffy and her nose is red, like she's recently been crying, and it's obvious she really did rush here as soon as she heard. She's wearing her running shoes, a pleated skirt, and the oversized tank top she usually sleeps in, as though she got dressed in the first items of clothing she pulled off her floor.

'I'm sorry,' I say, less sharply. 'You know I didn't mean that.'

'That's okay.' She moves off the bed and starts pacing, like she always does when she's thinking. For one second – one tiny fraction of a second – I almost wish I had never met Alex at all. I wish I could rewind back to the very beginning of the summer, when everything was so clear and simple and easy; or rewind even further, to the late fall, when Hana and I did our loops around the Governor and studied for calculus exams on the floor of her room, and the days clicked forward toward my procedure like dominoes falling in a line.

The Governor. Where Alex first saw me; where he left a note for me.

And then, just like that, I have an idea.

I struggle to keep my voice casual. 'So what happened to Allison Doveney?' I say. 'She didn't want to say good-bye?'

Hana whips around to stare at me. Allison Doveney was always our code, our name for Alex whenever we needed to talk about him on the phone or in emails. She draws her eyebrows together. 'I haven't been able to get in touch with her,' she says carefully. The look on her face says *I explained this to you already.*

I raise my eyebrows at her, like, *Trust me.* 'It would be nice to see her before the procedure tomorrow.' I hope Carol is listening, and takes this as a sign that I've resigned myself to the change in plans. 'Things will be different after the cure.'

Hana shrugs, spreads her arms. *What do you want me to do?*

I heave a sigh, and seemingly switch topics. 'Do you remember Mr. Raider's class? In fifth grade? How we used to pass notes back and forth all day?'

'Yeah,' Hana says warily. She still looks confused. I can tell she's beginning to worry that the bump on my head has affected my ability to think clearly.

I sigh again, exaggeratedly, like just reliving all the good times we had together is making me nostalgic. 'Do you remember how he caught us and made us sit across the room from each other? So every time we wanted to say something to each other we would get up and sharpen our pencils, and leave a little note in that empty flower pot in the back of the class.' I force a laugh. 'One day I must have sharpened my pencil seventeen times. And he never caught on, not once.'

A little light goes on in Hana's eyes, and she grows very still and super alert, the way that deer do when they are listening for predators, right before bolting – even as she laughs and says, 'Yeah, I remember. Poor Mr. Raider. So clueless.'

Despite her offhanded tone, Hana lowers herself onto Grace's bed, leaning forward with her elbows on her knees and staring at me intently. And now I know she knows what I'm *really* telling her, while I'm rambling about Allison Doveney and Mr. Raider's class: She needs to get a note to Alex.

I switch topics again. 'And do you remember the first time we ever did a long run? Afterward my legs were like jelly. And the first time we ever ran from West End to the Governor? And I jumped up and slapped his hand like I was giving him a high five.'

Hana narrows her eyes at me ever so slightly. 'We've been abusing him for years,' she says carefully, and I know she doesn't quite get it, not yet.

I make sure to keep all tension and excitement out of my voice. 'You know, someone told me that he used to be carrying something. The Governor, I mean. A torch or a scroll or something. Now he just has that little empty space in his fist.' That's it: I've said it. Hana inhales sharply and I know now she understands, but just to make sure I say, 'Will you do me a favor? Will you do that run for me today? One last time?'

'Don't be melodramatic, Lena. The cure works on your brain, not your legs. You'll still be able to run after tomorrow.'

Hana answers flippantly, just the way she should, but she's smiling now, and nodding at me. *Yes. I'll do it. And I'll hide the note there.* Hope pulses through me, a warm glow, burning off some of the pain.

'Yeah, but it will be *different*,' I whine. Carol's face flashes momentarily at the door, which is open just a crack. She looks satisfied. It must seem to her like I've come to terms with having the procedure after all. 'Besides, something could go wrong.'

'It won't go wrong.' Hana stands up and stares at me for a moment. 'I promise,' she says slowly, giving each word weight, 'that everything will go perfectly.'

My heart skips a beat. This time, *she* was giving *me* a message, and I know she wasn't talking about the procedure.

'I should get out of here,' she says, moving to the door, practically skipping now. I realize that if this works – if Hana does somehow manage to transmit a message to Alex, and if he somehow manages to break me out of my house-turned-prison-cell – this really will be the last time I ever see Hana.

'Wait,' I call out, when she's almost at the door.

'What?' She whips around. Her eyes are shining; she's excited now, ready to go. For a moment, standing in the fuzzy haze of sunlight still penetrating the blinds, she appears to be glowing, as though lit up by some internal flame. And now I know why they invented words for love, why they had to: it's the only thing that can come close to describing what I feel in that moment, the baffling mixture of pain and pleasure and fear and joy, all running sharply through me at once.

'What's wrong?' Hana repeats impatiently, jogging a little

in place. I know she's eager to get going and put the plan into action. *I love you*, I think, but what I say, gasping a little, is: 'Have a good run.'

'Oh, I will,' she says, and then, just like that, she's gone.

twenty-seven

He who leaps for the sky may fall, it's true.
But he may also fly.

– Ancient saying, provenance unknown, listed in the
Comprehensive Compilation of Dangerous Words and Ideas,
www.ccdwi.gov.org

I've known time to stretch out like rings expanding outward over water; I've also known it to rush by with such force it leaves me dizzy. But until today I've never known it to do both at the same time. The minutes seem to swell around me, to stifle me with their sluggishness. I watch the light move by centimeters over the ceiling. I fight the pain in my head and my shoulder blades. The numbness radiates from my left arm to my right. A fly circles the room, buzzing up against the blinds over and over, trying to fight its way outside. Eventually it drops from the air, exhausted, hitting the floor with a tiny pinging sound.

Sorry, buddy. I sympathize.

At the same time, I'm terrified when I see how many hours have gone by since Hana's visit. Every hour brings me closer to the procedure, closer to leaving Alex, and even as each minute seems to take an hour, each hour seems to fly by in a minute. I wish I had some way of knowing whether Hana successfully hid a note at the Governor. Even if she did, there's only the barest hope that Alex will think of looking there for word from me – the skinniest hope, the edge of an edge.

But still hope.

I haven't even thought about the other obstacles that stand in the way of my escape – like the fact that I'm strung up like a salami, or the fact that either Carol or Uncle William or Rachel or Jenny is always stationed just outside the door. Call it denial or stubbornness or craziness, but I just have to believe that Alex will come and rescue me – like in one of the fairy tales he told me about on our walk back from the Wilds, where the prince springs a princess from a locked tower, slaying dragons and fighting forests of poisonous thorns just to get to her.

In the late afternoon Rachel comes in with a bowl of steaming soup. She sits down on my bed wordlessly.

'More Advil?' I ask her sarcastically, as she offers me a spoonful.

'You feel better now that you've slept, don't you?' she returns.

'I'd feel better if I weren't tied up.'

'It's for your own good,' she says, making another gesture to my mouth with the spoon.

The last thing I want to do is accept food from Rachel, but if Alex does come for me (*when; when he comes for me; I have to keep believing*), I'll need to have my strength up.

Besides, maybe if Carol and Rachel really believe that I've given up on the idea of resisting, they'll loosen up my restraints or stop standing watch outside the bedroom door, giving me the opportunity to escape.

So I take a long slurp of soup, force a tight smile, and say, 'Not bad.'

Rachel beams at me. 'You can have as much as you want,' she says. 'You need to be in good shape for tomorrow.'

Amen, sister, I think, and drain the whole bowl before asking for seconds.

More minutes: a slow drag, like a weight pulling me under. But then, suddenly, the light in the bedroom turns the warm colour of honey, and then the trembling yellow of fresh cream, and then begins swirling away from the walls altogether, like water going down a drain. I haven't really expected Alex to show up before night – that would be suicide – but pain throbs deep in my chest anyway. There's almost no time left.

Dinner is more soup, topped with soggy chunks of bread. This time it's Carol who brings the meal to me while Rachel stands outside. Carol unties my hands briefly after I beg her to let me use the bathroom, but she insists on accompanying me to the toilet and standing there while I pee, which is more than humiliating. My legs are unsteady and the pain in my head worsens when I stand. There are deep grooves in my wrists – the nylon cord has left its mark – and my arms are like two dead weights, swinging lifelessly from my shoulders. When Carol goes to restrain me again I consider resisting – even though she's taller than I am, I'm definitely stronger – but think better of it. The house is full of people, my uncle included, and for all I know there are still some regulators hanging out downstairs. They'd have me secured and sedated within minutes, and I can't afford to be put under again. I have to be awake and alert tonight. If Alex doesn't come I'll need to generate a plan of my own.

One thing is certain: I won't have the procedure tomorrow. I'd rather die.

Instead I concentrate on tensing my muscles as hard as I can while Carol ties me up. When I relax again there's a tiny bit of wiggle room, just a fraction of an inch. Maybe enough to give me the chance to work my way out of my makeshift handcuffs. More good news: as the day has worn on, everyone has gotten a little more lax about guarding the bedroom constantly, just as I'd hoped. Rachel abandons her shift for five minutes to go to the bathroom; Jenny spends most of the time lecturing Grace about the rules to some game she has invented; Carol leaves her post for half an hour when she goes to do the dishes. After dinner, Uncle William takes over. I'm glad of it. He has a little portable radio with him. I hope he'll nod off the way he usually does after eating.

And then maybe – just maybe – I'll be able to bust out of here.

By nine o'clock all the light in the room has swirled away and I'm left in darkness, shadows draped like fabric over the walls. The moon is large and bright, coming through the blinds and barely outlining everything in a hazy silver glow. Uncle William is still outside, listening to the radio on low, an indecipherable static. Noises float up through the floor – water rushing in the kitchen and downstairs bathroom, voices murmuring downstairs and the scuffling of padded feet – the final coughs and shakes before the house will fall silent for the night, like a person in the middle of death throes. Jenny and Grace still aren't allowed to sleep in the room with me. I assume they're all settling down to sleep in the living room.

Rachel comes in one last time, carrying a glass of water. It's difficult to tell in the darkness, but it looks suspiciously cloudy, like someone has dissolved something in it.

'I'm not thirsty,' I say.

'Just a few sips.'

'Seriously, Rachel. I'm not thirsty.'

'Don't be difficult, Lena.' She sits down on the bed and forces the water to my lips. 'You've been so good all day.'

I have no choice but to take a few mouthfuls – tasting, as I do, the acrid sting of medication. Definitely laced with something – more sleeping pills, no doubt. I hold the water in my mouth, refusing to swallow, and as soon as she stands and turns back to the door, I turn my head and let the water run out onto my pillow, into my hair. It's kind of gross, but better than the alternative. Wetness seeps into my pillow, temporarily cooling the sting of pain in my shoulders.

Rachel hesitates at the door as though she's trying to think of something meaningful to say. But all she comes up with is, 'See you in the morning.'

Not if I can help it, I think, but I don't say anything. Then she leaves me, closing the door behind her.

And then I'm left in total darkness, with just the passing of the hours, the minutes ticking forward. And as I lie there with nothing to do but think – as the house settles and goes silent around me – the fear returns, a terrible fog. I tell myself he must come – he *has* to – but the clock creeps forward, taunting me, and outside the streets are silent except for the occasional barking of a dog.

To keep my mind from cycling endlessly around the same

question (*Will Alex come, or won't he?*), I try to think of all the ways to kill myself on the way to the labs. If there's any commercial traffic at all on Congress, I'll throw myself in front of one of the trucks. Or maybe I can make a break for the docks. It shouldn't be too difficult to drown, especially if my hands are still tied. If worse comes to worst I can try to fight my way to the roof of the labs, like that girl did all those years ago, dropping out of the sky like a stone, cleaving the clouds.

I think of the image that was beamed onto televisions everywhere that day: the small trickle of blood, the strange expression of restfulness on her face. Now I understand. It sounds sick, but generating these plans actually makes me feel better, beats back the terrible flutterings of anxiety and fear inside of me. I'd rather die on my own terms than live on theirs. I'd rather die loving Alex than live without him.

Please, God, make him come for me.

I'll never ask for anything again.

I'll give up anything and everything I have.

Just please make him come.

At midnight the fear turns, suddenly, to desperation. If he's not coming, I'll have to get out of here myself.

I work my hands in their restraints, trying to leverage that extra centimeter of space. The cord cuts deeply into my skin, and I have to bite my lip to keep from crying out in the dark. No matter how I pull and tug and twist, the cord refuses to relax any further, but still I keep trying, until sweat is dripping down along my hairline and I'm worried that if I thrash any harder it will attract someone into the room. Something wet trickles down along my forearm, and when

I crane my head backward I see a thick, dark line of blood streaking my skin, like an awful black snake: all my struggling has caused my skin to chafe away.

Outside, the streets are as quiet as they've ever been, and in that moment I know that it's hopeless: I won't be able to escape on my own. Tomorrow I'll wake up and my aunt and Rachel and the regulators will escort me downtown, and the only chance of escape I'll have will be into the ocean, or off the roof of the laboratories.

I think of Alex's molten honey eyes and the softness of his touch and sleeping under a canopy of stars, stretched out above our heads like they were placed there just for us. Now, after so many years, I understand what the Coldness was and where it came from – this sense that everything is lost, and worthless, and meaningless. Finally, the cold and the despair turn merciful, dropping down on my mind like a dark veil, and miracle of miracles, I sleep.

I wake sometime later in ink-purple darkness with the sensation of someone in the room, some loosening of the restraints on my wrists. For a second my heart soars and I think, *Alex,* but then I look up and see Gracie, perched at the head of my bed, working at the cords binding me to the headboard. She is pulling and untwisting and bending forward occasionally, to chew at the nylon with her teeth, giving the impression of a quiet and industrious animal gnawing its way through a fence.

Just like that, the cord snaps and I'm free. The pain in my shoulders is agonizing; my arms are full of a thousand pinpricks. But still, in that moment of release, I could shout and jump for joy. This is how my mother must have felt when she saw the first shaft of sunlight penetrate the fissure in her stone prison walls.

I sit up, rubbing my wrists. Gracie crouches against the headboard, watching me, and I lean forward and wrap her up in a big hug. She smells like apple soap and a little like sweat. Her skin is hot, and I can't think of how nervous she must have been, sneaking up to my room. I'm surprised by how thin and fragile she feels, trembling ever so slightly in my arms.

But she's not fragile – not by a long shot. Gracie is strong, I realize, perhaps stronger than any of us. It occurs to me that for a long time she has been doing her own version of resisting, and the fact that she is a born resister makes me smile into her hair. She'll be okay. She'll be more than okay.

I pull away just a little bit so I can whisper in her ear. 'Is Uncle William still out there?'

Gracie nods, then places both hands under the side of her head, indicating that William is sleeping.

I lean forward again. 'Are there regulators in the house?'

Gracie nods again, holding up two fingers, and my stomach sinks. Not just one regulator – two of them.

I stand up, testing my legs, which are cramping from being immobilized for almost two full days. I tiptoe to the window and open the blinds as quietly as possible, conscious of Uncle William slumbering only ten feet away from me. The sky outside is a rich, dark purple, the colour of eggplant, and the street is draped with shadows as though it has been covered over with velvet. Everything is totally still, totally silent, but at the horizon is just the faintest blush, a gradual lightening: dawn isn't far off.

I ease open the window carefully, feeling a sudden desire

to smell the ocean. There it is: the smell of salt spray and mist, a smell mixed, in my mind, with the idea of constant revolution, an eternal tide. I feel overwhelmingly sad then. I know there's no way to find Alex in the middle of this enormous sprawling, sleeping city, and no way for me to reach the border on my own. My best bet is to try and make it down to the cliffs, to the ocean, to walk into the water until it closes over my head. I wonder if it will hurt. I wonder if Alex will be thinking of me.

Somewhere deeper in the city a motor is running, a distant, earthy growl, like an animal panting. In a few hours the bright blush of morning will push through all that darkness, and shapes will reassert themselves, and people will wake up and yawn and brew coffee and get ready for work, everything the same as usual. Life will go on. Something aches at the very core of me, something ancient and deep and stronger than words: the filament that joins each of us to the root of existence, that ancient thing unfurling and resisting and grappling, desperately, for a foothold, a way to *stay here, breathe, keep going*. But I will it away; I will it to curl up again, to let go.

I'd rather die my way than live yours.

The motor is getting louder now, approaching. And now I see a solitary motorcycle, a dark black speck, coming up the street. For a second I pause, fascinated. I've only seen a working motorcycle twice before, and despite everything it strikes me as beautiful, the way it weaves up the street, barely glinting, cutting through the dark, like the sleek black head of an otter through the water. And the rider, too, just a dark shape massed on the back of the bike like liquid, like shadow, bent forward, just the crown of the head visible, drawing ever closer, taking on shape and detail.

The crown of the head: like the colour of leaves in autumn, burning, burning.

Alex.

I can't help it: I let out a little cry of excitement.

Outside the bedroom door, there's a thumping sound, like something banging against the wall. I hear Uncle William mutter, 'Shit.'

Alex pulls into the narrow alley that separates our property – a strip of grass, really, a single, anemic tree, and a waist-high, chain-link fence – from the next. I wave at him frantically. He cuts the engine of the motorcycle, turning his face upward, toward the house. It's still very dark, so I'm not sure he can see me.

I risk calling his name softly, into the yard. 'Alex!'

He swivels his head toward my voice, a grin splitting his face, spreading his arms as though to say, *You knew I would come, didn't you?* It reminds me of how he looked the first time I ever saw him on the balcony in the labs, all twinkle and flash, like a star winking through the darkness just for me.

And in that second I'm so filled with love it's as though my body transforms into a single blazing beam of light, shooting up, up, up, beyond the room and walls and city: as though everything has dropped away behind us, and Alex and I are alone in the air, and totally free.

Then the door to my bedroom flies open and William starts yelling.

Suddenly the house is noise and light, footsteps and shouting. Uncle William is just standing in the doorway, shouting for Carol, and it's like in one of those scary movies when a sleeping beast is woken, except now the house is the beast. Feet pound up the stairs – the regulators, I think – and at the end of the hall Carol flies out of her bedroom, her nightgown flapping behind her like a cape, mouth twisted open into one long, indecipherable shout.

I shove against the screen as hard as I can, but it's stuck. Below me Alex is screaming something too, but I can't make it out over the motorcycle engine, roaring to life again.

'Stop her!' Carol is yelling, and William comes to life, unfreezing, lunging into the room. Pain burns my shoulder as I shove against the screen again, feel it strain outward for a second and then resist. No time, no time, no time. Any second now William will grab me and it will all be over.

Then Gracie yells, 'Wait!'

Everyone freezes just for a second. It is the first and only time Gracie has ever spoken aloud to them. William trips over himself and stares at his granddaughter, slack-jawed. Carol freezes in the doorway, and behind her, Jenny rubs her eyes as though convinced she is dreaming. Even the regulators – both of them – pause at the top of the stairs.

That second is all I need. I give another shove and the screen shudders and pops outward, clattering onto the street. And before I can think about what I'm doing, or the two-storey drop to the street below, I'm swinging out of the window and letting go, the air sweeping me up like an embrace so for a moment my heart sings again and I think, *I'm flying.*

Then I'm hitting the ground with such force that my legs give way and the air gets knocked out of me in a rush. My left ankle twists and wrenching pain goes through my whole body. I skid forward on my hands and knees, rolling against the fence. Above me the shouting has started up again, and a moment later the front door of the house bursts open and two men spill out onto the porch.

'Lena!' That's Alex's voice. I look up. He's leaning over the chain-link fence, extending his hand. I fling one arm upward and he grabs me by the elbow, half dragging me over the fence; a bit of it catches on my tank top, tearing the fabric, nicking my skin. There's no time to be scared. On the porch there is an explosion of static. One regulator is shouting into his walkie-talkie. The other one is loading a gun. Strangely, in the middle of all the chaos, I have the stupidest thought: *I didn't know that regulators were allowed to carry guns.*

'Come on!' Alex yells. I scrabble onto the motorcycle behind him, wrapping my arms tightly around his waist.

The first bullet ricochets off the fence directly to our right. The second one pings off the sidewalk.

'Go!' I scream, and Alex guns it just as a third bullet whips by us, so close I can feel the air vibrating in its wake.

We jet forward to the end of the alley. Alex cuts the wheel, hard, to the right, so we spin out onto the street, tipping over so far my hair grazes the pavement. My stomach does a huge somersault and I think, *It's over*, but miraculously the motorcycle rights itself and then we're speeding forward down the dark street, while the sounds of shouting and the explosions of gunfire recede behind us.

The quiet doesn't last, though. As we turn onto Congress, I hear the wail of sirens, growing louder and louder, a scream. I want to tell Alex to go faster, but my heart is pounding so hard I can't speak the words. Besides, my voice would only be lost in the furious whipping of the wind around us, and I know he's going as fast as he can. The buildings on either side of us are a blur, grey and shapeless, like a mass of melted metal. Never has the city looked so foreign to me, so awful and deformed. The sirens are so loud that the noise is like a thin blade, vibrating furiously through me. Lights begin to flicker on in the buildings around us as people are roused from sleep. The horizon is touched with red: the sun is rising, a rusty colour, the colour of old blood, and I'm so filled with fear it is an agony, a shredding feeling, worse than any nightmare I've ever had.

Then, out of nowhere, two squad cars materialize at the end of the street, blocking our progress. Regulators and police – dozens of them, all heads and arms and screaming mouths – pour out onto the street. Voices boom, amplified, distorted through radios and bullhorns.

'Freeze! Freeze! Freeze or we shoot!'

'Hold on!' Alex yells, and I can feel his muscles tensing underneath me. At the last second he jerks the bars to the left and we skid sideways into another narrow alley, clipping the brick wall. I scream as my right leg gets crushed against the wall. Skin grates off my shin as we slide for several seconds along the exterior of the building before Alex once again gets control of the bike and we shoot forward. As soon as we burst out the other end of the alley there are two more patrol cars swerving behind us.

We're going so fast my arms are shaking as I try to hold on, and right then I have a momentary flash of calm and clarity and I realize that we'll never make it. Both of us will die today, gunned down or smashed up or exploded in some terrible moment of fire and twisted metal, and when they go to bury us we'll be so melted together and entwined they won't be able to separate the bodies; pieces of him will go with me, and pieces of me will go with him. Weirdly, the thought doesn't even upset me. I'm almost ready to give in and give up, ready to draw my last breath while pressed up to his back, feeling his ribs and lungs and chest move with mine for the last time.

But Alex obviously isn't ready to give up. He cuts down the narrowest alley he can find, and two of the cars following us come to a skidding halt, smashing each other as they try to follow and blocking the entrance so the other cars are forced to stop as well. Horns blare. The sharp stink of smoke and burning rubber makes my eyes water for a second, but then we're out again, bursting forward onto Franklin Arterial.

More sirens now, from a distance: reinforcements are on their way.

But the cove appears ahead of us, unfolding – calm and flat and grey, like glass or metal. The sky smolders at its edges, a growing fire of pinks and yellows. Alex turns onto Marginal Way, and my teeth clatter together as we bump over the old pitted pavement, my stomach yo-yoing every time we jolt over another pothole. We're getting close. The sirens whine louder, like a drove of hornets. If we can just get to the border before more squad cars arrive . . . If we can somehow make it past the guards, if we can scale the fence . . .

Then, like an enormous insect taking flight, a helicopter wings up ahead of us, lights zigzagging along the darkened road, the whirring of its propeller deafening, beating the air to waves, to shreds.

A voice cannons out: 'I order you, in the name of the government of the United States of America, to freeze and surrender!'

Tufts of long, sun-bleached grass appear on our right:

We've made it to the Cove. Alex yanks the bike off the road and onto the grass, and we go, half gunning, half sliding, down into the marshes, cutting a diagonal toward the border. Mud splatters up into my mouth and eyes, choking me, and I cough into Alex's back, feeling him heave against me. The sun is a half circle now, like an eyelid partially opened.

Tukey's Bridge looms to our right, black, skeletal in the half darkness. Ahead of us, the lights in the guard huts are still illuminated. Even from this distance they look so peaceful, just like hanging paper lanterns, like something fragile and easily dismantled. Beyond them are the fence; the fringe of trees; safety. So close. If we only had time . . . Time . . .

Something pops; an explosion in the darkness; the mud jumps upward in an arc. They're shooting again, from the helicopter.

'Freeze, dismount, and put your hands on your head!'

The patrol cars have arrived on the road that encircles the cove. More and more cars screech to a halt, and police begin to pour down the grass toward the marshland – hundreds of them, more than I've ever seen at one time, dark and inhuman-looking, like a swarm of cockroaches.

We're up again now, in the short strip of grass that separates the water from the old torn-up road and the guard huts, weaving around a tangle of bushes so quickly, the branches sting as they slap against my skin.

And then, just like that, Alex stops. I slam up against him, biting down hard on my tongue, taste blood in my mouth. Above us the light from the helicopter wavers a little, trying to locate us, then fixes us in its beam. Alex raises his arms above his head and climbs off the motorcycle, turning to face me. In the solid white light his expression is unreadable, as though he's been transformed, in that second, to stone.

'What are you doing?' I scream, over the noise of the propellers and the shouting and the sirens and beneath it all, the constant, everlasting groaning of the water as the tide slurps back into the cove – always there, always sweeping everything away, wearing everything to dust. 'We can still make it!'

'Listen to me.' He doesn't seem to be shouting, but somehow I can still hear him. It's like he's speaking directly into my ear even though he's still standing there, arms raised. 'When I tell you to go, you're going to go. You've got to drive this thing, okay?'

'What? I can't—'

'Citizen 914-238-619-3216. Dismount and put your hands above your head. If you do not dismount immediately, we will be forced to shoot.'

'Lena.' The way he says my name makes me shut up. 'They've electrified the fence. It's powered on.'

'How do you know?'

'Just *listen* to me.' Desperation and terror creep into Alex's voice. 'When I say go, you drive. And when I say jump, you jump. You'll be able to get over the fence, but you'll have thirty seconds before the power comes back online, a minute, tops. You have to climb as fast as you can. And then you run, okay?'

My whole body goes ice-cold. 'Me? What about you?'

Alex's expression doesn't change. 'I'll be right behind you,' he says.

'We're giving you ten seconds . . . nine . . . eight . . .'

'Alex—' Icy fingers are reaching up from my stomach.

Alex smiles for just one second – the briefest flicker of a smile, like we're already safe, like he's leaning in to brush my hair from my eyes or kiss my cheek. 'I promise I'll be right behind you.' His expression hardens again. 'But you have to swear you won't look back. Not even for a second. Okay?'

'Six . . . five . . .'

'Alex, I can't—'

'Swear, Lena.'

'Three . . . two . . .'

'Okay,' I say, almost choking on the word. Tears are blurring my vision. No chance. We have no chance. 'I swear.'

'One.'

At that second explosions start lighting up around us, bursts of sound and fire. At the same time Alex screams, 'Go!' and I lean forward and twist the throttle like I saw him do. I feel his arms wrap around me at the last second, so strong they might have carried me off the bike if I weren't gripping the handlebars so tightly.

More gunfire. Alex cries out and releases one arm from around my chest. I look back and see him cradling his right arm. We bump up onto the old road, and there is a line of guards waiting to greet us, rifles pointed. They're all screaming, but I can't even hear them: all I can hear is the rushing, rushing of the wind and the hum of electricity coursing through the fence, just like Alex said. all I can see are the trees in the Wilds, just turning green in the morning light, all those broad, flat leaves like hands reaching for us.

The guards are so close now, I can see individual faces, make out individual expressions: yellow teeth on one, a large wart on the nose of another. But still I don't stop. We plunge

through them on our bike and they scatter, fall back and
jump apart so they don't get mowed down.

The fence looms above us: fifteen feet, ten feet, five feet. I
think, *We're going to die.*

Then Alex's voice, clear and forceful and, incredibly, calm,
so I'm not sure if I hear him or only imagine him speaking
the words into my ear. *Jump. Now. With me.*

I let go of the handlebars and roll to one side as the bike
skids forward into the fence. Pain goes through every single
part of my body – my bone is being ripped from my muscle,
my muscle is being ripped from my skin – as I tumble across
jagged rocks, spitting up dust, coughing, struggling to
breathe. For a whole second the world goes black.

Then everything is colour and explosion and fire. The bike
hits the fence and a tremendous, rolling boom echoes through
the air. Fire shoots into the air, enormous tongues licking
up toward the ever-lightening sky. For a moment, the fence
gives a high, shrill whine and then goes dead again, silent.
No doubt the surge shorted it momentarily.

This is my chance to climb, just like Alex said.

Somehow I find the strength to drag myself to the fence on
my hands and knees, dry-heaving, vomiting dust. I hear
shouting behind me, but it all sounds distant, like under-water
noise. I limp to the fence and haul myself upward, inch by
inch. I'm going as fast as I can but it feels like I'm crawling,
barely making progress. Alex must be behind me because I
hear him shouting, 'Go, Lena! Go!' I focus on his voice: it's
the only thing that keeps me going up. Somehow – miraculously – I reach the top of the fence, and then I step over the
loops of barbed wire like Alex taught me, and then I tip over
the other side and let myself drop twenty feet to the ground,

hitting the grass hard, half unconscious now and incapable of feeling any more pain. Just a few more feet and I'll be sucked into the Wilds; I'll be beyond its impenetrable shield of interlocking trees and growth and shade. I wait for Alex to hit next.

But he doesn't.

That's when I do the thing I swore I wouldn't do. Suddenly all my strength is back, fueled by panic. I scramble to my feet as the fence begins to hum again.

And I look back.

Alex is still standing on the other side of the fence, beyond a flickering wall of smoke and fire. He hasn't moved a single inch since we both jumped off the bike, hasn't tried to.

Strangely, in that moment I think back to what I answered all those months ago, at my first evaluation, when I was asked about *Romeo and Juliet* and could only think to say *beautiful*. I'd wanted to explain; I'd wanted to say something about sacrifice.

Alex's T-shirt is red, and for a second I think it's a trick of the light, but then I realize he's drenched, soaked in blood: blood seeping across his chest, like the stain seeping up the sky, bringing another day to the world. Behind him is that insect army of men, all of them running toward him at once, guns drawn. The guards are coming too, reaching for him from both sides as though they are going to tear him apart, straight down the middle. The helicopter has him fixed in its spotlight. He is standing white and still and frozen in its beam, and I don't think I have ever, in my life, seen anything more beautiful than him.

He is looking at me through the smoke, across the fence. He never takes his eyes off me. His hair is a crown of leaves, of thorns, of flames. His eyes are blazing with light, more light than all the lights in every city in the whole world, more light than we could ever invent if we had ten thousand billion years.

And then he opens his mouth and his mouth forms one last word.

The word is: *Run*.

After that the insect men fall on him. He is taken up by all their snapping, ravaging arms and mouths like an animal being set upon by vultures, enfolded in all their darkness.

I run for I don't know how long. Hours, maybe, or days.

Alex told me to run. And so I run.

You have to understand. I am no one special. I am just a single girl. I am five feet two inches tall and I am in-between in every way.

But I have a secret. You can build walls all the way to the sky and I will find a way to fly above them. You can try to pin me down with a hundred thousand arms, but I will find a way to resist. And there are many of us out there, more than you think. People who refuse to stop believing. People who refuse to come to earth. People who love in a world without walls, people who love into hate, into refusal, against hope, and without fear.

I love you. Remember. They cannot take it.

Acknowledgments

To my wonderfully patient and attentive editor, Rosemary Brosnan, who is part mentor, part taskmaster, part therapist, and all friend.

To Elyse Marshall, publicist extraordinaire, for the immensity of her support.

To the best agent in the world, Stephen Barbara, for putting up with me (I don't know how you do it).

To everyone at Foundry Literary + Media, in particular Hannah Gordon and Stephanie Abou.

To Deirdre Fulton, for letting me stay for an entire summer while researching this book.

To Arabica Coffee House in Portland, Maine, for the deliciousness of your coffee and toast and the proliferation of your electrical outlets.

To Allison Jones, for her enthusiasm, advocacy, and general loveliness, and for single-handedly hand-selling *Before I Fall* to the entirety of Williamsburg, Virginia.

To my aunt Sandy, for years of constant love and support.

To all of my lovely blogger friends and fans, for making what I do worthwhile.

To my family, as always, for loving me.

And to my friends, of course, for being like family.

*Read on for an excerpt of Book Two
in the DELIRIUM trilogy:*

pandemonium

Unflinching, heartbreaking and totally addictive, this novel will push your emotions to the limit.

Lena's been to the very edge. She's questioned love and the life-changing and agonising choices that come with it.

She's made her decision.

But can she survive the consequences?

The eagerly anticipated sequel to the international bestseller DELIRIUM.

Available now in paperback and eBook.

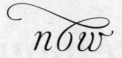

Alex and I are lying together on a blanket in the back-yard of 37 Brooks. The trees look larger and darker than usual. The leaves are almost black, knitted so tightly together they blot out the sky.

'It probably wasn't the best day for a picnic,' Alex says, and just then I realize that yes, of course, we haven't eaten any of the food we brought. There's a basket at the foot of the blanket, filled with half-rotten fruit, swarmed by tiny black ants.

'Why not?' I say. We are staring at the web of leaves above us, thick as a wall.

'Because it's snowing.' Alex laughs. And again I realize he's right: it is snowing, thick flakes the colour of ash swirling all around us. It's freezing cold, too. My breath comes in clouds, and I press against him, trying to stay warm.

'Give me your arm,' I say, but Alex doesn't respond. I try to move into the space between his arm and his chest but his body is rigid, unyielding. 'Alex,' I say. 'Come on, I'm cold.'

'I'm cold,' he parrots, from lips that barely move. They are blue, and cracked. He is staring at the leaves without blinking.

'Look at me,' I say, but he doesn't turn his head, doesn't blink, doesn't move at all. A hysterical feeling is building inside me, a shrieking voice saying *wrong, wrong, wrong,* and I sit up and place my hand on Alex's chest, as cold as ice. 'Alex,' I say, and then, a short scream: 'Alex!'

'Lena Morgan Jones!'

I snap into awareness, to a muted chorus of giggles.

Mrs. Fierstein, the twelfth-grade science teacher at Quincy Edwards High School for Girls in Brooklyn, Section 5, District 17, is glaring at me. This is the third time I've fallen asleep in her class this week.

'Since you seem to find the Creation of the Natural Order so exhausting,' she says, 'might I suggest a trip to the principal's office to wake you up?'

'No!' I burst out, louder than I intended to, provoking a new round of giggles from the other girls in my class. I've been enrolled at Edwards since just after winter break – only a little more than two months – and already I've been labelled the Number-One Weirdo. People avoid me like I have a disease – like I have the disease.

If only they knew.

'This is your final warning, Miss Jones,' Mrs. Fierstein says. 'Do you understand?'

'It won't happen again,' I say, trying to look obedient and contrite. I'm pushing aside the memory of my nightmare, pushing aside thoughts of Alex, pushing aside thoughts of Hana and my old school, push, push, push, like Raven taught me to do. The old life is dead.

Mrs. Fierstein gives me a final stare – meant to intimidate

me, I guess – and turns back to the board, returning to her lecture on the divine energy of electrons.

The old Lena would have been terrified of a teacher like Mrs. Fierstein. She's old, and mean, and looks like a cross between a frog and a pit bull. She's one of those people who makes the cure seem redundant – it's impossible to imagine that she would ever be capable of loving, even without the procedure.

But the old Lena is dead too.

I buried her.

I left her beyond a fence, behind a wall of smoke and flame.

In the beginning, there is fire.

Fire in my legs and lungs; fire tearing through every nerve and cell in my body. That's how I am born again, in pain: I emerge from the suffocating heat and the darkness. I force my way through a black, wet space of strange noises and smells.

I run, and when I can no longer run, I limp, and when I can't do that, I crawl, inch by inch, digging my fingernails into the soil, like a worm sliding across the overgrown surface of this strange new wilderness.

I bleed, too, when I am born.

I'm not sure how far I've travelled into the Wilds, and how long I've been pushing deeper and deeper into the woods, when I realize I've been hit. At least one regulator must have clipped me while I was climbing the fence. A bullet has skimmed me on the side, just below my armpit, and my T-shirt is wet with blood. I'm lucky, though. The wound is shallow, but seeing all the blood, the missing skin, makes everything real:

this new place, this monstrous, massive growth everywhere, what has happened, what I have left.

What has been taken from me.

There is nothing in my stomach, but I throw up anyway. I cough up air and spit bile into the flat, shiny leaves on either side of me. Birds twitter above me. An animal, coming to investigate, scurries quickly back into the tangle of growth.

Think, think. Alex. Think of what Alex would do.

Alex is here, right here. Imagine.

I take off my shirt, rip off the hem, and tie the cleanest bit tightly around my chest so it presses against my wound and helps stanch the bleeding. I have no idea where I am or where I'm going. My only thought is to move, keep going, deeper and deeper, away from the fences and the world of dogs and guns and—

Alex.

No. Alex is here. You have to imagine.

Step by step, fighting thorns, bees, mosquitoes; snapping back thick, broad branches; clouds of gnats, mists hovering in the air. At one point, I reach a river: I am so weak, I am nearly taken under by its current. At night, driving rain, fierce and cold: huddled between the roots of an enormous oak, while around me unseen animals scream and pant and rattle through the darkness. I'm too terrified to sleep; if I sleep, I'll die.

I am not born all at once, the new Lena.

Step by step – and then, inch by inch.

Crawling, insides curled into dust, mouth full of the taste of smoke.

Fingernail by fingernail, like a worm.

That is how she comes into the world, the new Lena.

*   *   *

When I can no longer go forward, even by an inch, I lay my head on the ground and wait to die. I'm too tired to be frightened. Above me is blackness, and all around me is blackness, and the forest sounds are a symphony to sing me out of this world. I am already at my funeral. I am being lowered into a narrow, dark space, and my aunt Carol is there, and Hana, and my mother and sister and even my long-dead father. They are all watching my body descend into the grave, and they are singing.

I am in a black tunnel filled with mist, and I am not afraid.

Alex is waiting for me on the other side; Alex standing, smiling, bathed in sunlight.

Alex reaching out his arms to me, calling—

Hey. Hey.

Wake up.

'Hey. Wake up. Come on, come on, come on.'

The voice pulls me back from the tunnel, and for a moment I'm horribly disappointed when I open my eyes and see not Alex's face, but some other face, sharp and unfamiliar. I can't think; the world is all fractured. Black hair, a pointed nose, bright green eyes – pieces of a puzzle I can't make sense of.

'Come on, that's right, stay with me. Bram, where the hell is that water?'

A hand under my neck, and then, suddenly, salvation. A sensation of ice, and liquid sliding: water filling my mouth, my throat, pouring over my chin, melting away the dust, the taste of fire. First I cough, choke, almost cry. Then I swallow, gulp, suck, while the hand stays under my neck, and the voice keeps whispering encouragement. 'That's right. Have as much as you need. You're all right. You're safe now.'

Black hair, loose, a tent around me: a woman. No, a girl – a girl with a thin, tight mouth, and creases at the corners of her eyes, and hands as rough as willow, as big as baskets. I think, *Thank you*. I think, *Mother*.

'You're safe. It's okay. You're okay.'

That's how babies are born, after all: cradled in someone else's arms, sucking, helpless.

After that, the fever pulls me under again. My waking moments are few, and my impressions disjointed. More hands, and more voices; I am lifted; a kaleidoscope of green above me, and fractal patterns in the sky. Later there is the smell of campfire, and something cold and wet pressed against my skin, smoke and hushed voices, searing pain in my side, then ice, relief. Softness sliding against my legs.

In between are dreams unlike any I've ever had before. They are full of explosions and violence: dreams of skin melting and skeletons charred to black bits.

Alex never comes to me again. He has gone ahead of me and disappeared beyond the tunnel.

Almost every time I wake she is there, the black-haired girl, urging me to drink water, or pressing a cool towel to my forehead. Her hands smell like smoke and cedar.

And beneath it all, beneath the rhythm of the waking and sleeping, the fever and the chills, is the word she repeats, again and again, so it weaves its way into my dreams, begins to push back some of the darkness there, draws me up out of the drowning: *Safe. Safe. Safe. You're safe now.*

The fever breaks, finally, after I don't know how long, and at last I float into consciousness on the back of that word, gently, softly, like riding a single wave all the way into the shore.

Before I even open my eyes, I'm conscious of plates banging together, the smell of something frying, and the murmur of voices. My first thought is that I'm at home, in Aunt Carol's house, and she's about to call me down for breakfast – a morning like any other.

Then the memories – the flight with Alex, the botched escape, my days and nights alone in the Wilds – come slamming back, and I snap my eyes open, trying to sit up. My body won't obey me, though. I can't do more than lift my head; I feel as though I've been encased in stone.

The black-haired girl, the one who must have found me and brought me here – wherever here is – stands in the corner, next to a large stone sink. She whips around when she hears me shift in my bed.

'Easy,' she says. She brings her hands out of the sink, wet to the elbow. Her face is sharp, extremely alert, like an animal's. Her teeth are small, too small for her mouth, and slightly crooked. She crosses the room, squats next to the bed. 'You've been out for a whole day.'

'Where am I?' I croak. My voice is a rasp, barely recognizable as my own.

'Home base,' she says. She is watching me closely. 'That's what we call it, anyway.'

'No, I mean—' I'm struggling to piece together what happened after I climbed the fence. All I can think of is Alex. 'I mean, is this the Wilds?'

An expression – of suspicion, possibly – passes quickly over her face. 'We're in a free zone, yes,' she says carefully, then stands and without another word moves away from the bed, disappearing through a darkened doorway. From deeper inside the building I can hear voices indistinctly. I feel a brief pang of fear, wonder if I've been wrong to mention the Wilds, wonder if these people are safe. I've never heard anyone call unregulated land a 'free zone' before.

But no. Whoever they are, they must be on my side; they saved me, have had me completely at their mercy for days.

I manage to haul myself into a half-seated position, propping my head up against the hard stone wall behind me. The whole room is stone: rough stone floors, stone walls on which, in places, a thin film of black mould is growing, an old-fashioned stone basin fitted with a rusted faucet that clearly hasn't functioned in years. I'm lying on a hard, narrow cot, covered with ratty quilts. This, in addition to a few tin buckets in the corner underneath the defunct sink, and a single wooden chair, is the room's only furniture. There are no windows in my room, and no lights, either – just two emergency lanterns, battery-operated, which fill the room with a weak bluish light.

On one wall is tacked a small wooden cross with the figure of a man suspended in its middle. I recognize the symbol – it's a cross from one of the old religions, from the time before the cure, although I can't remember which one now.

I have a sudden flashback to junior-year American history and Mrs. Dernler glaring at us from behind her enormous glasses, jabbing the open textbook with her finger, saying, 'You see? You see? These old religions, stained everywhere with love. They reeked of *deliria*; they bled it.' And of course at the time it seemed terrible, and true.

Love, the deadliest of all deadly things.

Love, it kills you.

Alex.

Both when you have it . . .

Alex.

And when you don't.

Alex.

'You were half dead when we found you,' the black-haired girl says matter-of-factly as she re-enters the room. She's holding an earthenware bowl with both hands, carefully. 'More than half. We didn't think you were going to make it. I thought we should at least try.'

She gives me a doubtful look, as though she's not sure I've been worth the effort, and for a moment I think of my cousin Jenny, the way she used to stand with her hands on her hips, scrutinizing me, and I have to close my eyes quickly to keep all of it from rushing back – the flood of images, memories, from a life that is now dead.

'Thank you,' I say.

She shrugs, but says, 'You're welcome,' and seems to mean it. She draws the wooden chair to the side of the bed and sits. Her hair is long and knotted above her left ear. Behind it, she has the mark of the procedure – a three-pronged scar – just like Alex did. But she cannot be cured; she is here, on the other side of the fence: an Invalid.

I try to sit up all the way but have to lean back after only a few seconds of struggle, exhausted. I feel like a puppet halfway come to life. There's a searing pain behind my eyes, too, and when I look down I see my skin is still criss-crossed with a web of cuts and scrapes and scratches, insect bites and scabs.

The bowl the girl is holding is full of mostly clear broth, tinged with just a bit of green. She starts to pass it to me, then hesitates. 'Can you hold it?'

'Of course I can hold it,' I say, more sharply than I'd meant to. The bowl is heavier than I thought it would be. I have trouble lifting it to my mouth, but I do, finally. My throat feels as raw as sandpaper and the broth is heaven against it, and even though it has a weird mossy aftertaste, I find myself gulping and slurping down the whole bowl.

'Slowly,' the girl says, but I can't stop. Suddenly hunger yawns open inside me, black and endless and all-consuming. As soon as the broth is gone I'm desperate for more, even though my stomach starts cramping right away. 'You'll make yourself sick,' the girl says, shaking her head, and takes the empty bowl from me.

'Is there any more?' I croak.

'In a little while,' she says.

'Please.' The hunger is a snake; it is lashing at the pit of my stomach, eating me from the inside out.

She sighs, stands, and disappears through the darkened doorway. I think I hear a crescendo in the hallway voices, a swelling of sound. Then, abruptly, silence. The black-haired girl returns with a second bowl of broth. I take it from her and she sits again, drawing her knees up to her chest, like a kid would. Her knees are bony and brown.

'So,' she says, 'where did you cross from?' When I hesitate, she says, 'That's okay. You don't have to talk about it if you don't want to.'

'No, no. It's fine.' I sip from this bowl of broth more slowly, savouring its strange, earthy quality: as though it has been stewed with stones. For all I know, it has been. Alex told me once that Invalids – the people who live in the Wilds – have learned to make do with only the barest provisions. 'I came over from Portland.' Too soon the bowl is empty again, even though the snake in my stomach is still lashing. 'Where are we now?'

'A few miles east of Rochester,' she says.

'Rochester, New Hampshire?' I ask.

She smirks. 'Yup. You must have been hoofing it. How long were you out on your own?'

'I don't know.' I rest my head against the wall. Rochester, New Hampshire. I must have looped around the northern border when I was lost in the Wilds: I've ended up sixty miles southwest of Portland. I'm exhausted again, even though I've been sleeping for days. 'I lost track of time.'

'Pretty ballsy of you,' she says. I'm not really sure what 'ballsy' means, but I can guess. 'How did you cross?'

'It wasn't – it wasn't just me,' I say, and the snake lashes, seizes up. 'I mean, it wasn't supposed to be just me.'

'You were with somebody else?' She's staring at me penetratingly again, her eyes almost as dark as her hair. 'A friend?'

I don't know how to correct her. My best friend. My boyfriend. My love. I'm still not totally comfortable with that word, and it seems almost sacrilegious, so instead I just nod.

'What happened?' she asks, a little more softly.

'He – he didn't make it.' Her eyes flash with understanding when I say 'he': If we were coming from Portland together, from a place of segregation, we must have been more than just friends. Thankfully she doesn't push it. 'We made it all the way to the border fence. But then the regulators and the guards . . .' The pain in my stomach intensifies. 'There were too many of them.'

She stands abruptly and retrieves one of the water-spotted tin buckets from the corner, places it next to the bed, and sits again.

'We heard rumours,' she says shortly. 'Stories of a big escape in Portland, lots of police involvement, a big cover-up.'

'So you know about it?' I try once again to sit up all the way, but the cramping doubles me back against the wall. 'Are they saying what happened to . . . to my friend?'

I ask the question even though I know. Of course I know.

I saw him standing there, covered in blood, as they descended on him, swarmed him, like the black ants in my dream.

The girl doesn't answer, just folds her mouth into a tight line and shakes her head. She doesn't have to say anything else – her meaning is clear. It's written in the pity on her face.